I0590509

WHISTLE PUNK FALLS

A FELIX CULPA

SHAUN ANTHONY MCMICHAEL

ALTERNATIVE BOOK PRESS

WHISTLE PUNK FALLS: *A Felix Culpa*

Alternative Book Press.
alternativebookpress.com
Copyright © 2025 Shaun A. McMichael
All Rights Reserved. First Published 2025

For permission requests, contact Alternative Book Press.
alternativebookpress.com

Cover Art and Interior Design by Roderick Brydon
This book contains limited material determined by the author
to fall under the "fair use" doctrine of copyrighted material
as referenced and provided for in section 107 of U.S. Copyright Law.

LIBRARY OF CONGRESS CATALOGING-IN-PUBLICATION DATA

Shaun A. McMichael / WHISTLE PUNK FALLS: *A Felix Culpa* / First Edition

Fiction, General. Fiction, Friendship

ISBN: 979-8-9924613-3-6 (Trade Paperback)

Printed in the United States of America

PRAISE FOR WHISTLE PUNK FALLS

"The hot drama of the youth, Loud's disintegration, Jeremy's jealousy... Shaun paints the most perfect and awful of teenage situations and communicates them as somatic experiences. His lyricism and literary verve result in Margaret-Atwood-quality sentences that demand multiple readings out of pleasure and awe."

ELI HASTINGS—Psychotherapist, Author of *Falling Room, Clearly Now the Rain*

"Shaun Anthony McMichael is the patron saint of the alienated and disaffected youth in Washington's post apunkalyptic grunge scene. His characters commune with Kurt Cobain's ghost while simultaneously embodying that same rebellious spirit. Like Cobain, Jeremy Sweet, the book's protagonist, is from the dying timber town of Aberdeen on the coast of Washington, pushed toward Seattle on a tsunami of desperate hope in search of his mentally disturbed friend known as Loud. McMichael's prose is simultaneously lyrical and irreverent. Whistle Punk Falls resonates deeply--an unforgettable reading experience."

DAREN DEAN—Professor, Author of *Beyond the Pale, Black Harvest*

"*Whistle Punk Falls* spins a hard-luck tale that could have been written by Kurt Cobain channeling a young Raymond Carver. It's a reminder of a Northwest beyond the sights of Seattle's high-tech winners, returning us instead to the left behinds and street rats of this rain-drenched corner of the continent."

DOUG THORPE—Professor, Author of *Rapture in the Deep: Reflections on the Wild in Art; Wilderness and the Sacred*

"Brilliant, lyrical, brutally authentic. The prose achieves poetic heights of poignancy. A remarkable achievement."

JIM THOMSEN—Editor, Book Reviewer

"A great time capsule of the last year of the tumultuous aughts, Whistle Punk Falls makes you remember and roll your eyes at your adolescence while making you want to relive it."

DENNIS STAPLES—Author of *This Town Sleeps*

"In his debut novel, Whistle Punk Falls, Shaun Anthony McMichael offers a clear conjuring of teenagers coming-of-age in post logging boom Aberdeen, WA and the surrounding region in all its beauty and desolation, its shattered economy and social degradation…Loud's harrowing mental collapse along with the escalating desperation of his friends' efforts to intervene in his descent provides the book's profound emotional power and compelling narrative drive. But it is the author's deft use of those strengths in service to his larger themes -- abusive judicial systems, familial and communal dysfunction, traumatic grief, class struggle, white savior syndrome, and rampant drug use, the troubling constants of America's late capitalist culture -- that truly sets the book apart. The resiliency of McMichaels' characters, the webs of friendship they weave, and the family bonds they struggle to rebuild provide the book's defiant promise of renewal."

HARRY KIRCHNER—Editor at Counter Point Press

"A moving and beautiful story. A great achievement."

GREGORY WOLFE—Publisher, Editor at SLANT

"McMichael delivers a haunting, coming-of-age race against time in a failing Pacific Northwest timber town. When seventeen-year-old Jeremy Sweet's attempt to help his troubled friend Loud goes catastrophically wrong, he's forced into an unlikely alliance to set things right. A fiercely empathetic debut about friendship, family, and the fragile ways we try to save each other."

THOMAS KOHNSTAMM—Author of *Supersonic*

"So much in the story mirrors the economic and social frustrations of many an American abode that the demise of social connections, niceties of caring about others, and struggles to stay alive under insane conditions and expectations make Whistle Punk Falls more than just another story of teen angst or apocalyptic survival…Filled with enlightening moments and fiery social and psychological realization, Whistle Punk Falls is a study in contrasts and experience. It deserves high profile in any library, to be recommended to young adult and adult readers interested in how relationships fracture and are rebuilt in small towns across America."

D. DONOVAN—Senior Reviewer, Midwest Book Review

for my mother

WHISTLE PUNK FALLS

A FELIX CULPA

"Whistle punk—The worker, often young and unskilled, responsible for relaying instructions between the remote worksite and the landing."

ANDREW MASON PROUTY,
More Deadly than War! Pacific Coast Logging,
1827-1981

"...he had come to the disconcerting conclusion that whistling was not an important theme in literature. There weren't many authors who made their characters whistle. Practically none of them did...no hero or heroine had ever crowned the high point of one of their epics with a magnificent whistle of the type that shatters glass,"

JULIO CORTÁZAR,
Hopscotch

PART ONE

Dear Malachi,

I'm writing because I don't know what else to do. If I send this to you, you probably won't read it. But in case you do, I'm writing to tell you that I see you. I see you, my child, the way I always do. A smile in that whirly go-round your dad built for you out of a cable drum. He'd lay you on your back and he'd spin you so gentle. Going round and around, you'd coo and giggle and I'd imagine you beneath blue sky, surrounded by the cedars and your daddy's love, and I could sleep. He was out of work again. Striking with all the other mill workers. But he was able to care for you while I slept off a late-night shift tending bar. I told you I was waitressing at a diner. Which would have been a lie because the Pour House wasn't serving food back then. I guess that was my first lie to you. I didn't like the idea of telling your baby ears that your momma was a barmaid. Not that there was anything wrong with it. I didn't have a problem when I started. Never sipped a drop. Though plenty of guys offered. I preferred serving them back their fire water. Which made them laugh. That one made your dad laugh too. I used to make him laugh.

I'm sorry for them. The lies. Though there've only been a few, I paid for every one. They lay beached and bloated on the shore of my insides, undying in their ragged breath and stink.

Some lies can be friendly for a while. You need them sometimes. Like the one I told you about me being a waitress. While I was working, you and your dad would play 'diner'. He'd be your customer; he made a little apron for you, and you'd pretend to bring him food, just like mommy. See? A friendly lie.

I think those times were the happiest in your dad's life. But to your grandpa, he was just a house husband, and he reminded your dad of that every chance he got. I had my job, and it wasn't that bad living with your grandparents. Even though they charged us rent and didn't have any money themselves to buy us any baby things or groceries.

Then everything started going belly up.

You stopped taking milk from me early. Don't know why. But I took it hard. Those times had been the only times that were just ours. I loved nothing as much as you falling asleep on me, milk-dudded while I stroked your hair, black like mine. Plenty of babies stop breastfeeding early. But I didn't know that then. And God knows nobody told me. I felt them looking at me and thinking things. But it was more than that. All that time with your dad, Grandma Gin, and Pappy Rue. You started preferring them. You stopped liking being close with me and stopped saying 'hi, mommy', all sweetness and smiles when I'd wake you up. Instead, you'd turn away, crying for daddy, even when he was right there. Which he always was.

Your dad had a spirit choked by the smog of that place. Bogged down. Tired so much of the time. But he sure did love you, and he clung to you because I think you gave him some of your fire. And he wanted to keep it that way.

I'd come home from the bar around four in the morning and sleep until nine or so and wake up like a shot to hold you. Your dad would be playing with you, his "best little buddy", and he'd tell me "You go rest, you go rest" and would take you out to a park or something. Right then. Like he was trying to keep you away from me. Me, this stranger that he had married. I didn't want to rest. I wanted to be with you.

I have a fire burning inside me just like you do. And when I can't get something I want, the fire leaps out.

That's what did it, I think. A fist of darkness closed around. And I started sneaking tastes at work to ease that tight, clenching feeling making a caged animal out of my heart. Buzzed was the only time I felt loose and light enough to smile and chitchat with the fat white guys and their dates while the only thing I wanted to do was run home and take you away from there, those sloughs and that harbor with its evil clouds and sour winds.

Aberdeen has always felt like a possessed place to me. Too many bad things have happened there. Too many people's ghosts linger, all restless and crushed up by the mills and the booze and the drugs and the depressions. Your dad was born into all that. And some of that spirit wormed its way into you.

I couldn't talk to the McCrowleys about any of it. Couldn't talk to anybody in town about it. They just thought I was weird. Weak. I was Indian after all. And they all thought they knew what that meant.

Funny thing was that your dad liked me at first because I was different than everybody else around. But somewhere along the line, he stopped trusting the part of me that was different. The Native part. Which I didn't think was that big of a part of me back then, me being as wayward as I was. But I looked Native. Just like you look Native. And we can't unlook like who we are. To them, we'll always be that over everything else. Which I think you're finding out even if you're not admitting it to yourself yet.

Anywho... I dove. Plunged. Headlong into that stuff like so many of us have. All I can tell you is that it got so bad I couldn't work and had to go on "vacation". It was a cheap-o DSHS place, but it did the trick. It didn't matter. By the time I came back, your heart was sown so tight to Grandma Gin's side that no light could shine through, and your dad had gotten work as a faller, which gave him the excuse of being tired so he could avoid talking to me altogether.

I couldn't go back to tending bar. And I couldn't find any other kind of work in that place. Pappy Rue said I just wasn't trying hard enough. Maybe he was right. My heart wasn't in my job hunt because I was done with Aberdeen. I'd come out there in the first place to find my dad and wound up marrying a white version of him that was going to end up leaving me too.

But I tried. I tried to get your dad to come with me. *Let's start over! I'll be good to you again. And you can be good to me too. We'll have us another spring!* But he wouldn't. Said he'd never leave the harbor. Said there wasn't a way in hell I was taking you, either. Said he'd take me to court and that he'd win because I was a drunk and now everybody knew it. He'd never spoken to me like that before. Being as docile and quiet as he was, I wonder where he'd gotten up the energy to utter such hateful words. It was like somebody else was speaking out of his mouth. Probably his dad. He'd never had it in him to resist Pappy Rue. I didn't either.

I tried to get you to come with me. Not for good or anything. Just for a weekend stay with your uncle. My brother up at the rez. To clear my head. To tie us back together, momma and son, to our place. To our people. But you wouldn't go with me. *Want Daddy. Want Daddy*, you whined as I tried to wave you into my car. So, I took your soft, little hand real tight. And I walked you back into that house by the mouth of the sloughs. And I said goodbye.

That's the truth. Same as the truth about what really happened to your dad. Same as I told you when you was up here for those days during the end of May. Before you ran off. But lies call to you sometimes. They offer themselves to you as a friend. And that's how it went in the McCrowley living room the day after 9/11.

I'd gotten the call about what happened to your dad. And I'd sped down the coast to come get you.

But you were at school. You didn't know anything was afoot yet. And there Pappy Rue was, staring at me with his wide, foggy eyes, rheumy as bubbled glass , and weighed down by all of Aberdeen's awfulness. He looked at me like I had a knife in my hand.

He told me to sit, his lips trembling.

I obeyed. It was his house. What could I do? I wasn't so wayward as to disrespect an elder. One that was housing my baby. I asked after Ginny. But he just shook his head.

"Let's be clear on something," he said. "You and I haven't always seen eye to eye. But on this, I think we can stand on common ground."

Standing on the same ground with him always made me give up more than I got.

He said we couldn't tell you what really happened. With your dad. That we needed a lie. A friendly lie. That things were going to be hard enough on you as it was without you knowing your dad was a cedar thief.

He raised a shaking finger at me and told me that I did not have a right.

"So help me God, I'll…"

And he could have, my son. Your pappy was, and is, well connected. He could have had them do whatever he wanted with me.

So, I agreed to his terms. I would tell you a friendly lie. And I did. I told you the lie to save your memory of your daddy. But by telling you the lie, it worsened your memory of me, because I was the messenger. And when the news is bad, everybody shoots the messenger. That's why there's that old saying telling you to not shoot them. But you were a boy. And you didn't know that old saying. But your Pappy Rue did. Which was why he had me be the one to tell it to you. Whatever I told you, he knew you'd hate me for it. And it's why I probably will never send you this letter. But I don't know what else to do other than write and think of you on that little makeshift merry-go-round in the McCrowley's backyard, spinning in slow circles, round and round.

Your mother always,

Leah Ledbetter

Forks, Washington

THE TIRE SWING IN THE SLOUGH OF DESPOND

The black frame of his bicycle feels heavier than ever in Jeremy's small white hands as he walks it down his steep driveway into the cul-de-sac. His hands tremble against the metal. The April morning air holds its chill like that popular girl who caught him staring at her in the 9th grade. As the bike's cassette clicks, Jeremy almost convinces himself it's the sound of Loud's bike approaching. But Loud's somewhere in Seattle. Lost to Jeremy, lost to himself. And it's all Jeremy's fault.

From where Jeremy stands, Aberdeen resembles a wadded newspaper slowly unfolded onto the wet, black earth. A freight train slithers along tracks, passing through the downtown warehouses and millworks. The grain silos line up like rows of gray Thermoses on the riverbank. Eastward, the mill towers give off slow, billowing puffs of white steam. At their base, piles of russet logs pine for their former lives as trees greening the Willapa Hills to the north. East, then north. The direction Jeremy needs to go to stop his friend from annihilating himself in a way that may flash in an instant or draw out over a decade.

With everything Loud has been through, it's miraculous he's still alive. If he is still alive.

Before Jeremy straddles his Clydesdale of a bike, he gives his car's bumper a farewell kick. It didn't start again. He's waited until now for his mom to come home so she could help him jump it, as she normally takes a morning break from her beat. Nothin' much doin' at six a.m. No perps to question, no eyewitnesses to interview. A good time to have breakfast during which mother and son avoid looking at each other, their eyes transforming into funhouse mirrors that evoke their respective humiliations of the last year. But she didn't come home. Now that he thinks of it, she hasn't come home the last several mornings.

Maybe it's just as well. Mom would want to know where he was driving to this early on the last Saturday of Spring Break. He wouldn't be able to lie to her, and she wouldn't consent to letting him go.

Jeremy pushes off and starts pedal-stomping, afraid now of her Crown Vic rounding the corner. In his effort to build up speed on his oversized mount, his foot slips. He goddamns the middle-aged hipster at the counter of the Olympia cycle shop who sweet-talked his mom into buying the bike. *He'll totally grow into it.* It wasn't the first time she'd been fooled by a man.

Jeremy realizes he's talking to himself and wonders if this is what it's like for Loud all the time. Nah. Loud doesn't talk to himself. He talks to *ghosts*. Kurt Cobain's ghost. Billy Gohl's ghost. Always famous dead people. Never Joe Schmo from Idaho who got too blitzed one afternoon and crashed his car into the Wishkah. That's one reason Jeremy thinks all Loud's talk of ghosts is a bullshit cover for some textbook mental illness. It amazes him that the pissed-off, out-of-work shitkickers around here haven't tried to lynch Loud. Seattle's lowlifes or trigger-happy cops might not be so kind.

As the sun rises, the pinkness of dawn recedes into the east. The elevation climbs as Jeremy makes his way toward Cal's house. His legs have to mash down onto the pedals to make it uphill. With each roll of the crank, Jeremy prepares his argument for why Cal should come help him look for Loud.

In uneven patches, clear-cut strafes across the saw-tooth hillsides where working men of the woods extracted the evergreen giants in a process as perilous as combat. In Aberdeen, Jeremy has discovered that logging is as time-honored as a religious rite yet growing just as infrequent. Somewhere to the west, Gray's Harbor opens to the sea. But Jeremy, huffing along on his bicycle, can't imagine any way out. When he first arrived in Aberdeen less than a year prior, that trapped feeling poured over him like a concrete overcoat in a mob movie. Meeting Loud that third day at Weatherwax High took a sledgehammer to that feeling. Yet the fire inside Loud is dying. Jeremy can almost feel it. That fire lit up the darkness of this place. That fire brought his friends together. Without it, they won't be able to see each other in the same light, and so, Jeremy fears, they will stop seeing each other at all. But it's more than that. Jeremy doesn't know how he'll be able to live with himself.

*

Loud's run away, Aurora group-texted to Jeremy and Cal the night before. *I did something awful to him and now he's gone. I don't know where to.* What Aurora didn't say was that the awful thing she'd done had been Jeremy's idea.

Aurora's thread continued:

He ran off a couple days ago. Didn't tell you because I was too much of a mess. But I'm in deep shit with the cops now for what I did, and a missing person report is out for him. So I figured you should hear it first from me.

Aurora's last text read: *I don't want anyone looking for him. I think we should be done trying to be his little white saviors. Which he doesn't need. Because we're just making everything worse. I don't want to talk, I need time. Try to move on.*

Every word infuriates him.

Move on? To what? How? Here? One look around sinks that argument. As if he had something better to do. Like get a job. Jobs were scarce before, but after the crash? The line outside the DSHS is longer than for a sold-out show. The laid-off workers' picket lines are thinner only because they've secured unemployment and are at home stewing around the kitchen table over what's next. Cal even got canned and the dude was practically born with cork boots on.

And 'white saviors? Is that what they've been trying to be?

They are white and Loud is Native. But Jeremy has never felt like anything more than a bystander to Loud's train wreck. But for Aurora, the white-savior phrase probably makes more sense, given how far she's gone to try to help Loud. Aurora became Loud's girlfriend over the last few months. The fact of their relationship still makes Jeremy want to blow hot chunks from his center, to try and expel the snake of jealousy that squirms inside him anytime he thinks of the two together without him. Which has been most of the time since November.

Aurora. In his favorite selfie with her, she's got her arm around him and she's smiling that smile with her tongue on the tip of her front teeth, her dark slinky hair falling over one side of her face, her skin the color of an almond's insides. She was just the drummer girl in overalls he had science class with. The girl like the hallway print he passed every day without noticing until he realized that it was the strangest, most beautiful painting he'd ever seen.

As he wheezes uphill to Cal's house, Jeremy thinks about changing direction. About throwing his bike onto the lawn of Aurora's house, busting down the door, and declaring that they don't need Loud. They have each other!

But that idea makes him sick too. He shakes his beehive of curly brown hair. Jeremy wouldn't be able to stand himself. Besides, even under normal circumstances, his tiny self could never fill a hole left by a larger-than-life somebody like Loud McCrowley.

Hole. Jeremy should have taken Courtney Love more seriously. What a perfect band name. Especially in retrospect. The hole in her life after the hole Cobain put through his head. A big, black circle that nothing could fill.

Jeremy isn't moving on. He's already spent too much of the last few months on the sidelines, watching the awfulness of Loud and Aurora's relationship play out. He can't move on. He has to move through.

Part of him wishes he didn't have to. He's the least streetwise person he can think of. The least equipped to spelunk into Seattle's underbelly to look for Loud. He wishes Loud had parents around to ground him or at least keep him off the edge. Where were they anyway? Loud never wanted to talk about family around him. Maybe Loud thought that he just couldn't handle it. This bothers Jeremy. It's not like he's a silver spoon kid. His mom and dad divorced when he was three!

All Jeremy knows about Loud's parents is what everybody said. That his dad died in some weird way when Loud was a kid. And that his Native American mom isn't around. Given the way Loud seems to treat the women in his life, Jeremy bets Loud pissed off his mom to the point where she wouldn't or couldn't help him anymore.

Whatever the real story is, unlike anyone else in town, Jeremy knows Loud is in Seattle. After he got Aurora's texts last night, he pulled up Loud's clandestine Facebook page under the alias Hawky-Mo. He saw new pictures posted of Loud's brown, bony bare feet dangling over the 99 Bridge.

*

When Jeremy rolls up, Cal Gearhart is changing his Forerunner's oil; Jeremy can hear the thick, black piss dripping into an oil pan. The truck's running boards are more mud-spattered than normal, as are the pant cuffs of Cal's Carhartts as they stick out from beneath the frame. But Jeremy doesn't think too much of it, as Cal has probably just been out muddin', bouncing his four-by-four through old logging spurs to take his mind off shit. Cal, after all, is a redneck of sorts. With a mullet and everything.

"Hey," Cal grunts. "You heard any more from Aurora?"

"No," Jeremy says and tells Cal about how Loud is in Seattle and how he wants to go look for him.

"What if we find him, and he runs from us again?"

"I haven't thought that far ahead," Jeremy admits. "We'll… tackle him."

"That didn't work out so well last time."

"We'll be ready this time," Jeremy says. "Plus, he'll be worn down from street life."

"Or more jacked up."

"We'll threaten to call the cops. Just threaten."

"The cops?"

"He *is* a danger to himself. Right? Talking to people who aren't there. Smoking his brains out. Not bathing. Wandering around half naked."

"You just described every homeless person in Seattle. That's not enough for them to do anything about."

"But Loud won't know that. It'll work! It's…it's got to work. Loud's not just another homeless person."

"Not yet."

"Because we can help him. For real this time."

Cal clicks his tongue. He wipes his face off with a rag and tosses it.

"Plus, my car won't start," Jeremy says. "And I need you to drive."

"You do drive a POS Tercel," Cal snorts. He then complains about how he always has to be everybody's fucking chauffeur. "But I don't have anything else going on today. It's not like I have a job to go to anymore."

A half-hour later, Cal's Forerunner is roaring up the highway out of Aberdeen, toward Seattle. Social Distortion's rockabilly bliss blasts "Mommy's Little Monster" out of Cal's stereo, punctuated by the sound of the windshield wipers. Rain clouds and sunbeams fight to win the day. Jeremy looks over the guardrail at the valley of Junction City. The peak of the rotten barn on Feller's Landing. The sloughs. And, left flying on a tower in Rhinehouse & Sons' Timber Co.'s abandoned lot, a tattered American flag.

*

Cal wasn't out muddin' last night. He was out looking for Loud.

A few days earlier, Cal found out he would not be inheriting Bullfinch Boyd's Papermill and Lumberyard from his dad. The mill's doors closed forever. This poured a ton of woodchips into the kiln radiating inside his barrel-chested core. Then Aurora texted. The news about Loud leaving dropped into Cal like a lit M-80. Sure, Loud had disappeared before. But this time felt different. More combustive and final. The kid seemed to be cracking beyond repair. So, Cal whipped up a search party, roping in Moreno and Weets, two off-duty cops. Cal didn't invite Jeremy because he wouldn't have been much help with his poor eyesight, shaky nerves, and fumbly thumbs. But Cal's not going to tell him any of this, because Jeremy will get butt-hurt and probably dive into his books for cover.

In Moreno's old fishing boat, they paddled around for hours in the sloughs outside of town. With nothing but the sculling of their oars in the brackish waters, they hoped to sneak up on any rough-shod camp Loud might have. After hours of getting turned around in the bends of the sloughs, bumping into creosote-coated pilings and black banks, and finding only shadows, they called it quits. The cops had to report for duty, so they gunned it back.

When they curved around the oxbow outside Preacher's Slough, Cal killed the motor. He saw the starlight catching on the silt of a familiar beachhead under a Sitka spruce overhanging the river. Cal could see the tire swing they'd hung there, its rope stitching a seam in the purple cloak of night; the empty circle of the tire framing the stars. It was Whistle Punk Falls, their hangout spot.

A quick pan from his Maglite showed nothing but moss-bearded branches and ferns. It was too obvious for Loud, even if he had been somewhere in Grays Harbor. Even if he was insane. Like Aurora said, he was gone.

BLACK TAPE

Loud has a dream of his mother calling to him in the night. Her hair is a raven's wing over one side of her face as she waves for him to get into the car and come with her. But he doesn't go.

He has always been sure the dream is not a memory but a whisper-trick of his mother through the miles, trying to fool him into believing that she loves him.

What he remembers is this:

His mom's brick-red Rabbit kicked up gravel as it pulled away, leaving little Loud and his dad, Pete McCrowley, to eat alphabet cereal for dinner. Which was okay with him because they were Letter-Betters—Loud's favorite. Dad sang LeadBelly's "Goodnight Irene" while Loud tried to read a message he thought he saw in the floating letters.

Dad was a timber faller who couldn't afford childcare and didn't want to burden his parents, so he brought little Loud toddling along with him as his whistle punk. Loud's only job had been to look out for falling branches and whistle a warning when the trees fell.

After long days in the woods, their ears still ringing from chainsaws and felled trees, and Loud's whistle warnings, Dad would do kid stuff with Loud like reading scuffed up overdue library books and teaching Loud how to ride a bike.

Though he always left the wispy strands of his thinning hair askew, Dad performed his toilet each morning, shaving with canola oil to save money. And so, whenever Dad would bear-hug him, which was often, Loud's nose was filled with the scent of the nutty unctuousness and sawdust, a potpourri that made him feel a calm certitude.

Eventually, Dad went to work at the Rhinehouse mill so he could get a more consistent paycheck. He would leave Loud with his McCrowley grandparents before dawn, then come home to him at dusk. This routine lasted until Loud was nine.

The day after 9/11, Loud rode the bus home from school, his mind reeling with images of planes colliding with the two towers on the other side of the country. The bus dropped him off on the dirt road near his grandparents' house. They lived in a clapboard house outside Junction City, right on the edge of the sloughs. When the house came into view, Loud found his mom's Rabbit parked outside, which told him something was wrong. She'd stopped coming around. Grandpa McCrowley, whom he called Pappy Rue, said she was a drunk.

Leah was exactly as Loud remembered her. With a dark mane as thick as horsehair, she wore shorts and sandals—even in the brisk fall air—and a red plaid shirt. Her sun-wrinkled face featured a man's heavy chin and though she had pretty eyes, they were small from crying. Her face was a mask of grief.

In the living room, his mother knelt and tried to press her forehead against his face, but he recoiled. Her breath stank of cigarettes. The ache he'd occasionally had for her had long since calcified to the point that she was worse than a stranger to him now, someone he didn't trust. He asked where Dad was.

"Malachi…Your dad had an accident," she told Loud. Her voice was low, hollow, and shimmering, as if it were echoing out of a gourd. Her eyes lingered for a moment on Pappy Rue, who sat in his armchair watching them in glassy-eyed silence. Leah took a breath and told Loud that Dad's accident was at the mill. "Oh, Ki. Your dad. Sweetie. He's gone."

Loud disappeared into a well of grief. When he emerged a few days later, his mom was gone too. Which didn't surprise him. He crept into the living room of his grandparents' house. Their old TV's wan colors played across Pappy Rue's bifocals while the old man's snores mingled with the onscreen dialogue.

An accident. Gone. Loud repeated it, but still, it didn't make sense. His dad's death yawned out silently like the mouth of a cave Loud couldn't enter, not because he was afraid, but because the magic spell of life forbade him. From deep inside, a drive to live hummed. Faced with the enduring reality of his life, Loud's nine-year-old mind searched for images from shows and movies to project onto the veil of his father's death.

Had it been like the scene of a tired man working at a machine shop? A gear catching his unbuttoned shirt cuff and pulling him in, sawblade whirring. Red chainsaw lube supposed to be blood splattered the man's face while he screamed and screamed. Somebody turned off the machine, but it was too late. The man bled out.

In Loud's mental reproduction of this scene, Loud shaved the actor's face with canola oil and replaced the actor's blue plaid shirt with his father's blue chambray. And the scene worked for a while.

But Pete had worked in a lumber mill. And Loud had never heard his dad scream. The scene was incomplete and silent, spurring Loud's brain to rework it, play, rewind, and replay. It became a compulsion. He could never get it quite right. Never could he construct a scene clear enough to understand how Dad could be gone.

For Loud, trying to make sense of his father's death became like scrounging through boxes of unmarked VHS tapes on the hunt for a good movie. Loud tried tape after tape. The reels turned and turned. The film jammed and spurted out, knotting Loud's consciousness in black film strips—lightless and silent, save for Loud's screams.

Loud clawed his way out of this incoherent hive of grief by, in the words of Pappy Rue, being a little shit.

When his grandparents bought him a stubby yellow Huffy at a pawnshop for a Christmas present, Loud used the bike to thunder down the stairs while standing on the pedals.

"The mill ate my dad," Loud said through clenched teeth during this daredevil feat. The phrase became a maxim of survival that fueled the fuck-the-man chorus on an endless loop through his brain. The thrill helped him feel something other than loss.

Pappy Rue chained up the bike as a punishment. In response, Loud launched himself from a mini-trampoline into a ceiling fan going full spin.

This incident precipitated Loud's relationship with drugs.

On the drive to the doctor's office, Pappy Rue explained in his flat, mucusy voice that it was the only way. *Each one of your little capers is an ulcer in my gut.* Loud had been twelve and too tender footed then to run away. The little orange pills the doctor prescribed helped his mind not pinball as much at school. His grandparents unchained his bike and granted him a few more years of shelter, despite his occasional tantrums about having to be medicated.

Eventually, they kicked him out anyway.

Pappy Rue had been the one to tell him. A former Marine, and union leader at Rhinehouse, Pappy had a giant hobnail of a nose growing by the minute as he aged. His aviator-form bifocals housed his sad gray eyes, and his flannel-shirt breast pockets were always heavy with his old man tits and bills he was trying to pay. A neck tattoo hid beneath his Pendleton collar. Loud thought it was probably an anchor but held out hope that it might be a naked lady. All he knew was that the tattoo was from a war Pappy Rue never talked about.

A few months prior, Pappy Rue had started opening the door for clean-shaven men who looked like golfers in their polos and creased khakis. These men said the word "property" a lot.

That morning, when Pappy Rue sat Loud down, he began by saying that they were getting too old to keep up with him.

Loud wondered about this. Sure, a week previously, he'd

embarked on an unsupervised, five-day escapade in the sloughs, uninterrupted despite police searches. But he had camped out in places his Grandma Gin had already shown him. Loud thought she could have found him if she'd really wanted to. He looked around for Grandma Gin, but she was off somewhere like usual.

"And we can't afford it anymore," Pappy Rue said, a thickening film moistening his eyes.

He cleared his throat and coughed. He'd just finished a cigarette, improving his mood but harshening the delivery. Smoke hung in the air. Loud looked at the floor.

"It's time for you to go be with your mother. She's been sober now for a while," Pappy Rue coughed again. The sound was like a heel-stomp on wet gravel. "We'll be moving too. So, you're not alone in this. But we'll be moving close by. Over to Think-of-Me-Hill. The retirement center. And we'll still see ya at Christmases. This is a time of change for all of us."

Loud gave the slightest of nods.

Pappy Rue thumbed his nose. "You gonna talk to me or what?"

This was the most his grandfather had said to him since Loud's dad died. Pappy Rue knew the art of silence. Whenever Loud derided him or Grandma Gin's decisions, Pappy would just clean his glasses and stare out the living-room window. This silent treatment would light coals on Loud's head, and his tongue would lash out in vilifications about them being against him, not being his parents anyway, and being racists. But, through the worst of it, Pappy's silence would hold, and Loud's anger would fizzle, leaving him sullen and remorseful.

This time, Loud decided to turn the whole routine over onto Pappy. And though he knew the stolid old soldier would never lose his cool, Loud knew it would make him uncomfortable.

"You can talk to me. Probably better to." Pappy Rue gave a single snuffle of his nose.

Loud shrugged.

"You can have a fresh start up there," Pappy continued. "Maybe learn a thing or two from your mother's people out on the cape."

Loud suppressed an eye roll. Dad had called it the boonies out there. Loud hadn't even been to a powwow yet. Not that he'd be the slightest bit interested or curious, but no one had ever invited him.

In the face of Loud's continued stonewall, Pappy Rue frowned and looked at his watch. He grumbled, making Loud smile inwardly.

"Okay, then. Here." Pappy lifted a blue envelope with a lanky blue dog running across it.

"Hold on to it. We'll drive you to the station in the morning. The bus will take you to Quinault. Your mother will be waiting to drive you the rest of the way."

Loud ran away that night. He left his pill bottle of Adderall, an act he'd later regret when learning about the drug's street value. He took but didn't use the bus ticket. His reliable heater of self-preservation advised him to hang onto it for a rainy day. It was summer, and biking would not be a problem. He'd biked to Olympia before on a Sunday afternoon he'd taken off his medication. He'd arrived at the state's capital the next morning and caught the bus back to Aberdeen, a friendly bus driver allowing him to walk on the bike. That had been two years ago. He figured that now he could go even further. Better, he thought, to save the ticket for another time.

As he pedaled, the August night breathed the warm breath of cedar on his skin. When he got onto the highway's shoulder, he threw his bike down, turned west, and gave a final look at the darkened town. The silent chimneys. The lightless blocks along the river.

He turned east. He was getting out of town and going to

the big city, the subject of an infinite number of punk ballads he'd already committed to memory. With legs rotating, he balanced his butt cheeks on his bike seat and lifted his arms high as he road, a devotee first of the eggplant-colored midnight, then the lavender lightness of pre-dawn. When the sun broke from the hills in a purl of orange, Loud shouted, feeling found by life itself.

*

Through a combination of biking and hitchhiking, Loud made it to Tacoma, though by that point, the plates of the chain links were so stretched that the chain caught in the back tire's spokes. When an old hippie in a Bug answered his thumb, Loud ditched the bike by the roadside. He watched the fallen Huffy's wheel spin to a slow in the rearview mirror while the old hippie drove him northward to Seatown.

Over the next year, which should have been his sophomore year in high school, Loud lived under Seattle bridges, sneaked into shows, and perfected his dance moves. His signature dance, the Flail, became a series of jerks, kinks, twists, and tremors synched to music. It was a postmodern fancydance that the bands liked so much, it led several to hire Loud as their "sideshow monkey". This provided him with places to crash, as well as access to what became his drug of choice.

At a post-show rager, he smoked his first joint, though the effect was latent until his third or fourth. When he did get that first high, the profane laughter that erupted from his throat earned him the 'Loud' moniker. He continued his stoned performances at shows, and the nickname stuck.

He sought occasional shelter in libraries. They reminded him of his Grandma Gin and of a more normal life, which he craved yet felt denied of. It was at a library computer where he started his Facebook profile under the alias Hawky-Mo.

He was studious that year on the streets. He learned how to

hop trains and look out for bulls—mercenaries hired by BNSF. Bulls had a sadistic fetish for bludgeoning stowaways' skulls, always claiming self-defense.

A few band members taught him how to make M-80s, and they drove through Seattle's hill-vaulted, old-money haunts, blowing up mailboxes.

Loud learned about heroin addiction and its music—the snaps of tourniquets, the clinking of spoons, the striking of Zippo lighters, the snores of the opioid stupors, and the sight of needles dark with residue, left in the tatted arms, thighs, and feet of bandmates and band-aids alike.

As an Aberdeen native, he had seen addicts before: they made their mats along the scuzzy storefronts of the downtown core like lepers along the walls of a decrepit temple. They moved in noctambulant shuffles, spanging and sweating with sleeping bags draped over them.

Seeing addicts from the safety of his pickup's cab on their way out to work the woods, his dad could never help but sigh: *fucking junkies*. It was the only time Loud ever heard his father overtly disdain a group of people. Loud promised himself he would never be one of them.

Of course, the scene kids made addiction look much cooler, their faces going all porcelain cherub after a hit. But Loud was never tempted. He told them he was scared of needles. They never bought that, though, because he wouldn't free-base with them either. Loud's ongoing refusals to ride the wave aroused suspicions and resentment from all the musos he'd been running with. They got bored of his sideshow monkey dances and resentful of his strange, ageless vitality. As the year went on, Loud found himself facing cold shoulders.

He made it through the winter via couch-surfing, but as the weather got warmer, his bandmates got colder and started turning him out. His favorite crash pads rolled up overnight and Loud started taking risks. He had long avoided shelters because they would ask too many questions. But even in the late April air, he worried about hypothermia under a wind-whipped underpass. Eventually, he dragged himself to a shelter, writing his name down on the nice white people's clipboards and later in the night, at their behest, giving them his real name and date of birth.

In early May, a squad car arrived at the shelter. They'd come for him.

Dad had always been wary around cops. He'd taught Loud a certain way to act around police. "Your life would be just another notch in their belt. So, you do what they say, whatever they say, anytime they say it. They think they own the air you breathe, remember, and will kill you for using too much of it."

So Loud didn't argue when the police told him they were taking him to Heather's Haven, a housing center for runaways. Loud calmly got into the car, his inner heater keeping him warm and telling him to shut up, be nice, and stay alive.

"It seems your mom would like you back at home," one of the officers explained.

"Please, don't take me back to my mom," Loud insisted.

"Son," the cop said.

"She's a crazy wino!"

"Son," the cop continued. "As crazy as your mom might be, she can't be worse than the streets."

*

From the outside, Heather's Haven looked like a clapboard apartment without many windows. Inside it was made up of colorful doors that suggested a box of crayons. There were couches, an outmoded big screen TV, a kitchen, and staff that acted like camp counselors, bringing food and activities and smiles.

Loud avoided everything but the television, which he'd

come out and watch from seven to eight p.m., making sure not to make eye contact with the three to five other kids being held.

He stayed in his room at all other times and ate his meals out of their recycled cardboard containers.

Loud thought about running, but he knew he'd get picked up again. Besides, the months of half-sleep under bridges and the traipsing through the city's wet under-dark had finally punctured his energy reserves, and he found it difficult to move. In his stupor and sobriety, scenes of his dad's death revisited his consciousness, and he soon found his mind tangled again in black film strips.

Three days later, up rolled his mother's brick-red Rabbit.

Leah wore slacks and a blazer now. Her coarse hair was in a neat ponytail. She wore a few necklaces that looked like they were made from bone, seashells or both.

She gave him a concerned look, and he made the mistake of making eye contact with her. Her brown eyes were the copper color of light on the waters of a clay-bottomed eddy. They were *his* eyes, and he couldn't bear to look into them.

"Malachi. Are you okay?" she asked in her deep voice.

Like before, her breath smelled like cigarettes.

"Yeah," Loud said. "How are you, Leah?"

She ignored him.

"I see the Rabbit's still alive and kicking," he said.

She continued to look at him.

"I'm so glad. I have such nice memories of this car," he said with venom.

She kept looking at him. He stared out at the window and winced as she leaned in and kissed him on the forehead. He smelled her Newport cigarettes and remembered the way the smoke clung to her hair.

"You look like something's eating you alive from the inside," she said, with that glinted edge that warned she was getting angry.

Upon his continued silence, she shifted into reverse, and the Rabbit made a high-pitched whine backward. "What's eating you?" Her voice trembled.

He failed to suppress a smile.

"Tell me!"

"No, Leah," he replied.

With a right turn onto the freeway, Leah drove over what had been Loud's neighborhood for nearly nine months. Loud guessed he was supposed to thank her. About ten minutes later, she said:

"I'm sorry I yelled at you, Malachi." She took her eyes away from the road to look at him again, "I'm glad to see you. You must have felt so alone..."

"I'm used to it," he said.

During the winding drive out to Forks, Leah hummed along with Stevie Nicks and Neil Young albums, and Loud held his head in his lap. The headaches had started at Heather's Haven and peaked in intensity as they neared Lake Crescent. In the last year, he'd eaten more weed than protein. Dry of THC, his brain ached like a parched throat. He swore he could feel each cell in his head throb for it.

The Rabbit's cab had one new feature: a trinket dangling from the rearview mirror—an ivory-colored tube. Blemishless. Smoothed. He pawed at it idly and realized it was a hollowed-out bone.

"You like it?" Leah asked with her eyes on the road. "One of the first people I helped get sober made that for me. On his fifth year clean."

Loud massaged his throbbing temples while Leah talked about how Makah children used such a bone as a game piece, only the other pieces were marked by ashen rings. The game's contestants had to guess in which hand the player held the plain piece even as the guesser passed the bones from hand to hand behind his back, while all sang at the top of their lungs and danced in circles. Similar circles as Loud's eyes rolling as Leah spoke.

"I've got no games with you," she said. "My piece is right here. Out in the open. For you to take."

MOMMY'S LITTLE MONSTER

Dad had been right. Leah did live out in the boonies! And it wasn't even on the rez out at Neah Bay. The town of Forks was a collection of mothballed businesses, parking lots, trailer parks, and modest ramblers on big, flat grids all bunched at the base of the Olympic foothills. Not that he'd asked, but Leah told Loud she preferred her own space off the reservation.

"A quiet place to call my own where I can rest after work and where I can keep my distance from tribal expectations. Still, it's close enough I can go participate when I choose too. I am your mother after all. Independent and…Well. Never mind," she said, seeing his attention drift.

That first morning, Loud woke and looked out the window of his mother's spare bedroom. His room, she'd said.

Mountainous hills surrounded the town. Key-shaped strips of brown cut across the slopes, showing where the logging crews had come through. Loud padded out into the living room of his mother's bungalow to find a plate of eggs and bacon ready for him. She was at the table reading the paper. He approached the plate of food warily, as if it were a trap.

"Good morning," Leah said without looking up from her reading.

"Hi, Leah."

"The eggs are fresh. From my neighbor."

Loud spooned in some eggs. His headache had faded, and he was hungry.

She asked him how he slept, if he enjoyed his room, what he thought of her house, and some other things, which Loud responded to by staring at his plate.

She touched him on his chin. He jerked away.

She shook her head. "What were you doing out there,

Malachi?"

"Being a little shit," he replied.

She shut her eyes. "And I've been so worried about you!"

"You didn't try to find me."

"I did!" she replied. "For *weeks*. As often as I could get away from work."

Loud snorted.

"The shelters wouldn't tell me anything... How could you even think I wouldn't go looking for you?"

Loud shrugged.

"Why do you hate me?"

"You left Dad. And me."

She folded up her newspaper. "What was I supposed to do?"

Loud shrugged again.

"Huh? You tell me that. He couldn't provide for the three of us. What was I supposed to do! He had gone on strike. Again. With all the others. We couldn't pay for anything! We had no money coming in."

She inhaled sharply into what Loud thought would turn into a sob, but when he looked up, her eyes were dry. "You know, you never asked what it was like for *me*! I don't know what they told you, what lies they twisted into you, but it was hard."

"I'll bet."

"You got a bitter root in you!" Leah pointed a finger at him. "You have always been bitter toward me. Even when things were good, and I would try to hug you, you would turn away. You refused my breast! I had to feed you from a bottle...And you didn't want to stay with me even after he died. You preferred Grandma Gin to me. Anyone to me!"

Loud's temples throbbed. He wanted to jump out of himself as if his body were no longer safe, as if it had been put over flames.

She put her hands down on the table, fingers outspread.

"I'm sorry I left you, Malachi."

"I'm not."

She rose, putting on a rain jacket and ID badge. "I have to go to work," she said.

She told him she worked at the prison as a chemical dependency counselor. But he wasn't sure. He bet she still drank. She was Native, and people said all Indians did was drink. Even the stories written by Indians were all about Indians drinking. While she was gone "at work," Loud snooped around the house, but didn't find any alcohol.

So, he slept and watched TV, finding new images to explain his dad's death while he hid under a heavy blanket. But the headaches from the pot withdrawals still found him. He thought about wandering around town to see if he could score, but when Leah came home, he was still there on the couch, not having moved in hours.

Her breath was hot and smelled sharp as she knelt by him.

"You know, we could be okay out here, you and me. I got people out here, Ki. My brothers. Their families. Our friends. They're good people. We have fun out here. We could ride bikes on the beach. Go see the sea stacks. You'd love it out here... if you tried."

A vision flashed in Loud's memory: his father sitting alone by the fire in their backyard. He was humming "Goodnight Irene" and whittling her face into a piece of wood that would not speak. Somewhere his spirit still did this alone, eyes blackened in death. Floating in white, the letters of the cereal spelled something. They always had, but suddenly Loud found he could read the message. *When love leaves, it don't come back.*

Loud clutched the blanket and stiffened his jaw.

"But you won't try. You hate me," Leah sighed. "I know you do."

She touched his hair. He forced himself not to flinch and stared straight ahead, trying to focus on the TV.

"But that's okay," Leah said. "Know that I love you. I named you my angel. My clamshell boy."

Loud continued to stare at the TV.

"You should know, though," Leah continued. "That if you hate me, you'll always be half hating yourself and everything you come to love. I'm half of you, you know."

"I don't hate you," he said.

"You do," she nodded. In Loud's peripheral vision, he could see his mom's face twisting like a hot rag wrung out. The face horrified him; it reminded him of that day he had come home from school, and she'd been there to tell him of his dad's death. It made him want to run.

As if sensing it, she got up and sat in a chair farther away from him.

"I want to go back to Aberdeen," he said.

"Why?" she asked, hands in her lap.

"To start a band and piss people off."

She sniffed. "And be another Cobain?"

"That's the plan."

"I just don't understand. Why would you want to go back there?"

"So I can make music about working people. People like Dad."

"You admire your dad," Leah commented. She lit one of her Newport's.

The smell made Loud's mouth itch for weed with its deeper musk.

"How do you think your dad died?" She pointed her cigarette at him.

Loud sat up. "You told me! The mill ate him. And they covered it up and didn't give us any money or anything."

She inhaled deeply and let out a strand of smoke through her nose. She turned off the TV. Tears shot up into her eyes, and her chin quivered. In a smoke-deepened voice, she said: "I told you a lie."

Loud blinked.

"Your father was killed in a cedar swamp on 9/11. It was midnight. He and Keith—you remember him—they were cutting where they weren't supposed to. They were stealing a tree. And then this wind…"

"No."

She shook her head, "A branch came down—a widow-maker. And he didn't have his little whistle punk to warn him…"

"How do I know this isn't the lie?" Loud asked.

"It isn't! They'd been on strike at the mill. They were desperate." Something inside Loud clicked on. The reels started turning.

"Why are you telling me this?" Loud demanded.

"I told you what I did because…" Leah sputtered. "Because I didn't want you to think badly of him."

Loud looked at the cradleboard above the fireplace, the one supposedly carved for him by one of his uncles. An uncle he'd never met.

"But I'm sorry for it now," Leah continued. "Because it made you hate that town so much you started loving to hate it. Just like your father had. He could have come up here with me. Uncle Philip works in forestry. Did he tell you that? Why would he? One of these 'I'll-never-leave-the-Harbor' people. He was *so* in love with that town of his, he couldn't see what else was out there. It's the same with you, I see it. But it's just a town, Malachi. People work there. People die there. People work and die here too! But they'd be your people. And if you don't want to get into all the tribal stuff, we live far enough away where you don't have to. That's part of why I live here! But here, you'd have a place to belong. Instead of where…"

"I don't want a place with you! I want my dad," Loud

hissed and shook himself free of the blankets and went to stand out in the backyard for a long time in the cold crepuscular air. The smell of heated coals hung heavy in the air, and somewhere, people were laughing long and hard. So hard that maybe they were crying.

Loud's viscera shook as if chilled by a great wind. His thoughts turned. The reels inside were rolling, but in different directions and this time with color and sound, and they said:

So you're not just a runaway mom, Leah Ledbetter Homewrecker. You're a liar. Too bad, so sad I wouldn't guzzle at your nip. Probably because you tasted like beer. You stole my eyes! Some counselor. Convenient for you to tell me now that dad's a cedar thief. Cooking me up a slab of beefy bullshit, trying to shove me back into your vagina. Hula-hooping with your driftwood circles. Sure. Sure, Leah. How about you shut your giant cunt, get off my junk, and let me be where I wanna be. Your 'people' aren't ever going to be my people. They'll do what you did. Shit me out whenever you get tired of me. When love leaves, it don't come back. *I see you clear and I'm steering south, clear away from YOU and what you did to Dad! What you did to us. You left him. You left me. You hated him. You hated his half of me. So, I guess I do hate you, Leah Ledbetter. Monkey can't see. Monkey don't get his dues. Monkey do the do do.*

*

Loud woke up in bed, not sure how he'd gotten there.

He sat up. His mind was moving, moving quicker than on the herb. His thoughts had glistening edges to them, like freshly sharpened butterfly knives. He was sure of one thing: he was going to get a map and head back to Aberdeen as soon as the moment presented itself.

It did sooner than expected. And he wouldn't have to walk.

Loud woke up the next morning to find his mom already dressed and seated by the door. No breakfast on the table.

She invited him to help himself to whatever was in the cupboards before telling him that she would be out all day. Her bike was in the garage; he could ride it around town if he wanted.

"I named it Neil Young," she said. "Because your dad and I used to…"

"Where are you going?" Loud asked, noticing she didn't have her work badge on.

She said she was going to talk to someone. Someone she trusted. To get some advice.

"About me?" he asked.

Her eyes glimmered, impressed, and amused. "Yes," she said.

"Have fun," he scoffed, tossing himself onto her sofa.

When she came back, it was late afternoon.

"Malachi," his mom said at the door. "I want to show you something."

He didn't reply. But she kept standing there.

"Malachi. Get into the car," she said.

He got up and went. Maybe somewhere along the way, he could jump out and run from her. She drove him over a white river to purple-barked trees that stood like pillars holding up the sky. When she stopped the car abruptly, he readied himself for her tears, her vindictive pleas— whatever might come. But she just pointed out her window down a road, nameless and bent, tunneling into a throat of wet, curling trees.

"That road, Malachi. If somebody was crazy enough, they could walk that road down to the big ugly town you love to hate so much."

Walk? he thought. *Why bother when I can just boost your bike?*

Malachi "Loud" McCrowley left that night. On the plushy seat of Leah Ledbetter's bike, Neil Young, he hummed self-spun songs about mills eating his dad while the bike wheels turned and turned. In this fashion, Loud traveled three-quarters of the length of the Olympic Peninsula. More than a hundred miles.

Days later, when he arrived back in his soggy hometown on his mother's bike, he discovered his grandparents' house still standing on the edge of the sloughs, abandoned and, from his perspective, vastly improved.

Boards were nailed over the windows, but for some reason, not the door. They hadn't even bothered. On the door, there was a single sheet of pink paper with broad, black lettering:

NO TRESPASSING—SIERRA PACIFIC INDUSTRIES

Loud snatched it off the door and put it in the left lapel of his vest pocket.

After trying the locked door, he saw the boards over the windows were thin OSB. Those cheapskates! The boards on the front windows, under the covered porch, were intact. But the boards over the windows along the back basement had been exposed directly to wind and rain. It didn't take long for Loud's inquisitive fingers to find a weak corner.

He spent the rest of the day prowling around Junction City, eventually boosting a pry bar and mallet from a demolition site. He took the tools back to the house, and in the time it took him to hum "I Fought the Law," he had cracked off the rotting board, bashed through the window glass, and climbed into his grandparents' abandoned basement. The basement he'd once lived in with his dad.

Gloom, dust, and the smell of cedar beams overhead welcomed him home.

A FIEND, A FRIEND

Cal's Forerunner cruises along the highway over the Nisqually wetlands on their way to Seattle. The April morning's sun, in full swing, breaks through the clouds and catches on the wet strands of the tidal flats and the slicks in the estuary.

They cross a bridge. Jeremy's eyes hurt in the light. The crisscross of the trusses cast an argyle pattern of light and dark over him. His stomach cramps up as he remembers the good and the bad about Loud.

*

Jeremy met Loud on his third day at Weatherwax High School, just in time to prevent his new-school despair from turning suicidal.

That first day still makes him shudder. Even though it was the start of his junior year, he felt like a freshman all over again. The new school towered with its arches and bollards. Its glass reflected his tight smile slipping into a sneer as the open doors emitted the malfunctioning jukebox sound of the student body. He took a deep breath as he felt their voices tidal-wave toward him.

Blue-and-gold Bobcat posters bannered the walls. Crowds of kids perched along the mezzanine. Girls ran down the stairs screaming, imparting urgent but fragmentary truths about boys, clubs, shoes, and Taylor Swift. Huge ox-like dudes in jerseys shoved each other and flexed. Peons in sweatshirts and Dickies huddled and pigeon-murmured at the base of the stairs or in the corners.

Jeremy knew the first day would be filled with get-to-know-you nonsense with kids he didn't want to get to know since he planned on doing Running Start. He would've ditched had it not been for the threat of Judge Spurgeon and Truancy Court. His mom had warned him that it wasn't like Olympia. On topics like absenteeism, Grays Harbor County didn't play. A newly created attendance court was sentencing kids to nights in jail for skipped school days and his mom warned him that his status as a police detective's kid was no Get-Out-of-Jail-Free card.

Weatherwax's library hadn't opened yet, which forced Jeremy into the lunchroom in search of an anonymous corner to wait in until class started. The smell of new paint and bad food added to his nausea. The tables were all full of established cliques, leaving Jeremy to shuffle around friendless, repeating in his head *it's cool, it's cool, it's cool,* and trying to embody the expression. He also refrained from drawing the Xs on his knuckles that identified him as straight-edge. He had dressed generically to avoid being seen, opting for corduroys, and a black hoodie over his The Doors t-shirt, a crowd-pleaser. Who didn't like The Doors? The shirt featured the iconic pic of a shirtless Morrison, gazing out with his hypnotic eyes. Though no girl would be checking out Jeremy, they might give Morrison a once over, which might just give Jeremy enough time to come up with something clever. He felt eyes on him, his narrow cheeks shining with his newness. He pressed on his fingertip calluses, reminding himself that he played guitar—which was cool, which meant he was cool. At least, sort of cool.

The bell rang. Jeremy got lost in the mass-scattering of bodies and was left wandering the hallways looking for Ms. Rigby's English class. He misplaced his transcript and didn't even know which floor his class was on. A school safety officer recognized Jeremy as "Detective Sweet's boy", put an avuncular arm around his neck, and dragged him to class where he tiptoed into the rows of his peers as if they were a bewitched wood.

As he eased behind the one empty desk, the image of the kid seated behind him flash-burned into his brain: two hundred pounds of bumpkin with bad teeth and icy blue eyes oddly avoiding him.

The man-child's tongue stuck out of the side of his mouth like a red steam lever as he sharpened his pencil on a piece of flint. The teacher took roll. The kid behind him was Brock Olander.

One of the many things his mom had told him to avoid in Aberdeen was anybody with the last name Olander. Known as the Ollanketos before being anglicized to the Olanders at Ellis Island bygone years ago, the family of Finns were something of a legend in their embodiment of the town's spirit of underhanded independence. Brock's father, William Olander, was a Rhinehouse millwright by day and proprietor of unscrupulous industries by night. Jeremy's mom was inclined to investigate but knew she'd never be able to cut through "all the good ol' boy bullshit." But even without his mom being a principled gumshoe, the Olanders had another reason to hate Jeremy.

Jeremy was the son of Malcolm Sweet, a former spokesman for Earth First!, the group whose lobbying helped label the spotted owl as an endangered species. This achievement effectively shut down logging operations in Western Washington, causing Aberdeen fathers to be without jobs for most of the '90s. Aberdeen children went without Christmas presents and, judging from Brock's snaggle teeth, orthodontia. In their jobless fury, the rifted loggers made a rag-and-sawdust-stuffed effigy of Jeremy's dad which they tossed into a bonfire. In one of Jeremy's monthly visits to his dad's house, Malcolm show-boated the pictures in his copy of *The Harbor Herald*. His dad told Jeremy that infamy was one occupational hazard he was all too happy to incur. He saw himself as ensuring Jeremy's generation a future with oxygen-breathing old-growth, free of molestation. He regretted the impact this would have on "the Workers of the Harbor." Though they were misguided in their misplaced, self-abasing affection for their corporations. The Aberdeeners, Malcolm felt, needed to see the writing on the wall or get left in the dustbin of history.

Easy for him to say. He wasn't being forced by Mom to live with them.

"Your dad thinks too highly of himself," Mom sighed. "It was fifteen years ago. Nobody remembers that."

When Jeremy continued to protest, she told him that it came down to a simple fact.

"You're not your father." Case closed.

Ms. Rigby continued rollcall. When she got to Jeremy, she said his last name as "sweat" like the kind that was running down his back. He told her it was "sweet." But as she was like ninety years old, she didn't hear.

"It's Sweet," Jeremy clarified loudly. "Rhymes with 'treat.'"

"Or teat," somebody said.

The other sixteen-year-olds snickered, but above their static, Jeremy felt Brock Olander's unamused silence.

As Ms. Rigby passed out syllabi, Jeremy felt a tap on his shoulder. He turned around to see Brock. He looked like he was twenty-five—with a beard and limbs thick as overstuffed sausages. He wore black Carhartt jeans and a hickory shirt. Jeremy turned back around to face the front, hoping it was a mistake.

There was another tap on Jeremy's shoulder, this one followed by a whisper.

"*Psst!* Douchebag. Just to let you know, if you're going to start any of that tree-hugging shit of your dad's, I'll beat your fucking face in."

"That was fifteen years ago!" Jeremy seethed.

"We don't forget shit here like they do in Olympia," Brock said.

"Well, I'm not him."

"You're worse," Brock commented. "You're a little faggot too scared to chain yourself to a tree."

The kid in front of Jeremy passed back a stack of syllabi. Jeremy took it and shook it in Brock's face. "Don't. Talk. To me like that."

The voice sprang from a place deep inside him where an idea lived. An idea— put there mainly by his mother—that he was entitled to respect.

"What?" Brock asked, recoiling.

Jeremy motioned for him to take the papers. Brock did not accept. His face was aghast. "I can talk to you however the fuck I want. I mean, you've got a half-naked guy on your shirt. You've got to be queer."

Jeremy dropped the stack of syllabi onto the ground and turned around.

"Excuse me!" Ms. Rigby whined and made Jeremy gather the papers while Brock continued.

"You have to earn respect out here, you yuppy little kike," Brock hissed.

Jeremy furrowed his brow. Brock either didn't know what kike meant or was commenting on Jeremy's curly hair, grown big in homage to At the Drive-In, a postpunk band from Texas.

"I'm… not Jewish," Jeremy replied.

"You're Jewish?" Brock turned to his peers, who were all intently watching the situation. "Dude, the little faggot is Jewish!"

A couple of kids laughed.

"I said…" Jeremy said.

Brock thwacked him on the back of his neck with a pencil. "Hey!"

Jeremy felt Brock's thwacks for the next forty-five minutes, the pencil leaving a red wand of shame. The bell rang. Jeremy resisted the urge to turn tail by gripping his desk and planting his feet on the carpet.

Brock rose and bulldozed Jeremy's desk out of the aisle.

"Oops. Let me fix that for ya," Brock said, and with a single jerk from his forearm, he slid Jeremy and his desk back into alignment. With the same motion, Brock's other hand batted Jeremy's glasses off his face and across the room.

As the soundtrack of Brock's heaving laughter faded, Jeremy picked up his glasses, wiped them off, and put them back on. Ms. Rigby, who was reading her computer screen through the lower semicircle of her bifocals, didn't say a word.

The next day, Jeremy came early to class and sat at the very back.

Brock sat right next to him. He rotated a black puck of chewing tobacco between his fingers and flicked it.

Jeremy flinched.

"Like that, pussy?" Brock said. He popped open the can of Skoal. He gathered a wad between his thumb and forefinger and stuffed it into his lower lip. Right in class. For Brock's casual drug use, there was no more censure than there was for his bullying.

Other students shuffled in. Jeremy looked ahead, trying to take notes. But he could see Brock giving him a zombie-like leer, with his jaw gaping open, revealing his mouthful of crooked teeth and hazing Jeremy with his chew-flavored breath. Jeremy couldn't think above Brock's mouth-breathing, broken only by the occasional suck on the blackening ball of tobacco bulging in his lower lip.

Jeremy turned toward him, wondering what the hell the hick kids ate to get them growing so big. Probably bull testicles. "Dude, what's your problem?"

"Don't look at me!" Brock snapped and returned to zombie mode.

Jeremy went back to his futile effort to focus, writing down the day's talking points. *F. Scott Fitzgerald, Lost Generation Typology, Roaring 20's, Symbolism…*

"Wanna fight?" Brock croaked.

"No."

"Cuz you're a pussy."

Jeremy's hands were shaking. Brock guzzled from a Coke bottle, then asked, "What would you do if I hit you in the face right now?"

"I guess…" Jeremy's voice went out like a match. "I'd ignore it?"

Brock laughed. "You guess? It'll be hard to ignore it with your teeth on the floor, you kikey faggot."

Class proceeded with Brock flicking his chew can. Every flick felt like a fan blade whizzing near Jeremy's head. As class wrapped up, Brock, wearing a look of contrition, offered Jeremy what was left of the black soda.

"No way," Jeremy replied.

"Fine," Brock said. He uncapped it and splashed a swig onto Jeremy's pants. A swig that Jeremy discovered contained pulpy discharges of saliva-soaked chew.

*

Chemistry offered an unexpected reprieve. He sat at a lab table with a girl, also bespectacled, wearing overalls over a Modest Mouse t-shirt, eyes locked on Jim Morrison from behind her sable-colored curls.

"I love The Doors."

"Who doesn't?" Jeremy had seen Modest Mouse at one of their early shows in Olympia. He and the girl, Aurora, talked through the bell.

Their first assignment was to review a concept from Biology in a creative presentation that could take the form of a play, a sculpture, a poem, or a song. The Chem. teacher, in her striped tights, jean skirt, and dreads, seemed more like a closet member of Riot Grrrl, which they both loved. Once Jeremy found out Aurora played drums, the choice was easy. A jam session was in order!

Between the two of them, they had the firmest grasp on cellular respiration. Jeremy reworded Weezer's "Undone-The Sweater Song" and sang, "when the air comes through your lungs (whoa-o-whoa-o-whoa!)." When she caught her breath from laughing, she helped him work out the rest of the lyrics. They agreed to meet at her house later that week to practice.

She wasn't the prettiest girl he'd ever seen, but the prospect of playing to her beat and rocking out to cool tunes sounded like a fun enough reason to keep living.

*

At night concerns about Brock returned. Jeremy couldn't sleep with the phantom feeling of the dark emission on his leg. He felt the big troll's hateful words in his bones, filling lacunas into who he was. Was he gay? He tried fantasizing about a guy for a change—some strapping senior he'd seen naked in the locker rooms before P.E. It didn't go anywhere. Was he Jewish? He invented a subplot in his Anglo ancestry involving a Jewish mistress. He would have embraced either identity. Either would have been far better than being what he was: somebody dumb enough to let a bovine yokel bully him.

Jeremy had been dumb enough to believe that reading all those books would get his father to like him. Yet whenever they got together, his dad would stare just above Jeremy's head and prattle on about the newest piece of legislation that would actually WORK FOR THE PEOPLE!, meanwhile never asking Jeremy anything about his life, how he was doing, what he was feeling, what his interests were, or if he had a girlfriend.

Jeremy had been dumb enough to believe that his dad's replacement, Keith Chevelle, loved his mom. Mom and Keith, her hubby of two years, boyfriend of four, had already been in Aberdeen a year by the time Jeremy arrived. She'd taken a job with Aberdeen PD for higher pay and the promise of a quick promotion to detective. Keith, native to Aberdeen, had followed. Jeremy remained in Olympia with Grandma so he could finish out his sophomore year at his old school. When Grandma dropped Jeremy off at the new house in Aberdeen, he found Keith with his shirt off, napping on the sofa while the TV glowed. It was eight o'clock at night. During the year Jeremy had spent separate from them, he had heard only veiled reports from his mom that things were "rough." Keith had been having some trouble finding consistent work.

That night, Keith largely ignored Jeremy while he unpacked. Jeremy fell asleep to the sound of the television nattering in the living room. Then, around midnight, Keith started up his motorcycle and drove off, leaving Jeremy alone in the house. He went out into the living room and sat up, waiting for Keith to return, which he did four hours later.

"Where have you been?" Jeremy asked triumphantly. In a way, he was ending a six-year tug of war over his mom's affection. He had gained yardage using pity and loyalty, while Keith used his handiness and sex. The contest had made life interesting, and Jeremy even liked it when Keith won sometimes. Other times, Keith dropped the rope, sending Jeremy and his mom into the mud.

With his eyes ringed in red and smelling dank, Keith looked at Jeremy and, with a straight face, said he'd been out purchasing some antacids. "Let's keep this between us," he said. "Some things are best kept between dudes is all."

Jeremy told his mom the next day, driving one more stake into the coffin of her second marriage—one that never should have happened. If only she would have put up with his dad's workaholism, erratic pay, and leftist views. If only his dad could have put up with Mom's conservative sympathies and need for stability.

It was a pyrrhic victory for Jeremy. He felt like a fink for telling on Keith and more of a momma's boy than ever. His mom's proceeding seizures of grief turned her face into one big, red welt. Jeremy sat with her while the tears dripped off her nose and stuttered out platitudes that he hoped would sound comforting. His attempts at encouragement were so ineffectual against her adult despair that it made him feel more than ever that his youth was a disability.

*

On the morning of his third day at Weatherwax High, Jeremy put on his Clash shirt and ripped-up jeans. He drew a fresh set of Xs on his knuckles. Why hide? He didn't know whether he was gay or Jewish. But he did know he was punk.

He walked into class and sat in the back again. Brock came in—today in a work bib and ball-cap toned in hunter-camo. He was chortling to Johnny Tayak. Short but stocky, Johnny had big, liver-colored lips and eyes so wide around they looked spooked. As if a big rig had just honked in his face. The two parked themselves right next to Jeremy.

"Hug any trees today, Nancy Jew-face?" Brock asked.

"I am tired of your shit," Jeremy said through a sneer.

"Me too! Which is why I'm done talking. Three p.m., today. You and me, Jack in the Box parking lot."

"Is that where you go to get head?" It came out of Jeremy like a spear slicing through layers of fear.

Brock didn't flinch: "You would want to suck my dick, wouldn't you?"

"I don't want to know about your fantasies."

"You know, I just might not wait to pound your ass until three. Maybe after class. What do you think, Johnny? Maybe after class, I'll just deck this kike and get it over with."

"Definitely," Tayak agreed.

The classroom door opened, and in sauntered the punkiest kid Jeremy had ever seen:

The shinies studding his jean vest, his freshly-styled mohawk, his Butthole Surfers t-shirt. But none of them were needed to interest

Jeremy. It was the kid's skin. He *was* something. Latino? Middle Eastern? Indian? As a well-read sixteen-year-old with a liberal father, Jeremy romanticized non-whiteness. Sure, in retrospect, you could say he fetishized it. But here's how his thinking went back then. Whatever ethnicity this kid was, he was brown—a color all people were supposed to be back before they hid from the sun. A color all people would eventually be again, or so one of Dad's theories went.

The newcomer's light brown eyes rested on him, in near recognition, spurring on Jeremy's suspicion that they were somehow alike. He plunked into the seat in front of Jeremy.

"Well, well. If it isn't Loud 'the Juker' McCrowley," Johnny Tayak said.

Brock let go of Jeremy's desk. "I see you didn't have balls enough to try out for football, McCrowley."

"Fucking around with summer rugby's all you could handle, huh?" Johnny taunted.

"Your mom keeps me too busy to handle much else," Loud said, then turned to Jeremy, "It's hard work humping a double deuce, huh?"

"He doesn't know!" Brock said to Johnny. Brock turned back to Loud and pointed at Jeremy. "Lil Sweet is more of a queer than you are, McCrowley."

Loud raised an eyebrow at Brock.

"Well, *ask* him," Brock shrugged, pointing to Jeremy.

"So what if he's gay," Loud said. "Love is love, dude."

Ms. Rigby shut them up, and the rest of class went by without incident. Brock and Johnny were quiet, other than occasional thwacks of their Skoal cans. Jeremy no longer flinched. Brock's vitriol seemed to bear no real malice toward Loud, as if, through the ostensible summer forays in roughneck rugby, Loud had won uneasy respect from Brock. Jeremy suspected Brock was even a little afraid of Loud. Whatever the case, sitting next to Loud, Jeremy entered an eye-of-the-storm cessation of cruelty.

At the bell, Loud and Jeremy stayed seated while the rest—Brock and Johnny included—exited class.

"Dude, where did you come from?" Jeremy asked.

"Here."

"I'm from Olympia."

"No wonder why he hates you."

"He's been at me all week!"

"Yeah…" Loud nodded. "He'll do that. So, *are* you gay?"

"So, do *you* play rugby?"

"Just be real about it," Loud said.

"No. I don't think I'm gay."

Loud shrugged. "Anything is cool if you own it. Try it. Say, 'I braid my butt hairs.'"

"Eww."

"I use mommy's compact mirror," Loud said, lifting his legs.

Ms. Rigby cleared her throat and motioned to the door with her chin.

They went to lunch together, straddling chairs at one of the octagon-shaped tables honeycombing across the cafeteria's linoleum.

Jeremy scanned for Brock.

"He's probably throwing the ol' pigskin around," Loud said.

Upon hearing this, Jeremy shook out the contents of his sack lunch: an apple, a turkey sandwich, a Capri-Sun.

Loud was looking at Jeremy's sandwich. It had provolone cheese. Peppers instead of tomato to avoid sogginess. But no matter what combo Jeremy tried in the morning, the journey inside his backpack always rendered the crispiest, most appealing grinder into a soggy, gluten-wrapped abortion by lunchtime.

Loud was still looking at the sandwich, a smile playing across his face.

Jeremy slid him half the sandwich and watched. As Loud

worked his jaws, the sandwich's sad triangles folded in on themselves and disappeared like a cardboard box in a trash compactor.

Jeremy picked up the remaining half, only to notice Loud guiltily eyeing it as well. He relinquished it with an eyeroll. Loud pounced and devoured again, finishing with a belch.

"So," Loud said. "What's with the X's?"

"It means I'm straight-edge."

Loud looked at him blankly.

"Like, I don't do drugs."

"Oh. Right on," Loud said.

"What, that's not as cool as braiding your butt hair?"

"No, it definitely is," Loud said. "I don't touch the shit, myself."

A pachyderm-sized racket boomed up from a far corner of the cafeteria as Brock and his bros paraded through, giving nuggies to second-string linemen and bra-snapping the spaghetti straps of their girlfriends.

"Hey," Loud said. "Want to fuck with him?"

"Yes. No. Is it…you know, legal?"

"Of course!" Loud said primly. "Meet me at the classroom at the very south end of the first floor right at the two-thirty bell."

LOUD'S LITTLE FOOL

Running out of homeroom a few minutes before the bell rang, Jeremy arrived at a door in a quiet, unadorned wing of the school. He wasn't shaking with fear, but ambition. Why? Just because of this guy, Loud? The self-doubt, Keith's waywardness, Mom's misery—they were all still there. But now Jeremy had something to do, some small revenge to extract.

Loud appeared moments later. "What does he do to you that bothers you most?"

"Calling me a fag and a kike."

"You're Jewish?"

"No. Well… I don't think so! But…"

"Okay, something else. I don't do anything biggoty."

"He stares at me funny. Like this."

"Like a zombie."

"Perfect."

The dismissal bell rang. The door opened, and a series of kids meandered out. One had a sizable ledge clefted into his skull. Another had big, air-catching ears and a vacant stare. Another girl laughed snarkily at nothing. Other kids looked normal, but they were the kids Jeremy only had gym with. Then out came Brock.

Jeremy and Loud made their faces into zombie masks.

All the heft and swag seemed to drain from Brock. He seemed genuinely disdain-filled and brushed past them.

*

Loud had a bike too! And they had unknowingly locked up at the same rack at the ass end of the school. They both agreed skateboarding was cool but impractical as transportation. Helmets weren't even on the table. Mess up Loud's mohawk? Flatten Jeremy's white-boy fro? No discussion! Sorry, Mom.

They cruised along Weatherwax High's blocky edifice, following it south toward the downtown sprawl, the water somewhere beyond. The new school stood like a mall, all corrugated steel and glass cinctured by brick. The old school, which Cobain attended, had gone up in flames years prior.

As Loud stood on the toothy jaws of the pedals, he towered over his Diamondback Outlook's eighteen-inch frame. After countless days left out in the rain, his bike chain had oxidized into a bumpy, orange snake that oddly complemented the frame's hunter-green color.

"I call my bike Clyde. As in Clydesdale. Cuz it's so fucking big. Does your bike have a name?" Jeremy asked shyly.

"Yeah," Loud said. "Neil Young."

Neil Young's rear derailleur convulsed any time Loud shifted, and the shocks rattled as he hopped on and off curbs. But his long legs hammered the rusty rig forward in a strident but leisurely pace so they could talk.

"Brock's…not really in Special Ed, is he?" Jeremy asked.

"Just for his homeroom. He's got some kind of reading issue thing."

Jeremy's stomach turned. "I thought you said you didn't do anything biggoty. That was…kind of fucked up of us."

Loud shrugged. "It's no more fucked up than him calling people names for being gay or Jewish. He calls people 'retard' too. All the time. Thinks he can say anything he wants just because he's big and his dad's some kind of muckety-muck."

"You ever seen him? William Olander?"

"Yeah…The guy's a beast."

During the summer, Loud said he'd gotten so bored that after reading a dozen books in as many days, he'd wound up playing on the Aberdonkies, the same rugby team as Brock. William Olander had rolled up to one of their games in his big truck with its lifted tires. He's brooded behind the windshield, on the phone the whole game.

Jumping a curb, Loud said that rugby was the closest thing to a mosh pit you could find in Aberdeen. "Right now, at least."

Loud said how there were always assholes like Brock in mosh pits, anyway. At least in the Seattle ones.

"You know the Seattle scene?" Jeremy asked, keeping Clyde steady on the sidewalk.

"Sort of. I was in a band out there. A few, actually."

Jeremy tried to keep his eyes in their sockets. "What kind of bands?"

"Punk ones, of course. Some psychobilly."

"Why did you leave?" Jeremy asked.

They skirted across Wishkah Street. The diesel engines of the enormous trucks idled impatiently for them to cross the street's width before the light changed. Back on the sidewalk, they rolled into the shadow of the Becker Building. The east side of its haggard visage with its exposed façade and boarded-up windows looked like it just survived a shelling.

"Scenes can be like an old sweater," Loud explained. "They scratch and choke the life out of you."

"I can see that," Jeremy said, thinking all the shows he'd been to in Olympia. They were frequented by the same group of ten people who acted like they were too cool to talk to him.

"Plus, most of those Seattle cats were strung out on skag," Loud said.

"I've read that stuff can kill you."

"You've read," Loud said with a grimace. "But I've seen."

It sounded like Jeremy's five-word autobiography.

"Speaking of getting killed," Loud said, abruptly cutting across the street. "We better slip into the cut."

"Brock did threaten to kick my ass today."

They crossed when the traffic cleared. Loud stood on his pedals again, and Neil Young's little frame listed from side to side as he picked up speed. Black duct tape zebra-striped across his shoes. Stretching over his shifting hips, his skinny jeans were shredded and frayed in just the right places.

"So. Do you know a place I could get some hip threads?" Jeremy said.

"What you need is a thrift store," Loud said, pushing on. "In a place where cool people drop off cool clothes. Definitely not here."

They decided on St. Vincent De Paul's in Olympia. For five bucks, Loud said they could bus there and back, and Jeremy was more than down to spring for the fare.

The bus stop, which Loud called the Smoke Hole, was demarcated by green archways and old bums sucking on snipes. Loud seemed to know them and nodded discreetly in their direction. Loud started looking from side to side and moving his shoulders like someone getting ready to box.

Jeremy wondered if Loud was embarrassed being seen with him.

"You sure it's okay to leave our bikes here?" Jeremy asked as they locked their frames to a streetlamp. Aberdeen bus stops didn't have bike racks apparently.

Though Jeremy's U-lock and Loud's chain would ward away any amateur thieves, a pair of bolt cutters would be enough to rob them of their rides.

"Nobody's going to fuck with your rig when it's tied to mine," Loud said and faced the oncoming bus.

Jeremy didn't have time to ascertain how Loud was able to have such nonchalance in a downtown drug den like Aberdeen. Was it all just bluster? If it wasn't, was Jeremy ready to face the implications of involving himself with someone who could command the respect of downtown rascals great and small? He asked too late. The bus pulled up, and his feet followed Loud's, his body more aware of what he wanted than his mind could admit. If he couldn't immediately possess the free-wheeling saunter Loud maintained in this oppressive place, Jeremy wanted to be around him long enough at least for some of it to wear off.

The bus chugged up the hill away from Aberdeen.

Jeremy decided to broach the race issue. And did it like a drunk in a paint store, splashing unfortunate whiteness everywhere. "So…You're like…Well…Where are you from? I mean, where is your family from?"

"I'm Native American," Loud said, looking annoyed.

"Cool," Jeremy said.

"It's not really," Loud said. "I don't thread dreamcatchers or hunt whales on the weekend or anything Native. So, it's like being born with a tattoo on your forehead with the sign of a club you're not really that into. And most white people hate your club. So, you get none of the benefits and all the static."

"I…like your club. I think Native peoples are…"

"Well, good for you. But I don't do clubs. Of any kind. And don't expect me to be your one non-white friend so you can say you're not racist. Because *all* white people are racist, no matter what they say."

"No doubt," Jeremy said.

"All people everywhere are racist," Loud said.

"Yeah they fucking are." It was easy to agree with Loud because Jeremy didn't know what he thought about the whole race issue, yet. Then again, he didn't know what he thought about much of anything yet except which bands he liked. And that he liked Loud and wanted to be his friend.

*

Returning to his hometown of Olympia after a two-month leave made Jeremy realize that it was a lot more like Aberdeen than he thought. There were old brick buildings and a river with pilings sticking out like rotten teeth in an old person's skull. Except that in Olympia there were record stores, ironwork esplanades, and a dirty capitol dome.

At St. Vinny's, Jeremy riffled through the racks. It was tedious yet addicting. Though he asked for the changing rooms, Loud seemed to have no shame, taking off his shirt in the aisles, revealing his hairless and undernourished torso before putting on whatever tee he was looking at. Loud's stomach had the man-creases and abs of the dudes in underwear ads—definitions Jeremy did not possess yet sensed he was supposed to have.

Everything they tried on seemed too big or too smelly or too lame.

"These jeans aren't torn up enough," Jeremy mumbled.

"Tears are a good thing?" Loud asked.

"Well, it's…you know…the style."

Loud shook his head. "Noooo. I don't know."

"But… your." Jeremy pointed at Loud's holey jeans.

"These are my clothes. Please tell me you're not one of those people who buy jeans worked over with carpentry tools. Life will tear your jeans up for you."

With Loud's help, Jeremy scored a couple of good finds, including a vintage Rancid shirt with WWI soldiers wearing gas masks.

On their return ride home, the sun was a blast of energy slowly exhausting itself in the big September sky. It filled the bus with white light, making the rattling metal walls feel thin like they were riding in the exoskeleton of a giant locust.

They sang favorite punk anthems. Social Distortion's "Mommy's Little Monster." The Misfit's "Last Caress." NOFX's "Don't Call Me White", which Loud never had to worry about.

The twenty-year-old tunes, dated and obscure, were all the more deliciously theirs.

Jeremy always gravitated to punk as ballast against his mom's career as an authoritarian, but also because he didn't see himself in much of the top-charting songs of his time which were mostly about chasing tail at dance clubs and being a badass. As a minor, he had never been to a club. Any confidence he possessed manifested in a snide, sidelong amble on the outskirts of center stage. Edgy, aggressive music always seemed the best soundtrack for his internal rage. Paradoxically the music helped him hide more comfortably.

Of course, as a cop's kid, Jeremy had to cobble together his punk façade from carefully chosen principles. Ian MacKaye's straight-edge mantra—*don't smoke, don't drink, don't fuck* –interlocked with Mom's ardent belief in the evils of marijuana and premarital sex. The punk movement's pacifist wing appealed too as it allowed Jeremy to quietly sneer at the authoritarian nature of police without doing anything about it. The truth was, he didn't really mind cops or that his mom was one. So long as they left him alone. This was what he wanted from most people. Except for a stray wish that if he looked cool enough, one day a cute girl might come over and talk to him.

Though punk's uniqueness differentiated him, Jeremy was noticing that it further alienated him from most other kids, who didn't share his oddball interests. Until he met Loud. Meeting a kid in 2008 who liked the same music he did, to the same intensity, was unexpected. It made Jeremy want to reach out and grab Loud to make sure he was real, to make sure not to lose him.

But then Loud started rolling his neck round and round in slow, unsteady circles, whispering words that flowed and sometimes sputtered. These unknowable utterances must have belonged to some off-kilter melody Jeremy didn't recognize.

Though he had his preferences by then, he had a vast awareness of music— thanks mostly to his dad, but he couldn't tease out what Loud was humming. Maybe it was Loud's own warlock mix, whipped up in the pinball machine of his mind.

Loud's face—with his butt chin, heavy nose, and perfect skin—shifted expressions as often as the shadows of the trees falling over. His brows would arch into a look of apprehension. Other times he'd laugh for no reason, or the side of his face would pinch together as if letting out a fart. For stretches, Loud didn't seem to know Jeremy was even there.

Loud sat up with a start. He rubbed his hands and smelled them.

"Man, it's been forever since I've been to a show," Loud blurted out.

"There are shows we can go to in Olympia," Jeremy said. "There's a scene there."

"What's better than being part of a scene," Loud gave him a suggestive look, "is starting one."

"You think *we* can start a punk scene? In Aberdeen?"

"Oh, no doubt," Loud said. "I mean, Kurt Cobain was born here, dude."

"Nobody cares about that anymore. Nirvana's cliché. We'd have to make something totally new. Anyway, what do you play?"

"I scream into microphones," Loud replied. "Plus, I do the Flail. It's basically my impression of an epileptic seizure set to music."

Jeremy lied and said he played a little guitar and some bass. But Jeremy could play anything. Green Day, Red Hot Chili Peppers, AC/DC, Mars Volta, whatevs. But he couldn't create an original lick to save his life. He rubbed the calluses on his fret hand, as if the calluses were rosary beads from which he could milk divine forgiveness for being such a no-talent hack.

"Well," Loud said. "Play more. Get good, and we'll see."

"That is if Brock doesn't break my hands first."

"He'll probably just break your nose."

Jeremy didn't laugh.

Loud stirred in his seat. "Seriously, don't worry. If I'm around, he won't do anything."

When they got off at the Smoke Hole, they exchanged Facebook profiles.

"I'm never on there," Loud said. "I use it sometimes when I'm at the library. And I only give out my profile name to people I trust. Swear you won't tell anybody?"

*

The next day, on the way into English class, Jeremy found himself hurtling toward a wall. He caught himself but felt Brock Olander's tobacco-juiced breath wafting into his ear: "Better hope your boyfriend is here today."

Jeremy sat down in a collection of trembles. Brock sat at the other end of the room, the threat of him magnified by the sudden distance.

Nine-fifteen bell, nothing. Nine forty-five, nothing. Ten a.m., nothing. No Loud. Jeremy's Rancid t-shirt gave him no comfort.

The bell rang, and Jeremy bolted for the door. He ran down the empty mall of the school until it started filling with bodies. He slipped through them and didn't slow until he was near the exit. Truancy Court be damned, he was getting out of there and running home. He put his hands on the push bar to the exit, but he couldn't reach it.

Faster than he could scream, they pulled him by his coat around a corner. He shouted once in the bathroom, but Johnny Tayak's hand was over his mouth.

"Move," Brock said. Johnny let him go and got clear.

Brock had smudged a line of black shoe polish below his left eye. The bathroom fluorescents glinted off that black line like the metal stay on the hood of an eighteen-wheeler that was barreling right toward Jeremy.

Brock looked at him sadly. "You don't pick on people for having a learning disability. It's ignorant, cheap, and mean. Especially when Loud's supposed to be in that class too!"

Jeremy's eyes captured only a fraction of the lightning movement Brock's big body made. A black spot dropped in his vision. He was on the floor, getting kicked in the ribs, the hits pounding like a double bass in a death metal jam. It ended in a slow fusillade of wadded paper towels descending from an upturned trash can. And Brock shouting, "Tell your boyfriend I know where he lives, and he's got it coming!"

When he was sure they were gone, Jeremy got up and went to the mirror.

A ring around his eye was reddening. Questions circled too. What Brock had said… Was Loud really supposed to be in Special Ed? Or was Brock just insulting him? Regardless, Jeremy felt he'd been a fool to think of Loud as some kind of protector. His black eye would remind him of that fact in several colors over the next few weeks. His Rancid shirt had ripped in the tussle. Loud was right. Life would tear things up for him.

ALL OF LOUD'S LADIES: OVERALLS AND THE COUGAR

Instead of going to school the day Jeremy got beat up, Loud inadvertently expanded his love life.

On the mat in the empty living room of his grandparents' abandoned house, Loud awoke that morning to his usual alarm: the gurgling emptiness of hunger. Being hungry was like burping backward. Instead of a bulging propulsion of gas outward, a hunger pang drew you—your air, your muscles, your bones—inward to try to fill up the emptiness.

So, he did what he'd done every morning since coming back to the Harbor: rolled out at the crack of dawn for Sweet Nothings Popcorn Factory. There, he'd get handouts from café manager Molly Donahue, a silver-haired lady with green eyeshadow and paint-on eyebrows.

On one of his mornings cruising around downtown, Loud had passed the coffee shop—the one inviting business on the strip. Warm, sugar-scented air piped out of its storefront with a caramelly promise that sent his stomach into pleading. He trolled by it a few more times before Molly called him in. She gave him coffee and a bowl of rainbow-colored popcorn on the house. When she asked him about his life, and he told her about his dance, the Flail, she laughed and gave him a sandwich.

Loud squirmed in the gooey light of this generosity. The older woman's wile and arching eyebrows reminded him of Grandma Gin. But her soft smell and batting eyes made him worry. She could be a cougar. Loud told himself he wouldn't overuse the hookup. But of course, he had. He was living in a squat house without running water or electricity, and so, he kept slinking into the coffee shop, his big brows worrying upward in leading lines that betrayed his hunger. Instead of telling him to scram, Molly kept feeding him. She enrolled him in school. She bought him a backpack and school supplies and got him an Obama phone at a Boost Mobile. Each morning, Loud's anxiety ticked louder with fear that any day, she might cut the cord or call his mom or ask him to give her a back rub.

It wasn't raining that morning as Loud set out, but heavy clouds herded across the sky. The sun rose and mellowed the gray imperceptibly into the pale light of day. Neil Young's shocks groaned as the tires rolled and bumped along the trail by the railroad tracks between the highway and the Chehalis River.

Downtown opened to Loud like the rusty, tangled insides of a garage in which an unrelenting restoration was taking place. Mornings in Aberdeen smelled of smoke and freshly broken wood, a smell that rose from the houses and lingered in brown clouds over the river valley until a wind ran it out to sea.

The downtown buildings wore faded signs, gutters filigreed with moss, and rusty fire escapes. Foam sealant oozed into yellow liquid that trickled out from the crumbling exteriors. Meanwhile, the twin barrels of Heron and Wishkah streets funneled a barrage of big rigs and beach tourists towards their bliss-point destinations unbroken by the townspeople's pain.

Given the length of the line of the bums in front of the Union Gospel Mission, it wasn't quite seven. Sweet Nothings wasn't open yet. So Loud killed time by taking a tour of the eyesores along the mouth of the Wishkah River. It all made him hungrier, and he crushed the pedals through the remaining blocks to Sweet Nothings. But that morning, instead of finding Molly bustling around doing her opening tasks, Loud found a pair of closed doors and a girl standing before them.

As Loud leaned Neil Young on its kickstand, he saw the girl wore overalls—rolled up to reveal a pair of striped socks (bands of pumpkin, teal, magenta) and red Converses. Her fingers moved outside of her sleeve-length glomits, tapping at the door handles, having given up tugging. The duct-taped glasses, wrinkled buttoned-up shirt, tangly hair uncurling from her purple beanie, the half-moons of grime in her fingernails, the sooty stains in the denim. Loud wondered if Molly had taken on another pity case. Maybe the woman was trying to make a second soup kitchen out of the coffee shop. One for the young, pale angels of the street.

The girl turned and looked at him.

*

Aurora Lee Loftner had fleetfooted her way through the purple polygons of the dormant downtown and let herself into Sweet Nothings an hour prior. Like every teenager in Aberdeen, she was conscious of how hard it was going to be to find a job. Uncle Lyle was doing all he could to assuage this fear and was starting her opening at his café three days a week.

For the last several years, she'd volunteered at Think-of-Me-Hill Retirement Community: a five-story brick building just north of Weatherwax High. Because she had never known her grandparents and had time on her hands with Lyle always busy at work, she loved spending time there watching old TV shows and having the seniors teach her things. Over the years, she'd learned how to swing dance, play pinochle, and lead bingo games. And, since she was also learning the drums as a hobby, she learned some fifties-era rock and swing beats in the retirement center's band, the Fidget-Bridgettes. But there was no money in it. And Uncle Lyle recommended that she get some more transferable skills with the job at Sweet Nothings.

As on most things, Aurora didn't fight him on it. She worried about his health, his heart. And he was her only family.

Lyle Blanchard was black. Hefty. Handsome in his bowtie. One of only a few black people living in Aberdeen. His blue eyes were gems that glowed from a pair of heavy brows, his skin the color of a mug of milk poured over the last grainy swig of the day's coffee and stirred and stirred into a beige cream. Though they were not blood, though they looked nothing alike, Aurora knew Lyle considered her his daughter, especially after her mother's passing. In his view, vision and belief ran thicker than blood. What had blood mattered in Lyle's life? A childless Episcopalian couple, the Caldwells, had adopted him as a toddler, along with a little white baby girl who grew up to be Aurora's mother.

The night before, Lyle's friend and café manager, Molly, had trained Aurora how to disarm Sweet Nothings' security system, turn on the lights, and start up the drips and poppers. But that morning, when Aurora opened the doors, the piquant smell of garbage assaulted her senses. Baked overnight in the darkened box of Sweet Nothings, the coffee grinds, the banana peels, the discarded cakes, and the spilled milk had mutated into a smell so strong it almost had sentience. In the hustle of training her, Molly had forgotten to take out the trash.

Aurora pushed through the hurdle of smell, into the dim space, and punched the code into the alarm just before it sounded. She dumped out all the coffee grinds and dragged the bags of rotting food outside. On her way out to the dumpster, the locked doors closed. The bags, as she wrenched them from the trash cans, ripped open onto her—the filters full of grinds and the sandwich halves with putrid mayo. It was then she realized she'd forgotten the store keys inside, locking herself out. She found herself covered in trash at the unyielding doors of Sweet Nothings, trying not to cry.

When the figure parked his bike and shuffled up, her hands gripped the door handles. It could be anybody, she thought. A customer maybe. Not necessarily a deranged dawn walker. Semi-trucks were blasting past on Heron, along with the mammoth pick-ups of the working men commuting to sites in the surrounding hills. A patrol car trolled by. Though she was most likely safe, she shivered at the stranger's approach.

The figure stalled and stood slightly askew. She put on her unassuming smile, one she practiced in the mirror. The one she would show her dad were he to walk back into town. The one she would show her mother's ghost if it visited. She knew that people—dangerous people especially—hated to see fear and suspicion even when warranted. So, she turned, looked up at him, and showed this stranger her smile.

It was some guy. No—a boy. She looked away, her fingers relaxing to tap on the door. She dwelled for a moment on that first impression: his rough face, with its mischievous curvatures hidden in a hood.

"Not open yet?" came the boy's voice.

"Guess not," she said, letting herself look at him again for the slightest second. Longer looks from girls told boys they were interested. She knew that much, though she'd never given any boy a look long enough for them to notice.

They stood in the wind and the tentative morning light, the leaves already starting to flutter in slow zigzags down.

After introducing himself, Loud asked, "So does Molly hook you up too?"

"Uh. Kind of." Aurora gave him another half a glance. The patches of old band names adorning his jacket didn't interest her, yet the patches told her that he was an interesting person.

"Cool," Loud nodded. "Me too. She must be late, cuz she's usually here by now."

"Well," Aurora hesitated. "I'm supposed to be getting the store open for her. I work here. Yeah. But I locked myself out." She gave a little laugh. "After spilling garbage all over myself. See my keys?"

She pointed to them, gleaming on the counter, realizing too late that she'd given him a reason to get closer to her. He smelled. Like pine, body odor, and dirt. Then again, *she* smelled like trash.

"Sucks to be locked out," Loud said.

"Yeah."

"I feel locked out a lot in this town."

"That sucks," Aurora said.

"You got a quarter?"

Seriously? "Look, Molly will be here soon. We can give you…"

"A button then?" he asked.

His face stayed insistent, so she ripped one of the extra buttons sown onto her shirt and flicked it to him. He caught the button and rounded the corner of the building. He walked with his hands in his vest pockets and sauntered like he owned the place.

She heard the sound of feet plodding on a dumpster top and clunking up a fire escape. Minutes later, she saw him emerge on the other side of the glass. Opening the door from the inside, he came out, and she smelled the garbage again, thinking that this time, it had fleshed itself in a body. He was smiling.

"How did you…."

"Skylight." He flicked her back her button.

She tried to walk in.

He stepped in front of her. "What are you going to give me?"

"Uh…" She felt a flush of heat on her cheeks. "A punch in the face?"

"I know," he said and took off her glasses. "You could let me clean these for you."

In the fuzziness, she saw him wipe the lenses on what must have been the cleanest corner of his Butthole Surfers t-shirt. "There, Overalls," he said and put the glasses back on her. She thought she could feel his touch linger along her earlobes, now red hot as stovetops.

Looking through her lenses clearer, she saw the space between his teeth, eyelashes and the roundness of his cheeks and chin emerging from the angles of his face.

"Thanks," she said. "I wish sometimes my glasses had windshield wipers."

"Sometimes, I wish the sky had windshield wipers."

*

Grandma Gin had taught Loud how to steal.

She wore great billowing sashes that could wrap, fold, cover, and obscure her girth. Her hair was a puff of ecstatic cotton, and her dark blue eyes, almost purple, were always wide as if she'd just stuck a fork in a socket. She hovered above him in her arabesque wrappings. On the ground, she was a nimble-footed pasha of mischief and mystery, taking him on long walks through deer trails in and around the sloughs' inlets, showing him where to find groves of mushrooms and copper-colored pools of spawning salmon. She showed him how to make tea from stinging nettles. Nettles that had to be picked right, with your bare hands. She taught him early on that the best things in life required blood.

She had taught Loud that the key to filching was in distraction. She would berate a convenience clerk at Safeway for not having her favorite brand of scratch, while Loud would swipe the clerk's key. When the clerk would feign an excuse to draw away, Loud would unlock the cabinet where they kept the cigarettes. At the Hollywood Video, Loud would cry at the counter for his "Oma" while she slipped discount DVDs into the many folds of her loose coverings.

On Sunday sunset walks, Grandma Gin had taught Loud how to vault up dumpsters and fire escapes onto rooftops and how to use a coin or a button to screw open one of the old skylights, so he could rappel into an unguarded building and take whatever it was they needed: a bolt of fabric she'd been wanting, grease for his bike chain, a bag of flour. Having only meager social security and Pappy Rue's retirement checks, it was how they survived.

*

Molly arrived forty-five minutes later. Aurora was cleaning the counters. And there was Loud McCrowley lounging at the barstools, reading yesterday's copy of *The Harbor Herald*.

"Shit," Molly said to herself.

She'd forgotten about Loud, her other morning charge. In allowing Aurora to open alone, Molly had ensured their first meeting. When Loud had started coming around, Lyle had made a passing comment about how he was fine with Molly giving the young man handouts, but didn't want him getting mixed up with his niece. But meeting a stranger was inevitable in a small town. And Molly didn't think anything would come of it. Aurora was a good girl with her head on straight. And Loud...well.

As Lyle was an accountant for Rhinehouse & Sons' Timber Co. by day, Molly managed his café for him. On her opening shifts, she'd seen Loud wandering around downtown, hobnobbing with the panhandlers. As she'd continued to watch him, she recognized him as Pete McCrowley's boy. People loved Pete. Until they found out he was a cedar thief and by then, he was dead. Rather than let his kid get sucked into the septic tank of homeless life, Molly welcomed him in. Now she worried she was in way over her head.

"I see you showed yourself in," Molly said to Loud.

Loud glanced at her without so much as a nod.

"Anything good in the paper?" she asked.

Loud shrugged. The headline said something about another Laura Law ghost sighting.

Molly shooed Aurora off for school, but not before Loud made plans to meet her at lunch.

"Bye, Overalls," Loud called out to her as she left, leaving him to stand there like a blue-tick pointer doing all he could not to run after her.

"Hey," Molly said.

Loud sat down but didn't look at her.

"I hear you skipped your first two days of school."

"I went yesterday."

"You know there's a Truancy Court in this town…"

"Yeah," he said.

"And that with one more absence, you'll have to appear before Judge Spurgeon."

"I won't have any more absences, though!" He pounded the counter, and his face twisted.

Molly stepped back from him.

"Sorry," he said after a minute. "I'm just…I'm just kind of hungry."

She closed the panini grill on a premade sandwich. "Why are you so hungry all the time?"

"I told you."

"Hmm. Must be my old age because I don't remember."

"I stay at my grandparents'. They're broke, okay. And I don't want to talk about it."

"I just get worried," Molly said, slapping down a washrag. "A young guy. Showing up every morning, starving."

He shrugged. "You don't have to give me anything."

She blinked slowly. "I want to."

"What's the problem then?"

"I'm just not sure that what I'm giving you is what you need."

She smelled the first batch of raspberry popcorn. She watched his nose perk up, and his feet squirm.

"How isn't it what I need? I'm hungry! And you have food. What's the big deal?"

Her mouth pinched up. "Lyle thinks I should call CPS."

Loud clenched his teeth and looked at the ceiling. "Don't. Don't call fucking CPS! They'll send me back to Mom's. She's a drunk!"

Molly's eyes narrowed, and she teared up, pretty sure he was lying through his teeth.

"I hate CPS," she said.

Loud shook his head and clenched his fists. He felt a door inside her creak open. If he asked her why, he knew she would tell him. And the last thing he wanted was another adult's sad story.

"I won't call them," she sighed, "if you let me help you."

"You can help me by giving me a goddamn breakfast sandwich."

He pounded on the counter again, making Molly jump. But she bounced back at him. "I can't afford to do that every day! This place is barely inching by. Just to let you know. I can take you somewhere that can help you for real."

"You mean a mental institution?"

"Like DSHS, wise guy."

Loud stood up. "Yeah, but you know… Truancy Court and all."

"I'll call the school and get you excused."

"Sweet! A day off."

"Half a day," Molly corrected.

*

The Laura Law headline had got Molly thinking.

In 1940, Aberdeener housewife Laura Law had been found dead in her home, her head having been bludgeoned four times and her breasts stabbed with a stiletto or an ice pick. Police investigations, state-prosecutor theories, and journalist speculations dead-ended in dubious suspects. In the absence of a likely culprit, the cold-trailed crime swelled as a specter that inhabited local imagination, manifesting in paranormal reports on a biannual basis as reliable as a windstorm off the coast. Laura Law's visage appeared in the heatshield on a trucker's muffler, it rippled across the scoreboard at a Bobcat football game, it lurked in pothole puddles, lapping at school children's galoshes, always with a raincoat over her pinafore dress and a cigarette between her fingers.

When Molly saw the headline about Laura Law and looked at virginal little Aurora all flushed in the presence of this rakishly handsome boy, unstable and smelly as he was—she thought: *If any harm comes to her from this kid, Lyle will never forgive me.* If she could just get him square, he might quit coming around. Though she would miss him, it was probably best.

ALL OF LOUD'S LADIES: THE FEMALE

Loud let the old lady take him to DSHS. It was getting colder already, and it was only September! He also went along with it because of how she squinted when he told her the lie about his mom. It was those eyes. Even with all the green eye shadow, Molly's eyes remained small, shifty, and smart. She was shrewd like a grandma. Loud didn't know if she could tell a lie. But she knew a lie when she heard one. He realized he'd have to say less around her from then on.

The visit to DSHS—the newest, nicest building on Heron Street—was more perfunctory than a doctor's visit. Because he was over twelve, he got interviewed in private by a man with eyeglass chains and a gray mustache.

Loud told him a truth, a half-truth, and two lies in the following order. He'd had food stamps with his grandparents, but no longer stayed with them. He said he'd stayed with them up until spring when they let their house go, so he went up to stay with his mom for the summer. He told the man his mom had sent him back in the fall because Weatherwax was better than the high school in Forks (Go Bobcats). He told the man he was staying with a family friend. Loud gave the man Sweet Nothings' address.

"I'll have to double-check this information with Mom," he told Loud.

Loud nodded. If they were able to get a hold of his mom, she'd either tell them the truth—which would yield a CPS call and, possibly, a report against her having custody. Or she'd confirm his lie. A far more likely option, Loud guessed, given how they parted and given what they both knew about CPS's penchant for taking Native children away from their parents.

Loud left the office with a sigh of relief and a two-hundred-dollar increase in income that would arrive in Sweet Nothings' mail the following week like a credit card. He came out to an open street and a sunbreak turning the wet pavement into bars of gold.

"Where is your mother!"

Loud whirled around. Molly was leaning against the DSHS building with her arms crossed.

"Why do you care?" he demanded.

"Because. You don't live with your grandparents."

"You don't know that."

"I do because I had grandparents. Even if they were poor and mean, there's no way they'd let you run around in those same clothes every day. There's no way they'd let me—a total stranger— feed you breakfast. They'd starve first!"

Loud started walking away from her, across the street. But she caught up with him, even in her pumps and stubby legs.

"My grandparents are dead," Loud said.

"They can't be dead. They were claiming your food stamps."

"You weren't supposed to be listening in! That shit's confidential."

"I can't help it. I got ears."

Gusts of wind scythed above their heads, causing them to yell louder.

"Okay. So they're not dead. But they're dead to me. And I'm dead to them."

"Could you slow down, so we don't have to shout?"

"Why don't you go back to work?"

They were walking past scuzzy motels with rusty marquees. Old motor homes dozed in their parking lots.

"Where are your parents?" she asked again.

Loud heard desperation in her voice. She didn't have much left. He could win this one with a quick blast of bullshit: "They put bath salts in my cereal when I was a kid, and I got sent away."

"That. That sounds terrible. Bath salts. My gosh. How'd you turn out so sharp?" Molly said, shaking her head. She was tearing up.

"Fuck if I know," Loud said. He heard feminine laughter echoing off-kilter from somewhere. Maybe an open window of the hotel to his left.

"If you don't want to tell me your autobiography, fine," Molly said. "Just don't think I was born yesterday."

"K," Loud said.

"Well. It's been fun, kid. But I got to tend my bar."

"Yup."

"Just… don't be a stranger, okay."

He looked back to see her crying. Her colorful makeup was beginning to run like a rained-on Mardi Gras.

*

Loud started schlepping toward Weatherwax High but realized it was nearly noon. He'd only have two or three periods left, and would they really jail you for missing two or three classes? Plus, he still felt hungry. Not for food, another type of hunger—one deeper down. One that itched unscratchably between his thighs. One that a friendly but overbearing old barista or a food voucher couldn't solve.

During his year as a homeless sideshow monkey for noise-grind bands in Seattle, Loud received payment not only in the form of free schwag but also, access to groupies—pale, tattooed waifs, usually semi-conscious. During post-show parties, these band-aids let Loud shed most of his sexual naiveté on them, and, once practiced in the basics, he was more than happy to satisfy their need for fast and usually rougher forms of release.

Having had such frequent access to tail and tokes, he ached to blow his load and soak his brain in some hash smoke. His saliva grew thick, and he doubled back around to the motel. He wanted to find where the strange laughter came from. He thought about the girl from earlier, Overalls. He wished she were homeless. He knew she wouldn't put out right away, but that'd be okay. They could sit at a park for a while and talk and *maybe* kiss a little.

The T and H had long ago gone out on the buzzing sign of the Thunderbird Motel. *Underbird*, Loud whispered. Tear-like rivulets of motor oil ran from the parking lot.

Loud's nose caught a whiff of the twangy green smell of pot. He looked up, scanning the outer walkway of the second floor. He saw peeling paint and a mattress against one window, a piece of particle board against another. The others framed crooked sets of blinds that gaped out at him like mouthfuls of bad teeth.

A hoarse voice called out. Loud turned. A man in a wife-beater was b-lining toward Loud, brandishing a broom. The man's body looked like a cigarette butt. Track marks bruised his forearms. His face looked like it had been crushed between two cinderblocks. Smashed up by two goons when he couldn't pay up, was Loud's guess.

"No! Trespassing! Allowed!" the man yelled.

"You couldn't pay me to stay in a place like this," Loud said.

The laughter again. Loud heard a door open.

"I. Will. Call. Law enforcement," the man huffed, catching his breath. "I am trying to run an establishment."

"Larry, he's mines! He's mines!" a voice rang out. It was the same as the laughter—shrill, inane, alive.

Coming down the stairs was a girl in fuzzy pink sandals, sweatpants two sizes too big, and a white tank top two sizes too small. As she came toward him, Loud saw that she wasn't a girl exactly. But not a lady either. Her hair was a dirty blonde tangle, and her wide face was agape in something between mirth and pain. Her pants slid a little further down with each step, and as her hands went to hold them up, her speed-bag breasts seemed that much closer to exploding out of her top.

"Is he an associate of yours?" Larry demanded, pausing his broom thrusts at Loud.

"A what? Speak fucking English, Larry."

"A friend. Is he a friend of yours?"

"Yes! Right, friend?" She grabbed Loud's arm. "Let's go."

Loud smelled sour sweat and bubble gum. He felt her bigness grab him roughly by the arm; her bosom bounced against his, making it impossible for him to not look down her shirt.

Larry was still yelling. "Because I've warned you that your guests cause a nuisance. Complaints have been filed!"

"Yeah right, Larry. You don't have to lie. He's not a cop!"

"Cease and desist or I will be forced to evict," Larry raised the broom to her, his eyes buggering.

"I'll go to the cops!" she said.

"Then I will call the landlords association!" Larry proclaimed as he shrank into a room marked *Office*. "I have rights!" he screamed from behind the door.

"And I'll tell 'em what you use our vouchers for!"

She turned to Loud and burped, "Larry's my bitch. Oh my god, these pants!" She growled as she pulled the sweatpants up. She did it slowly so Loud could see down her crack.

"I'm Karla," she said. Her eyes, hanging big, lazy, and brown, grew out of sockets purple from lack of sleep.

"People call me Ki," Loud replied.

"Aren't you special?"

"It's my road name."

"You're one of those traveler kids, aren't you? What are you doing out here?"

He shrugged, "I took the bus from Olympia where our squat is. I wanted to see the Cobain memorial."

She let out something between a hiccup and a laugh. "You're weird!"

Loud looked around. They were walking south, back toward the DSHS.

"What are you worried about, pretty boy? About the po-po?" she asked, mockingly. "They don't even mess with me no more. Oh. My. God!" She hiked up her pants again.

Loud felt that unitchable itch itching. "This is way better than school," he blurted.

"I go to school," Karla said.

"What grade?"

"I'm a senior this year," she said.

Loud looked at her. She didn't have any acne like kids his age did. And she talked bigger. She had long pink nails. Plus, you had to be eighteen to rent a hotel room by yourself. He knew from trying in Seattle.

"A super senior, maybe," Loud said.

"Ha! Asshole," she said, pushing him into the street.

A passing car honked as it swerved away. She laughed. Then she got serious. "You got any weed?"

"I was about to ask you that," Loud confessed. "Know where we could get some?"

"What do I look like?" she asked.

"Like someone who'd know where to get some."

"I don't even want to mess with any of those creeps right now."

"I smelled it at the hotel."

"Let's go see the statue thingy!" she said. "Come on."

With eyes widening, she dosey-doed him around in the direction of the Young's Street Bridge. He saw the spaces in her teeth as she gave him an ear-to-ear smile.

He wrenched free of her. "Let's get some fatties first."

"What's more important?" she said, arms akimbo. "A girl taking you to see something or…"

"You're not a girl," he said, reaching to pants her, but she deflected.

"Wanna bet?" she said, starting to run.

Loud gave chase.

"Anyways, guess what my last names is? Potts!"

*

Underneath the bridge, the damp planks smelled like pitch and mildew. All he could feel was the warm wet and the tangles of her hair.

He said he'd say when.

He lay on the bank below the names. Even in the dark, the names floated on the concrete above him in green and pink spray paint as things in his vision shifted. Karla was quiet and like the river and the river sucked along the sand and the stones.

He said he'd say when.

There was all of him tugging down, down, down in the warm wet.

On the concrete wall above him, he thought he saw his name sprayed over by Cobain's name. Suddenly the letters shifted, and Loud couldn't see, but could feel Cobain standing there in a baggy sweater, shrugging.

"Hey," Loud murmured, but the shade swirled back into the letters.

He said he'd say when, but he didn't because she was just tangles of hair sucking under the bridge.

*

Loud left Karla under the bridge, mumbling through a mouthful: *You asshole!* He could hear her saying it as he jogged downriver. He could hear the echo of her weird laughs. The clouds were unfurling to blue sky, and in the clear blue, he could see flashes of what he'd done to her. Of her drain-clog of dirty blonde hair, her pearl-jammed mouth, her wet eyes, the soaked knees of her sweats, rump half hanging out while Cobain's ghost watched on in silent mirth.

Where the itchy craving had been, there was nothing. Loud felt empty. But not a hungry empty. An empty-empty, at the bottom of which he could see her—hurt and alone now—and it made him sick.

Loud retrieved his bike from behind Sweet Nothings and biked over to school.

He found Jeremy Sweet on the stairs between the school and the upper terrace of the tennis courts, between the old folks' home and the school. The tall, drab brick building of Think-of-Me-Hill Retirement Community shadowed them the same way old people and their needs seemed to overshadow everything else in town. Jeremy was listening to music and staring at nothing, glasses bound on the bridge by duct tape.

Having leaned Neil Young against Jeremy's bike, Loud sat next to him on the mossy lips of the stairs. Jeremy nodded at him, though his headphones were blaring from his mp3 player. Loud motioned, and Jeremy gave him a headphone, and they sat listening to The Clash live, performing "What's My Name?"

"Sorry," Loud said. "That I wasn't there today."

"Where were you?" Jeremy asked.

Loud squinted and tried to play back the events of the day. There'd been a cute girl in overalls, food stamps, an overweight hooker in her late teens, and a blow job. Oh yeah, and a Kurt Cobain ghost sighting. Great lyrics for a punk anthem. But he knew none of it would make sense to this normie kid.

"Being a little shit," Loud summarized.

Jeremy was quiet.

Loud risked a look at Jeremy's face and quickly turned away. A blood vessel had popped in the kid's eye from Brock's fist. A deepening crimson circle hung around the eye. He had a wad of tissue over his nose, stopping up the still-running trail of red humiliation.

"It doesn't hurt that bad," Jeremy said with a tremble in his voice.

Loud looked down the stairs. He wondered how fast it would take him to run down the stairs and away from all this pathetic shit—this kid, his big words, his excuses for not playing better guitar, his glum need of a buddy, his weakness.

Loud got up. There wasn't even a murmur from the kid about where he was going. Loud figured maybe the kid didn't want to bother him. Or maybe he was just too weak. But either way, Loud liked the fact that the kid wasn't trying to lasso him with any tether of brotherly commitment. Loud felt like he could easily stay or go without a scene. He turned back around.

"Want to go see a waterfall?" Loud asked.

"In this place?" Jeremy sniffled.

"It's a local secret."

Jeremy let out a sickly laugh and shook his woolly head.

"Come on. What else are you gonna do? Sit around waiting to get beat up again?"

"Fuck you," Jeremy gave a rueful snort before getting up to follow.

THEATER OF THE OPPRESSED

The ridges on the Forerunner's steering wheel cup Cal's carpals as he drives one-handed on the I-5 North passing the low-slung strips of decay outside of the big army-navy base, all harshly lit by the mid-morning sun. Check-advance places, pawn shops, seedy motels. It reminds Jeremy about how he learned about Loud's side-squeeze, Karla Potts. Cal must have been reminded of it too because he asks about the Morck Hotel.

"Did you check for Loud there? Just curious."

"You couldn't pay to set foot in that crack den again," Jeremy shakes his head.

"Don't blame ya. Just askin'," Cal says.

Yet here he is going to rappel down into Seattle's nether regions to look for Loud. Sometimes, he thinks he would have been better off giving Loud the finger and walking away from him and his invitation to go to see Whistle Punk Falls.

*

A waterfall in a fucking estuary? The idea made Jeremy snort more snot-blood. Jeremy's whole head griped from Brock's blow only a few hours earlier. But a quixotic run-around with Loud would prolong presenting his wounds to his mother.

They rode their bikes between Walmart and the river. When they biked out of the box store's shadow, the sun fell full on them, smarting Jeremy's eyes and worsening his headache. The light panged off the blue river and the white buildings of the mills: some silent, others chugging out their own cumulonimbus clouds. The cattails and reeds breathed their green smelling pollens while the yellowing leaves of vine maples waved to the boys as they entered another shadow: the richer dark of the sloughs.

Wasn't Loud cold, in his jean vest and old band tee? Loud's

brown skin was free from goosebumps as he pedaled ahead.

The river thinned and became black tentacles leaking out from the emerald rushes toward a sea so distant it seemed theoretical. The trail narrowed, running along eddies bowered in canary grass and alder suckers. Spruces stood askew like the sails on ships frozen in their yawing on the sea. The banks were covered in giant, rain-catching fronds. As the waters ate into the trail, their bike wheels rolled warily; they stood up and forced their bikes through, flecks of sediment flicking up into their faces from the tire treads.

Rows of planks stood straight out of the river.

"What are those?" Jeremy asked, not expecting an answer.

"Pilings that used to hold up logging platforms. All this used to be industry too," Loud said.

"How do you know all that?"

"My family were all loggers. And all of them got eaten by the corporate machine."

The statement hung in the marsh and drifted up into the silent stratifications of the forest. It made Jeremy feel more than ever like a spoiled city brat who didn't belong in Aberdeen with all its labor loss.

They stopped at the trail's turnoff for Feller's Landing, the main boat launch into the sloughs. They leaned their bikes against trees, not even bothering to lock up because they were so far outside of town. Jeremy traipsed after Loud along a deer trail that opened to an oxbow, right on the marsh's green waters. From its eastern bend, a thin beach of black sand spread before the waters. A Sitka spruce stretched out over the river before bending skyward. Notches gouged into the tree's shaggy purple bark.

"Here it is," Loud said, walking toward the water.

Jeremy set a tentative foot onto the silty ground, almost expecting to sink. "Oh, BTW. Brock says he knows where you live."

Loud paused.

"He could be full of it… *I* don't even know where you live."

Loud shook his head. "Those guys have this weird way of knowing about everything."

Olander had known all about Jeremy: his dad, his background.

"Do you need somewhere to stay?" Jeremy asked.

"You got a free couch? I'm a gold-medalist couch-surfer."

"Maybe… if you show me this supposed waterfall."

Loud's eyes widened, showing his curlicue eyelashes. "You can only see the falls at sunset! So, I'll have to hurry."

Loud approached the buttswell of the great Sitka. His limbs hoisted themselves up the trunk using the notches he'd made in the summer with a hatchet and a hammer.

"Wait for it," Loud called down, as the sky above the slough bloomed into sunset.

There was no misting, no rushing of water. Whatever waterfall was there clearly existed only in Loud's mind. Loud was almost halfway up the tree now and was pausing on a thick branch facing west. The colors purpled.

Wait for it.

Jeremy was a collection of bruises and doubt on the bank of an unnamed tributary, yet he trembled in anticipation.

Wait for it…Now! A single stream geysered out from a place in the tree-tower that seemed halfway to the sky: Loud McCrowley pissing off a tree.

*

They lit a fire on the beach. A little while later, Cal scared the shit out of them by trolling around their campfire on his dirt bike for a few minutes before he gave up the gag. He introduced himself to Jeremy and the three had their first hangout.

Cal had played ragtag rugby over the summer with Loud and Brock, but Cal gravitated to Loud because of his novelty and need. Cal had taught Loud the basics of the game to which Loud added his own flair, including a pogo-jump of a sidestep Loud used to help Aberdeen win a showdown against the rival team in Hoquiam. Though neither talked about it in front of him, Jeremy suspected the two bonded over smoking pot, pounding beers, pounding pussy, or all of the above.

In Cal, Jeremy saw another potential friend. Another potential protector. But potentially, just another dude who knew more than Jeremy—about everything. Another dude who wouldn't be there for him. Another Loud. Another Keith. But what choice did he have? It would be better than being alone.

*

"So. Why are we doing this again?" Cal asks at the wheel. His Forerunner follows the I-5's cut through the emerald hills, full with spring leaves.

"I don't know," Jeremy says. "The Theater of the Oppressed, I guess."

"Oh yeah. That. Whatever that is," Cal says.

Jeremy tells Cal how in his uber-liberal school in Olympia, one of the teachers, a chubby, pony-tailed guy in an All-Things-Considered t-shirt and a wool-sock-sandal combination had led his entire Freshmen class in an exercise on Budd Inlet beach. The teacher stood in the parking lot while the students stood on the water line. He shouted to the class a series of statements confirming their privilege and each student had to take a step toward him for every question they could answer 'yes' to. *Can you see your race represented in movies? In government? Can you walk around in neighborhoods without being worried about being stopped by the police? Can you go through an airport without being worried about being deported?* By the end of it, even with his divorced parents and dead-beat stepdad, Jeremy ended up walking all the way up to the teacher with all the other white kids, while the couple kids of color lingered by the waters.

"We've got to learn from those close to the water, friends," the teacher told Jeremy and his fellow whities. "They've stayed close to the water, to the sea. To life. While we're stranded in a concrete field of our own privilege."

But Jeremy hadn't had many friends in the first place. And never a kid of color. Ever. Not until Loud.

"That's a really dumb story, dude," Cal says. "I feel like Loud would punch you in the face if you told him that story. And spit on you for trying to make him your token brown friend."

"He probably would. And he'd probably spit on me a second time knowing I was the one that told Aurora to do what she did," Jeremy says. "I basically made her chase him away. So I guess I'm wrong. I would have to go find him no matter what race he is."

"I guess I would too," Cal admits.

LADY COP

After their first hang out at Whistle Punk Falls, Cal agreed to drive Loud and Jeremy back to Jeremy's house. Mostly because when Cal asked where they wanted to go, Loud looked at Jeremy, his big brows getting puppy doggish.

Jeremy gave Cal directions to his house in Canyon Court while he thought about how he was going to square everything with his mom: his black eye and his would-be bunk buddy.

*

After all the reports were typed up and she'd clocked off, Detective Charlotte Sweet was glad at least that it was past midnight. Jeremy would be asleep and she wouldn't have to face his plaintive, if understandable, confusion about what was going on with Keith. All she'd said was that Keith was staying at the Guesthouse Suites, a hotel by Walmart. She walked into her rambler with only one ambition: to polish off a bottle of wine in the dark by herself to try to forget about all the things she couldn't fix. With Aberdeen, with her marriage to Keith.

A mangy-looking kid sat in Keith's armchair with his feet up on the table, slurping up a bowl of cereal.

She stammered, just about drawing her gun.

The kid avoided her eyes like a scolded mutt.

"Hello?" she asked.

"Hey," he said to the floor in a surprisingly deep voice.

Tall, dressed like a Sex Pistol, and smelling unshowered, he had an uncanny look to him. Like somebody who'd been beaten. Or done the beating. She called for Jeremy.

"Mom," he said, coming out of the kitchen. "Gosh, you're home late. Are you hungry? I made spaghetti."

"You want to tell me what happened there?" she asked. All

questions about who the strange kid was and why they were up so late were held at bay by the sight of the bruise painting the side of her son's face. She watched her son exchange looks with the kid in the chair.

"It's my fault," the kid said.

Charlotte noticed his fully formed Adam's apple.

"And you are?" she asked.

"People call me 'Loud.'"

"Loud?"

"Yeah. Like…a lot of volume."

"My eye isn't his fault," Jeremy cut in. "He's a friend I made in class…"

"You shouldn't lie to a cop." Loud smiled.

"What were you doing?" Charlotte asked.

"Just shadowboxing," Loud said. "You know, messing around. Only, I got too close."

Charlotte inspected her son's darkening bruise. He winced when she touched it.

"Well… Loud. Thank you for trying to save my son some embarrassment. But this is too big to be made by a swipe. Somebody hit you hard, Jer. Guess I'll talk to you about it later. What are you boys doing up so late?"

Jeremy shrugged. "Couldn't sleep. Worried about you."

"That's why he had me come over. To keep him company," Loud said.

Charlotte smiled tightly, eyes hardening like lava. She smelled insincerity. "That's sweet. This is a scary town. But I'm alright. So, Loud, let's take you home."

Jeremy asked if Loud could spend the night.

"It's a little late for that," Charlotte shook her head. "And I'd have to call and ask…"

"Oh, my uncle won't care," Loud piped in. "He works the

night shift at the Safeway, and I'm on my own like every night anywho."

"You'll have to put me on the phone with him. So I can ask if it's all right," Charlotte said.

"He can't take calls at work," Loud said. "He's been written up for it before. And I'd hate to cause him more trouble. I'll ask ahead next time, I promise."

"Well…" she began, watching Jeremy's face. No reaction. It was possible Jeremy didn't know whether any of this was true or not. "I'm fine with you staying over…but first, I'm taking Jer to the ER to make sure he doesn't have a concussion from whoever beat him up today."

After doing a mental check that there wasn't anything out and available in the house that Loud could steal, Charlotte asked the kid to guard the place while they were away.

"Oh, you already know!" Loud nodded.

"Thanks," Charlotte said. "Oh. And do me a favor. Can you find someplace else to sit? My husband is pretty territorial about that chair. And I wouldn't want him to come home and clock you for sitting in it."

She guided Jeremy by the arm out the door and into her blue Focus.

The rambler she was renting sat in a cul-de-sac on Canyon Court, named after the small, alder-filled gully on the north side of the street, over which the 6th Street Bridge stretched. An open concrete culvert cut the culdy in half, forcing cars cruising in to pull a U-ey to do it slowly. She and Keith talked about how it'd be a great place to have a baby.

She noticed Jeremy's body decamp from its composed position and slump against the passenger window. "So. Why'd you make a big deal about Loud sitting in Keith's chair? Is he coming back?"

"Don't ask me that right now."

She hadn't spoken to Keith in two days and didn't know what made her say the thing about the chair. She didn't really care if Jeremy's new friend sat in it. Hell, he could mark his territory on it. Maybe it was because Loud put her on edge, and she wanted him to think there was a man around in case he tried anything.

While the doctor looked at Jeremy's head, Charlotte walked back to the car. All of her work worries came flooding back.

Meth use was down. The hills had been cleared out years ago and last year, APD had teamed up with the Feds to do a big bust downtown, temporarily shutting down the cartels' harbor for their new dirty. Plus, Sudafed had recently changed its formula so their pills couldn't be cooked; Purdue Pharma was coating Oxycontin with a nullifying agent released when smoked. Meth would take a hiatus for a spell until the cartel's chemists could tweak the formulas.

Heroin came creeping back in of course. But there was something else. Just about everywhere Charlotte walked or drove, she could smell an intense, befuddling fug. She could see it in the red eyes of the dazed perps brought in with pounds and pounds of the stuff in their trunks and trench coats. The dispatchers' phones were ringing off the hook with tips about it. Marijuana. The chronic was becoming the number-one drug trafficked in the Harbor.

She broached the subject with one of the cops she trusted, Officer Javier Moreno, her old partner from her brief stint on patrol.

"Somebody's growing around here," Charlotte said.

They were sitting in his squad car, the one they'd shared during her training. Moreno had parked in an alley facing Heron where they watched for car prowlers. The streets were quiet.

"Best to let sleeping dogs lie," Moreno said.

"Somebody's protecting someone."

"A lot of people are protecting someone."

"And I bet none of them are Latino."

Moreno laughed. "If they were. Well. You know they'd be on the next plane to Tijuana."

"You know who it is."

Moreno scoffed, "The breadcrumbs are big enough. And you're quick. You'll figure it out."

Rain started spattering onto their windshield.

"But there's no point, Char."

"Why not?"

Moreno stared straight ahead and let out a long exhale, the future a long, lightless tunnel he'd have to crawl through. "Look, I'm no Mr. Popular. Having grown up around here, couldn't have been. But, what the bigshots let through and what they don't? Sticking your nose in all that? It'd make you so unpopular, you couldn't get anything done."

He said they had to keep their heads down on street level. "Our jobs? We're just sweeping up." It'd all be legal in a few years anyway.

Charlotte figured he was right, though it didn't sit well. How long would it be before Jeremy got into that stuff? And what came after that?

Charlotte was snapped out of her brooding by a phone call from Keith. She went out to the chain-link fence in the hospital's parking lot. Set on the hillside, the lot overlooked the river, the granaries, the coiling aluminum tower of the biodiesel plant, and to the west somewhere, the elusive expanse of the Pacific.

"Yeah," Charlotte said into the phone.

"Good to hear your voice, babe." He was eating something soft. "I thought about what you said. And I think you're probably right. Maybe I am trying to kill a good thing cuz I'm scared."

"I just don't know why you'd leave your stash out," Charlotte said. "It's like you want me to find it. I don't know whether it's to hurt me or…"

"I would never do something like that just to hurt you."

"Then why leave a wad of hash out like that? Right on your workbench. Where Jeremy could have found it. You can't be that stupid. Even on that stuff."

"I think I'm just that stupid all the time, Char."

"Yeah well, have you figured out what to do about it? We've been over this again and again." And they had been. All last year. His reasons why it wasn't that bad, her reasons why it was. She repeated what it all came down to: "I can't be Detective Ms. Pothead!"

"I know, I know! Fuck. There are groups. That DSHS guy… He wants to hook me up with the Wednesday group there. But. I don't know."

"You never do…"

"Just let me talk, Char. I don't know if that'll be enough for you, is all. Fuck."

"*Tomorrow's* Wednesday. Go and then we'll talk more. But don't call until you go."

"Sure, sweet thing."

And just like that, his raspy, Marlboro-ed voice made her go skittish as a sixteen-year-old. Her knees buckled, and she clutched the fence to stay standing. "God damn it Key," she said through gritted teeth and eyes scrunched in angry tears.

"Can I take you to a movie on Thursday?"

She laughed. She couldn't believe it. She was laughing with this asshole.

"Okay… *If* you go to the group."

"It's a date then."

She put her phone away and turned around slowly to see

Jeremy standing there with an ice bag around his purple eye.

"No concussion," he said.

"Oh? Good," Charlotte said, wiping her eyes and nose. "Now you can tell me who did it."

"K. When you tell me what you're doing going to a movie with him on Thursday."

"He's my husband, Jer."

"Then why is he staying in a room at the Guesthouse?"

"I told you. There's stuff going on. What does this have to do with your eye?"

Jeremy pointed to his heart. "There's stuff going on."

He got in the car.

She brooded on this a minute. Her actions were allowing her son to climb a dubious moral high ground over her where he felt he could omit things from her. She ran a hand through her hair, got in the car, and started it.

"I just don't understand any of this," Jeremy said.

"Neither do I."

*

What Charlotte didn't tell Jeremy was that the whole thing with Keith felt like a sorry sequel to her first marriage.

When Jeremy was three, she'd divorced his father because of his chronic toking on sativa-stuffed cigarettes that serrated and sustained his intellect into the wee hours. Long after Charlotte had called it quits for the night, even after they'd had Jeremy, Malcolm would be up yammering to himself, finger-goading his typewriter into stenographing his latest manifesto on climate change, on prison reform, on legalization. And they were brilliant. Malcolm was brilliant. He was the only person she'd ever met who'd actually read *Das Capital*. Though she disagreed with him on legalization and plenty of other things, she found it impossible to argue with him. There had been a season where she'd been entranced, sitting beside the whitewater of his philosophizing spirit. He'd taken her to art museums, operas, and fine dining he couldn't afford. But his gaze was never at her, always just over her head and outward to the leaden circles of society's systems at play in the arts, or even on the menu—the systems that, according to him, were constructed to constrict the individual. Malcolm honed himself on deconstructing these systems with such focus that his energy and attention never turned toward her, and never toward their son.

Only a few years after the split with Malcolm, Charlotte locked gazes with the hungry green eyes of the mechanic who'd changed her oil and pulled her in like a tractor beam by asking her out in a voice as intriguing as incense. She was so flush with attraction that her bloodhound nose failed to sense that Keith Chevelle's incense of intrigue was laced with the same smoke as her ex-husband's.

When Jeremy asked her the whys about Keith, all Charlotte heard was *why did you dump Dad for this guy?* The answer was unutterably simple. Sex.

*

Charlotte went to that movie with Keith. And back to his hotel, where she gained more empathy for down-and-out prostitutes than she ever thought possible. When she told Keith this, he reminded her that she got to go home while she was making him stay at the hotel.

"So, who's the whore here?" he asked.

"How's that Wednesday group going?" she asked.

Keith was suddenly very interested in checking texts on his phone.

"You said you'd go," Charlotte said.

He looked up. "Maybe if you'd lemme move back in, I could get up the motivation."

"Is it that you're ashamed to go?" This was one of those

moments where she felt more like a mother to him than a lover.

Keith shrugged again.

Charlotte tipped over the table and shouted at him to stop making excuses if he ever wanted to see her again.

Yet when he called a few days later and invited her to dinner at Billy's Diner, she'd agreed. Jeremy was distracted with his new friend who was now staying with them. And though she worried about Loud's influence on Jeremy, she now had a bargaining chip over Loud: the roof over his head. Plus, Charlotte was going to keep this short.

Keith entered wearing his camo-colored cap, navy-blue shop jacket, and Dickies of the same color. She saw changes in him she hadn't noticed before. The hollows of his face had a purple tinge to them, and, along with his stringy goatee, he had a few days' worth of scruff on his cheeks—which he was scratching. He looked thinner. Almost gaunt. They got a table, ordered, and waited.

"I noticed you checked out of your hotel."

"Yeah."

"Where are you staying?"

"With Carl from work."

"You're lying."

"I swear on my mother's grave I'm not."

"She must have been cremated."

"Call Carl."

She looked at his hands. The rims of his nails and the wrinkles around his knuckles and wrists were clean of the grime from head gaskets and intake manifolds and timing belts. She also noticed the cologne of grease on his clothes was fainter than usual.

"You're not working at the shop," Charlotte said. "Your hands are spotless."

"I just had the day off, is all," he said.

"You haven't shaved," she observed. "They make you shave every day."

Hollow-sounding reasons and excuses began spilling from Keith's mouth. She didn't hear them. And she no longer saw him through the tears welling up. Back in Olympia, when she'd told him about the APD job, he'd been uncharacteristically enthused. *Oh, it's a great place, babe. I got all kinds of people there who would love to set us up. It's a great town. Big, new high school for Jeremy. Way cheaper than here.* Charlotte had known Keith was from Aberdeen and had had his troubles there. But she didn't know what kind.

While she pretended to read the Billy's Diner menu, she asked him if she could search his truck.

"You don't have no warrant," Keith said as he got up and left.

*

Charlotte felt nothing as she let Keith go. She needed to think more about the situation with Jeremy's new friend. Loud had been staying with them for nearly a week. Reportedly because his uncle was out of town. No, Loud didn't know when he would be coming back. Family emergency having to do with a relative living in Kansas.

Charlotte hadn't bought a word of it but figured that the closer she could keep Loud, the closer Jeremy would stay and the safer they would both be, and the more she could find out about what was really going on. Don't spook the suspect, went the detective rule book. Keep them close. The more she found out about Loud McCrowley, the more she could do about it— eventually. But with everything being so crazy with Keith and work, she hadn't the time. She didn't know Loud's real first name or legal guardian.

The whole situation reminded Charlotte of why she needed to cut things off with Keith: Jeremy. A mother needed to be above reproach so she could protect and correct. She just hoped she wouldn't be too late.

*

When she got home, she was relieved to find Jeremy alone. Loud was "going to clear his head."

"So…what's going on with Keith?" Jeremy asked.

"Things are going to be up and down for a little while, Jer," she told him.

"What does that mean?"

She breathed in while pulling her hair back and looking up to keep the tears in. "Don't ask me right now."

"I'd like to help you," Jeremy said.

"I'd like that too," she said. "But I have to do this alone."

THE CRASH

Meanwhile, Aurora was helping her Uncle Lyle set up an emergency meeting he'd called at the Chinook Elder's Lodge.

Aurora had never been interested in any of Uncle Lyle's work with the stuffy fraternal order of the Chinooks. But Uncle Lyle said it was an important meeting and that he needed her there. A big investment firm in NYC had collapsed, and this lit a fire under him to call the Chinooks together. But as the men filed in, though they were all soaked from a September downpour, Aurora noticed they all looked and sounded like they'd just invented the two-by-four. As she unfolded the chairs on the Lodge's parquet of varnished cedar, she heard them chortling about Aberdeen's Green Revolution: about how useful steam could be when harnessed. About how much countertops made from compressed wood particles were selling for in markets all over the world. About the lucrativeness of biodiesel. Their bubbly optimism made Aurora wonder if Uncle Lyle was making too much of Wall Street's bad news.

Aurora set out carafes of fresh coffee and hot water and realized she was the only female in the room. She felt miffed at Uncle Lyle for proffering her the "opportunity" for some community service hours helping him with his good ol' boys club. Granted, Uncle Lyle was the only black man in the room, but still a man. Except for Principal Campbell and Mayor Anders, she didn't know who all the men were and didn't really care. They were all high muck-a-mucks. She'd always thought she'd never leave the harbor, but what kind of future was there for her in a town where women didn't or couldn't attend meetings like this? What Loud had said about feeling locked out in Aberdeen suddenly resonated.

Among the smiling, clean-shaven men, there was one glowering face. The dad of that bully Brock, William Olander. He was a short, stocky man who wore thick Carhartt work pants, a hickory shirt, and a black POW-MIA cap. He had a fat red face and a blond walrus mustache. He didn't smile or joke with the others. He seemed to be holding everything in, like someone trying to quash a vicious bout of hiccups by not breathing. Or a poker player trying not to smirk while holding a winning hand. Or a fat grenade about to explode. To Aurora's relief, he avoided the refreshment table.

*

Uncle Lyle felt similar to Aurora about the Chinooks.

Calling an emergency Chinook Elders meeting was a damned-if-you-do, damned if-you-don't kind of situation. His fellow Aberdeeners would be averse to the warning he was about to give them. But were he to stay silent, he'd be left with guilt that he'd done nothing in the face of a foreseen storm.

Then again, what did he owe them?

The Caldwells, his adopted parents, were long dead. They'd been upright children of local fortune; they'd nourished him with that fortune, and loved him like a son, leaving him their turreted Victorian farmhouse on the hill and their esteemed seat at the Chinook Elders Lodge. But the rest of the town? Aberdeeners held Lyle to a degree of esteem, perhaps even fondness, because of how he had committed himself since age seventeen to civic life, organizing food drives, voting, petitions, fundraising efforts for historical projects, all on his own time. After the Washington Public Power Supply System threw in the towel on their colossally mismanaged nuclear cooling tower project, they tried to stick Grays Harbor residents with the tab. Lyle had organized protests, which led to a lawsuit that eventually brought relief to everyone's electric bills. So, everybody in Aberdeen more or less owed Lyle, and knew it, even if they would have normally been biased against someone like him: a heavy-set Black intellectual who liked jazz and had remained unmarried for reasons that spurred frequent barroom speculation.

But had he not bent his being to the good of their fair town? He shuddered to think. By the time he was Aurora's age, he had subconsciously understood that if he did not love the town more than it was inclined to hate him, it would eat him alive. So loved it, he had.

Lyle had played his cards well. His membership in the Chinooks as a man of color was an accomplishment, though no one ever spoke it. But he was used to nothing being said about how his blackness led to different treatment: long stares as he ambled down the aisles at the grocery store; invitations never received to drink with other Chinook brethren; racial slurs written about him on bathroom stalls. All of this he would have to publicly shrug off while telling himself it was just ignorance. He white-knuckled his way through some days until he could be alone and feel the pain with his only Black friends: long-dead authors and musicians: Dubois, Hurston, Ellison, Baldwin, Morrison; Ellington, Coltrane, Davis—Miles and Angela.

But everybody in Aberdeen loved his niece, Aurora. In his presence, even the most hostile eyes softened. Both men and women alike would stoop and coo at Aurora during each stage of her growing up: the little pony-tailed girl with her drumsticks, her books, her gaggle of old people. Townsfolk would look up at Lyle and give him watery-eyed nods of approbation. He'd done right by his sister, may she rest in peace. This affection by proxy had been a balm to Lyle for much of the past fifteen years.

He was therefore unprepared for how uncool and annoying his civic commitment would make him in his niece's eyes. How tiresome and middling he seemed to appear to Aurora, as she sulked behind the drink table. It pained him when he saw himself through her eyes: a sad, old trustee too busy, too awkward to love her as the father figure she needed.

And so, as the Chinook Lodge filled with white faces, Lyle felt even less sure of himself than normal and it took more effort than ever to muster up his voice to the necessary levels of orotundity.

*

As Cal's dad drove, he explained the importance of going to a Chinook Elders meeting. It was a fraternal organization of town businessmen. The regional manager of ITT Rayonier was a member. So were the CEOs at Imperium, Dahlstrom Timber, and Mary's Lumber.

"Competitors?" Cal knew to ask.

"Not directly," his dad replied. "But you could see why we would want a seat at the table. If you're not at the table, you'll be served up on the table."

The Chinook Elders had a common interest in the health and well-being of the town. Together, under Lyle's urging and direction, they'd started Visions 2020, and their collective ability to problem-solve, work together, and foresee threats would determine Aberdeen's future and, thus, Bullfinch Boyd Inc's ability to do business.

Despite the late hour and the tediousness, the invitation made Cal sit up straight and feel self-conscious about his mullet. Going to this Chinook thing confirmed that his dad was grooming him to take over. This likely meant he could avoid college—a prospect more exciting to him than girls, football, or good weed. He never wanted to leave the Harbor.

The Chinook's Lodge sat across from the Rhinehouse & Sons' sorting yard in South Aberdeen. The building was con-structed of sturdy timber with few windows. As they entered, Cal's eyes gravitated to the one girl there. Beneath her overalls, glasses, and ponytail, Cal saw potential in the vivid green eyes, taut shoulders, and the cream color of her slender neck. Following his dad's lead, Cal introduced himself.

Aurora tried not to look at him as she told him her name. Indie girls like her never looked at him directly. Most of them were probably intimidated by him: his size, his confidence, his status as a local son of fortune. But with Aurora, Cal thought, she was trying to save face, as if to say, *I know I'm not your type and I don't care.*

"Don't you hang around with Loud and Jeremy?" Cal asked.

"When I'm bored," Aurora acknowledged.

"Have they shown you Whistle Punk Falls?"

She shook her head. "Maybe it's a 'guys only' thing... They're staring." She motioned with her pebble-smooth chin to the podium where an older, heavyset Black guy was adjusting his bowtie and clearing his throat into the mic.

"Do you think any of *them* care if we are listening?" Cal asked.

"Well, that's my uncle. So, yes," Aurora said.

Aurora's uncle shuffled up to the podium and introduced himself. Cal sat by his dad, who elbowed him and nodded toward Aurora. Cal shook his head.

"Well," Blanchard began, running a hand over his neatly cropped curls. "I've called this meeting because the country is entering a financial crisis that I believe will rival the Great Depression."

The gist of Lyle's concerns, as Cal understood it, was that on Monday, a big NYC investment firm had gone bust. Following this, the federal government had bailed out a similar investment firm to keep the world's economy from collapsing. All of it made Cal wish he'd paid more attention in his econ class, but, according to Lyle, this was a problem for everybody in the room because this investment firm specialized in real estate. And because the investment firm was going to be operating on government funds from now on, they would be collared with tighter regulations, as would all similar firms. This meant that the heyday of home loans and development bonds that everyone in the country had been living in for the past decade would be coming to an end.

"This is about the demand for lumber, that precious cash crop of ours," Blanchard said.

There was silence. His dad shifted in his seat. Cal understood this was the important part, the time not to check his phone or give Aurora another once-over.

Blanchard predicted that because new laws would make it harder for banks to loan people money, people wouldn't be able to buy as many houses or finance development. This would drive down demand for timber to the lowest levels that Grays Harbor had ever seen.

Some guy in a Mackinaw vest stood up and shouted: "Blanchard, you're being a doomsdayer. You've lost your head, just like all those fellas hanging themselves in their Armani ties in New York City. Who had it coming, by the way."

There were murmurs of agreement.

"Shut up, Jorgensen," a voice said. It was Brock's dad, William Olander. "He's trying to tell you something and you're interrupting like an idiot."

"Thank you, William. But it's all right. Doug, go on," Lyle said, opening a hand to the Mackinaw-vested man.

"Well. Uh. Yeah. So... I was saying," Jorgensen continued. "It's fellas like that that use our downtown buildings as tax shelters. They built fortunes on rotten products, and they're reaping what they deserve! We'll keep our heads up and work hard. The way we always have."

Cal jumped a little when he heard his dad speak: "And Lyle, if I may, demand for timber is already low. The housing bubble popped months ago when Freddie and Fannie went south. But demand for byproduct has increased! As I've been telling you all, companies around here will be fine so long as they diversify."

"I hope you're right. Truly, I do," Lyle replied. "But my contacts in the industry have shared with me some most unsettling models. The biggest earners in New York are failing. The biggest ones here will likely fail too. Or leave. Including Sierra Pacific. Perhaps even Rhinehouse & Sons."

There were murmurs among the Chinooks. Jorgensen's voice was first to break out:

"This coming from a Rhinehouse accountant?"

"I balance their books for them. I'd be the last to defend them. No more than you would."

"Something's not right with this," Jorgensen continued. "You're just trying to make us sell our shares, so you can buy up."

"Rhinehouse released a statement back in May saying they had no plans to move or do any layoffs," Cal's dad added.

"I know the PR strategy of my own company," Blanchard said. "If Rhinehouse is considering moving or laying off anyone, it would not inform any of us ahead of time. Least of all me."

The retorts and rebuttals continued.

"I've heard enough," Olander announced after a while. "Thank you for trying with these people, Lyle. Good day to you." And with that he huffed out, shaking his head.

Cal loosened his collar, blushing, knowing he couldn't add a word to this conversation. It was like everyone was talking about the intricate details of a highway in the sky visible only to those over forty. As Lyle shifted his weight at the podium, Cal felt a little worried for the old guy, surrounded by all these ruffled white people, including him and his dad, whom Lyle no doubt thought of as tighty-whities.

But the bookish old Black dude held his own. *He's used to it*, Cal guessed. He continued doggedly with a laundry list of recommendations to all the business leaders in the room. He told them to save. To lay low. To halt any expansions or purchases that would require loans or liens on personal property. Otherwise, they'd go bottom-up. He also told them to diversify their retirement funds, because real estate wasn't going to be the safe-bet investment it once was.

Jorgensen and several others left halfway through Lyle's speech out of disgust. Cal's dad stayed and listened politely.

When Lyle was finished and they all stood up to leave, Cal went over to say goodbye to Aurora.

"I'll put in the good word for you. About coming with us to Whistle Punk Falls."

She shrugged.

*

The invite came sooner than she expected. A week later, on a clear Friday after art class, Loud invited her to pile into Cal's Forerunner with him and Jeremy and light out for their hangout spot. At a gas station in Junction City, Jeremy, Cal, and Aurora pooled their money and stashed up on snacks and firewood.

They arrived at the oxbow in Preacher's slough with a few good hours of daylight left. The October air had stayed crisp and dry. They built a fire. Using an old spare in Cal's truck bed, they built a tire swing and used it to dive out into the murky slough, doing backflips off the rubber into the icy waters. They would flail frantically against the slow current back to the beach where the fire waited to warm them.

As the sun's rays went amber into dusk, they clambered up the Sitka using the hatchet-cleaved holds. Then, while the boys were finding branches at the same height and whipping out their chill-shrunk dicks, Aurora, perhaps suspecting what was coming, jumped.

The boys heard the splash.

"Dude. She's a total badass," Cal said.

"If she's not dead," Loud said.

"I'm clear," she shouted up to them a few seconds later, and they took their collective whiz. Then they too plunged in.

They spent the better part of the night stoking the fire, talking music, noshing on cheap food, and breathing deeply of the thrilling air—cold enough to keep them awake, dry enough to cull them into staying longer. Out there on the silty bank, they felt a continent away from fraternal orders, old town ghosts, and adult anxieties. It wasn't until about 1am when Cal decided it was time to head back.

"When we get back into cell service, our phones are probably going to be flooded with parent texts wondering where we are."

Loud didn't seem concerned.

As they packed up, Loud lounged, using his feet to roast a marshmallow on a stick balanced between his toes.

"Aren't you coming?"

"I think I'll stay. You guys go on ahead."

"What if it rains?" Aurora asked.

"My uncle's place is close enough. I'll be fine."

Loud assured them he'd done it a hundred times and that they didn't need to worry. They turned towards the darkness of the woods, Cal's truck, and their disquieting timber town, the image of Loud's roguish smirk as he stoked the fire, flickering in their minds as they left.

CHERRY BOMBS AWAY

Gridlock impedes the Forerunner's procession around Tacoma's arenas and casinos and bridges. Adding to Jeremy's nausea is the hot, acrid twang in the air that his mom has likened to the smell of a dead body.

"Tacoma's a big ass city," Cal says, frowning at all the cars. "Seattle's an even bigger ass city. How do you plan on us finding Loud again?"

"Well, there we're in luck. Dude sticks out like a sore thumb wherever he goes. People will remember seeing him."

"Yeah. That fucking hairdo," Cal acknowledges. "You know, I asked him about the whole mohawk thing one time?"

They were hanging out in the grubby intermural field's locker room post rugby scrum and Loud was doing up his famous fin with a can of five-finger-discounted hair grease.

"Will you hurry up with that shit?" Cal had asked.

"Don't get your pubes in a knot," Loud snorted.

"So, you're Native. And you wear a mohawk. Isn't that kind of… I don't know. Basic?" Cal asked. Derivative would have been a better word, but Jeremy hadn't been around back then to help with useful things like that.

Loud had turned around, lip curled and asked Cal, "What the fuck do you know about being Native?"

"About as much as you know. You said it yourself."

"Exactly. About all this world has taught me about being Native is that some of them wore mohawks and all of them have a drinking problem. And I don't drink. And the funny thing is that if I was white, we wouldn't be having this conversation. Even though whitey was the one who stole it. Like he did everything else."

"Well, sorr-ee! Fuck. White kid bringing up race. Dumb plan."

"Yeah, whatever. What is the plan for tonight anyway," Loud had said, turning back to coaxing his stirp of hair into attention.

But as Cal went to drop a deuce, he could hear Loud talking to the mirror, muttering and retro-activating a comeback: "You know what's basic is for a redneck to be walking around with a dab of chaw in his lip."

"Never brought that up again," Cal laughs and thumps the Forerunners dash.

"You got more guts than I do," Jeremy says.

"Yeah, well, I dunno. You're the one hot to trot on this little quest of ours."

The Tacoma aroma is still curling their nostril hairs. One of Jeremy's dad's diatribes replays in his head. *The I-5 corridor. More like the I-5 drag. The infrastructure was never intended to handle round-the-clock volume!*

"I could get out and run faster than this!" Cal says.

"Sorry dude," Jeremy says and repeats again how all this is his fault—Loud running away and everything.

"How?" Cal asks.

"Too many ways to say."

"Try me. We got time."

Jeremy shifts in his seat. "I guess it would have helped if I had seen the writing on the wall earlier. About Loud."

Cal shrugs, "We all made excuses for him. Looked the other way to keep things chill."

Jeremy continues, "Instead of seeing his issues for what they were, I saw him as my muse."

A smile worms its way onto Cal's face. "Is that why you blew up that toilet?"

*

The rest of October, one of the driest on record, passed much the same way as their first collective night at Whistle Punk Falls—after school and weekend hangouts at the oxbow. The weather held out and Loud made them endure joke after joke about how they were enjoying the most Indian summer of their lives. Loud would disappear for a few days to a week at a time, but they were too busy with school and other things to think much of it, assuming Loud was just a free spirit.

Jeremy, for one, didn't mind having a break from his bunk buddy, who had been arousing all sorts of suspicions from his mom and creating a bit of a mess around their modest rambler. With Loud gone, back at his uncle's Jeremy assumed, Jeremy could devote more time to school and guitar.

Then, the last week of October, Aberdeen weather woke up and remembered itself. Rains misted, showered, and pounded the Harbor.

During a particularly somnolent English class, Loud asked Jeremy if he could resume coach surfing and though Jeremy worried about his mom, he was stoked to have his bunky again.

That first day back together, they stayed up all night watching cult favorites like *Fight Club* and *A Clockwork Orange*.

A couple days in, they had their first fight. They'd gotten their *Great Gatsby* tests back in English, and Jeremy was pissed. In response to a short-answer question, he'd answered that the glasses on the big billboard symbolized Nick Caraway—the silent, uninvolved narrator watching everything go down. Ms. Rigby had marked it wrong, writing in red pen that the glasses symbolized God.

"Fitzgerald *says* the eyes are God. No duh," Jeremy fumed to Loud. "That's so obvious it's not even an answer. Rigby's so… dumb."

"Wait, which character is Fitzgerald?" Loud asked.

"That's the writer, dude."

"Well, forgive the fuck outta me. Anyway, what'd you get on the test?"

"A-minus."

"Fuck you!"

"What?"

"No, seriously, fuck you. Are you just saying all this to make me feel stupid?" Loud asked.

"No… I'm just," Jeremy stuttered. Loud hadn't even come to class on test day. Loud hadn't been in class for weeks and now that Jeremy thought about it, he'd never even seen him reading the book. Why had he bitched about his A-minus to *Loud*?

Before Jeremy could think of anything to mollify him, Loud was halfway out the door, saying he needed a minute.

A "minute" turned into three days. Jeremy tried to pass the time doing homework. But each time he put pencil to paper, he would replay his exchange with Loud and kick himself in time to the pounding rain.

On the fourth day, Jeremy cut a quick path through the rain to Weatherwax High, Fugazi for his soundtrack. Though walking took longer, biking in the rain stung his eyes, rusted his chain, and soaked his ass through. As he walked, Ian MacKaye's vocals hit his ears like a cold, hollow pipe while the mean-street distortion on his rhythm guitar crunched and whapped out catchy melodies bristling with social commentary on issues ranging from conformity to consumerism to homelessness to environmentalism. With their ear-wiggy choruses and range of lyrical content, the band was beyond punk. Even seven years after their last album, they sounded contemporary, arranging the score for the coming apocalypse. With their music as an accompaniment, Jeremy's feelings of aggression and woe broiled.

Jeremy had been introducing Loud to Fugazi just before their fight. Now Jeremy doubted he'd ever get to play him the rest of their discography. Loud seemed like one of those people you should prepare to lose.

But when he walked into the cafeteria for lunch, there Loud was, at their usual table with his feet up, reading a copy of the school newspaper, drinking a large coffee, compliments of Molly Donahue. The Halloween-themed paper had its cover story about Laura Law and Billy Gohl ghost sightings.

"Hey," Loud said, folding his paper and slapping it on the table. "Sorry I bailed for a couple of days. I just… needed some space."

Jeremy shrugged while applying fresh Xs to his knuckles with a Sharpie.

"But," Loud said. "The time was well spent."

"Whatever," Jeremy said, swiping the paper.

The main story reported more people seeing Laura Law's ghost. Laura Law lying on a cloud of smoke like a fainting couch. Laura Law smoking wistfully while crossing her legs atop a logging truck's crane. Laura Law rocking herself in the reflection of one of the dark windows of the Ninemire building.

"I bet it was some random drifter," Jeremy said, thinking about who had killed her.

Loud ignored him. He was looking over his shoulder. "I've thought of a way for you to get back at Olander."

"Brock?"

Jeremy's black eye had yellowed. Brock had been taken out of Rigby's English class and switched into a more rudimentary reading program. And, with everything else going on in his life, Jeremy hadn't thought about Brock much.

"What? You don't care anymore? That guy kicked your ass and got off scot-free!" Loud said.

Jeremy shrugged again. But he felt the hurt returning suddenly, along with a latent rage over how this world was constructed in such a way that a guy could call you 'fag' and punch you in the face without any kind of reprisal.

"Well, you might not care. But I do. I'm not letting anybody just beat up my friend," Loud argued, his face souring in displeasure at the very idea. "And." His face went calm. "They've been circling outside my house."

"You went back?"

"Yeah. My grandparents called me. They're on a road trip to see their family in other parts of the country—Nebraska. I think I told you. They wanted me to check on things."

"So, Brock and his posse came by?"

"Yeah. Him and the Tayaks. The whole fucking clan. They drove by real slow, looked around, and drove off. They're planning something. And if they don't hit my grandparents' house, they might hit us at your mom's. I saw them prowling around this morning."

Jeremy's breathing quickened. "Call the police! Or, fuck it, let's just tell her. She *is* the police."

"She's just one of many... The other cops won't back her up if she wants to do something about it," Loud said. "Old man Olander...He's got the cops in his back pocket, dude."

Jeremy put his head in his hands.

"The point is this." Loud looked over his shoulder again. He muttered and scrunched up his brows as if a stiff wind was blowing in his face. "We can't let them cow me. Us, I mean. We've got to hit them first."

"Hit them?" Jeremy asked. "How?"

"Here's the plan," Loud said.

"You're...serious."

"If you back out from this, what kind of punk are you?"

Jeremy squirmed inside, feeling pigeonholed. "What's your idea?" Jeremy asked.

"Brock has IBS. Irritable Bowel Syndrome."

"Eww. How do you know that?"

"I found out in the locker rooms after rugby practice last summer," Loud whispered, looking over at Brock. He was in his hickory shirt and work boots, flicking his Skoal can. He made a joke to his friends before trundling his wide ass down a set of stairs that led to the gym and a seldom-used student bathroom.

"There he goes. Okay, we have to be quick! Brock, with his IBS, has to take like ten shits a day," Loud explained.

"That's why Ms. Rigby let him go so much," Jeremy said.

"Stay focused, man. This is it!"

"What?" Jeremy asked, grimacing. An uneasy feeling was creeping in, as if the rain that had seeped from the sidewalk into his shoes, socks, and skin were rising to his knees and waist and into his mouth.

Loud gripped Jeremy's shoulders.

"This is your moment," Loud said. He looked around the lunchroom again, then reached into his leather jacket and pulled out a red cylinder about the size of a spool of fine thread.

"What the fuck is that?" Jeremy asked.

"It's an M-80."

"Where did you get it?" Jeremy whispered, looking over his shoulders now too.

"I learned how to make them."

"Where?"

"Street-Kid High School. I graduated Val-e-DICK-torian."

"You want me to explode it on him?"

"Not *on* him. Fuck, I'm not a psychopath. In a urinal! While he's in the bathroom. Freak the shit out of him…Now."

"What?" The pulse in Jeremy's neck beat like a countdown. "But what if I kill him?"

Loud shook his head. "He's in a stall, dude. And you're going to plunk it in the next-door urinal's little hole."

"So, I go in, light it, drop it in and run?"

"The old in and out."

"The old in and out," Jeremy repeated. It was a line from *A Clockwork Orange*. "Can't I think about it?"

"Did you *see* the look he gave us a minute ago?"

"I didn't see him give a look!"

"Well, he did. He's going to hit us after school, I'm telling you. Now's our chance to hit first!"

"Won't this make him madder?"

"Maybe."

"What's the point then?" Jeremy asked. "To scare him?"

"That…and to make him look stupid. The cameras will catch you going in and out, but when they pull you…"

"Pull me?" Jeremy asked.

"The principal's going to question you, but you'll stay strong. You'll say you walked in and saw Brock light it, and you ran."

"He'll argue back," Jeremy replied.

"His word against yours. Troubled jock against straight-A student. An open and shut case."

"That's why you can't do it."

"They're already itching to pin some piddly shit on me," Loud said. "They'll never think a good kid like you would do something like this."

Jeremy suddenly doubled over in a nervous glee. "It's a good plan."

"Jeremy." Loud gripped his shoulders again. "This will be the worst thing you've ever done."

Jeremy sat up straight. "Oh, shit."

"But I really need this. It'll buy me—us—some distance from them. They'll realize we're a threat. Make them know! DO. NOT. FUCK WITH US."

It was a line from *Fight Club*. Fugazi choruses barraged through Jeremy's brain. "Yeah," he nodded. "They shouldn't fuck with us!"

"Because of you! Here are the matches. Don't look back."

*

Holding the cherry bomb in his pocket, Jeremy walked down to the bathroom. His gaze was straight and steps certain. He didn't think, knowing that thinking would put a wrench in the wheels Loud had set in motion. The one image Jeremy kept in his head was that ugly moment under uncaring fluorescent lights in a similar bathroom when he'd been pummeled by this very same sonofabitch that he was going to get back big.

As he opened the bathroom door, a thought chilled him: what if there were others in the bathroom? No one. All clear except for Brock's work boots showing from under the stall. Jeremy could hear him hocking and spitting—chew, probably—onto the bathroom walls.

Jeremy took out the sulfur-smelling cherry. He struck a match. With shaking hands, he held the devious little flame to the green visco tail and the fuse popped into life.

Brock shuffled urgently in the stall. "Hello?"

One, two, three, Jeremy counted as he turned in and tucked the cylinder into the urinal.

When he turned around, Brock was standing in his way.

"What the fuck?" Brock said, peering around him.

"Duck!" Jeremy screamed and launched himself onto Brock.

They stumbled back into the stall the instant the bomb blew.

The explosion sounded like an anvil striking the porcelain. There was a popping sound within the watery hollow, followed by sound of the bowl shattering on the tiled floor.

Reeling from Jeremy's charge, Brock fell with his full weight unto the unflushed toilet he'd been using. The bowl in the stall broke, and they fell, legs kicking, in an expanding lake of shit.

Jeremy wrenched free from Brock.

"Get back here, you little fucker!" Brock yelled, getting up and charging forward.

Jeremy slammed the stall door in Brock's face and ran.

*

The next day when Jeremy passed beneath the school's arch, he was a shivering mess. He held his breath for when the administration would descend upon him. He circumvented the front office and made his way to first period.

Moments after Ms. Rigby submitted the attendance, an office TA delivered a summons from the principal. On his way to the office, Jeremy imagined the scene: Brock in tears blubbering about how they'd tried to blow him up.

When Jeremy opened the door to the principal's office, there was no sign of Brock: just Principal Campbell. Something inside Jeremy fell away. He knew he wouldn't be able to maintain a bald-faced lie against a stern, sober adult. So, he whipped up the next best thing: a half-truth.

"I blew up the toilet," Jeremy stammered.

Principal Campbell sputtered as he crossed out the line of questioning he'd formed in his head. Jeremy felt him correct course; he asked if McCrowley had put him up to it.

Jeremy said he hadn't.

"Brock said he saw the two of you talking before he went to the restroom."

"We're always talking."

"Then why'd you do it?"

"Brock and his friend Johnny Tayak beat me up a few weeks ago. After calling me 'faggot' for a week," Jeremy said, pointing to his yellow eye. "And I found out about Brock's… condition. Some of the other football players were making fun of him behind his back. But when I heard them, I thought about getting back at him with the toilet bomb."

Principal Campbell asked where he got the explosive.

"What does it matter where I got it?" Jeremy asked. "I did it."

"You seem awfully eager to fess up," Principal Campbell observed. "Which tells me you're protecting somebody."

"Are you really going to ignore hate speech and assault?"

"You're trying to blame shift. I'm calling your mother."

"K…" Jeremy said, giving an unimpressed look.

"And you'll be spending a night in juvenile hall."

Officer Javier Moreno appeared. The gravity of what Jeremy had done descended, calving into him with glacial weight and irrevocability. The cold glint in Moreno's eyes and his badge intensified the freeze.

*

There was no way his mom would even try to get him off the hook. She was a career woman with a reputation to protect. Not that Jeremy would have asked.

Officer Moreno didn't cuff Jeremy or flip on the siren. But he did put him in the squad car just as school was getting out. Jeremy buried his head in his hands, but it was no use. Everybody saw his big curly head getting hauled off to the slammer. He heard laughter and expletives. The chilly pangs of conscious had thawed. Everything inside him became a flavorless gray wad. An over-chewed piece of gum. He wanted to fall asleep or dissociate from his body so that he wouldn't have to live the slow, sad procession of what was coming.

The Juvenile Detention Center was a low, aluminum-roofed hexagon-shaped building outside Junction City. The heavy doors opened to low ceilings, clay-green walls, and low-stim fluorescents.

Jeremy had to strip and put on a jumpsuit with orange flip flops. A guard slapped a yellow bracelet on Jeremy's wrist. Yellow, the color of Gatsby's car. The color of a coward. They took Jeremy's keys, mp3 player, and wallet, but let him keep *The Stranger*—his class's next book. He'd finish it that night. A perfect companion, really.

Officer Moreno walked Jeremy to a cell at the dim end of a row of white bars, his big hand on Jeremy's arm. Jeremy kept his head down as he marched. He didn't want to see his fellow jailbirds, muse upon their petty crimes, or exchange identifying information they could use to find him when he got out. Moreno's hand started to feel like a mitt fresh out of the oven as the officer guided him into the open cell. Jeremy wanted Moreno to leave. His cell closed with a cavernous clang, and as the sound's reverberations faded, he could still feel Moreno's tall shadow on him, along with his beady, dark eyes.

Jeremy looked up at him from his seat on the wall-secured single bunk.

Moreno leaned his forehead against the bars. "I… know you got stuff going on in your life…but. That doesn't give you permission to destroy property."

Jeremy nodded and pressed *The Stranger* between his hands just to feel something solid that wouldn't give way. It helped as he felt the fog of detachment clearing away to reveal the wreckage of what he had done to his life. This wouldn't be over tomorrow. Maybe not ever. He'd have a record now.

"Just between you and me, she blames herself," Moreno said.

"I don't." Jeremy looked at the ceiling to keep the tears in. "Mom didn't make me blow up the toilet."

Moreno shifted and clutched the collar on his bulletproof vest. "You should choose your friends better."

Jeremy lowered his face. Who cares if the tears fell? "Loud

chose me. And that's enough to make us BFFs."

"Why?"

"Because," Jeremy said, wiping his nose. "I'm not the type of person that has people lining up around the corner to be friends with him."

Moreno nodded. "Did Brock Olander give you that black eye?"

"And called me 'fag' a bunch of times."

"I'm sorry that happened to you."

Jeremy shrugged. "I didn't have to blow up a toilet over it. But it is stupid that nothing's going to happen to Brock."

"I got called 'spic' a lot when we first moved here," Moreno said, looking at his boots. "'Wetback', too."

"How did you get them to stop?" Jeremy asked.

The insides of Moreno's eyebrows met as he looked up. "I got big and learned to beat the shit out of them."

From between the bars, Jeremy could see the stiff leather holsters weighing down Moreno's belt. From watching his mom take apart and clean her utility belt, Jeremy knew Moreno had a commando's worth of weaponry on him: two pairs of handcuffs, Taser, Glock, expandable baton, flashlight, mace. He couldn't imagine anyone calling Moreno a name now, but he knew there were people crazy enough to insult cops. And that when they did, the cops—the good ones, anyway—had to just kind of take it and laugh about it later.

"But now," Moreno said. "When somebody says something shitty to me, I don't have to beat on them. Because I know who I am."

Jeremy nodded and thanked him and said he'd think about it, knowing it was the quickest way to get the guy out of his face. He would never be able to beat anybody up. He would never wear a big, heavy belt with a badge. He wouldn't ever be able to choose who his friends were or be confident enough in his own skin to let an insult wick off. But he could learn how to make the most of whatever shitty situation he landed himself in, something his friend Loud McCrowley seemed to be pretty good at. So, he lay down on the thin foam mattress of his cell and opened *The Stranger* to face Meursault's mommy issues while he hummed "I Fought the Law."

THE DANCING SKELETON

While Jeremy had passed October doing homework and partaking in autumn bliss at Whistle Punk Falls, Charlotte had been extricating herself from her former lover.

She peeked into Jeremy's room and saw his Weezer poster, Fender Strat laid on his bed, and his guitar amp accidentally left on. Her breath hit speed bumps of emotion as she exhaled. She simply couldn't have a pot smoker as a husband. Couldn't keep entertaining his half-hearted claims of wanting to reform. Couldn't let him sink her reputation and her career and hook her boy on that brain-cell-melting trash. No matter how great the sex was. She turned the amp off.

That last week of October, Charlotte called Keith and told him to come by the next morning to pick up his stuff at the curb. She wouldn't be there. The divorce papers would be served to him soon. The druggies might have their grip on the city, but they didn't have to govern the morality of her home.

With one case file closed, another opened. The McCrowley kid was back to stay with them. With Keith out of her life, Charlotte would have the bandwidth to check out what his real story was.

*

The next morning, Principal Campbell called her with the news: her son had blown up a urinal. The Olander boy, Brock, had been in the stall next to it. In an ensuing scuffle, they'd broken a toilet. Principal Campbell believed Jeremy had intended on pinning it on Brock but faltered under pressure. Brock claimed Loud McCrowley had put Jeremy up to it, and Campbell believed him. Campbell and admin were still deliberating Jeremy's punishment while he spent the night in juvey. She understood and thanked him.

Charlotte sank to the floor, processing the news. She nodded off.

I don't understand any of this, Jeremy's voice echoed in her head.

Later that afternoon, she called her son in the tank.

"I have a lot of questions for you," she told him. "There's a lot I don't understand. But I did want to start by telling you that Keith is gone."

The line was silent. "For good?"

"I'm so sorry, Jer." she said. "I never should have let him into our lives."

"It's…whatever."

He told her he didn't want to talk. "I have to do my penance."

"We'll talk about it later," she said and hung up to try to smooth things over with the school. She called Principal Campbell back and asked him to consider the circumstances. She told him she was sure he'd been acting out because of family instability. She admitted working a lot of overtime while making bad decisions with her soon-to-be ex-husband. Not to mention the fact that Jeremy had been beaten up recently—by Brock, obviously. Why else would he have wanted to frame him with vandalism? These events, plus the McCrowley boy's toxic influence led to Jeremy's heinous actions, which she was so sorry for. The principal said he'd factor all this in when meting out Jeremy's punishment.

*

When he was released the next morning, Jeremy wished he'd told his mom he loved her on the phone the night before. And that he was sorry for making trouble for her. He wanted to tell her how in *The Stranger*, all Meursault feels after his mom's death is numbness. *If you died, I'd cry*, Jeremy felt like saying.

While his mom waited in the car, Jeremy dressed. His head

hummed like a hornet's nest. Entering again into the natural light—gray as it was—felt like a slap. He winced, and his shoulders tightened around his neck, preparing for the lecture that was coming.

On the car ride home, she gave him the third degree. He could have hurt himself. He *had* hurt himself! He could have hurt someone else. Sure, the big asshole had beaten him up, but he could have gone to her and the principal for a legitimate chance at justice. Instead, he'd destroyed property. Though he was out of the slammer now, she warned him, he might be prosecuted criminally. Not to mention that he had probably ruined her reputation. From then on, she'd be known as the cop who couldn't control her kid.

"I'm sure all of this is because of me," she admitted.

"No," Jeremy shook his head.

"You're just trying to tell me something," she said.

"Then I would just tell you!"

"I don't like who you're acting like, Jer."

"Who am I acting like?" Jeremy asked.

"You know who," she said, mouth trembling.

After pulling into the driveway, she told Jeremy to go find Loud.

On his bike, he found Loud at the Smoke Hole. Loud went all kid-in-a-candy-store giddy when he saw Jeremy, asking him what it was like *inside*. Had he dropped the soap? How many tattoos had he gotten? Was one of them a naked lady? Was the said naked lady tattooed on a part of the body he'd feel comfortable showing him?

"Dude, you are a bonafide badass now! I'm so jealous."

It surprised Jeremy that Loud had never been arrested. In the same instant, Jeremy realized it was probably bad that he was surprised and caught himself before he said anything.

Loud continued: "You can sing the most anti-establishment barn-burner now and not look like a poser!"

Jeremy shrugged him off. "I probably can't go to college

now. And my mom is probably going to kick your ass out. Oh, and they know you gave me the idea."

Loud didn't seem concerned.

They biked back to Jeremy's house in Canyon Court and found Charlotte sitting in Keith's armchair with a rage as steely and pinpointed as the ejection port on her Beretta.

"Jeremy," she said. "Go to your room. You…" she addressed Loud and pointed to an empty chair directly across from her.

"I have a name."

"Which I don't know," Charlotte said.

Jeremy was still standing there.

"Go, Jer," Loud said. "I'll see what she wants."

Jeremy left, mumbling about how he didn't need permission to do anything.

Loud sat down, and Charlotte began:

"Now. I can tell by your face you know what this is about, and that you're pleased with yourself."

"It was the kid that gave Jer that black eye, Detective Sweet," Loud said. "Plus, he was creeping around my house with his dad and those other redneck donkey-punchers. They don't like me cuz I'm different. Like everyone else around here!"

Charlotte thought for a second. "The Olanders are no friends of mine. But you've put my son into the crosshairs of danger. And I can't just let this go."

"So, you're kicking me out."

"No."

Loud raised an eyebrow.

"You can stay," Charlotte said. "If you agree to two things."

"Let's hear 'em," Loud said, cracking his knuckles and thinking *This broad's gonna be harder to kick than Cougar Lady.*

"First, you have to call your mother."

"That right there is a dealbreaker. I live with my grandparents for a reason."

"I thought you said you live with your uncle. The one in Kansas. Or is it Nebraska?"

Loud held up his hands. "Okay, you got me. I live with my grandparents. They're old. They don't have much money. They've never been able to take care of me that well. I don't want you calling CPS on them. So, I lied."

"You're lying again. You don't live with them either," Charlotte said.

"Yeah, because they fed me bath salts when I was little."

"Right… Bath salts. So. When you're not here, where do you sleep?"

"Can't tell you," Loud said.

"Then you got to call Mom."

"I'm not calling my mom. End of story. What's the second thing?"

She exhaled out her nose. "You need to go to counseling." She reached over and handed Loud a card.

EVERGREEN MENTAL HEALTH SERVICES
DR. LEANN PAUL
Psychiatrist

"A shrink…" Loud said.

"A therapist," Charlotte said. "I have an appointment for you tomorrow."

He snorted.

"I've heard you out in the backyard talking to yourself…"

"Those were…song lyrics. You…You wouldn't get it."

Loud let the card fall to the floor. He stood up.

Charlotte realized Loud had his pack with him, full of all his things. He'd anticipated this. She stood up.

"Know before you leave that you're on Judge Spurgeon's radar."

"No shit."

"If you leave, I'll have to stop protecting you from Truancy Court."

Loud paused at the door. He cupped his hands and put them over his mouth before taking a deep huff from his palms. He let out a little laugh and turned to her.

"Did I ever tell you..." he paused, winking at her, "how much I love a woman in uniform?"

He walked out the door laughing and talking to himself. The skeleton patch on the back of his vest danced as he hustled off on that little green trail bike of his. With mirth? Or maybe he was starting to shiver in the November chill.

*

At the wheel of his Forerunner, Cal Gearhart cusses in the stop and go traffic in the narrow corridors beneath Seattle's convention center. In the alcoves above cement pilings, blue and gray tents perch like nests.

"Think one of them is Loud's?" Cal asks. Jeremy shrugs.

Bumper-to-bumper, Cal might as well get out and push his truck through the city's caverns of steel—somewhere inside which Loud wanders along the edge of a great void they imagine has the power to extinguish his fiery spirit.

Jeremy checks his texts to see that he's in the clear for missing his shift at *The Harbor Herald*: his boss either buys his lie about being sick or doesn't care that he won't be showing up.

"Why are you still interning at that paper, dude? It's spring break," Cal asks.

Jeremy's "internship" at *The Harbor Herald* has consisted

of dialing lists of phone numbers, asking for subscriptions and donations. The internship started as part of his punishment for blowing up the toilet: a two-week suspension, a thousand-dollar fine, and six months' community service. Lyle Blanchard made the arrangements with the town's well-respected but floundering paper, which had been offering a paid internship for a high school kid to do some cold-call marketing. The position was to be funded through a grant from Visions 2020, the renovative project Lyle presided over. Fulfilling the paper position with free labor from Jeremy enabled Lyle to re-direct the funds to upkeep costs on the paper's ancient press. It also ensured that Jeremy got rejected over one hundred times a day in the back office of the paper's brick building while the Chehalis River surged slowly by out of the office window.

"Tough break. The Rejection Factory," Cal laughs, using Jeremy's epithet for the job.

The first week had been kind of fun, as Jeremy got to upsell people on buying the paper with him on the front page: *Read now about a troubled youth vandalizing Weatherwax High, only in* The Harbor Herald! Besides, Jeremy would get to claim the internship as an extracurricular on college applications.

Still in the shadows of Seattle's overpasses, Jeremy checks Facebook on his phone for updates on Hawky-Mo's page. There's been nothing for days. He has no idea where to start looking for Loud in the sprawling city. No idea if Loud is still on the streets or even still alive. But Jeremy's emotional center sloshes in a doldrum of nonchalance. In his year of knowing Loud, they'd gotten separated numerous times, yet their paths continued to cross. It seemed inevitable to Jeremy that they would meet again as if they were walking the same single-pathed, circuitous maze.

AIN'T THAT A SHAME

Minutes after leaving Sweet's house in the harshening November air, Loud McCrowley was chaining his bike up to the 'Underbird Motel's balcony railing, outside Karla's room. Strange, he could already hear cackling. Only this time, it wasn't coming from Karla inside the room, but from inside his head. He felt his thoughts turn, the reels moving in their eccentric ways, the warped film of his life's movie rippling and fading in and out. The thoughts overpowered him and he slumped against the railing in a trance swirling with memories and feelings which distorted each other in an endless cycle: Grandma Gin letting Pappy Rue salt him with ground up bits of Adderall, the highway miles, the shitkickers and their trucks whirling rings around his house, Jeremy's mom, that Lady Cop, wanting to drug him up just like his grandparents had. He pictured himself as an Adderall-flavored Thanksgiving turkey and all the white people dressed in Pilgrim hats, licking their lips, ready to eat him. The highway called. It spoke. *Come.*

"Where have you been?" a voice asked.

It was Karla, peeking out of the hotel room she lived out of. She was wearing a bathrobe that resembled pink insulation.

Loud smiled at her.

She pulled him into her room and pointed to a green brick wrapped in purple cellophane laying on the middle of her bed. "Would you like to meet my new friend?"

Loud barely heard that the grass originated from the Olander's family farm. He certainly didn't ask Karla what she'd done to get it. He just moved hypnotically towards the brick, tractor-beamed by its presence, salivating for the smell, which he knew would momentarily replace his ache for his father.

It had been a couple days since Loud had a toke. Since he'd run out on Jeremy after that little tiff. And since, his thoughts turned on wheels becoming wobblier and wobblier the more school assignments piled up and enemies grew from the trees surrounding his grandparents' house. But the instant the smoke from the silver-tipped cannabis hit his lungs again, all that noise dimmed. The silence hovered over the rain-filled potholes in the parking lot. The silence floated over the low roofs of the wide streets and up into the hills going russet in the deepening autumn. Loud watched the smoke leave his lungs and believed he could feel it join the fog caught in the canopies of the trees and the steam from the mills, and he felt he could will his spirit to leave his body, rise high enough, and maybe even catch a glimpse of the sea.

*

Loud stayed with Karla at the 'Underbird for a week. Though the weed was almost worth it, Karla kept making him go down on her for it. He'd swallowed so much of her cum and post-cunnilingual toothpaste, just about every part of him was nauseous. And she pawed at him to go all the way with her. Loud knew it was only a matter of time before he gave in, and he did *not* want to deal with a baby or a baby's momma now or ever. So Loud decided to try his grandparents' again, hoping the shitkicker revenge storm was over.

Loud decided on bringing Aurora, whom he called Overalls, with him to survey the damage the Olanders and the Tayaks had no doubt by now inflicted on his squat.

"It's so weird that Jeremy blew up that toilet," Overalls said on their walk out to the sloughs.

"Yeah," Loud said.

They were walking, Loud having loaned his bike to Karla as a kind of pay-it-forward for the weed.

"You know why he did it, don't you?" Overalls said.

He shrugged.

"Fine, don't tell me." She smiled.

"I really don't know."

They kept walking.

"Why don't you go to any of your other classes? Except for art," Overalls asked. "The one you have with me?"

"What are you, writing a book?" Loud said with a smile.

"Maybe."

"I don't always know why I do the things I do," Loud began. "It's like…You know how when you're sleeping, and you wake up saying something weird. Or thinking something weird. Like you convince yourself that a spider is crawling in your socks. And then you get up half asleep, pull off your socks and wonder, halfway into the second sock why you're doing what you're doing."

"Well, I never sleep without my socks. I get way too cold. But I know what you mean."

The Chehalis River snagged itself in a series of marsh-bearing curves. These siphoned the river down into a stream that hid in and around the lumber and pulp mills outcropping along the banks. They saw the corpses of trees, their red, cleaved faces piled into bristling heaps, waiting to be homogenized into something people could use. The clustered roundness of the heaps looked kinetic, and Loud wondered if one big push could send the booms rolling into a stampede that could flatten the whole of Junction City. Not likely. The mills were indomitable, corrugated steel pavilions that in some form or another would always fill up the Harbor sky with their weather system of steam.

After Art class, Loud had told Aurora that he needed her to do something for him; she'd warily agreed. No boy had ever needed anything from her, and maybe that was the appeal. But as they walked, she was glad she was wearing her raincoat and layered underneath with her overalls and a flannel long-sleeve so that he couldn't see her shaking: part from the cold, part from nervousness. She didn't ask him where they were going. She continued to feel an unspoken need emanating from him, and she kept worrying about whether this need was something she could fill.

She hummed a tune she'd picked up drumming with the Fidget-Bridgets:

Ain't that a shame
My tears fell like rain.
Ain't that a shame
You're the one to blame.

"Is that Weezer?" Loud asked.

"Fats Domino." She laughed and told him about her times with the octogenarians at Think-of-Me-Hill Retirement Community.

"Why do you like hanging out with old people?" Loud asked.

"I guess it's because they know so much. They've lived so much life! They have so many stories."

The Chehalis River seemed easygoing, but beneath, she knew, there was a shoving contest between the inland freshets and the heavy saltwater. The dirt road bent left and out of sight of all industry. The mills' ticking and roaring dirge grew quiet. The rain stopped, yet the earth stayed dark, hinting at water on all sides. The thinning leaves on the alders were yellow as dandelions. They rounded the bend in the road, and in a glen, she saw a house. In the center of the second story, a boarded-up gable waited like blinded Cyclops's eye. The sun and the rain had long ago exfoliated the house's powder-blue paint to reveal gray, parched wood. The surrounding grasses had grown tall. Fearsome looking weeds bloomed. The overgrown yew on the west side of the house rested its branches on the covered porch's rails and the porch swing, which creaked along with the open front door.

Red spray paint hissed messages across the clapboard siding: *fag, freak, fuck-up.* The front windows were black gaps; the boards formerly nailed over them had been ripped down. A trail of books with broken spines led to a nearby eddy where a slashed sleeping bag and an overturned trunk bobbed in the current.

"Oh my gosh, Loud!" Aurora said.

"Fuck me," he said.

She felt so stupid for being afraid of him, standing there in his soaked jacket, looking at his ruined books. He sniffled and turned his face from her to start picking things up. She helped him make a pile. Then Loud led her to the back basement door, which was also open.

"Good thing there wasn't much to trash," Loud said, once inside.

Strands of spider-web tickled her arms.

In the dim of the basement, Loud felt around with the toe of his boot. A board wiggled. He lifted the board and unearthed a few books sealed in plastic bags.

"Glad I hid a couple," he said. One of the books was the Kurt Cobain biography *Heavier Than Heaven.*

From the cover, the heavy-lidded eyes of Aberdeen's anti-hero stopped Aurora in her tracks. Framed by flaxen hair, the slender face boasted its strong chin. The weak smile seemed to be holding back a grimace or a smirk.

"The books are all my grandma's," Loud said. "Mostly stolen from the library… Maybe some butt-hurt librarians did this to pay us back for late fees."

Aurora gave a dry laugh at Loud's quip as she shoved them in Loud's bag. Along with the books was a toolbox.

She followed him upstairs. Fallen swatches of wallpaper lounged on the floors. Vacant appliance outlets yawned out from holes in the cobwebbed kitchen. Somebody—multiple somebodies— had peed in the fireplace.

"What a bunch of…assholes," Aurora said.

The wan light of the overcast day crept in from the window and door frames, laying bare the waste of what had been the McCrowley family home.

They found the boards that had been ripped off the windows. Aurora held the boards while Loud used a hammer to drive through a few nails.

Then they sat on the porch and looked out at the slow-moving water snaking around the dogwoods and squat cedars. She thought about the bare floors, the holes in the wall, the missing appliances, the dark, empty rooms, and the boards they'd just re-nailed over the windows.

She fussed with the cuff of her multi-colored glomitts, failing to contain her question. "Why are you staying here?"

"Cuz my grandparents are on a road trip," he said flatly, his lips heavy and parted.

"I don't believe you," she said.

"That's your problem," he said quietly. "Brock and his posse wouldn't have ever fucked with this house had my granddad been here. They're all members of this Chinook thing."

Aurora nodded. "My uncle. He's in that same thing. Only I'm not supposed to tell anyone. It's kind of like the Masons, I think."

"Yeah, I think so too. They're all white people and weird. Well…except for your uncle."

"They *are* all men," Aurora said. She tried again to pull her black hair back into its ponytail, four or five irascible strands escaping to dangle over her face.

Suddenly Loud turned to her. "Don't tell anyone I'm living here. Not Jeremy, not his mom, not Cal. Nobody! Please."

Before she knew it, he was pressing his head into her

shoulder. She raised her arm slowly, reflexively, to pat his back. "Okay," she found herself saying.

"I'd have to go to Tumwater or Pasco or Des Moines or some stupid place like that and live in a foster home."

"Okay, okay," she said.

He lifted his head up and looked at her with the heavy eaves of his brown eyes.

They walked out of the sloughs to where Aurora had cell reception so she could call Uncle Lyle to pick them up. Loud hung out at their house until 9pm, then lied saying he was going to stay at Cal's.

Loud had yet to meet Cal's parents. But he knew they were super bougie and would never let him couch surf there. So he obeyed the highway's voice whispering *come,* setting back out for his squat in the sloughs, a growing storm at his back.

GOING DEEPER

Cal parks the Forerunner on a hill overlooking the freeway's course through Seattle. He nudges Jeremy awake. Twisted shore pines darken the hill, and below them, people squat in tents, the tent flaps listing in the wind created by the northbound cars. Shielding their eyes from the noon sun, they scan the tents for signs of Loud's mohawk.

"So… Where are we going to sleep?" Cal asks.

Jeremy pulls a beanie over his bouffant. "Homeless shelters."

Cal shakes his head. "So, we're going to be voluntarily homeless. Isn't that. Like. Lying."

"No. We truly won't have anywhere to sleep. Unless you want to cuddle up in the truck bed."

Cal looks again at the tents. Mangy-haired people mill in and out. Wisps of smoke plume out of the tent openings.

"I… can't do this," Cal says. "I can't become McCrowley. Not even for a weekend."

"You're backing out?" Jeremy asks.

Cal turns away. "I guess you can say that."

"Don't you want to find Loud?"

"Not enough to risk becoming like him."

"He's our friend," Jeremy says.

"I don't think he's able to have friends…with how he is."

Jeremy feels exhausted. His calluses are soft. He wants his room, his bed, his guitar. But he grabs his backpack wedged in the back seat and wrenches it free.

"So, you're still going?" Cal asks.

"One of us has to! Something might have happened to him." *I'm not going to be a Nick Caraway to his Gatsby*, Jeremy thinks.

"How long are you going to look?" Cal asks. "Your mom is

going to ask me."

"As long as it takes."

"No. I'm giving you two days. Then I'm coming back for your ass," Cal says.

"Okay, tough guy."

"There's one more thing I've got to say. Other than I think you're crazy."

"Yeah?" Jeremy rolls his eyes.

"I..." Cal falters, clenching the steering wheel. "I kind of like Aurora."

Jeremy laughs at first. But Cal's expression stays serious.

"You...what?"

"I haven't like...done anything with her. Because of... all of this." Cal stares out the window at the homeless people puttering around the squat trees. "And I won't...Until you've... had some time. But..."

Jeremy gets out of the cab and slams the door. "Go back and date her for all I care."

He starts walking toward the tangled trees, preparing himself for Cal to shout something after him. But the Forerunner's engine revs. The power steering gives a thin growl as the wheel turns, and the truck takes off.

Jeremy starts shaking. The argument with Cal made him forget his bike in the back of the truck. His face reddens. He's alone. Just like Loud. That feels real. He's going to walk the same streets Loud has walked, sleep in the same doorways Loud has slept. And in that way, his search can't be anything but a success. If he doesn't find Loud, he'll at least discover something about what it's like to live like him.

Jeremy walks past the tents, the tarps, the crushed bicycles, and the silent pit bulls. It would take one whole day just to explore the shelters. He doesn't want to betray his normie status by asking every bum if they've seen his friend.

That sick feeling of jealousy slithers into Jeremy's stomach. Off goes Cal to seal the deal with Aurora—the girl Jeremy put so much of himself into.

"My mom was so pretty," Aurora told him. They had been talking on the phone, each in their separate beds, Loud gone on one of his wanderings.

"She was so pretty, and so many guys wanted to date her. You can still see her name carved in the trunks of trees out in the sloughs. *Marcy May Loftner.*"

"I've never seen them," Jeremy said.

"That's because you never went as deep in as Loud took me."

Well, Jeremy thinks, descending a set of stairs beneath the freeway, *here's to going deeper.*

Dear Malachi,

I'm writing because I don't know what else to do. The power's still out. Powerlines are down everywhere. Trees too, blocking the highways. That gale sure was a doozie. I can't go into work because of the roads. And so, I've got nothing to busy myself with to keep me from thinking about you.

Mothers are strange creatures. I know mine was. When my dad was out, all she'd do was complain that he wasn't around enough. When he was home, she'd complain he was home too much. That's probably one of the reasons why he left us for good. And one of the reasons I left to find him.

Did you know your name means 'messenger'? It's an angel's name. And you were my little angel. I never loved anybody as much as you. Except for maybe my dad.

I know I'm saying 'sorry' a lot, but there's so much I'd do differently if I could go back. For parents, regrets are the children that never grow up. I should have made you go with me when I left. Being that young, you would have gotten used to me. And if I'd surrounded you with everybody from the tribe, you wouldn't have grown up feeling so bitter and separated and maybe you would have been okay sharing yourself between me and your dad. Then, when he died, it wouldn't have been so hard.

But I didn't want to become my mom. Cooking food for every naming ceremony, wedding, and funeral. It all brought her so much joy. But it took it out of her too. She'd come home overburdened and short-fused. And she wouldn't have much left for us.

Then there was the fact that I'd had you in Aberdeen. If I'd have been smart and had you on the rez, you would have been born Makah. But as it stood, I would have had to drag you through a tribal meeting and have you voted in. Something I worried about getting you through.

Mothers are strange creatures, like I said. We worry a lot. You know that one? Worry's like a rocking chair; fun to sit in, but you never go nowhere. But what that old joke doesn't say is that sometimes it's the only chair you have to sit in.

When I first saw the finished skeleton of that gray whale our hunting party brought back in '99, I knew it was a female without anyone having to tell me. Such sleek, proud bones! Hanging beneath her tail are these two little nubs. The museum people say those are the remnants of legs that her ancestors used to walk the earth. But I think they're the leftover worries over her children that hardened and refused to pass even as she aged.

I've always said I live here to have my own space apart from the rez. But I'm starting to change my mind about all that. Look at us, Malachi. Both of us. Living so far from the sea. They say we get our power from the sea.

I should have gotten lawyers involved with the McCrowley's hold over you. Your Uncle Phillip told me so! With all the laws around keeping tribal kids with parents, they could have helped me.

Lawyers! The idea gave me a weird feeling. To think I needed lawyers to make my own kid love me. No. No lawyers. I wanted you to choose. I did not want to rip you away from the family you decided to be with. Even if you were only a boy. Especially because you were only a boy.

Anywho, I come back to your name. Malachi. Messenger. Maybe this has all happened for a reason. Maybe you've got something to tell all those people down there.

Wish you could hurry up and tell them so you could come back to me. But there are some things I can start doing while I wait. And then maybe my waiting can be done. This downtime in the power outage has made me realize that.

Nothing gets wasted. Our people have always made a lot from a little: spun clothing out of dog fur, polished seal clubs out of whale bone, weaved baskets out of bear grass, sewed skirts from cedar strips. Finery from the pieces of dead things. Maybe there's something yet to come out of the mess I've made of our lives.

Your mother always, whether you like it or not.

Leah Ledbetter

Forks, Washington

A VOICE IN THE STORM

An hour or so after leaving Aurora and Lyle's, Loud McCrowley was walking through the rain-pelting darkness and cold toward his squat house for the second time that day, his bike still on loan to Karla. This time he was taking the highway, an atypical route home for him because of its lack of shelter from the road and its belligerent drivers who had the habit of throwing things at hitchhikers. But the Chehalis River had no doubt risen in the rain's endless slaughter, washing out his usual dank path along the water's edge. Plus, it was a little faster.

Loud was so drenched already, the additional sprays off the wheels of the occasional truck rushing by could have been the brushings of butterfly wings for all he cared. Grit and mud smattered onto his face, but his cheeks were numb from the cold. The sight of himself in the dingy mirror back home would give him a good laugh. He laughed just thinking about it.

At the crest of the hill, he stopped and looked back at the town. It was a huddled enclave of shoddy buildings clinging to the harbor as the rivers writhed around it, and the rain whipped down from above. From the tops of the silos, pale green industrial lights flickered feebly in the deluge. More than ever, Aberdeen seemed like the last futile outpost of humanity—a group from which Loud was divorcing himself yet again.

Come as you are, read the town's welcome sign, quoting the Nirvana lyric. *Unless you're me,* Loud thought. He thought about that similar evening over a year ago when he'd fled his grandparents for the city. Why had he come back? The reasons were lost to him like his father, like his tears.

The sky thundered. Loud laughed. The clouds took on a malignant green that looked like how a sick stomach might feel. How his stomach started to feel as he heard a siren yip behind him.

Though he didn't turn around, he could hear the V-8 engine smoldering in its first gear. He kept walking. The film of water over the highway conducted the patrol car's revolving lights onto the ground ahead of him. A voice sounded through the loudspeaker:

"Stop walking."

Loud stopped.

A hand cranked the e-brake.

"Turn around."

Loud turned around to see a tall, lean figure step out of the squad car.

He swallowed and breathed, and the little heater inside him whispered to him reminders of his dad's advice. *They own the air you breathe…*

The officer was a Latino dude with a big black mustache and small, steady eyes. The figure said something into the walkie on his shoulder but did not approach. He propped his arm on the squad-car door.

"You wouldn't happen to be Malachi McCrowley, would you?" the officer asked.

"Nah, I'm his good twin." Loud gave a little smile that he hoped looked charming.

The officer smiled back. "The twin who goes to school every day?"

"Every day."

"You just happen to have a matching leather jacket with all those do-hickies on it," the officer said, waving at Loud's patches.

"No. That asshole stole it from me. I just stole it back. He's at the 'Underbird now if you want him. Him and his crazy skank, high on hash."

"All right, all right," the officer said. "Why don't we get out of the rain."

Another squad car pulled up.

"Am I under arrest?"

"Probably. Why don't you step toward the hood for me?"

Loud did as he was told. The officer frisked him, cuffed him, and explained about the truancy warrant. Loud saw from his badge that the man's name was Moreno.

*

Officer Moreno took Loud to the juvenile detention center, the same way he'd done with Jeremy a few weeks prior.

Juvie was just a stone's throw away from Loud's grandparents' abandoned house.

"So, I can make myself feel at home, huh?" he said as he was made to strip.

Moreno walked him to his cell. It was the one closest to the guard's station. The guards let him keep the book he'd been carrying in a Ziplock bag—the Cobain bio—but took his CD player. Too bad. In the CD player's disk deck was a long-over-due library copy of Nevermind. But he'd listened to the album so many times, he scarcely needed it. He would beatbox the drum track and scream out the lyrics for as long as his voice lasted.

Loud sat on the cold floor, likening his situation to the Wobblies of nearly a century before who'd been jailed for protesting. Hardly an exact comparison, but enough to make him feel better. How he wished he had a cohort of crumb-bums and drifters from around the countryside to sing with and bemoan the establishment. Instead, he'd have to pass the night alone like usual.

Officer Moreno told him he'd have a hearing with Judge Spurgeon the next morning. Moreno said some other things to him, but Loud didn't pay attention.

The night was his, and he was dry. Drier than he probably would have been at home.

He flipped open his book, and he began to read, the rain dripping to a momentary cease-fire.

*

The calm would indeed be momentary in the war of electrons waging in the sky that night. Two tropical typhoons had created a low-pressure system over the Pacific. Winds carried the expanse of air eastward until it had amassed a life of its own. It cruised into the Washington coastline and the high-pressure air mass floating overhead. As heavy as the plates beneath the earth, the two masses hit each other with tectonic force, producing eighty-mile-an-hour winds that shook the Harbor dark.

The lights in Loud's cell flickered and failed. His hands went for the cell door. No good. The manual locking mechanism was still engaged. A whirring deep within the building yielded a crackle of light, which blinked a few times, then held—yellow and dim, but enough to read by.

Loud would read a few pages about the legendary punk band's inception, then break to watch the storm. In the inner ear of Loud's imaginings, Cobain's voice was caterwauling the song "Stay Away" while the very real wind provided a frenetic strings accompaniment to the thrash in Loud's mind.

The combo delighted Loud, and he made his own mosh pit off the four bare walls, slamming himself against them in crooked cartwheels. He skanked scuffs onto the cell's egg-shell paint. Through the rectangular Plexi-glass window, he saw the wind bending the crowns of the trees toward the ground. Loud saw their trunks form parabolas. He swore he saw the tree-tips touch the earth. He swore he could feel his bones bending with them.

Almost in time with Grohl's snare cracking in his head, a tree snapped and Loud watched its trunk crash down. Try as he might not to blink, on the impact—wet and heavy—Loud's eyes fluttered, and in that darkness, he saw the figure of his father disappear beneath a similar tangle of whip-like branches nailing him into the earth.

Something inside Loud clicked on. The reels started spinning in a way even more unusual than their customary witchy turnings. He stopped jumping. The world seemed to warp, and he felt dizzy. He shrunk into the corner and shoved his face into his book until the image went away.

He did not hear so much as feel a voice saying hello. The voice didn't so much speak. It pressed upon his body. Hello. Hello three times. Then, in a long, dirge-like grating, a finale time. Hello.

Loud looked up at his empty cell. Someone. Something. Was there, whispering.

Loud tried to stop the sounds going on in his head. He went to remove a pair of headphones that weren't there. "Hello?" Loud demanded. "What's going on?"

Cobain's shade seemed to unfold from the cell walls. A carnivorous flower from a dark thicket.

The shade didn't speak. It stirred. Stirred into Loud the message it wanted. *Is it me? Is it you? Monkey-see? Monkey-do?*

"Who? Who's there?" Loud demanded. He was shaking. "Is it you?" Though he knew the answer.

Cobain's shade smirked, lifted its death-purpled limbs, and showed Loud signs. Of love. Of blood. Of cutting. Of being cut. Of umbilical cords and the necessary dangling. All of it too much. Too close. Too hot. According to the ghost, Loud should not have returned to Aberdeen, but should have stayed in Seattle. This place was too much. Too heavy.

"I saw you that time!" Loud smiled. "Under the bridge! Where... Where are you?"

Monkey, do, the shade replied. *Monkey, see. See, Monkey?*

Loud looked at his book cover. Cobain's tired, rueful face looked up at him from beneath the unkempt strips of blonde hair. The face was silent.

Loud threw the book at the wall and then he fell asleep.

*

Loud's arraignment with Spurgeon wouldn't occur until two days later.

That night's storm would become known as the Great Coastal Gale. That next morning, Aberdeen woke up late. Their phones were all dead; the power out. No alarms sounded. The town walked outside to find clear skies, seagulls gliding in the air, and telephone poles and trees making big X's in the road. Renters in the flats south of Heron got out of bed only to find themselves knee-deep in water. They waded out of their flooded homes in shaken stupors to their cars and started the treacherous drive, having to circumvent new tributaries of the Wishkah and Wynoochee that had formed overnight, flowing over roads, highways, and hillsides. They tried the heights, but there too, the trunks of firs impeded their path. The bridges were banjaxed with overturned trucks that tried to cross in the winds, only to be bashed against the trusses.

Police couldn't complete their patrols, and the municipality courts could not commence trials for the many petty offenses of vagrancy and car prowling that had accumulated over the week. But this wasn't much of a problem. The adult jail in the center of town was built on a concrete block and became the only functional homeless shelter in the county. As for the juvenile detention center in Junction City, built in the same low-level trench as the Chehalis River, there was a slight risk of flooding and discomfort to any youth inmates. But no one was in custody that night. No one except Loud McCrowley, who would have to wait an extra day in the dampened cell before he could be tried. More time to get to know the ghost of Kurt Cobain.

*

The ghost stirred. It was thirsty for chocolate milk to settle its stomach. It wanted aspirin for its raging headache. And so, these were the first things Loud cried out for.

"Anything else?" the guard asked.

"Oh, and…can I get my phone call?" Loud said.

"K. Who do you want to call?"

"I don't really want to call anybody. That's just what they always ask for in the movies."

As the ghost was down in the mouth, Loud did his best to cheer it up by doing The Flail while the song "Aneurysm" played in his head.

The ghost divulged that he was so low when he wrote that song. *Lower than worm meat. Wanting to be high. Wanting to be with people. People and their love and blood and heat. And their mistakes mistaking love for want.* Yet, the ghost missed taking. *Take, monkey. Take.*

*

Judge Spurgeon arrived the next morning. He slipped on his robe, and he had the bailiff call for the boy. He'd tried his hardest to make it the previous morning. He'd known about Loud's case and knew that acting quickly was the most essential thing in dealing with these types. But the roads had been blocked by trees, and his Buick only made it a few blocks until he'd had to turn around. He'd had to delay the arraignment and ordered the boy to spend another night in the cell. Overnight, Spurgeon thought about the boy. Spurgeon's best intentions, having been thwarted, turned into sleep-depriving annoyance.

When the boy was marched out into the carpeted court-room, Judge Spurgeon took note of his appearance: tall with bad posture, mohawk drooping like a captive whale's dorsal fin and a face muddied either by tears or a build up of filth. The boy glared at him and blinked hard while gritting his teeth.

Loud's take on the judge: an old Republican with liver

spots, jowls, a white mustache, and that pre-Parkinsonian shake of the head, anticipating his answer to every request: no.

Spurgeon read the file on Loud while Loud sat listening impassively.

"You're technically in the custody of your mother?" Spurgeon asked.

Loud shrugged. "Haven't seen her in months."

"Well, she lives up in Forks," Spurgeon snorted. "Why aren't you there with her?"

Loud grimaced. He thought about the brick-colored Rabbit driving away. He thought about the lie she'd told about the mounds of branches falling on his father. Or the lie about the mill eating him. Maybe both were lies, and his father was still alive somewhere, whittling her face into a chunk of wood and eating alphabet cereal. Either way, when Loud thought about his mother, he thought of womb-juice, infants hung by their own umbilical cords, cigarette-butt breath, and behind her, a group of real Natives who would reject him as half the minute he opened his big fat trap.

"We both think it's best not to live together," Loud scowled.

"Would she say that?" Spurgeon asked.

"Dunno."

"Well, I intend to find out," Spurgeon said and picked up the phone at his desk and, by some miracle, hoped enough lines had been repaired for his call to go through. But no such luck.

Spurgeon was arching into real anger now. "Who are you staying with?"

The lie came out reflexively. Just another turn in the merry-go-round of Loud's mind:

"I am staying with Lyle Blanchard. His daughter's a friend, and she's letting me crash on her couch."

As Loud stood in the echo of his lie, he reassured himself. It made sense. It was his last option. It would work. It had to work.

Spurgeon's brow furrowed. "Blanchard? Aurora?" Spurgeon mused, thinking of the sweet little girl with glasses who played drums in the Senior Center's band a few years ago. "Well, I can't just take your word. Why were you wandering on the highway? In the middle of the night?"

"I was going to be staying with them. But I had to go to my squat first."

"Your squat?"

"Yeah. I have this…place in the slough where I keep my shit."

"I will have to call Lyle and confirm all of this."

"Go ahead."

Again, Spurgeon picked up the phone with a liver-spotted fist, punched in Blanchard's number, and received the out-of-service message.

Spurgeon gave Loud a look that indicated he was both extremely peeved and a little nauseous. Detaining Loud without cause was fodder for a sure-fire lawsuit, and though he doubted Loud had the acumen and resources to mount a case for himself, people could surprise you.

"You're being released," Judge Spurgeon relented.

"Thank you," Loud said.

"But if you miss one more day of school or are seen wandering around again, I'll have you transported to your mother's house in Forks so fast it will make your head spin."

"Thank you."

"And I'll be contacting Blanchard in the next week to corroborate your story."

"By all means," Loud replied, making a mental note. The judge said "in the next week". Loud had seven days to convince Aurora and her old, fat, Black uncle to let him stay with them.

*

Much to Jeremy's chagrin, the storm only took out two days of school. In what seemed like no-time, Jeremy was back in History class, wondering where Loud was, wondering if he was mad at him for his mom kicking him out.

The prior evening, for the first time ever, a girl had called. But it was just Aurora, calling to talk about the Chem. final coming up.

After they'd talked through the content, Aurora, to Jeremy's surprise, kept talking.

"I'm drinking tea and listening to Rocky Votolato. Completely out of character for me, I know. I just need some knitting. I'm basically an old lady. What are you doing?"

Jeremy said he had to go and hung up. But the conversation lingered, along with the feeling of wanting to talk to her more. *Why did I hang up? Rube move, dude.*

He was thinking about her as Loud McCrowley slammed himself down in the seat next to him, just in time for History class to start.

"Dude, where have you been!" Jeremy asked. Loud was covered in dried, clay-colored mud and smelled like the boy's locker room with a dash of septic tank.

Other students were outright gawking and covering their noses.

"Oh, you know…" Loud shrugged.

Jeremy messed with the corners of his paper before broaching the subject.

"Look, I'm sorry about my mom, okay," Jeremy said.

"Why should you be sorry?" Loud wouldn't look at him. "It's me that's sorry. Sorry for you that she's your mom."

"Yeah… Uh. Thanks. It's just…"

"Dude. I don't hate your mom. I *did* make you blow up that toilet."

"You didn't *make* me."

"That's nice of you to say… But I did. You don't have to defend me from what I am. Even to yourself."

But Jeremy did. On a day between units a few weeks ago, their hippy Chem. teacher had them read "Unpacking the Knapsack of White Privilege." Though he hadn't a clue what it had to do with Chemistry, Jeremy found himself embracing the essay; he had a rucksack full of privilege. Through Jeremy's safety net of powerful adults in his life—his mom, Lyle—he'd been able to turn an act of vandalism into a volunteer gig that on paper would look like an internship. If Loud had done the deed himself, it likely would have gone way worse for him just because of his skin color. Plus, Loud didn't have safety nets. His mom had been putting a bug in Jeremy's ear lately about how Loud had a mom; he wasn't an orphan in need of rescue. Okay then, where the hell was this mom of his?

Jeremy cleared his throat, trying to get up the guts to ask Loud this very question.

"Anywho, what's been going on here? McCarthy? Roosevelt? Rich, dead white people power-grabbing and blah blah blah?"

Loud was a few decades ahead, but more or less correct. They'd been reading about the Gilded Age and had been assigned to do a poster on a tycoon.

"Sweet!" Loud said. "I've been getting back into drawing. This project sounds like a cinch."

Yeah, but they had to cite sources. And write an accompanying five-paragraph essay about the historical figure and their impact on the times.

"Easy. I'll do Rhinehouse," Loud said.

"That'd be good," Jeremy admitted. "Ulmer Rhinehouse bought like…all of Washington forests for a million dollars or something. Do him."

"Oh, I'm going to do him all right. Just like he did us. Dirty," Loud replied.

By 'us' did Loud mean Native Americans? Working-class Washingtonians? Teenagers? There were so many groups Loud was part of and apart from.

Loud took out a soggy composition notebook and made lines on a crinkled page.

"So…," Jeremy said aloud.

"What, dude?" Loud looked up. "I'm kind of in the middle of something."

"So," Jeremy began again, wanting to ask about Loud's mom.

Jeremy's resolve faltered. Any of these questions might light a fuse under Loud and send him running.

"So, you know we have a big test soon, right?" Jeremy asked

"Aren't we passed this? What does Aurora have next period?"

Jeremy shook his head at the non-sequitur. "Uh. Jazz band made state. Aurora's in Olympia for the competitions. Why?"

"I wanted to talk to her about joining our band," Loud asked, looking up.

"Our band?"

"I think it's time for us to start practicing. No more waiting around for you to 'get good.' You're probably better than any of the Sex Pistols were when they started."

"Yeah, okay. Whatever," Jeremy said. But his heart did a somersault. He'd been twiddling his thumbs for the last week, waiting to broach the whole band topic again. The school talent show was in a month, and Jeremy fantasized about winning.

"Wrote any songs?" Loud asked.

"Actually…" Jeremy began. He'd had plenty of time to tease out a riff from his six-string. Yet all the strumming and stretching and picking led him back into other people's music— Neil Young ballads, Pearl Jam anthems, Fugazi barnburners, Buzzcock ditties.

With music, Jeremy was lost in the woods, walking in circles, constantly returning to the same untenable slough of what had been done before. Jeremy's two-hour tinkerings would all end the same way: with him beating off and going back to schoolwork.

"Actually, no," Jeremy concluded with a sigh. "No songs yet."

"You've been a good boy. Busy with homework. I get it. Don't worry, I've got some stuff. As long as you can put music to it."

"But where are we going to practice?"

"Working hard over here?" It was Mr. Brenna. "McCrowley, nice of you to join us."

"You're right, it was nice of me," Loud quipped.

"Okay, you can take yourself to the principal's office."

"What?" Loud asked. "For *that*! I didn't even say anything!"

Mr. Brenna did not want Loud's smart-aleck remarks in class, distracting his students. He could wait in the principal's office and get his assignments there.

"Won't bother. I'm outro!"

Loud turned to Jeremy before leaving. "I'll think of a place to play, I swear."

Jeremy watched Loud leave. He'd become way more of a quick sketch of movements and motives since Jeremy had last seen him.

Mr. Brenna told Jeremy to pick better friends. He nodded and went back to reading. A neighboring table of kids kept looking over at him.

"Can I help you all with something?" Jeremy asked, putting his textbook down and showing teeth. "Would you like to ask a bigoted question pertaining to my taste in associates?"

The kids all looked back down at their books. Even the kids that were bigger than him.

"Didn't think so," Jeremy seethed. His two-week suspension for blowing up the toilet and his front-page notoriety had one unforeseen benefit: mystique. It meant that kids stayed out of his way. It meant that a couple of seniors with tattoos and cigarette addictions said "hi" in the hallway. It meant that nobody was stepping up to echo Brock's taunts, which had lost frequency and sting. But what good was mystique when it came to songwriting? Or being a friend?

*

Three months later, Jeremy still wonders this as he descends the stairs beneath downtown Seattle's I-5 colonnade, looking for Loud.

A crowd of kids banter on a ledge between the overpass and the loose gravel scramble of ground. They are unpacking and repacking their rucksacks. Travelers, Jeremy concludes.

Having returned from the Rainbow Gathering—a fringe festival somewhere in Okanagan, the travelers twiddle their thumbs for Seattle's Hemp Fest to start. Then Hump Fest. Then Hop Fest. Through Seattle's endless string of fests, they plan on riding through April and maybe even May. They think Jeremy is too until they see the X's on his knuckles.

"Oh, you're straight-edge. Right on," they say.

They've never met anyone named Loud or Ki or Hawky Mo. "There are usually raves down here around midnight," they tell him. "You could try looking for him there. You'd be welcome."

Jeremy has until midnight now to try other scenes and visit some service centers.

He walks along Seattle's bridges and under its overpasses. He walks down trails and through entryways. He fills out orientation forms for homeless youth service centers. He snacks at a church basement, hangs out in a yellow clapboard house with a TV and laundry, then has dinner downtown in a trapezoidal brick building painted rave-green. Tweeners with clipboards greet him. Jeremy answers their questions: no, he doesn't do drugs or alcohol; no, he's not interested in case management. In turn, he shows them Loud's Weatherwax High school ID, pointing to the photo of Loud looking away from the camera with lips half-open, showing his gap-teeth, looking a little lost, and surprised. Jeremy shows them Loud's Facebook profile, vow-be-damned. He's tired! He wants to find Loud already and go home.

The staff members shake their heads, but call over youth after youth: a stocky dude wearing baby-blue bead bracelets over cut-up wrists and a dog-collar around his neck; a fat girl with faraway eyes and oily black hair beneath a furry hat with cat-ears; a pale-eyed guy with dreadlocks and a beard, a holey A&F polo for a shirt and nothing but an old knit blanket for pants; a black chick with perfect painted-on eyebrows, aqua nails, and designer jeans studded with imitation rhinestones; a weary-looking kid who calls himself Stacy with track marks up and down his arms, bad teeth and socks stuffed into his shirt; a brother with a bone through his nose and a tuxedo t-shirt; and others with dyed hair, thick necklaces, lip piercings, big backpacks, hasty tattoos, mismatching clothes and tan skin from hours passed out in the sun.

But none of them recognize the picture of Loud. Except for the brother with the bone through his nose.

"Native kid. Gap teeth. Yeah! That's Link-nut. Link-nut. Sigh. He's the new kid on the block. He seems okay. A little out there. A bunch of us were hanging out with him and the Rat City crew the other night. A cool enough dude, like I said, but a little paranoid and, you know, wee-oo-wee-oo. But whatever. Good luck finding him, man. Yeah, I'll let you know if I see him. Got to go!"

Jeremy boards a bus for White Center, a.k.a. Rat City.

THE BRAWNY MAN™ KILLED HIS FATHER

With Aurora gone at her band thing, Loud's last hope of a couch-surfing spot in Aberdeen had yet to materialize. He had only a few more days until Judge Spurgeon sicced the police on him for being a homeless minor, fewer if he was caught wandering around. So, that Friday evening, Loud was trying to keep a low profile by spending the night in the hospital waiting room.

It was a place he'd tried before with some success. It was cleaner than the 'Underbird. It was warmer and drier than his grandparent's house, albeit more of a hassle. At the 'Underbird, no one asked why you were there or who you were there to see. Not even Larry anymore. Lately, Larry was either in a heroin coma or so strung out he couldn't see straight. But the winds from the Great Northwest Gale had blown apart the 'Underbird's decaying roof. Karla had absconded with the bike and was nowhere to be found. His grandparents' house was no longer an option, considering that the rains had flooded the Chehalis, and Preacher's Slough had risen to the house's first floor. So, for the moment, the hospital waiting room would have to do.

The raindrops fell slow and continuously. Loud watched it from the waiting room's wall of windows. The rain fell so slowly that the distant lightning caught the raindrops midair in a second so drawn out, Loud felt he had time enough to count each and every drop. They numbered the same as the lives of workers taken by the saw blade, the donkey engine, the whizzing belts, the widow-makers. They numbered the same as his fears.

As he stared out at the darkness through the windows, the darkness stared back. The windows were as big as an aquarium's, built as if to observe the darkness: a creature that had outgrown the tank to the point that all you could see was its mouth. And the lightning gave that mouth definition. For Loud, the hills with their sawtooth pines became the inner sets of the beasts' jaws. Grays Harbor was its belly of acid. And in the darkness, the thunder groaned in rumbles of hunger.

"Are you alright?" asked a voice.

It was the front-desk lady. She had auburn hair and a face like a Yankee bean.

"Are *you* alright?" Loud asked. "All right, alright?"

"May I ask you who you're waiting for?"

"For a friend."

"What's your friend's name?"

"It's. Um. Why does it matter?"

"So, I can look up which room he or she is in. So you can visit them."

"Pete McCrowley," Loud replied. "It's my dad, actually. Yeah, and can you go check on him? Like now, please?"

She gave him a dubious expression before walking off, her pants swifting as she went. He sunk as far down as he could into the chair, wondering if she'd come back in a few minutes, with his dead father in tow. He laughed.

He walked down the hall to the bathroom. He would try hanging out in there a while, hoping the desk lady would just forget about him. Maybe by tending to an actual emergency.

*

A few streets down from the hospital, Aurora was asleep, exhausted from the state jazz competition which Aberdeen had lost miserably. Even in her sleep, her wrists twitched from the 4/4, 5/4, and 9/8th beats she'd had to tap, jerk, and jiggle out.

She woke. Uncle Lyle was calling her.

She turned on the light. Uncle Lyle stood at the door, looking at the floor. He asked if she'd drive him to the hospital again. Just in case.

She pushed her covers aside to grope for some clothes in

the pile at the foot of her bed. She found her alpaca-wool sweater and her trusty pair of faded overalls. She moved with a deliberateness that was free from the desperation of an emergency. Lyle had asked her to drive him to the hospital almost every week since the market crashed.

"I am sure it's just acid reflux again." Lyle gave her a tight smile.

They got into Lyle's Chevy Longhorn, and she drove him up the hill. He apologized again. She tried to cheer him up by telling him he was helping her get some practice hours in for her driver's license, to which he gave another tight smile.

Aurora bet people thought Lyle drove the classic old truck around town just to appear normal—normal being Aberdeener for white. But they would be wrong. Lyle washed it with religious frequency once a month and she would help him sometimes. Lyle would scrub the bug guts clean off the truck's beveled hood while humming Duke Ellington like he hadn't a care in the world. But Lyle didn't like the truck to appear normal. He liked it because it made him feel normal.

Aurora and Uncle Lyle passed through the waiting room, which at that moment was empty, and waited while Lyle explained things to the ginger-haired receptionist, who looked somewhat frazzled as she checked Lyle into an exam room.

While the doctor examined Lyle, Aurora sat in the hallway, reading *Heart of Darkness* for class. In Conrad's murky, dream-like writing, it didn't take long before she started dozing.

*

When Loud came out of the bathroom about a half-hour later, the desk lady was gone.

He congratulated himself by pumping some free coffee from a carafe at a corner table. He took a swig of the lukewarm swill and felt grains of coffee catch on his tongue.

"Like mother's milk," he said in disgust and took another drink.

He bathed in the staleness of the waiting room. Next to the black, aquarium-sized window, the white room was yang to the darkness's yin. He picked up a magazine and a pen to doodle political cartoons on the ads he found. He'd gotten stuck on his Rhinehouse sketch and needed some comic inspiration.

He came across an ad for Brawny Man paper towels.

Out of his bag, he took out a pair of scissors and a Mod-Podge bottle he'd purloined from Weatherwax's art room. He cut out Brawny, slapped him in a blank page on his comp. book and, in a terse, scrawling hand, wrote:

BRAWNY MAN™ RUNS FOR MAYOR.

Brawny Man knows the woods. A man of the people. Good with an ax. Worked felling the last of the timber. Lost his job like the rest of the town when the conservationists shut down the woods. Like the rest of us, he did the food stamp circuit, the welfare jig, and, let's be honest, the depressed rummage through a 24 pack of Icehouse. But Brawny Man is through with all of that. He comes into town with his flannel and russet curls, promising to put Aberdeen back to work. And with his big hands wet with the sap of freshly felled firs and sawdust, he's going to wipe everybody's ass with his fresh brand of political TP.

But they don't know the truth. Brawny Man is a Trojan horse. He's just a puppet for...Ulmer Rhinehouse, back from the dead! Dun, dun, duuuuun! Rhinehouse house-user—the people eating timber baron! Using Brawny Man as his stooge, ol' Ulmer wants to take over the town. This time for good! And make everyone his work force of zombies that never strike and never stop working! Pete McCrowley found out about all this, but too late. Brawny Man axed him in the back and ate him and shit him out, and now he's sawdust. Poof! The one thing Brawny Man didn't count on... Pete's son knows everything!

"Young man."

"Hang on a second. This is getting good," Loud said, refusing to look up from the drawing he'd started.

"Young man!"

"What? Jesus, desk lady!"

"My name is Laurel. And I'm a receptionist."

Loud took a sip of coffee. "Good for you. My name's Loud, and I'm a bum."

"I'm afraid I am going to have to ask you to leave."

"I'm a graduate of B-U-M University! You can't talk to me like that."

"There's no Peter McCrowley here, sir."

"Check under Pete!"

"No patient has been admitted this evening with P as a first name."

"Whoa. You think I'm waiting for a patient? Pete's a surgeon here."

"We don't have any surgeons on staff tonight."

"A nurse?"

"We don't have any nurses named Pete or Peter. Or any male nurses for that fact."

"You know that?"

She nodded.

"Off the top of your head. Just like that?"

"It's my job."

"Sucks for you," Loud picked up his coffee and started walking toward the bathroom.

"You can't just hang around here all night. You have to go."

"Why not?" he asked, turning around.

"This area is for patients only."

"What if…" Loud said timidly, "what if I'm here to be a

patient?"

"Are you sick?"

Loud dropped his coffee. The woman gasped and jumped back. Loud felt the liquid on his pant cuffs. "I'm going to have to call security," she said, backing away slowly.

Loud stomped on the cup, which made a popping sound. The woman turned and ran.

Loud looked at the spilled coffee—its yellow-brown disorder expanded slowly across the linoleum, splats of it dappling in pools where the floor sank toward the swamp on which the rest of the town was built. Under the lights' clinical fluorescence, the liquid seemed to ooze into words that Loud could read as plainly as the darkness outside.

The words read: *Follow her.*

*

Aurora woke up again to Uncle Lyle standing above her. Uncle Lyle's broad face was calm and more himself. With his sad, light eyes, Lyle looked to her like a distant relative of Booker T. Washington. He smiled wryly. "Acid reflux again."

"Well, I'm glad you're okay," she said, hugging him. She felt his belly inhale. She remembered resting on his lap as a kid with that belly rocking behind her like a Spanish galleon, the two of them eating their crazy concoctions of popcorn while watching Discovery Channel.

"All that great popcorn of ours has gotten to my gut, I suppose," Lyle said. "That and the stock market."

"At least you're not like some people who just don't go to the doctor," Aurora said.

They walked out into the waiting room, and there was Loud McCrowley, staring at a puddle of coffee.

"Hey!" she said.

He looked up slowly. "Oh. Hey, Overalls. You're back!"

Loud had on only his jeans, leather jacket, and a damp Nirvana t-shirt—sans sleeves. Through the low arm loops of the tank top, Aurora could see his ribs.

"Young man. You look terrible," Lyle said.

"I haven't been sleeping."

"Where have you been?" Aurora asked.

"Around."

"And where have you been staying?" Lyle asked.

Aurora saw a wince pass across her uncle's face as he asked it.

The three of them stood in the silence, broken only by the wall clock ticking.

"Uh." Loud gritted his teeth and snapped his eyes shut. "Do I have to answer that?"

Lyle looked at his niece. The receptionist burst through double doors, a groggy, white-haired security guard bringing up the rear. "That's him." The receptionist pointed at Loud.

"Oh, don't tell me. This one," the security guard said, seeing Lyle. "Lyle, you big troublemaker, running around trying to tell people stuff that makes too much sense. I'm going to have to give you a good paddle for it. Hi, Aurora."

"Hi," Aurora said.

"Burt!" Lyle said. "It's very good to see you. But I don't believe for a second they'd trust *you* with a nightstick."

The two old men laughed.

"No, him." The receptionist grabbed Burt's shoulder and pointed to Loud. "He's been hanging around all night. And he just threatened me."

"She's a liar," Loud said quietly.

"Threatened you with what?" Burt asked.

"He threw a cup of coffee at me!"

"Looks like he missed," Burt surmised.

"Burt!"

"He with you, Lyle?" Burt asked.

Lyle turned to Loud. "Aurora and I were just about to drive him home with us. We've had a long night. But I think he's had an even longer one."

Aurora nodded slowly while keeping her eyes on Loud.

"See, I told you I was waiting for a friend," Loud said to the receptionist.

"Let's go, young man," Lyle said.

Lyle gave a shallow bow to the trembling receptionist and Burt before chuffing his hefty body out of the automatic doors. Loud sneered at the receptionist, grabbed his backpack, and followed Lyle out. Aurora walked in step with him. "Are you okay?"

"That receptionist is a bitch," Loud said.

"Shh."

"As if it were my fault I lost my housing."

The second set of sliding doors opened and conveyed in a confluence of air that cut through Aurora's sweater.

"Lyle hates me," Loud said.

"He doesn't hate you. He just doesn't like BS."

"What BS?"

"You weren't waiting for us."

"But I was, Aurora. I was. I really, really was."

"O…kay."

"I was waiting for somebody. I just. I just didn't know who."

The words made Aurora's mouth twist into chagrin. "Make me feel like a jerk, why don't you?"

"You don't have to take me in," Loud said.

"Yes, I do," she said quietly.

Thunder roared, and Loud jumped. She grabbed his hand and led him to Lyle's truck. She had parked it near the overlook at the edge of the parking lot. As she walked, the lightning flashed, and the Harbor's wide waters lit up like an ocean of mercury.

*

While Lyle rode shotgun with Loud between him and Aurora, he thought about what he was doing. He knew about this boy's erratic behavior. Knew that Detective Sweet would censure his decision. Pessimistic whispers arose in Lyle about his sister—Aurora's mother—and her sordid history with men. Lyle waved away these concerns like flies. Aurora was different. Lyle shook his head and scratched his beard. Aurora had a strong head on her shoulders, and Lyle just couldn't see her becoming romantically involved with a classmate so obviously troubled.

Besides, as an adopted child, he felt an obligation to intervene. Who knew who his biological parents had been, or not been? Though constant, Lyle Blanchard considered the question vulgar and irrelevant. The fact was, he had been spared from an unthinkable fate, from chaos by the goodwill of others. The real question—the one that gnawed at and goaded him—was why fate had bestowed the gift of stability to him over the mass of others functionally orphaned by their neglectful parents. As an echo of this enigma, Lyle made a point to give back every day of his life.

Lyle caught whiffs of Loud's body odor and heard the fatigue and fear in the boy's voice. How big was their vision for 2020? If it didn't have room for people like Loud McCrowley, what kind of vision was it? Not one that he could accept. No, Visions 2020 was about creating a place at the table for everyone. Because, Lyle thought, if there wasn't a place at the table for someone like McCrowley, there couldn't be a place for someone like him.

*

"So he's staying with you now?" Jeremy typed into a Facebook chat with Aurora. A wave of squirmy nausea was sending flu-like chills throughout his body.

"Yes," Aurora typed back.

"Where is he sleeping?" Jeremy typed instantly.

"Couch. Why?"

Why *had* he asked that?

Facebook chimed a few minutes later.

"Jer. This is Loud." Jeremy swallowed. "Do trustworthy friends talk behind their friend's back?"

Jeremy stared at the ceiling for a second. "No," Jeremy typed into the computer, lying with every keystroke.

Loud typed back immediately. "No, they don't. So think about that before talking to her about me again."

MAGIC LUNCH

Though the feeling of jealousy overpowered into an existence-crippling nausea, Jeremy answered their invitation to jam.

It was the morning after the big snow, only a few days into the New Year.

"You *have to* come," Aurora told Jeremy on the phone. "It's Loud's birthday."

So Jeremy got over himself, packed up his gear and readied Loud a birthday present: a box of his favorite cereal, Letter Betters, and a burned CD of underplayed punk anthems: "That's When I Reach for My Revolver" by Mission of Burma; "I Apologize" by Hüsker Dü; "Orgasm Addict" by the Buzzcocks; "Suspect Device" by Stiff Little Fingers; "Sound System" by Operation Ivy. Jeremy presented these offerings to Loud as a "happy seventeenth." Loud hugged him and said he was the best while Aurora watched, cooing about how sweet they were. This prompted Loud to order they quit the cutesy shit and make some noise.

Their three-piece consisted of Jeremy on guitar, funneled through a new Orange amp he'd gotten for Christmas as an *I'm-sorry-for-marrying-that-asshole* reconciliation effort from his mom; Aurora on the flimsy drum kit she was borrowing from the retirement center; and Loud, their budding frontman. In the absence of a PA and mic, they had Loud using a bullhorn resurrected from Lyle's '70's heyday as a protest organizer against the Satsop nuclear towers. In high spirits, they practiced on a thick, buff-colored rug in the cold garage's painfully white fluorescents where they generated a feedback-filled screed all their own. And with Lyle away at a Rhinehouse corporate retreat, there was no one authority present to politely suggest the pandemonium be turned down.

They bypassed any lengthy and hazardous discussions

about band names since such discussions were likely to kill the band before it began.

"We've got to put a couple of songs together before the talent show," Jeremy said. "What are you guys smirking at? We can do it!"

Loud had no shortage of lyrics. In fact, he had so many, he couldn't stop mumbling them, occasionally having to step into a corner of the garage, put his hands on his ears, and spew them into a heating vent before returning to the bullhorn. Hadn't Bob Dylan and Leonard Cohen done similar things? Wasn't eccentricity a prerequisite of genius?

The initial progression involved Loud screaming into the bullhorn, Aurora following with a few tentative cracks on the cymbals before she locked into a rhythm and Jeremy jumping in a few bars later trying to chord-change along with Loud's erratic banshee.

The trouble was that Loud's yowling failed to cohere with anything close to a tune. Jeremy was about to say something when Loud paused and, without warning, launched into an actual melody—a barnburner fueled by Loud's tuneful, hiccupping drone:

Add!
some sugar,
add!
some spice,
a dash of guilt in rice,
Nix the sunshine, bring the spite
and don't forget, don't forget!

And here Loud paused. He clapped out a change rhythm and began shouting what Jeremy supposed was the chorus.

ADD HER ALL
ADD HER ALL
ADD HER ALL
ADD HER ALL

Loud repeated this chant long enough for Jeremy to whip up a half-decent riff while Aurora thundered out some rhythm. The strings sliced through Jeremy's fingertips, sliding up and down the frets. The noise synced and pitched toward greatness, and for almost a full minute, they were a band.

Then Loud spat, *And you got a Maaaaaaaagic lunch. Thanks, mom!*

Loud dropped the bullhorn on the rug. Its pop reverberated, whistling from the amp. Loud went into the corner to rub his hands over his face. A kind of artistic ritual? Aurora and Jeremy looked at each other. What they had just played resembled a song. Maybe even a good song. Jeremy clicked off the volume knob. Doubtful of Loud's ability or willingness to repeat the act, Jeremy retreated to a nearby journal where, with fingers throbbing, he wrote down the exact words with line breaks. He recorded the title as "Magic Lunch."

Aurora tightened her snare. Jeremy fussed out a Misfit-like guitar lick to match the verse. Aurora began ticking her high hat. They played "Magic Lunch" a few more times until Loud got bored, and stormed off somewhere for a while, returning to the bullhorn with a completely different song, his voice a tremolo reminiscent of Jello Biafra of the Dead Kennedys:

It all started
With a rose and a bear
they made it under a fruit tree
and spent the night there.

Then along came a worm
It'd been eating through a Bible
It ate up all the bloom
and charged the beast with liable.

As with the first song, Loud abruptly changed rhythms.

Myth pitch, wiggle dick.
A maggot on your dish.
Call me a faggot? Call her a bitch?
Will it make you itch?!!!

This choppy, acidic burst sounded more like a pre-chorus, especially as Loud's voice growled and built the foundation for something bigger. But Loud dissolved into a strange, toneless monologue that dead-ended in another bullhorn-drop.

Jeremy sighed and made a few more notes, blood from a popped blister punctuating the page. Aurora put down her sticks. "I really liked that one. The first part sounded like mewithoutyou."

"I was thinking the Dead Kennedys." Jeremy looked up from his notes. "But, could you… do it again so we can get some chords down. I was a little confused about where you were going with it."

"Not today," Loud shook his head. "I've got a lot more stuff in here. I just got to get it out, and then we can go back over it later." His lip trembled a little bit, and his face scrunched into that wince like he was trying to clamp down on something inside him about to spill out.

"Yeah, but we don't need to get out everything now," Jeremy said, sucking his sore finger. "We only need two or three songs for the talent show."

"Don't put me in a box, dude! That's not how a band works."

"Okay," Jeremy relented. "Does that one have a chorus?"

"I don't really think in terms of chorus-this, verse-that," Loud said. "I don't really even think in terms of songs. They're more like sonic brain shits."

In his notes, Jeremy titled the tune, "Chorus-less Song No. 1."

They floundered a while, with Loud just spewing more of his screed into the bullhorn without a pattern they could pick up. Jeremy and Aurora shared sheepish glances at each other and shrugged. Was this how Led Zeppelin felt the first time practicing with Robert Plant?

When Loud got tired, Aurora suggested Jeremy try starting them off with something.

Loud shrugged. Jeremy stalled by messing with the settings on his amp.

"Common motherfucker," Loud said. "Play that guitar!"

Jeremy started fingerpicking a speedy little melody he'd been working on.

"Jer," Aurora said.

Jeremy kept picking. "Wait for it…"

"Jeremy!" Aurora said again.

"What? I was just about to start the verse!"

"That's the Backstreet Boys," Aurora said.

"Fuck you, no, it's not."

"Don't talk to her that way!" Loud barked. "And it *is* the Backstreet Boys! It's 'I Want it that Way.'" Loud said with a shit-eating grin. "You're just playing it fast."

"Fuck!" Jeremy shouted, looking at his bloody hands as if they'd just strangled somebody.

"It's okay," Aurora said. "It happens."

"I'm a complete hack!" Jeremy groaned. "A backwater wannabe, and I don't even know it."

"Let's take a breather," Aurora said.

"Yeah, fuck it. Let's just go down to Jack'n the Crack and kick the can," Loud said.

Jack'n the Crack was Loud's nickname for the downtown Jack in the Box. They "packed up," which involved Loud putting the bullhorn in its hard-shelled case and Jeremy zipping up his gig bag. Loud excused himself to take a shit.

"Be sure to make it a sonic one," Jeremy jeered.

Loud made fart sounds as he walked out of the garage.

As Jeremy curled up his guitar cord, he sank below the shame of his gaff into the murkier feeling of intrigue. That first song was awfully ear-wiggy. *Add her all, add her all.* There was something there, some hidden meaning he couldn't understand yet. The best lyrics were the elusive ones, whose meanings grew into meaning for you years later. But there was something urgent in Loud's words. The face Loud made when he sang—scrunched up and desperate as if suffocating. It was like he was trying to tell them something.

Why doesn't he just tell us what's going on? Jeremy wondered.

"Hey, don't look so worried." Aurora jabbed him in the shoulder. "We got like two songs started. That's pretty good for a first practice."

Jeremy sat down. "Yeah, but…the talent show's in like two weeks."

Aurora sat next to him. "I don't think we should aim that high."

"That high? It's a talent show. At Weatherwax."

"You knew that being in a band with him wouldn't be… like, normal. Right?"

"I guess."

"He wants to change the idea of what a band is. He's talked to me about it for hours. I think it's a cool concept."

Aurora was sounding like Jeremy's mom had sounded about

Keith. *Keith is a brilliant mechanic. You don't understand yet, but a good mechanic is worth his weight in gold. He's going to open his own shop one day.*

Jeremy shook his head. "I just want to come up with some songs so we can play a gig."

"I know, but we can't count on it. We're together. Can that be enough for you right now?" Aurora said. "It's what he needs."

"Yeah, I guess."

"Relax," she said, rubbing his shoulders. His face reddened and fumed at her. Yet when she took her hands away, he wanted them back.

Loud's housing arrangement with Aurora had made Jeremy so sick with jealousy, he'd avoided them during most of the holidays in spite-filled hermeticism, letting his mom treat him with the amp and lots of meals out. He also gave himself over to the pre-college anxiety rituals encouraged by his guidance counselor: he took an SAT test prep course online and aced a pre-SAT, while also getting ahead on his reading in History and English. Meanwhile, he ignored Aurora's texts inviting him to have s'mores with her and Loud over the fire pit or to go see *The Dark Knight* with them and Cal.

New Year's Day, Jeremy woke up to the futility of avoiding his friends. His absence had caused them to grow closer. Aurora and Loud had probably been up all night every night without him, picking each other's brains, finishing each other's sentences, and who knew what else in an endless sleepover. Jeremy couldn't help but feel that part of it was his fault for isolating.

They emerged from Lyle's basement into the snow and looked down at the valley of flat ramblers with white covered roofs. The blanket of white made the town look quaint. Innocent.

Jeremy felt a cold thrill in his neck as Aurora spiked his hoodie with a handful of gray snow. They pounded each other with snowballs until Loud reappeared. He chided them for wasting time. They had important cans to kick. They took off walking, and Jeremy reassured himself that Loud's weirdness during the practice was just an artist's affectation. No big deal.

NETTLE TEA

After band practice, they kicked the can at Jack'n the Crack. Jeremy and Loud had been abusing the hook up lately with Cal and his ride-sharing friendliness, so they bugged Aurora to call him. *See if he'll drive us up into Willapa Hills. We could go tubing in the snow!* But no dice; Cal had to work a shift at the mill. Jeremy left a little while later to do homework. As he was leaving, he gave Aurora a smirk shaded green with nausea—the kind you give to someone who's driving you at insane speeds down a series of switchbacks.

As the snow melted, downtown went back to resembling a war-torn city in southeastern Europe. Aurora and Loud wandered the streets. They decided to follow the traces of snowpack remaining, which led them up into the mist-wrapped hills overlooking Aberdeen, and they kept going along century-old train tracks that ran along dynamited hillsides and cut through granite gullies.

Carried by rust-coated bridges, the train tracks crossed over tributaries of the Wishkah and Wynoochee rivers, now rushing with snowmelt. This prompted Loud to tell Aurora about John Turnow, The Wildman of the Wynoochee. Everybody thought he was crazy or stupid or both, but he was a total genius. He could shoot a deer through the heart while running. He lived off roots and berries and built himself an Ewok village of tree forts.

"Why did he live alone?" Aurora asked.

"Scared of people."

"It's funny what we're afraid of," Aurora said.

"What do you mean?"

"Well, the Wild Man was brave enough to live by himself in the woods. I'm not brave enough to spend a night in the woods by myself."

They were quiet for a while. Rain began to fall, the drops sizzling pockmarks into the snowbanks, dissolving them into streams.

"So, what happened to the Wild Man?" Aurora asked.

"Well, he pissed off his family. He had an argument with his brother over putting down his favorite dog or something, and so Turnow shot his brother's dog out of revenge. Then Turnow didn't go to his parents' funeral. His brothers wanted him committed to an insane asylum. They talked about going into the woods and bringing him in. Then, Turnow's two twin nephews went out 'hunting' one time. Their bodies were found full of bullet holes near the Wynochee River where Turnow's tree forts were. Everybody blamed Turnow."

"Who else could have done it?" Aurora asked.

"Anybody. The woods were full of people roaming around, killing people for money or because they were bored. There was a lot less law back then. But, whatever. Nobody had any proof. They just blamed the only person they knew who lived nearby. A person who just happened to not fit in with them. A person who they were already mad at."

"So, what'd they do? Form a posse? Pitchforks, torches, guns?" Aurora asked.

"Definitely with guns. A couple of times. But like I said, Turnow was a dead-eye. He'd pick off dozens of them from his free forts, which scared them off for a while. A band of dudes finally tracked him down, shot him up, strung him up, and took a bunch of trophy-photos with his corpse. Geez, are you cold?"

Aurora nodded, chin quivering. He put an arm around her shoulder.

"It really sucks," Aurora said, thinking about the Wild Man.

"Yeah. But it's okay. He's a pretty chill ghost."

Aurora raised an eyebrow, but didn't pry, assuming it was just his weird humor.

By the time they got back to Uncle Lyle's house, Aurora felt chill to her bones.

"I know the perfect thing to warm you up" Loud said. "Nettles! I saw some around here the other day. On the other side of that garden-path thing."

The double plot of Lyle's house was situated by a tract of trees. As a border marker, his adopted Episcopalian parents, the Caldwell's, had planted a garden centered by a prayer labyrinth, modeled after the ancient maze on the floor of the Chartres cathedral. The Caldwell's used smoothed stones to create a concentric network of lines that wrapped around an inner circle. Unlike normal mazes, there were no dead-ends. Only one path that you walked in and out, without stepping over the lines. The point, Aurora explained, was that when a pilgrim walked along the lines, praying all the while, they drew alternatingly closer to and farther away from the center circle. According to tradition, God's spirit dwelled inside the center circle and would embrace you when you arrived. In fact, it had led you all the while, as the same lines that formed the entrance, formed the innermost circle.

Though Lyle had long left the church for reasons all his own, he maintained the labyrinth in his adopted parents' memory. While Aurora helped him weed it, he told her the original Greek version of the story. In that version, the inventor Daedalus made the labyrinth to imprison King Minos' bastard son, the minotaur. Enemies of the king were doomed to fight their way through to the center, only to have the monster devour them.

"I like that version better," Loud said and strode over the concentric circles to a stickery patch of weeds. Loud got on his knees and started nipping at them with his fingers. He told her to pluck some of the thorns.

Aurora followed around the outermost line of the labyrinth, approaching the nettles gingerly with her soft, pale fingers. But her hesitance made her compensate by gripping too long in the wrong places, and after the first few tries, her fingers were covered in slowly swelling pockmarks. Loud did nothing to help her when she winced. Instead, she had to watch his fingers work in little pecks. She mimicked the motions until she had a modest handful of nettles.

They went inside and added the nettles into a boiled tea kettle. While it steeped, they ate a bowl of Letter Betters—an off brand of Lucky Charms and Loud's favorite cereal, which he was down to eat any time of day.

When it was ready, the tea tasted a little like matte—a box of which her father had sent her once. Her father, a man named George Stamos, was a mountain guide somewhere in Chile. He wrote her letters a few times a year. He sent her things—the alpaca sweater she was wearing for instance. She told Loud all of this without knowing why. He was focused on making a fire in the fireplace. She sipped her tea and wondered if he'd even heard her.

When Loud sat down to admire his fire, his big brows were furrowed, and through the part in his lips, she could see the gaps between his teeth.

"Have you ever met him? Your dad?" he asked.

"No."

Loud took a drink. "Do you write him back?"

She nodded, cupping the warm sides of the porcelain with her swollen hands.

"I wouldn't," Loud said into his cup.

"I never thought not to." She shook her head. "It's what I have."

She wrote her father short letters. She wrote knowing he would read them, but not answer directly. Who knew who he really was or what he really did in Chile? He was probably just an English teacher who made up all those stories of guiding gringos through glaciers and Patagonian steppes and Nothofagus forests.

She knew she'd never know. Why? she wondered. What was so awful about her that made him avoid her, his daughter? She could never bring herself to ask him, fearing that he wouldn't write back if faced with such a question. His letters were the only semblances of love she had from him.

Loud whispered something and smelled his hands. He looked into the fire, and she saw how lightly colored his brown eyes really were.

"Where's your mom?" he asked her.

Marcy May Loftner had been killed by a logging truck not far from Ocean City on the windy hairpin turns of the 101. She'd been drinking, which surprised no one, least of all her older brother-by-adoption, Lyle Blanchard. But in the end, the meth in the truck driver's veins left Marcy's fatal flaw in the shade. No Aberdeener found fault in Marcy's memory the way they might have if circumstances had been different. The funeral was well-attended by Marcy May's many admirers and Lyle, who adopted her surviving daughter—a beautiful, green-eyed girl with curly black hair who had just turned four.

Loud's brows were knotted together as Aurora finished her story. He sighed and shifted his legs as if getting ready to leave.

"I'm sorry," she said. "I shouldn't have shared all that."

"My grandma taught me how to make this tea." He looked straight at her. "She told me about the Wild Man. Taught me everything, actually. My dad died when I was nine, only I don't really know how it happened. My mom said this, then that. Everybody in town says that. I don't know what to believe. I wish I knew what really happened. I wish that he was here still."

Aurora blinked. "I don't know what to say…"

Loud shook his head. "It's just crazy. We have kind of the same…"

He trailed off. Aurora sipped her tea. She told him she was

glad his grandma had taught him how to make it. She was about to ask where his grandma was.

"Damn, Overalls!" Loud said suddenly. "Those nettles got you."

He inspected the red pockmarks at the center of the puffy blotches on her hands, but he didn't do much other than rub them a little and hold them. She let him.

It's what I have, Aurora said. The weird boy, the wild man, the storyteller with the ripped-up vest, patches, and fuzzy mohawk.

Long after they finished their nettle tea, Lyle came home. It was around one a.m. Aurora saw the dour expression on his face as he came in. She saw his face go graver as his eyes passed over the scene: her holding hands with Loud by the dying fire. Lyle tried to soften his expression. But his pillowy cheeks seemed to weigh as much as the moon, and he couldn't manage more than a half-smile at her before retreating upstairs without a word.

TATOOSH

There was so much going through Phillip's head.

What to do about the salal poachers. Large swaths of salal had been cleared in the hills not a mile south of town. The tire treads veered toward PA. He wanted them to be a bunch of white guys. But his contact at Port Angeles PD said he'd seen salal used in Navidad wreaths sold by Latino migrants at a popup stand outside the Walmart parking lot.

What to do about Valentine's day. He knew Shirley didn't give a shit. But he always got her something anyways. What kind of husband let an excuse to do something for his wife go by like that? Not his kind, that's what.

What to do about the pointy, hot pain in his chest. It made him wince, take off his bifocals, and rub his eyes. He'd slept well. He hadn't been putting in more hours than usual. He didn't get it.

What to do about his sister, Leah's crazy kid. He'd turned his phone to DO NOT DISTURB, worn out by all the texts. Could he do this? Could he do that? Could he talk to the tribal elders about the other thing? He had too much to manage already. 12,145 hectares to be precise. And his own kids. Grown now. Each of their possibilities and challenges showing themselves in his mind on Rubik's cube pivots. They still needed tending. Gracie studying polysci at UW. Dating a white guy. He worried about her focus. Phil Jr. at Central working on his psych. degree. Was he being assertive enough? Calling those internships back? Emailing them back? You couldn't just wait around. Your dumb old dad knows what he's talking about.

Hanging from his office wall was a woodcut of Tatoosh standing tall, legs on the gunnels of his canoe, spear in hand. Legend said he could spear salmon and seal from that position, then dive right in to retrieve his spear and his week's food supply. But now that Phillip looked at it, he thought Tatoosh saw something out in the distance. Something coming.

He winced at the pain again and grimaced, rubbing at his pecs.

Latino salal poachers. Skimming off their sacred, sovereign forest. Phillip ran a hand over his stiff gray hair as he checked his email again. How long did a tire tread analysis take in such a sleepy corner of the state?

"Owww." But nobody heard him. Everybody'd left already.

With everything going through his head, he was surprised there was room for pain. But there it was, breaking out from his torso. And out everything inside him seem to come, swirling together like vomit: Gracie, Phil Jr., Shirley's V-day gift, the fleeced salal groves, Tatoosh's aquiline gaze south. His sister. His nephew, lost out there somewhere. The hardwood floor of his office. White pine in that pretty herringbone pattern.

Too bad he hadn't listened to Rhonda, who'd suggested carpet. Warmer. Cheaper up front. But he hadn't wanted to have to pay to get it cleaned every year. Hardwood was easier for the cleaning guys. And prettier. But it was going to hurt to fall on. Because Phillip Ledbetter was falling. Falling, hand clutching his left breast.

TAILING THE SHADOW BOXER

They never played music together again.

Jeremy called a practice a few days after their "Magic Lunch" jam session, but Aurora said they couldn't. Loud was sick. Jeremy tried a week later after a shift at *The Harbor Herald*. But when he showed up at Aurora's, Loud wasn't there. It was late. Aurora had been crying.

"Where is he?" Jeremy asked.

"I don't know," she said.

"K. Well. I'm out." Jeremy turned to leave.

"You don't have to go, you know," Aurora said, wiping her nose. "You want to watch a movie or something?"

Why not? His homework could wait. But the feeling of cold, wet tentacles tickled Jeremy's ankles and threatened to pull him down into something. He looked at Aurora with her smudgy glasses and tear-wearied face. Where was this feeling coming from?

He said he had to go. She shrugged and said she'd see him in psychology class.

The icy air sliced through his jean jacket as he walked home. The full moon shone like a spotlight, glinting in the windows of the dim churches and empty buildings. Even the dive bars seemed dead.

Then a glimmer of light flashed in Jeremy's peripheral vision. A moonbeam had caught on an erratically moving leather jacket. Loud was walking west and shaking his head. Jeremy thought about calling out. Instead, he trailed Loud, staying about a block's distance behind. It was easy keeping his cover. Loud was laughing, punching the air, and yelling at nothing.

Jeremy followed Loud through Heron Street, then down

the block-long edifice of the Morck Hotel. The past century had twisted all quaintness and class out of the great brick behemoth. The apex of Harbor refinement in the '20s, a respectable, if stuffy, bastion of old glory in the '60s, the former luxury hotel was, by the '90s, rezoned for low-income housing. Now it was a drug den for addicts who cooked up and shacked up on the other side of thin plywood tacked over the purple-trimmed windows.

Loud paused at the broadside of the hotel, painted a garish highlighter yellow. He sidled up to one of the plugged door frames. He pushed in on the right side of the plywood board and disappeared.

Holding his position, Jeremy listened for laughter, shrieks, or moans, but heard nothing.

A train was coming. He heard its ferruginous horn whistle above its heavy chugging. He walked toward the sound, turning to walk along the building's lone intact edifice. He looked up at the terracotta cornices, still boasting barkentine-bearing shields. The tall ships etched into the stones sailed on a sea smooth and blue. He wanted to sail on those ships and that sea. He wanted to be carried to another shore, free from the violent incongruities of this stinking town. From cracks in the upper-level plywood, he saw a flicker and felt a sick sloshing inside, knowing that Loud was the source of that inconstant flame. The feeling of dread and anxiety grew with the sound of the train in its boring path through downtown. The train sounded like a leviathan on wheels and shook the Morck's walls with its rumble as if something was tunneling through the ground beneath it. Jeremy saw the train's grimy quadrilaterals flash between the downtown warehouses, carrying its freight seaward.

He went home and tossed and turned in bed, wondering whether he should tell Aurora where Loud was hiding out or keep it to himself. He opted for the latter. He wouldn't be able to stand himself if he snitched on Loud.

The next day, the day before the talent show, Loud group-texted them: *Sorry I can't be your fuselage into fame. I just can't. The band is over. Burn all those lyrics you wrote down. If you ever perform them, I'll sue you. Tootles.*

Jeremy buried himself in his studies. He imagined Loud and Aurora playing music by themselves. Or maybe even with a more competent guitarist that Loud had found squatting at the Morck. The thoughts dipped Jeremy in a vat of acid; his skin felt like it was burning off.

Then Aurora called him.

"I told him not to send that text," she said. "It was way too harsh. I'm sorry."

"I don't care."

"He is way too fragile to have any commitments right now. I tried to tell you that."

"Fragile from what?"

"From…from so much. He's been opening up to me a lot these last few weeks. I'm getting somewhere with him. Okay, he's waking up. I got to go! I'll call you later."

"Aurora," Jeremy said.

She hung up.

"I'm worried about you," Jeremy said.

*

The next day, Jeremy found Loud sitting in the back of English class with his head down and hood up.

"Dude," Jeremy began.

Loud looked up. His eyes had a mercurial shine. There was a sick glee in his face as if he were holding an M-80 with a lighted fuse in his hand.

"Don't talk to me right now please," Loud said. "I don't hate you. I just don't want you to talk to me right now. Or sit by me…Or look at me."

Loud winced and clenched his teeth as if speaking was a form of self-flagellation.

"Can… I ask why? Is it something I did?" Jeremy asked.

"No. Well. I don't know. Other than be a person? No, there's nothing you did." Loud pulled up his hood and put his head down again.

While Jeremy tried to hide his nausea and found an open desk up front, Loud continued to mutter. He spent all class like that. Even when Ms. Rigby approached him and prompted him to start work. Even when the safety officer came in and poked him, Loud remained catatonic. Only when Principal Campbell came in and threatened to remove him, did Loud respond by bursting out: "Judge Spurgeon the Honorable dishonorable can make me come here. But he can't make me do any work, and you can't make me leave because I'm not doing anything."

He resumed his position: hood up, head down.

The principal, the safety officer, and Ms. Rigby silently triangulated in their ineffectuality. The standoff concluded with Principal Campbell telling Ms. Rigby that from here on out, she was to take a daily note on Loud's behavior and report it to him and the head of Special Education.

When the bell rang, Jeremy left Loud to his corner of stupor and hustled off to psychology class, anxious to see Aurora. When he rounded the doorway into class and saw her already there, he felt like he'd just skinny-dipped in a mountain stream.

Her black hair, glistening in its Greek oil, was pulled back like usual, but she wasn't wearing her glasses. A pair of new jeans clung to her crossed legs. Though she wore big purple galoshes, she also sported a red peacoat and lipstick.

As he sat down next to her, Jeremy wished some collective fugue could fall over the whole classroom, morph their memories, make them strangers. He could ask her name and take her out to a movie.

Aurora looked up and gave him a relieved smile, tongue on the tip of her front teeth. "Hey," she said.

Unnerved by her verve, Jeremy opened his textbook. "After seeing Loud all morning, I sure am ready for *this* class."

Aurora's face turned grave. Jeremy kicked himself for bringing Loud up.

Aurora asked him what happened. But the teacher, Ms. Pickett, started talking.

While Ms. Pickett lectured, Jeremy flipped to Chapter 9: *Abnormalities*. While a video about Phineas Gage played, Jeremy read and re-read the section on mood disorders, pausing particularly long on the bipolar part. About the time the tamping iron lanced through Phineas Gage's frontal lobe, he abandoned his hypothesis and shut the book.

When class ended, Aurora grabbed Jeremy's arm. "I have a lot to tell you."

From the hallway, a voice was singing Nirvana's "Drain You."

Loud slouched against the wall outside of class, watching them.

"I've got to go," she said.

"Wait!" Jeremy said.

Her tight jeans made her hips saunter like a woman's. Loud smiled as she strode toward him. They turned and walked down the hallways together, holding hands.

Jeremy remembered being eight years old and his mom leaving on a date with Keith, the sleazy, mustached mechanic who always tousled his hair while giving him a weird little smirk that seemed to say *I'm going to do something with your mom tonight that your daddy ain't done in years.*

*

Jeremy pedaled into Bullfinch Boyd's lumber yard feeling like a messenger entering the court of a hostile country. Scaffolded in gangplanks and stairwells, the central tower billowed steam. Just left of the tower was a tall, scuzzy block of vats and machine housing. From there, a massive chute sloped down behind the tower to form the scalene triangle of the building's profile, which made it appear to be leaning to the left and on the point of collapse. But according to Cal, the building had stood that way for almost forty years, despite shutdowns and corporate takeovers. And if he and his dad had anything to do with it, it would stand for forty years more.

Jeremy walked his bike the rest of the way in. A light snow of sawdust was falling. Inside the mill's yard, the sky was taken over by shed-shaped buildings on stilts and various chutes and pipes angling toward each other in an eccentric geometry. Yet swallows dipped in and around the millworks. And there was Cal, driving a block of cut timber into a garage-sized box emanating heat. The steam on the freshly cut cedar smelled like pumpkin.

Jeremy knew better than to call out to Cal. He wouldn't be able to hear over the sounds of the planer mill: the roar of the tram sending the log booms in and out, the pops and crashes of the booms getting flipped by the tram's pronged arm, the whizzings of the laser-sighted ban saws regularizing the irregular, conforming the circular into the square. All this gave guys like Cal a hard-on. But to Jeremy, the whole thing sounded like a county fair ride gone haywire. His neck turtled into his shoulders, bracing for something to come flying out.

A steel-drummed conveyer was slowly moving lines of bark-stripped, golden logs into the mill. Jeremy looked at them like his environmental-lobbyist father did. He didn't see money or jobs, but cattle to the slaughter: cedar and hemlock kings being reduced to cabinets in IKEA kitchens.

Cal walked out of the corrugated steel walls of the dinky office, cork boots first, his torso still turned, his big arms lifted in farewell to his coworkers. He let down his greasy hair, pulled off his gloves and spat, all with a self-assured swagger that only a big working man could have.

After Cal helped Jeremy toss his bike into his truck bed, they got into the truck's cab, and Jeremy vomited out his worries to him while he nodded.

"Aurora and Loud are being really clingy together and not talking to me. Or anybody else."

Cal sighed, "You know, in a way, there might not be anything that weird happening."

"Nothing? Are you blind, dude?"

"Just think about it," Cal began. "Loud has a tough couple months. Then Aurora scoops him up and gives him a place to stay. Why are we surprised he's starting to get into her? She's his cute little savior."

"But the Morck! I think he goes and does drugs there. And I *know* he isn't doing any schoolwork."

"A lot of people do drugs and don't do schoolwork. Myself included," Cal said.

"Yeah, but…Aurora…"

"Maybe they'll even each other out. Opposites attract."

Was it something in the water that turned everyone here into idiots? Jeremy wondered. He took a deep breath. "I'm just worried about her."

"So that's it!" Cal said, chew on his breath. "You like her." He poked Jeremy with one of his grimy, sawdust-speckled fingers.

"No way," Jeremy said with a sinking feeling inside.

"Way!"

"You're stupid."

"Stupid, but right."

Cal put his car in gear. Jeremy slouched and looked out as they passed the Morck. In the daylight, the sickly neon yellow of the building's botched paint job didn't seem as baleful. The hotel was just another sad totem of daily Aberdeener reality.

"Is my concern just an acid reflux of jealousy?" Jeremy asked himself aloud.

"If it is, I'm not judging," Cal said, thwacking a can of Skoal into submission. He offered some to Jeremy who waved it away, his knuckles still lined with Xs.

"The only way to find out," Cal continued, "is some R&R time together!"

"I'm done peeing off trees."

"No, I mean the beach! Ocean Shores."

"It's January."

"Yeah, but it'll be warm in my beach house. Next weekend's MLK day. Three-day weekend and my dad's out of town. There's nothing stopping us from crashing on the coast."

"I don't feel like hanging out with Loud and pretending we're all good."

"You might not, but getting them out and away is the only way to tell what's *really* going on. Is he doing drugs or just being Loud? Is it weird between him and Overalls, or just young love? Smooch, smooch."

"You're asking me to willingly watch a train wreck," Jeremy said.

"They're our friends, dude."

Jeremy sank down into the bucket seat in Cal's truck. He squeezed his eyes closed and tried to think of life without Loud. If that ragged mohawked hooligan hailed him from the sidewalk, would he be able to look the other way? Pretend not to know him?

THE SEA

Their trip over to Ocean Shores started with some swings and jolts. Downtown Aberdeen was in foment. And Loud was missing. Aurora and Jeremy met up and texted Cal to find Loud and meet at Jack'n the Crack. It was raining. As they walked downtown, a black energy hissed from the old pipes of the machine shops and crackled in the engine blocks of the big-bedded trucks luffing by on Heron and Market Street. Other than the usual trickle of tourists en route to Westport or Astoria, there were clumps of working-aged men in Carhartt jackets, camo caps, and brogans gathered on sidewalks and scrunched together in booths at the Pour House. Plumes of ganja paraded through the misery. A line of regular-looking folk lined up outside DSHS. In the rain. It was nine a.m. on a Saturday.

"It looks like the Great Depression," Aurora said.

"Cal's dad says a bunch of shutdowns are going on," Jeremy said.

"Uncle Lyle told me Rhinehouse is leaving. And like two hundred people are getting fired."

Jeremy had no familial connection to the town's legal cash crop. But from what he'd read in *The Herald*, the crash went something like this: banks had stopped loaning money, companies were halting building projects, lumberyards stopped getting orders, and timber companies had to stop paying people.

He and Aurora veered off the sidewalk and cut through an alleyway where electric wires hummed above while garishly painted cartoon characters—Woody Woodpecker, Elmer Fudd, Mighty Mouse— winked at them with leering grins.

"I hope everyone will be okay," Aurora said.

"Cal didn't seem that worried," Jeremy said. "He says even if his dad stops selling lumber, he'll keep selling paper. People always need paper."

"I don't like it," Aurora said.

"Me neither," Jeremy admitted, thinking about how the town's tectonics created the same squirmy uneasiness that he'd felt during the throes of his mom's relationship with Keith.

Jack'n the Crack hummed like a union hall. Through the fogged-up windows, they could see the place was swirling with burly, dark shapes. The doors opened, and out came Keith himself in his camo ball cap and plaid shirt.

Keith's pale, hollowed-out face grew open sores like poisonous berries around his lips and cheeks; he thumbed and scratched as if wanting to pluck and eat them.

"Hey, Jer," Keith said, reaching to tousle his hair.

Jeremy recoiled. "Don't touch me."

"Ooh, I forgot. You're a badass now. Blow up any more toilets lately?"

Jeremy didn't answer.

"What's this?" Keith asked, pointing to Aurora. "Got yourself a girlfriend?"

Aurora had dressed down for the day: sweatshirt under her flannel-lined denim overalls and Columbia raincoat. Her skin looked pale and cold in the January morning's bluster. Jeremy wished she was his girlfriend so he could put his arm around her and tell Keith to go fuck himself.

"It's none of your business who my friends are," Jeremy stammered.

"Got your own secrets now, I guess," Keith said, while picking at a sore on his forearm. "Well, good for you." His voice had a ruefulness to it that came from constant self-betrayal.

Loud approached, his gangly body hunched up. Though it had stopped raining, his face winced as if still being pelted by precipitation. His mouth was moving, but when he looked up and saw them, he smiled.

Aurora stiffened. Her eyebrows bunched, trying to hide her relief. "You took off again last night. Where did you go?"

Loud picked her up and spun her. She laughed as he set her down.

"I just had to get some stuff from my grandparents' place, and when I got there, I was too tired to walk back."

"I could have driven you," Aurora said. "And I thought the house was flooded out."

"Well. Uh. Yeah, it was. I swam right up to the second floor…"

Aurora's face contorted, and her eyes watered. Keith was still standing there, watching.

"Hey. Sorry about…" Loud called to Jeremy. But as Loud was about to clasp him on the shoulder, Keith stepped between them.

"Ki?" Keith asked. Loud shook his head. "Ki," Keith repeated.

"Who the fuck are you?" Loud asked, his big brows furrowed.

"Ki, you got to remember me," Keith said, putting his hands on his hip.

Loud shrugged.

"Well, I'll be damned," Keith ran a hand over his goatee. "Pete's little whistle punk got himself a lobotomy."

Jeremy and Aurora looked at Loud.

"You knew my dad?" Loud said.

"Whatever, Malachi. So long, Jer," Keith said. He got in his pickup and drove off.

Jeremy turned to Loud. "Your name is Malachi?"

Loud's face was blank and ashen as he stared off in the direction of Keith's departing truck. A sharp wind blew, and he snapped his gaze to Jeremy. He put an arm around his shoulders and said they needed to talk.

"Overalls, wait for Cal!" Loud commanded.

"Sure," she said, looking small and alone beneath an overcast sky, in the parking lot of the big trucks across from the block of grimy buildings with broken windows.

"So you're talking to me now?" Jeremy asked, mockingly.

"Don't be a bitch," Loud said. "I just needed a little space the other day."

He steered Jeremy inside where lines of men waited to cop a burger. Others milled around, making signs in red letters. They sat in an open booth. Above the din, some guy in a Mackinaw vest told his layoff story to a group circled up around him while they cajoled, *Calm down, Doug.* Yet his marijuana-blazed eyes shivered incredulously.

"Two hundred of us got laid off. They called us all out into the parking lot and fired us. They didn't even let most of us back into our lockers to get our things. With as much regard for men as mules! Then they called us, begging us to stay on and help them shut down. Help them leave! And we'll do it! Take the scraps from those corporate sonsabitches."

Jeremy turned to Loud. "Look, if this is about the band thing. I'm over it."

"It's not that," Loud said, looking around. "I have to tell you something."

"Yeah?" Jeremy said, rubbing his eyes.

"I've been seeing him," Loud said.

"Who?"

"The ghost of Kurt Cobain."

There were the sounds of meat sizzling, registers sliding open, people ordering and complaining, microwave doors opening, bills trading hands for baggies.

The hairs on Jeremy's neck rose. "You're...what?"

"Crazy, huh?" Loud asked. "Since the storm, he's been

coming around a lot more."

"You can't be serious."

Loud scoffed and flung himself back in the seat bench. "You and Overalls...You're both *so* much alike. Such shitty friends." His expression sobered instantly.

"I'm just trying to understand," Jeremy said. "I've never heard of anybody seeing..."

"There have been multiple sightings in Aberdeen since he offed himself," Loud said. "He only appears to the malcontented sons of winos and loggers, so you wouldn't know."

"I've never heard or read anything about that," Jeremy said. *Laura Law and Billy Gohl sightings sure, but then again,* Jeremy wondered, *what was this difference? It was all cockamamie, wasn't it?*

"Because you don't want to know," Loud said, pointing his finger into Jeremy's temple.

"How do you know the ghost is real?" Jeremy asked.

"Of course it's real. What else would it be?"

A fucking hallucination, Jeremy thought. He shook his head in exasperation. "Okay, okay. You're seeing Kurt Cobain's ghost. It's just...everything is a lot to take with you. You know, it's never, like, 'my pet cat died' or 'I've got a big test to study for' or something normal. It's always some major shit, and it's just...tiring. And hard to believe."

"Well, sorry I can't be more normal for you."

Jeremy put his hands over his face. "So, tell me about this...ghost."

"He's pretty happy. Most of the time. And I'm getting a lot of inspiration from him, so I think we can resurrect the band soon."

"Uh-huh." Jeremy looked outside for Aurora. She had her hands at her sides. Working men who knew her or her uncle stopped to say hi.

"I just wanted you to know," Loud said. "So, if I start talking to him, don't freak out. If you see him, don't freak out. He's not going to hurt you. He just seems stuck. Like he doesn't have a place…"

Cal's truck pulled into the parking lot. Jeremy leapt up, rescued from the burden of being alone with Loud.

*

And to think that Loud hadn't even told Jeremy about The Wildman's ghost! Then he'd have really freaked out. John Turnow's ghost didn't say much, just drooled blood on himself and poked at the bullet-holes polka-dotting his chest. But neither the Wildman or Cobain followed Loud into Cal's Forerunner, allowing him to settle in and enjoy the trip with his friends.

The highway cut through Hoquiam and the dilapidated bungalows that huddled on the flats along the Chehalis. The weekend traffic started and stopped, and overhead clouds swirled like exhaust, making them wonder if they would ever see the sea. But after an alder swamp and the cove of pilings from abandoned mills, the highway opened. Free of the pall of steam from the paper mills, the sky widened and rolled out ahead, a distressed tapestry of marbled blue-gray. The light of the late winter sun shone off the river, the slicks of dried tar, and the broadsides of the Freightliners chuffing by.

The stereo blasted Pearl Jam's *Live on Two Legs*. Aurora beat-boxed and tapped out rhythms on their knees as she sat between them. Jeremy tried to sing along, listen, and pretend like everything was normal. Loud's mouth murmured along with the lyrics at first, eventually going its own way. His mouth moved independent of the melodies but burbled quietly into ballads of his mind's own making.

*

The ocean silenced them. It even shut Loud up. As Cal drove his Forerunner over the wet volcanic ash of the beach, the unending, undulating horizon of dark blue tore open the earth and stretched to the sky. It gave Jeremy the same feeling he got when a pretty girl said 'hi' to him in the halls. Cal stopped the truck and suddenly, there was only the wash of the salt waves, the listing of gulls on the wind, the smell of seaweed roving in knots like floating nests.

Though they still felt like their noses were going to fall off in the freezing air, the day had turned fair. The clouds overhead were high, billowy, and white as a dreamed-up city.

Aurora volunteered to make dinner. She walked up the dunes to the house, leaving them to play some Ultimate Frisbee on the cold, hard sands.

Aurora watched them from the garden-box window of the Gearhart beach house. She turned up Rocky Votolato's "White Daisy Passing" on her iPod and murmured his lyrics to herself: sad words that came out light and dripping with heart from Votolato's boyish voice box.

She was not going to let this moment pass. She was not going to let him go. He'd snuck out again last night and showed up that morning at Jack in the Box like he always did: looking guilty, like he'd either seen something or done something awful and smelling of pot, refusing to shower unless she shoved him in.

It had all happened so fast. It had only been a few months since she'd taken him in, and now she was monitoring his bathing and spooning him letter-shaped cereal and not going to her job at the Popcorn Factory while he moaned on and on about the ghosts. There were two now. Yet he held her hand, thanked her, apologized for being so weird, and pleaded with her not to kick him out or leave him alone.

The ghosts. He'd been talking about them for over a week now. She wasn't sure what she believed about them. All she knew was that Loud was seeing things. Things that were luring him away from her. She looked at herself in her new push-up bra, as she pressed on lipstick, overalls discarded at her feet. Did the ghosts look like this? she wondered to the mirror.

When Loud pleaded with her not to kick him out, he seemed to be on the other side of a set of invisible bars. And after everything he had told her about his grandparents, the highway miles, the Seattle streets, his wheeling thoughts, the walls of juvey and the ghost, she understood how his past could seem like a prison. But now?

You're safe, Malachi, she thought. *You've got friends. A place in this world. I know you don't believe me, but I'm going to show you.*

*

Tired of the wind interfering with their frisbee throws, they sat on a driftwood log shooting the shit. In their big coats, they looked like shorebirds miserably burrowing into their plumage to hide from the chill. But they perked up when Aurora in her red dress flamed up and over the gray-green dunes. She'd put contacts in, allowing her green eyes to radiate their jade-hue onto their stupefied faces.

Cal didn't even try to hide it. He stood up and stared slack-jawed.

Jeremy didn't do much better. "What happened to you?"

"Did you burn up your other clothes when you were making the food?" Loud wondered.

Though she wore leggings, Aurora must have been freezing. Her sleek jawline shivered as she parted her lips, painted thickly in cherry red. "Dinner's ready," she said. "Better come get it, though. I'm hungry enough to eat it all."

The wind quieted momentarily, letting her chocolate curls fall and contrast with the smooth vanilla of her clavicles and, dear god, cleavage! Three freckles over her sternum drew their eyes hesitantly but obediently downward.

"Do we have to dress up too?" Cal asked.

"Come as you are," she said as she turned back toward the house. Loud ambled after her. Cal and Jeremy brought up the rear.

"So, nothing is weird with this?" Jeremy accosted Cal. "I have never ever seen a picture of her in a dress. Not even the pictures of her at those old people events. And now she comes out here in freezing weather in *that*."

"Love works in mysterious ways," Cal shrugged.

Jeremy felt like taking his coat off and smothering her with it as if she were on fire.

"Speaking of love," Cal continued. "I should tell you, Ashley, a girlfriend of mine, is coming over tonight."

"So, I should get acquainted with my right hand, is what you're saying." Jeremy seethed, realizing he was about to become an enormous, aching fifth wheel.

"I'm sure it's not a first for you."

The whole thing had been Cal's lame set-up for a booty call. In thinking with his dick, Cal had inadvertently created a scenario in which Jeremy would be the only thing stopping Loud from being alone with Aurora, sans parental supervision. And, knowing Loud's domineering will, Jeremy was going to get run over like an early daffodil by a dune buggy.

*

For the first time since maybe middle school, since before his grandparents started feeding him bath salts for breakfast, Loud's mind was serene. It was the first time he felt at home, possibly ever. He was eating spaghetti with meatballs that his girlfriend made. He was sipping a whiskey-Coke his friend had mixed with some of his rich dad's stash. His best friends were sitting to his right and left, and he could stare, unabashedly if he wanted, at his girlfriend's chest. He hadn't smoked pot in almost two days.

He was tempted the night before. Even made it to the Morck. But when he saw Karla and smelled that hot ganja, he couldn't stop seeing Overalls' hazel eyes and smile, tongue touching her two front teeth, and suddenly, he didn't want it. He told Karla he never wanted to see her again.

"You'll be back, ya bullshitter," Karla sneered.

Loud then spent the rest of the night walking the streets, writing new songs in his head, riding the free bus, and talking to the tired Harbor prostitutes about how not to be an abusive boyfriend. He didn't miss the fuzzy blanket of weed when he was with Overalls. Around her, he didn't feel the same impulse to control or be controlled that he felt with other people, mostly because she seemed to give up all control from the start. Almost as a precondition, she seemed to be saying "I'm yours." She smelled like Grandma Gin.

After dinner, they washed dishes together, then broke into Ron Gearhart's stockpile of fireworks. They bundled up, slipped mortars into their coat pockets, and ran out onto the beach—mauve against the jet-black night. The beach was all theirs. They lit the shells and threw them into the tide pools as they jumped across. The explosions blossomed into teal pompoms and spun Catherine wheels of fuchsia, making a Mardi Gras of the salt-sodden sands. Their faces were gleeful through the smoke of strontium and sulfur. They ran in the light and sound.

Loud couldn't stop laughing. He was not alone. There were no ghosts. He knew where he was staying that night and when his next meal would be. He knew who loved him.

When they got back to the house, Loud saw the ghost of Laura Law at the door, bleeding from where her breasts should be.

He cried out.

"What is it?" Aurora gripped his arm.

He stammered.

"Loud," Jeremy said.

Loud blinked and shook his head and the apparition shifted. It was a tall, skinny ginger at the door. Cal called out to her. Her name was Ashley.

"Hey," she said from her throat, Adam's apple dangling down. She took a pull off the bottle of Jack that Cal had used to make the drinks earlier. She capped it and carried it loosely over her shoulder as she sauntered inside.

Cal ran up the stairs after her like a golden retriever, his mudflap of hair wagging.

"Sorry," Loud said in her wake. "I… thought she was someone else."

"Guess we're on our own," Jeremy said. "The three of us. Like the fucking 'Kiss Me' video."

Loud laughed.

"Oh, who cares?" Aurora said. "Let's go watch *Garden State* on the big screen."

They watched Aurora's favorite movie on the old 65-inch, turning up the volume so they didn't have to hear Cal and Ashley. Sitting between Aurora and Jeremy, with the emocore innocence playing across his face, Loud felt like a king. The feeling made him super sleepy.

"We should get the band going again," he said before he closed his eyes.

He woke up to the sound of someone moaning.

"Oh, poor ginger girl. Did Cal do you too hard with his big Clydesdale dick?" Loud asked the darkness. But the moan continued like wind creaking at the planks of the house.

Aurora and Jeremy were asleep on the couch. The movie's credits rolled up the walls from the hulking oak panels of the old TV. In the names of the key grips and lighting directors and camera men, words appeared. *We need to talk.*

"About what?" Loud asked the TV.

He felt Cobain's ghost nearby, calling him.

Loud followed the moans and groans out onto the balcony.

"What the fuck?" Loud said.

The ghost was sitting there, head in its hands. His groans joined with the crashing of the waves. He was soaking wet as if he had walked for hundreds of miles in the rain.

"What happened to you?" Loud asked.

The ghost looked up. It was Cobain's face, but the skin was purpled, and the eye sockets were hollowed-out nests of maggots. The teeth of the face were intact, but the lips had been eaten away.

The ghost showed him signs of umbilical cords and a hot, wet, red sack. It was a womb. The ghost pressed its concerns on him. By getting so tied up with these people, these 'friends', Loud was crawling into another womb.

The ghost stirred. And showed him new signs. Piss. After-birth. Dirty diapers, fly-invested heavens. Sour, curding breast milk. Vomit. And Aurora, Jeremy, and Cal were face down in the revolting, brown stew. *His* stew.

"Hey," Loud said, incredulously. "I've been through a lot. They get that. They don't care that I smell."

The ghost groaned and shook its head. It told Loud to leave for Seattle before he hurt them. Before they hurt him. Hadn't he had enough? The ghost showed him Aurora's bloodied hands.

If you leave now, everyone can just forget each other.

"Hey, you know what? I'm having a great fucking time without your weird ass. So why don't you just go to hell already!"

The ghost shrugged and rolled its maggot eyes. *Have it your way, Burger King. But first, I need to show you something.*

"No!"

Then I'll show it to them. The ghost started to crane its neck so that Loud could see the dark purple hole at the back of its head, still wet and seeping with life.

*

"Jer."

Jeremy was having a dream where he and Aurora sat in a cold, dark restaurant. The waitstaff shuffled in and around the place, but none of them came to take their order.

"Jeremy!"

It was Aurora, standing in the cold dark of the beach house's basement.

"Loud's gone," she said.

Jeremy rolled out of his sleeping bag. *Can't we just forget about him?* Jeremy wondered. *Let him run, let him babble his brains out, and get hit by a logging truck. Let him follow whatever ghost he was seeing into the ocean and swim away to some island big enough to contain his misery.*

But Aurora turned on the light, and Jeremy saw her soft face set in a polished stone of resolve.

Outside, the wind howled over the cedar shakes and metal roofs of the Newport mansions facing the beach. But through the wind and the distant tearing of the waves at the shore, they could hear somebody wailing.

The farther they walked through the frozen dune grass and the louder the wailing became, the more Jeremy's temples throbbed. Over the northern sky hung a curtain of retreating clouds lit purple by an enormous whaler's moon, emanating wild light. The stars were pinpricks in the shuttle box of existence; they hinted at the fluorescent lab lights of God's grand experiment, the center of which seemed to be a dark figure on the edge of a field of dune grass, flinging himself up and down upon the sands—a devotee at the mercy of a muezzin he alone could hear.

Loud clutched his head while he shouted to the sky:

"Shut up! Shut up! I don't want to see your hole. I'm not going to be like you, you fat fucking hole. I'll never be a fucking junkie like you! You left! I'm not going to hurt my people the way you hurt yours. I've got to tell them about Brawny Man. This is my land! This is my coast. This is my home and I am never leaving!"

The tableau, like a shrill, atonal guitar riff, sent a cold, sharp pain through Jeremy's stomach and ears.

"Loud's crazy," Jeremy said. Saying it was popping a blister: a small satisfaction giving way to pain. Aurora's eyebrows arched, pinching the skin above her nose. She breathed heavily beneath the broken calliope of Loud's screed.

"He thinks he's talking to Kurt Cobain," Aurora said, clutching Jeremy's arm.

"He needs help," Jeremy said.

Aurora rushed to Loud, calling his name.

Malachi stopped himself mid-fall, and with his hands raised, he turned around slowly. His shoulders were bent, hair windswept, and tossed with sand. In the moonlight, his face wrinkled raisin-like in shame.

"Stay away!" he hollered. "I smell! My smell! My smell's gonna suffocate you."

"We don't care about that," Aurora said. "I've told you before."

"We're just glad we found you," Jeremy said. "You could freeze out here!"

"Guys..." Loud moaned. "I'm sorry." His big brows hung over his tear-stained eyes.

His jump boots in the sand made his long legs topple. Aurora ran to him, and Jeremy followed. Loud clutched them by the shoulders. He looked at them wide-eyed, face aghast as if on fire. His mouth moved.

"What?" Jeremy asked. "What, dude?"

"Help me. Help me! Bro…help me."

Jeremy looked around for someone to take over or give him the words to say. Loud squeezed Jeremy's shoulder and asked him again for help. Jeremy could only nod.

"We will," Jeremy said. "We're going to help you."

Loud's face soured, and he sobbed, "No, no, no!" He babbled some more about Cobain and the Brawny Man and John Turnow and Laura Law.

"Let's get you to bed," Aurora whispered. "Come on, up we go."

She picked him up. Jeremy lifted too, and together they led Loud back to the house.

Loud's babbling became plangent, regular and soft, broken by occasional "thank-you guys" and "I love you both."

"I don't want to leave you guys. I don't. I don't want to be this way," he sobbed.

Yoked by Loud's arms, they pulled him forward through the sand and wind. Across Loud's quavering chest, Jeremy looked at Aurora. They were together at least—even if it was doing a chore no one else wanted to. But by the time they got Loud into the basement bedroom, Loud whispered to Aurora that he wanted just her.

Loud put his head onto Aurora's chest, his neck curled like a little boy's while his large body dwarfed hers.

"You can go," she said to Jeremy. "I'll be fine."

He left them on the bed together, the springs squeaking at the slightest movement. Before he shut the door, the last thing he saw was Loud lifting his head and Aurora taking both of his round, welt-like cheekbones in her hands.

GUESTS OF THE MORCK HOTEL

That night on the couch in Cal's beach house basement, jealousy was a freshly beheaded snake writhing and spurting itself dry inside Jeremy's stomach. A pair of earbuds plugged his ears and pumped them full of punk melodies to muffle any sounds coming from Loud and Aurora's room. He fell asleep around three a.m. But his mp3 player died and he woke up to Loud shouting.

"I've got to leave! I've got to leave. I've got to get back. He's going to hurt them!"

Aurora was trying to calm him down, but Loud was stomping through the house waking everyone up. He pulled Jeremy's sleeping bag off and marched upstairs. A few minutes later, a door opened, and Cal's girl, Ashley, screamed.

"I've got to go!" Loud kept saying. "I can't be away. Rhinehouse house-user's about to make off with all of it!"

Jeremy found Aurora in the kitchen, head in her hands.

"He's been like this since like five a.m.," she said.

He patted her shoulder.

"What do we do?" she asked.

"We need to take him somewhere."

"Like where?"

"I don't know… a hospital?"

"A hospital is for sick people," she said.

"And he's well?"

"We could ask someone," Aurora suggested.

The adults in their life flashed before Jeremy's eyes: his mom, Charlotte, phone in one hand with her divorce lawyer, the other hand on her badge flashed at a perp she was preparing to interrogate. Uncle Lyle carrying his big briefcase into his turret-house at one a.m., face ashen from the commotion at Rhinehouse he couldn't talk about.

Ashley was arguing with Cal.

Then the slider opened, and Loud started shouting, "You can't be here! I don't want you here! I don't know who killed you. You've got to go. Go. Go!"

Ashley screamed and ran downstairs. Loud wasn't far behind, yelling at her until she ran from the house. Loud stood looking at them from the bottom of the stairs. He smelled his hands, then shook them.

Cal called to them, "Put him in the back of my truck before I knock his lights out!"

To their surprise, Loud complied and jumped into the Forerunner's covered truck bed.

In a half-hour, the three of them packed and made a loose plan to go with Jeremy's idea: take Loud to Grays Harbor Hospital back in Aberdeen. Surely somebody there would know what to do. Then they got in the truck, which rocked from the back as Loud crab-walked in a frenzy.

"This was a bad idea," Cal said as he drove, his face red and jaw rigid. "Things are weird. Seriously weird."

Jeremy figured that was the closest thing to an apology that guys like Cal ever gave.

Cal looked at Aurora. "You need to be careful."

Aurora nodded, tearing up.

They were silent in the Forerunner's cab while Cal drove and Loud discoursed with the ghosts, apparently huddled in the truck bed with him. He opened the truck-bed window into the cab and gave them occasional updates.

"Lock that thing!" Cal shouted.

"Dude, Cal," Loud said. "I know this stuff is hard for you. But it's okay."

"Don't talk to him right now, Ki. He's... driving. Bye." Aurora closed the window.

Cal's forearms were rigid as pipes on the steering wheel. Instead of turning to aggression, Cal seemed to become a mere extension of the machine.

Back in Aberdeen, Cal took a left on Oak Street and downshifted to climb up Hospital Hill. The engine revved. It started to rain.

"Hey!" Loud called and flung open the truck-bed window.

"We should tell him," Aurora said.

"Loud, uh… something's wrong, man," Jeremy said, wiping his glasses.

"Yeah, you guys are judgmental as shit!" Loud barked. "Where the fuck are we going? This isn't the way home. I have a home, you know. Overalls knows."

"No, I mean, like, I think you need some help."

"Jer. Jer-e-meeee! I'm fine. Things are okay," Loud said. "I just can't handle your guys' bougie expectations, okay? I can't live this happy-go-lucky, face-saving lie you guys live. I'm…just realer than you. I see what you guys don't want to see. The reality this whole rotten town is built on top of, and I'm trying to expose it."

"Loud," Jeremy said. The truck rattled in its ascent. "You asked me to help you last night. And I don't know how. So, we're taking you to the hospital, so a doctor can help you."

"Overalls?" Loud asked her, his big brows arching.

"I think he's right, Ki."

Loud's lower lip quivered, spittle forming on the corners of his mouth. "No. No!" He shouted for Cal to turn the truck around. He wanted to go home. Home! But Cal didn't answer.

"Overalls, no!" Loud yelled. "You're going to take me back and leave me there."

"No!" Aurora yelled back. "That's not what I'm doing."

"I would have expected this from them, but not you! You're the girl who knows."

"We're going to stay with you the whole time," Aurora coaxed.

"You were right, Kurt! You were right," Loud screamed, his fists making popping sounds as he punched the roof of the truck bed canopy. "You know you're right!" he sang.

"Dude, he's freaking the fuck out!"

A red light. "Shit," Cal said as he heard the back hatch pop open.

"Go!" Aurora said, pushing Jeremy out.

Jeremy tore around the corner in time to catch Loud's sleeve. Loud shook him free and kept running toward the guard rail.

Cal's big hands caught Loud by the back of his leather jacket and threw him to the ground. Cal fell onto him, but Loud's legs kicked out. The two scrambled against each other on the wet asphalt, their limbs and hands struggling to push and hold in the rain. Before Jeremy could reach them, Loud wriggled free, and tossed himself over the guard rail and down the embankment.

They looked down and saw Loud's body roll, scrape, and slide before coming to a stop on level ground. He got up and fled into the tree line. Jeremy put a leg over the guard rail when Aurora caught him by the shoulder, "Let him go," she said.

Cal stood on the wet road catching his breath. He had a red mark on his neck, and his right eye was shut and reddening. "He...he got away from me," Cal said in confusion. He looked down, the rain beading on his brow. He walked toward his truck, waving off the honks he was getting from the cars. He waited in the cab for them.

Cal drove along the outskirts of the woods along the base of the hill, but there was no sign of Loud. He drove Aurora back home first, and she ran inside. Lyle's truck wasn't in the driveway and the windows of the turret house were dark.

"Think she'll be okay?" Jeremy asked.

"I don't know," Cal said and drove him back to his cul-de-sac in Canyon Court.

The lights in the rambler were off. Charlotte's car wasn't in the driveway. She was working swing shift probably and wouldn't be home for a few hours yet.

"What are you going to do?" Jeremy asked Cal.

"Go the fuck home."

"I'm going to look for him," Jeremy said.

"He's gone, Jer. Just let him go. He wants to go. We tried. But he likes his crazy, fucked-up life."

"I can't do that."

"Why?"

"Because like you said, he's my friend! And I'm not quitting the instant things get hard." He wasn't going to be like Keith with his mom. Or like his mom with his dad.

Jeremy burst from the truck. The rain tore down in diagonal sheets in the headlights of Cal's truck as he pulled away, leaving Jeremy to traipse off to the Morck Hotel.

*

As Loud fled from them, his mind howled, thoughts flaming so loudly he thought they might burn through his skull. Out from his inferno, he noticed someone was following him.

The figure was tall, wide-shouldered, but gaunt with a shaven head and wearing a white, prison-issue work shirt; his arms seemed perpetually crossed in a useless figure-eight, as if by a straitjacket. It was the ghost of Billy Gohl.

Loud tried to dodge him through an alleyway.

"You don't need to be afraid of me," the ghost said in Loud's face.

Loud fell, then scrambled up and away.

With syllables laced with traces of Bavaria, Gohl called after him, "I've never murdered anyone."

"I don't give a fuck," Loud said to the alarm of passersby. *My best friends just tried to drop me off at the cuckoo's nest and now this!*

The ghost of Gohl shook his bald pate and intimated to Loud that having friends in high places was useless. The boss hogs and their children would band together and chase him off or else, pin a murder on him.

Loud sang and cartwheeled and did The Flail to try to show Gohl that he was a useless imp that nobody would listen to. Yet the white, angular pall of Gohl's shade continued his pursuit.

Gohl's ghost cut. Its presence was a wind scything into Loud's mind, imparting a biting sense that he was being targeted and should leave Aberdeen. His voice made Loud spin in circles. He was angry. Angry at having been set up by "pettifogging boss hogs."

Heart pounding, Loud jumped a fence and crumpled in a heap. He held his hands over his eyes red and wild with tears. *This can't be happening. This can't be happening.* He wanted Grandma Gin. He called out for her.

Billy Gohl had been a favorite subject of Grandma Gin. Gohl was known by most as the worst serial killer along the Pacific coast. It was believed that Billy had lured voyaging sailors up into his second-story bar and, after promising to keep their money in his safe until they returned, bludgeoned them over the head with a two-by-four, sending their bodies down a hidden shaft into a dinghy that waited in the Harbor below. But Grandma Gin also told Loud another story about Gohl. Billy was a fearsome union organizer whom the local captains of industry conspired against. They concocted the story about him murdering the sailors to explain the bodies of drunks and bar-fight victims that frequently bobbed up in the Harbor's waters, unrestrained by railings, streetlamps, or sturdy boardwalks. The boss hogs' story about Billy worked wonders. He was arrested, charged, and shanghaied out to Walla Walla Pen. He spent the rest of his days there and the unions floundered without his leadership.

"My grandfather told me both stories about Billy and so I tell them to you. You'll have to decide which one is true," Grandma Gin said.

Now, it seemed, was Loud's time to decide. Loud lifted his hands away and sure enough, there was Gohl, huffing and puffing through his bushy mustache about the robber barons of the Harbor.

"No place is safe in this town. No place they don't have their spies! Even the whorehouses."

"I think I know somewhere you can hide out," Loud said. "And chill out."

*

Jeremy's soaked shoes slopped over the slick, broken slabs of sidewalk. The rain had stopped, but overhead was a starless sky. The Morck Hotel, with its sickly yellow paint and purple window frames, stood like a half-done funhouse. Its rusted fire escapes twisted up toward boarded up windows with cracks in them just big enough to reveal the flickering lights of the hive of squatters inside. He approached the lower doorway he'd seen Loud push open. He pressed in, and the plywood gave.

The cavern of the once-grand lobby echoed with unhinged laughter and harsh voices set to a beat of dripping water. Cracks and chipped paint marred the Corinthian columns. A sour-smelling pond of liquid pooled in the center of the great room while scattered bonfires illuminated a court lined with balustraded balconies and rail-less staircases.

Jeremy crept up one set of stairs and started combing the floors for Loud.

Most of the doors were nailed shut. NO TRESSPASSING signs were tacked everywhere. Yet holes were made, and through the many openings, Jeremy saw Aberdeen's lost: an obese, double amputee in a wheelchair nodding to himself. A balding woman petting a whimpering Dachshund blind with cataracts. A man in a soiled suit and tie with a patch over one eye, mumbling about Bill Clinton and looking for something in a pile of broken wood. In each room, somebody was nodding off in the corner, tourniquet wrapped around their arm, needle still in.

Each room was tattered with a similar assortment of supplies: foil, needles, little wads of cotton, clear glass tubes, hollowed-out pens, ashen steel sponges, Zippo lighters, and wood fires smoldering in corners. Each person had a story, Jeremy thought. Each had somebody who loved them, wishing they'd come home. Each had a friend who'd given up looking for them.

A ragged-haired woman with a gaunt face running rings around her room stopped, cocked her head at Jeremy, then charged forward, mouth-frothing in profane vitriol. He recoiled and braced for her to sink her teeth in, but when she reached the threshold of her feces-smattered room, she stopped instantly as if held in by invisible wire.

He wondered what line he'd have to cross to get one of them to hurt him. Maybe they were all so lost in their own hurt, they were no longer capable of hurting anyone else.

On the third floor in what had been a ballroom, Jeremy found the pale, mole-covered back of a fat girl on her knees before the crotch of a tall, skinny kid leaning back into the cracked leather of an orange chair. The kid was moaning absently while staring at the dilapidated ceiling, lit doobie hanging out of his mouth. It was Loud.

Loud startled, seeing Jeremy. He pushed the fat girl off him and sashayed over, bare-chested, jeans still around his ankles, and the dark meeting of his legs showing. He gave Jeremy a look of terror as if he was an armed posse of men sent to lynch him.

"Hi, Ki's little friend," the girl said numbly and hiccupped. She wiped her mouth on the back of her hand.

In a corner, Loud's bike, Neil Young, balanced upside down on its seat and handlebars, its wheels turning lazily in the drafts that ran through rafters black with mold.

Loud pulled up his pants shakily and motioned for Jeremy to follow him. He walked ahead, keeping his distance. Jeremy followed him down the halls of torment in silence until they were back downstairs at the rotten board he'd used to enter.

"So, you're a total pothead," Jeremy said.

"Smoking pot is, like, the least of the problems in here," Loud said.

In here? Did he mean in the Morck? Or inside himself?

Loud trembled, and his eyes watered with tears. He held up his hands. "You've seen. Now please, go."

Jeremy had never felt so powerful. Or ashamed. Or angry.

"I don't need your doctors or your concern. I don't need your judgment or your normie life's requirements," Loud said in a choked-up voice. "So get the fuck out of here. And if you tell her about this, I swear to God, I'll kill you."

ROMANCING A GHOST

Loud quit coming to school. So did Aurora. Jeremy tried Facebooking and texting her and got nothing. Safe to say they were an item now, but were they also Siamese twins? Had Loud dragged her into the Morck? No way. She wasn't corruptible like that. Was she? Jeremy distracted himself with all his classes, but in their continued absence, he was practically breaking out in hives from curiosity. Where *were* they? Jeremy tried texting Cal, but he was in the dark too.

"Come have lunch with me, kid," Malcolm Sweet said on a voice message.

A date with his dad in Olympia seemed like a way to get his mind off it all, but as he brooded on the bus northward, Jeremy felt brittle and thoughtless as a shell disconnected from its white and yolk, Aurora and Loud respectively. He kicked himself over and over again for it all: for not understanding earlier that Loud had a serious mental problem, for not telling Aurora…something. That she was in it too deep. That *he* was starting to have feelings for her.

Instead of distracting him with nonsense as a good dad should, Malcolm made it all worse by monologuing about heavy shit.

They ate at an outdoor table at Seasons—a beatnik café on the banks of Capitol Lake. Though it was dry, a harsh wind up from Budd's Inlet buffeted them. Jeremy was cold and could barely hear what his dad was saying the whole time, not that it mattered. Malcolm didn't so much talk to you. He didn't even talk at you. He talked around you and above you.

Malcolm expatiated about the baked-in racism of the U.S.'s incarceration system: non-parity between crack and cocaine sentencing, maximum sentencing laws, recidivism in felons.

"We're creating a pariah class of people who have served their time in our supposed system of penance," Malcolm sneered.

Sun glinted off the gray waters. Gulls flew in the face of the wind, hovering at a standstill until they wheeled away in resignment.

Jeremy felt he could have been anyone or no one and his dad would have said the same things.

As if sensing this, Malcolm blinked and began his excuses for why he worked so much, for why he was so unavailable. *I'm doing this for you, Jer. So you have a better world to live in.* His lobbying firm was seen as legitimate now. He was making real inroads with legislators. He was going to change things. "I hope you understand," he said.

Jeremy said he did. But he didn't. He didn't need a better world. He needed his dad to love his mom so he didn't have to as much. He needed someone to teach him how to fight, how to love, and how to help a friend. But Jeremy said he was fine, thanked his dad for lunch, refused a ride, and rode the bus back to Aberdeen.

Jeremy walked to Sweet Nothings to see what he could find out from Molly. But the wonky yellow popcorn box was dim. Lyle Blanchard's Chevy was parked beneath it. The single roll on the back of Lyle's head was a curl of pumpernickel dough. He wore a plaid tattersall and directed movers in placing the fridge, the icemaker, panini grills, and file cabinets into the stake-body of his truck.

It had been the first black-owned business on the strip, a fact that Lyle hadn't felt it necessary or advantageous to crow about.

"You closing too?" Jeremy asked him.

"Yes," Lyle said, drawing out the word. He took out a hand-kerchief and padded off sweat from his brow. "I'm throwing in the towel. Finally. Shuttering without ceremony."

Jeremy wondered if he'd just been bankrolling the whole thing to keep Molly and Aurora employed. "What'll Molly and

Aurora do?" he asked.

"Molly's gotten a job as a case manager at Teenage Graceland," Lyle said.

Teenage Graceland was a youth crisis center in the basement of a nearby church. Runaway youth from Ocean City to Elma could stay a night or two and get some case management help. A place someone like Loud could have stayed at had he not been so allergic to getting help.

Lyle cleared his throat. "And Aurora...well. Something's not right."

"What's wrong?"

Lyle said he didn't know and invited him to come by but cautioned that she might not want to see visitors. For the last week, she'd done nothing but lay in bed day and night, plugged into her headphones. "I assume it has something to do with McCrowley flying the coop."

So Loud was still submerged. Was he still lost in the Morck's dank corridors of addiction? Or had he left the Harbor altogether? *They weren't together,* Jeremy realized, a part of his heart feeling freed to fly again.

"In any case," Lyle said with a sigh, "feel free to come by. You might have more luck than I've had pulling her out of this rut."

Jeremy said he'd think about it but had to go work a shift at *The Harbor Herald.*

"Tell her I hope she's okay," he said.

"Will do," Lyle said.

Making his way to the paper, Jeremy walked cautiously beneath the green grime miring the cornices of the old buildings, which seemed like they could crumble any minute. He saw himself in its darkened windows and caught a sick smile in his expression.

He'd fantasized about Aurora every day since the beach. Jeremy dreamed that Loud had gotten stuck out on the couch that night and that he had been the one invited into her bed. The rational side of Jeremy's brain knew these daydreams were just that: idle imaginings. But upon hearing about Loud's continued absence and Aurora's bereft state in his wake, Jeremy wondered. Was this the time he could be more than the artsy-fartsy doofus in Aurora's life and she, more than the cute drummer girl in his science class? Maybe this was the time they could come together and be different than their parents: alive, happy, and free from death and its cousin, rejection.

Yet the cold writhing current he felt over Loud's condition continued to churn to the surface of his thoughts. Jeremy had tried to enlist his mom to help Loud. Did she have any clue what they could do?

She said she would ask the beat cops to do some sweeps of the Morck.

"A kid with as much truancy as Loud probably has a warrant out from Judge Spurgeon," Mom said. "But in terms of getting him treatment? He would have to show he's a danger to himself or others. And that's a really high bar."

So what else was there to do but to forget about Loud and try to be happy? If they could be.

That night, after his shift, Jeremy met Cal at the Jack'n the Crack where he caught him up: Loud gone, Aurora lonely.

Cal wasted no time drawing up a game plan:

"Make a move on her while Loud's gone," Cal said. "That's what she's waiting for. After what she's been through with him, she'll be ready as fuck."

Did Cal's crass tone have something to do with things at his dad's mill? Jeremy wondered. He hadn't seen steam from its tower in a few days, as if steam were a barometer for how much money they were making.

"I'm serious," Cal said. "Just go in there and break down

her door one day. *I* would."

"I don't really think that's my style," Jeremy said.

"What is your style? Waiting like a pussy for *her* to make the first move?"

"She *did* just get ditched by Loud. I want to give her some time."

"Time to what? Think about what an asshole Loud is?" Cal took an angry bite of his double Jr. bacon. "Quit thinking about it so much. You two have way more in common than her and Loud, and you're not batshit."

"Are you okay?" Jeremy asked.

Cal's mouth soured into a downward frown. "Who cares about me? I'm just the chauffeur."

Jeremy blinked and cleaned his glasses. Sprays of vindictiveness from Cal?

"How's Ashley?" Jeremy asked.

"She dumped me."

"Oh," Jeremy swallowed. "Because of Loud screaming in her face?"

"Why else?"

"I'm sorry, dude."

Cal took another bite. "If she can't accept me for who my friends are, she can't accept me."

"Sounds like you're through with Loud, though."

"I'm just pissed at him right now. And worried. But that's sort of irrelevant. I think you and Aurora would be good together. And I don't think all of Loud's nuttiness changes that."

But Jeremy wasn't so sure. Only a fink, only a mook, would nab his best friend's girl while he sequestered himself in a den of vice. Was he Loud's rival or his friend? He went home, did homework, and tried to sleep.

The next day when Jeremy went in for a shift of rejections

at *The Harbor Herald*, the three or four newspapermen at their desks waved. They were honest-looking dudes with beer bellies and horn-rimmed glasses; wrinkled collars and pocket protectors; beards and repose. For decades, they'd chronicled their town's seedy past and bleak present honestly. By that point, in the boredom of the backroom where he made calls, Jeremy had read most of *On the Harbor* and each new issue of the paper. Sometimes the journalists would exit out the back door and invite Jeremy for a smoke and a slug of whiskey. Ignoring the X's on his knuckles, Jeremy joined them. He was thinking about going for journalism when he got to college. Of course, the paper was sinking, hence his position. As were journalist jobs everywhere, they warned. But they didn't know that Jeremy was drawn to train wrecks and sinking ships.

Once seated, Jeremy pulled out a fresh list of phone numbers and dialed:

"Hi, this is Jeremy with *The Harbor Herald*. And I'd like to offer you a year-long subscription of honest, accurate, local reporting for this limited-time price of $59.99."

No, thank you.

Go to hell.

Uh, not right now.

How did you get this number?

Please, don't call again.

More lib-tard media? I'm good.

Fuck you, I was asleep.

No.

I paid to be taken off these goddamn lists! Goodbye.

No thanks!

I'm okay for now.

Rrrrr.....

And so it went for the next three hours. Sometimes Jeremy found a number that just rang continually, and he would keep dialing it. He'd spend a half-hour reading the paper as the dial tone pulsed inanely, hypnotically in his ear. Tone-silence-tone-silence.

His cell phone rang. Aurora.

"Hi!" he answered then winced. Picking up on the first ring? Why not just say, *I love you, I'm desperate?* Then again, why not? Why was he protecting dignity he didn't have?

"I'm…ready to see people," she said.

"Oh…Great," Jeremy said. He could hear music coming from her end: Cat Power. Chan Marshall's soul-rousing tone was unmistakable and sublime. He told Aurora so.

"*You* like Cat Power?" she asked.

"Yeah," Jeremy said again, wrapping the cord on *The Herald's* landline around his finger. Chan Marshall also always sounded like she was in heat.

"I guess I just thought she wouldn't be punk enough for you. Not catchy enough. Not enough bar chords and dick…"

Aurora's voice sounded different. Remixed. A coarser, more raw, McCrowley-salted version of her. Maybe she was upping her attitude in an effort to fill in for him.

"She's more badass than Rocky Votolato," Jeremy said.

"Oh, she could eat Rocky for breakfast."

"Or dessert. I always feel like Votolato's name sounds like, you know, a type of ice cream."

"You mean, gelato?" she asked. "You dumbass…"

Jeremy paused. "Uh, I'm at work."

"Does each minute you're on the phone with me count against your community service hours?"

"You're sassy today."

"Sorry," she said. "I just haven't talked to a living person for a while."

"Been talking mostly to ghosts?"

"Yeah," she said. "I guess you could say that."

Jeremy twisted the phone cord. Sultry Cat Power droned on.

That last image of McCrowley flashed in his mind—him at the Morck, bare-chested, high, trembling. *How much should I, could I tell her?*

As Jeremy looked out the back window, he saw the Chehalis drawbridge raise its arms. A flat-bottomed barge was passing, carrying vats, chutes, belts, and forklifts—the leftover pickings from one of Rhinehouse's shuttered mills. The ship's wake rippled out, blurring the blue water. The Chehalis River was blue. How could such an oil-logged waterway be blue? It was blue.

He remembered Loud's threat. The creak the plywood made as he slipped out of the Morck.

"Okay. Well…I got to go," Jeremy told Aurora, putting his glasses up on his forehead, and rubbing his palms into his eyes.

"Talk to you later, I guess," she said softly.

"Bye," he said.

It was all just too complicated.

Jeremy watched the barge crawl toward the obscured Pacific. Jeremy picked up the Herald's phone, punched in the numbers, and let the rejections drench him like rain.

But the next afternoon, there was a knock at the back door of *The Herald*. It was Aurora in her multi-colored glomits, purple galoshes, and red peacoat.

"When you're done…go on a walk with me?" she asked.

It was overcast but dry. Cold. But they had coats.

"Lemme finish this call, and we can go. You okay waiting out here?"

She nodded. Jeremy went back in and used the landline to call Cal.

"Where are you calling from? I didn't recognize the number," Cal said.

"From work. She's here… What do I do?"

"What the fuck do you mean? Take her on a date, dipstick!"

"That can't be what she wants right now."

"The opposite could also be true," Cal said.

"Huh?"

"Just stop thinking about it so much, bookworm. And don't fuck this up, or I'll drive over there right now and take her out myself."

Jeremy hung up. Why had he called *Cal*? That giant muffler. He talked about girls like they were hydraulic engines. As if you could apply just enough pressure and get them to move how you wanted. Besides, *would* Cal want to date her? The idea seemed impossible. *He's probably just trying to egg me on*, Jeremy thought.

He looked at himself in the mirror. Then he signed off on a clipboard and opened the door to Aurora.

She led Jeremy up into the hills. They passed weary retaining walls with gray rainbows stained onto their facades by time, wind, and rain. Cracks worked through the concrete with ferns growing out. Atop one of the retaining walls was an old billboard. Rain warped and framed by morning glory, the billboard was a hand-drawn scene from the 1950s: a man held a cigar in his mouth and winked at the viewer while a woman looked down at the protuberance of the cigar, intrigued as she lit its tip with a match. *Think of me…* the sign read. Think of Me Cigars. The hill had been named after the billboard, and the name stuck even when the billboard had been moved. A group of Reaganites had petitioned the mayor to have it taken down from the hill's crest and relegated to its backside—out of sight, out of mind.

"Have you heard from Loud?" Aurora asked under the shadow of the cigar.

"Sure haven't," Jeremy said, the woman with her lit match floating above.

"I don't care."

Rain started to fall. The drops made them squirm as if they'd been shaken from the fur of a tick-infested stray. Aurora popped an umbrella. They huddled under it with their hands intertwined.

"It's okay if you're sad," Jeremy said. "I'm sad."

"I am."

"He could reappear anytime," Jeremy found himself saying. "In a week or two."

"Or in a year. But it's not like he's my boyfriend or anything. So…"

"He's not?"

"I don't think I even want a boyfriend," she said. "Ever."

Jeremy looked away, worried she'd see the greenish coloring come into his face.

"Besides," she continued. "We never did a DTR…. Define the relationship."

"DTR, huh? Sounds like a corporation. Loud would hate that."

"He sure would."

And this began a twenty-minute conversation where they reminisced about Whistle Punk Falls, and their making of the tire swing. How they had wandered through the trails and tributaries on foot, making up songs, and telling old stories of the town. When they realized Loud's memory had taken over the whole conversation, they got quiet.

The trees were oxygen chimneys breathing freshness into the air. A century ago, workers blasted apart the dun-colored innards of the hills and laid train tracks through. Aurora and Jeremy ignored the craftsmanship as they tightrope-walked on the copper-colored rails.

"I guess we have to make new memories to reminisce about," Jeremy said.

Aurora didn't reply but continued walking her wobbly line. The drizzle gave way to mist. She lowered her umbrella. The afternoon clouds gave up their slate gray for the purple smoke of a winter's dusk. They crossed a trestle bridge across the Wynoochee River, and she told Jeremy the story of the Wild Man and his similarities to Loud.

Jeremy suffered silently with unspoken worries of wandering through shit-kicker country in the dark. But then the railroad terminated, its gully walls opening to Grays Harbor Hospital. They rested at the chain-link fence overlooking the Harbor.

"That was a sick trail loop!" Jeremy said.

"Loud showed me that," Aurora said. She clutched the fence and turned to him. "This is where I first took him in. He'd been hanging out in the waiting room. That's why, when we were coming back from the beach, he was scared I was going to dump him back off here. That's why he ran."

"You were trying to help him. We were trying to help him."

"I don't care," she murmured. "It didn't work."

The lights from the grain silos shone green in the gloaming sky. The coiled tower of Imperium and the brown scalene triangle of Bullfinch Boyd's were quiet. The houses looked like the crummy hovels of a Van Gogh painting.

"I hate this place," Jeremy said, looking at her. "I can't wait to leave."

"I'll never leave the Harbor," she said.

*

The whole time, Jeremy thought they'd been trailblazing together. But he had been watching her retrace the steps of her times with Loud. The whole time, for her, Loud's face had been rippling over the basalt cliffs. His figure had been lurking in the trees. His laughter had been on the wind, wild and antipathic. Aurora had been more interested in the ghost of the past than in Jeremy. How could he compete with the past? The past was permanent and severe. It belittled him. Especially because Loud was still at large and likely to re-emerge at any time. And if he found them together? It made Jeremy's desire for Aurora seem half-hearted and dim-witted. It could never happen. Jeremy wandered heavy-headed down the northeast side of Hospital Hill toward his Canyon Court home, feeling like a sleepwalker.

The instant he got home, Jeremy planned on nose-diving right into bed. He assumed Aurora would just stay on the hill, fingers fixed around the links of the fence: a mermaid caught in a tuna net. But, as he crossed the 6th Street Bridge, over the little cul-de-sac with its culvert running down the center, there she was, following him. Aurora Lee Loftner. Her hands were in her pockets. She was looking out through the bars of the tall fence erected to stop suicides.

Jeremy wanted to scream at her.

He walked down the bridge's stairs, into his cul-de-sac and into his mom's rambler. Aurora followed. Mom was working late. Jeremy didn't turn on the light. He sat down on the couch, and Aurora sat down in the big chair. Keith's chair. They sat in the dim light.

"What are we doing?" Jeremy asked.

Aurora, black hair tied tightly back, seemed to barely breathe. She was twirling a strand of her hair slowly around her pale fingers. She was looking at him, past him.

"What do you want to be doing?" Aurora asked him.

Jeremy felt her pushing him onto an edge. He was standing on a diving board and either needed to jump off or back down. He shook, his skittish lizard brain telling him to get away from her while his heart pumped loudly in his throat, wrists, and ankles, drumming him forward.

He pointed to Van Gogh's "Starry Night". Maybe that could be his entry point into telling her how he felt. He started to tell her it was his favorite painting.

"That's, like, everyone's favorite painting," Aurora said.

It was "I Want It That Way" all over again. The drums of Jeremy's pulse stopped, and the lizard of his motivations skittered away.

"Unless there's something special you wanted to tell me about it," she said.

"No. It's...stupid."

"O...kay."

Jeremy mumbled something about wanting to play guitar. "Do what you want," she said.

"Well...Uh. You could come too."

"To your room?"

"Well yeah. Uh. No. There's no drum kit in there."

"Too bad," she said and looked away.

His saliva thickened into a chalky protein shake. His mind was stone. He breathed slowly, trying to get enough oxygen to think.

"K. I'm going to let you go," Aurora said.

"No. Uh, I mean. What do you want to do?"

"I *don't* want to bother you," she said. "You probably... have stuff to study. I'm... Yeah. Bye."

*

Two months later, in his wander through Rat City looking for Loud, Jeremy walks past the neon lights of the tattoo parlors and the pawnshops. Alone, he feels like Travis Bickle. Jeremy replays the weird scene with Aurora from that night. *What do you want to be doing?*

A scraggily couple stumbles out of a dive bar. They laugh hysterically in their leather and sway, drunk already. They kiss. The guy lights both of their cigarettes.

The girl lighting the man's cigar. *Think of me...*

It hits him. That night, Aurora wanted him to kiss her. To make a move. To show her with his body what he really wanted. *Do what you want*, she said.

Cal had been right.

Kissing her would have been a jump-off, into her. Jeremy had known that subconsciously, but fear stupefied him. A jump into her could have been a jump into a pool drained of its water. If he had leaned in, she might have screamed or laughed or pushed him away. She might have rejected him. Not to mention what Loud would have done whenever he decided to waltz back into their lives. Jeremy hadn't thought Loud would actually kill him— probably just give him a black eye. He'd already had his black eye for the year. So he had backed down and climbed off the diving board Aurora had made for him. He'd played it safe. Safe and alone. Jeremy's autobiography in three words—until now, where he is wandering in a city of multitudes without a clear plan or place to stay.

The weight bowls him over suddenly and now he's swaying, overcome by the idiocy of his past and the precariousness of his present. A passerby asks him if he's good.

If he had bought himself a pair of brass knuckles to defend against Loud... If he could have grown a pair... If he had just kissed her, he could have prevented all the shit that came afterward. Instead, he is wandering through downtown Seattle looking for Loud, who reappeared, who became her boyfriend, and who ruined her.

The passerby asks Jeremy again, "Are you good, bro?"

"No, actually," Jeremy croaks. "I'm not good."

They hand him a dollar before turning away.

NOBODY'S GHOST

Avoiding a police raid on the Morck, Loud found himself wandering the highways south of the Chehalis. The rain hissed relentlessly. Louder than thought, the sky's vindictive tears drenched his leather jacket, jeans, and jump boots.

On a hill above the road, in a clearing of trees, there stood a longhouse from which great songs drifted to his ears and the songs rent him in two. One piece of him knew that if he approached, those inside would send him away. Another part of him strode forward anyway. The songs stretched out toward him in plumes, along with smoke that billowed from the longhouse's unhinged door. The smoke uncoiled voluminously, becoming round and heavy, ambulatory, and supple. Within were people moving and murmuring as the songs quieted. The smell of cedar and kinnikinnick reached into his nose as colorful fingers curling and drawing him deeper in.

A young man stood at the door. Clean-shaven, bare-chested. Browned-skinned, like him.

"What's your name?"

"I'm nobody," Loud said.

The young man nodded. "What do you want?"

"Nothing."

"Then you may have it."

Loud faded out of consciousness. He came to back on the highway. As before, he was soaked, trudging, and alone.

Nothing? Why had he said nothing? He looked into his tangled heart, a knot of black tape. He wanted to untangle it all and play it until it was a song surging as a river through whiteness, through the muddy banks, away from the broken bodies and trees inhabited by all the ghosts to the ocean beyond. It's not that he didn't want anything. The problem was that he wanted so much! Everything! *Can I have that?* He asked it again and again while the Oldsmobiles and Toyotas and Hyundais and Fords and Mazdas and Saabs rushed past and crested hills, disappeared, and then came and came again.

*

Clinging to the fence line on Hospital Hill above the Harbor, Loud looked up to the sound of a pair of brogans approaching.

"Heya," a man said.

"Heya," Loud said, wiping his nose. It was dripping. Not because he'd been crying but drip-drying because the rain had stopped.

The man was Native, Loud realized, and looked away. He wore a thick, plaid coat—a Pendleton like his father had. Only the coat was dry. Untouched by the rain. The hairs stood up on Loud's neck. Another ghost!

This ghost must have had bad eyesight because he wore bifocals. He looked old, hair the color of salmon scales, steely with patches the color of pitch, snow, and ash. He had heavy cheeks like his mother and, behind his bifocals, the deep, brown darkness of his eyes were unnervingly bright and keen. His leather-colored skin warmed in the streaks of sunlight sifting through the diffusing clouds.

"Whose ghost are you?" Loud asked.

The man smiled foxily, "I'm nobody's ghost."

"You're lying is what," Loud replied.

Nobody's Ghost kept the small smile on his face.

Nobody's Ghost offered him a ride somewhere, but Loud declined. He couldn't fly or do whatever it was ghosts did to get around.

"I thought Natives were too smart to come around here."

"Our people would come through here sometimes. They used to come through everywhere and anywhere there was trade."

"That why you're here? Hoping to trade?"

"What've you got?"

Loud shook his head. "Nothing," he said, realizing he was giving that answer a lot. He looked at his hands. Was *he* the ghost now?

"Me neither," Nobody's Ghost said. They listened to the rain dripping while all Aberdeen lay before them, teeming with its effluence and misery. "I guess you have to have a trade before you can have something to trade."

"You don't work?" Loud said, playing along. Some ghosts didn't know they were dead, he figured.

"Not anymore," Nobody's Ghost sighed contentedly. "I just retired."

"That's one way to put it," Loud laughed.

"How about you?"

"Do? For work?" Loud grinned. "I don't."

"A guy like you? Come on. What are you good at?"

"Being a little shit," Loud sneered. But Nobody's Ghost didn't budge. "Doing the Flail."

"The Flail? Hm. Show me."

So Loud did a few of his best Flail routines: *The Tornado, Reach for the Sky, Dog-Shitting-Razor-Blades*. Nobody's Ghost laughed and clapped.

When Loud was out of breath, Nobody's Ghost asked, "Where are your people at?"

"My people?" Loud asked with venom.

"Your mom? Your dad?"

"Nowhere. They're nowhere, okay."

"Sounds like a hard place to find."

Loud nodded. He was getting a headache. He needed a hit righteously bad. He looked down to where the Morck Hotel stood in all its dingy purple and yellow glory. The siren flashes and squad cars were gone. The coast was clear. He took a step toward it.

"Look at us all," Nobody's Ghost said.

Great, a monologue, Loud thought.

"All laboring after more instead of turning toward what we have."

Loud wasn't laboring after anything. And he didn't have much to turn toward. Except Overalls. Aurora. After a couple of minutes, he figured it wouldn't hurt to tell Nobody's Ghost all this. So he did.

"Guess you better go to her then," Nobody's Ghost shrugged.

"Yeah. I probably should. Or she'll think I'm dead."

"Say. You're pretty funny," Nobody's Ghost said. "Want to hang out again sometime?"

"Sure. Whatever. Just don't come around any of my friends," Loud said and made off down the hill to go get high at the Morck. But he found himself skipping. None of the other ghosts asked what Loud wanted. None of them asked him to go toward his friends. Maybe Native people's ghosts were different.

FUNNY VALENTINE

Upon leaving Jeremy's rambler in Canyon Court, Aurora's head was spinning. Jeremy didn't want her. That much was clear. *She's damaged goods,* she could almost hear him say.

Or maybe he just didn't know how to want her.

It didn't matter.

She went home and did the same thing she'd done the night before: masturbated and fell asleep to Elliott Smith. Around midnight she woke up feeling a cold ache coming from her center. She wanted Loud. She craved him.

It had been over two weeks since they'd been together. In her room, under Uncle Lyle's roof, she had rubbed Loud's shoulders and back. She let him kiss her and touch her breasts and rub himself off on her in burbles, his pants still on. It had been almost fraternal. He was beautiful. Frottage calmed him, put him to sleep, and made her glad. She was using her body as a poultice to entice him to stay so he could get better.

Her body had been her main way of communicating with him. Not her words. Not her intellect. Not her music. Just her body. Though this bothered her, how else was she supposed to draw Loud back into a safe and secure life where he could realize what mattered?

But the ghosts appeared, all that drama at the beach happened, and now he was missing.

Aurora woke up the next day angry. It was Valentine's Day. It was a Friday and school was a windstorm of classes full of new material, missed assignments, and makeup work from being out "sick" for two weeks. As she was packing her backpack, a song Loud had written for her fell out of a notebook.

The girl that knows
how to stop my hands from shaking
and to keep me from wasting.
The girl that knows
where the rivers start
and when the trains run.
The girl that knows
when the coffee shop opens
and the corn pops.
The girl that knows
where my heart is
and what my mouth needs.
The girl that knows
how to make tea from thorns
just like me.
The girl that knows
is just like me.
The girl that knows
is the only one for me.

Rereading it was like laying on a bed of knives. It made her wrack her brain for what she could have done differently after Loud had freaked out at the beach. His voice echoed in her head: *You're going to take me back there and leave me!* He must have been so scared. The sight of her late-assignment-stuffed backpack made it worse. She melted into a sniffling mess, burying her head between her knees. She intertwined her fingers and with her combined fists, pounded on the papers in a mad prayer to make it all go away.

*

At the bell, Aurora hurried out of school, bound for a final shift at *Sweet Nothings*.

Overwhelmed by a series of long and painful meetings at

Rhinehouse Corporate, not to mention his coffee shop's closure, Lyle had been too exhausted and distracted to harangue her about her absenteeism from school. He spent long hours in his study or pacing the prayer labyrinth out in the garden. Aurora felt so guilty about taking advantage of his state of mind that she volunteered to clean up at *Sweet Nothings* before Lyle turned over the keys. He consented just so she could get out for an hour or two.

Though Aurora was eager for the chance to busy herself, she worried about leaving Lyle alone. He looked so tired lately. The Rhinehouse corporation had opted to relocate the bulk of its operations to Brazil, where they could log without bureaucratic red tape or unions asserting its workers' rights. It was the last straw for Lyle. He had put in his two weeks' notice in protest. A careful man's protest, as he was still helping transition their accounts.

Aurora remembered a time when she would have been thrilled at having Lyle home more often. A time when she would have been happy to heat up TV dinners and turn on the History Channel, which they'd watch until they fell asleep. But they were both too distracted with their separate griefs to enjoy each other's company the way they once had.

She opened the doors of Sweet Nothings and felt the incongruousness of seeing a special place stripped down to its basic parts.

As she was vacuuming and wiping down the empty countertops, presiding over the hollowed-out core of Lyle's dream, she got the text. It was Loud.

She hadn't seen or heard from him in over two weeks.

She restrained herself from checking the text. She reached deeper into the crease of a booth's bench seat to wipe it free from kernels, crumbs, and coffee grounds. She wiped down the grimy bottom corners of the stainless-steel prep tables. All so she could tell herself she didn't need to check her phone.

She had checked it every five seconds the first week he'd disappeared. She'd sent lifelines out to Loud in the form of texts. The messages varied in subject and length, though she crafted them to sound as deferential as she could while still showing affection:

I think my favorite Beatles song is "Two of Us." Heard it today. Hope you're okay.

Picked some nettles for tea today. Didn't bleed. Wish you were here.

But there'd been no reply. Where had he been? What made him reach out now? Had he been with someone else? Had they dumped him so they wouldn't have to buy him a Valentine? Was he just desperate? Would any of that change how she received him? Probably not, she admitted to herself, disconcerted, infuriated.

After mopping the floors and standing in the dim center of the vacuous moth-balled shop, the ghosts of dreams slowly descending to the floor with the dust motes, Aurora caved and checked Loud's message on her phone.

The screen showed his Facebook avatar: a mohawked emoji.

Meet me at D&R tonight. Free, all-ages show.

She tried to busy herself cleaning some more. Cleaning anything. The windows. The blinds. The ceiling tiles. Anything that could occupy her fingers. It was like trying to hold her breath.

Another buzz came from her phone:

…Unless you're mad at me. I'm sorry I haven't called. Or been around. I was just really angry at you guys for what you were trying to do. I'll tell you more later. If you're mad, that's fine. But I'll be at the show if you want to see me. I would like to see you.

A warm feeling filled her, like an injection of chocolate fudge from her fingertips down to her knees. She hated Loud for it—this feeling that debased her. He was helping her save face, but also leading her on. *Was she mad at him?* Shouldn't she be?

The asshole hadn't called. Had abandoned her. Had treated her the way a rock star treated some band-aid. The way her father treated her. Was she going to put up with it?

Her words floated back to her. *It's what I have.*

Okay. She'd be a sucker for his shenanigans, but she was at least going to let him sweat a little. Without texting him back, she locked up and walked as slow as she could back home.

The big Victorian farmhouse with its turret by the trees. The house stood like a fairytale castle of clapboard, its ochre paint, its chocolate trim making it appear neat and cheery against the gray skies and the silent, looming evergreens behind it. Even though she had lived in the house all her life and would inherit the property, it seemed like someone else's house to her. She felt alienated from it now as if the thing she was about to do had already estranged her. She tiptoed upstairs to her room to change.

Black miniskirt. Strapless black bra. Skintight white tee with red polka-dots: backless.

She pulled up her overalls and drew her Columbia rain jacket over the ensemble.

She walked into Lyle's office. His three monitors were on. There was a stack of papers to his left, one in front of him. He was wearing his white button-up and bowtie, as if still at the office. He was muttering to himself.

"Hey," she said.

He swiveled around, and she saw a calm pass over him as he observed her overalls, her jacket, her unmade face, and her thick greasy glasses. "Hi," he greeted warmly. Though the warmth seeped out as he remembered where she'd returned from.

"How was it?" he asked.

Aurora shrugged. "It didn't feel like Sweet Nothings anymore. So, it just felt like some place I was cleaning up."

Lyle nodded. "It will always exist in our memories," he said and hummed a bar of "They Can't Take that Away from Me."

"Whatcha up to?" she asked.

"Trying to reinvent this town."

"If anybody can do it, you can."

"Going out?" he asked with a look of concern.

"Just to the D&R. There's this old Seventies cover band playing. Jeremy invited me."

"Jeremy Sweet?"

"Yep."

"I haven't heard you talk about him in a while," Lyle purred.

"Cal will be there too. And lots of other people. It's all-ages."

"Huh."

"Want to come? It's music from your era," Aurora asked.

"My era was over by 1970 but thank you for the invite. I think I'm onto something here. Do you want me to drive you?"

No.

Downtown was still dangerous.

Yes, she knew that.

"Okay... Well, have fun now. But be careful, my funny valentine," Lyle said.

She left, hearing him hum the Chet Baker tune. She could tell by the warm, open way he had spoken that he was pleased. He would nod to himself in a satisfied way and tell himself that she was a good girl. He could convince himself that McCrowley had just been a phase and cull himself back to his figuring. She was glad he hadn't asked her what was in her purse.

She felt a pang of guilt for her guise—her denim-Gortex lie—and how the heavy old moose had fallen for it. Her sixteen years of goody-girl behavior had lubricated the lie so that it slid like truth. The fathers of all the trollops at school would have made them take off their coats, twirl, and roll up their pant legs to reveal any fishnets. But Lyle had no experience with such subterfuge. It wasn't a fair game.

She worried about leaving Lyle alone. With his heart. With his age. With his worries. But they were all alone with their hearts.

The clouds above were dark granite cliffs: they seemed unmoving, impenetrable, and lethal to any who might try to scale them.

Aurora walked through downtown: the broken windows showing crooked sixteen-candled chandeliers; the art-deco cornices greased with gull droppings. She'd lied. Not even someone as smart or good-hearted as Lyle could change the town on their own. The only way the town could change was if people—lots of people—could just take a risk for the good. But, one at a time was better than nothing, she reasoned. Lyle was trying on his own with his computer, his schemes. And so would she tonight with Loud, with her body.

The D&R theater was just around the corner from what had been Sweet Nothings' Popcorn Factory. Most kids who were into music preferred to go to shows at a Hoquiam venue simply known as The Building, which doubled as a karate studio by day. Aurora wondered what was special about this 1970s cover band that was drawing Loud's attention, other than it being free and on Valentine's Day. Beneath the marquee flashing its blue-and-pink decree of light into the gray, people were slowly feeding into its recessed front entry. She hid in her coat's hood, hoping not to be recognized.

An attendant in the curved-glass ticket booth stamped Aurora's hand. Once through the double doors, she b-lined for the women's room. She didn't want to scan the seats or the bar for Loud. Not yet. She wanted his first look at her that night to be her in her outfit. She wanted him to be immediately taken and tricked into wanting this stranger. In a stall, she flensed her overalls, slipped in contacts, powdered her face, donned a black choker, and smeared on black lipstick. Then emerged into the darkened theater.

Following the floor lights, she picked her way through the crowd: families, kids, fellow teenagers. Crinkly, heart-shaped balloons floated up from the seats. There was laughter, jawing, and theater chairs squeaking as middle-aged husbands and wives leaned back and sighed from the jagged day they'd spent over kitchen tables, haggling out bills, and unemployment forms. There were people she knew: from school, from the retirement center. People that waved to her. People who noticed her outfit, her pale skin exposed and svelte. People who leaned their heads together and whispered about her and Loud.

People. So quick to notice, to whisper, to judge. So slow to befriend. No one offered her a seat. And Loud was not there.

She slid herself into a back corner. The velour of the bucket seat felt lascivious on her bare skin, and she squirmed to think about all the beer-fattened Aberdeeners who had sat there. She put her jacket back on and hood up, so she could hide. She felt instantly foolish. Why had she thought that she could hurt *Loud* by being incommunicative? Evasion was his most reliable character trait.

The house lights went down. The stage lights cast cones of golden white on the middle-aged guys with goatees and big hair. The lead singer—a paunchy version of Eric Clapton—introduced them as The Boon Doogles. With a four-four drum count, they were off, wagging their heads in abandon as they sang "Baba-O'Riley", "Black Dog", "You Shook Me All Night Long"–songs she knew almost against her will because she was an American kid who'd seen commercials, stepped into auto-parts stores, and watched movies about baby boomers growing up, doing drugs, and having unprotected sex.

The Boon Doogles rocked "Won't Get Fooled Again." The crowd clapped off rhythm and sang off-key and off-lyric to melodies everyone knew, but whose actual words no one knew precisely, no one taking the stoned rock gods of the past seriously. As she watched them, Aurora found herself wishing that the deception she'd told Lyle had been real. She wished she was surrounded by everyone: Jeremy, Cal, and Lyle too. And her father and Loud's grandma. That they could all be together, mediocre, and alive. The source of everything wrong in the world she understood then, was being alone.

A shirtless Malachi "Loud" McCrowley jumped up onto the stage during "Misty Mountain Hop" and started doing his impression of an epileptic seizure. The poor dope. He probably didn't even realize it was Valentine's Day. As the lead guitarist wrung out a solo from the guitar strings like juice from a vine, Loud shimmied and twisted his pelvis to the twangy guitar riffs. His eyes rolled back toward his big brows, his lips hung open, exposing his gap teeth, and his arms waved back and forth to the groove. He was a brown-skinned Mick Jagger. A homespun Robert Plant. A disaster.

On his bare, hairless chest, Loud had drawn a lumberjack holding an ax, the shaft of which following his man-crease down into his pants suggestively. Someone had written across his back: *Brawny Man wants you!* Loud was gyrating into the guitarists and the drum kit, stepping on toes, and accidentally gouging his fingers into the bandmates' eyes and ears.

The Boon Doogles smiled and played along, trying to make it look like this was all a scripted part of the act, but Aurora watched them during the guitar solo talking to each other with faces glowering.

"Loud! Loud," she called to him.

He saw her and waved but kept doing his thing.

"Get down!" she urged above the music. He didn't respond. The Boon Doogles cut the song short. The lead singer thanked their guest. "Whoever he is," he said.

Loud bowed.

Aurora looked out into the theater seats. People were frowning and shaking their heads. The women were squirming uncomfortably. The kids were watching blankly. The teens were snapping photos with their phones, no doubt uploading the pictures onto Facebook in seconds and adding pages of commentary just as quickly. The Valentine's Day balloons were already starting to sag.

The band was signaling toward the back of the theater, where there was a mill of activity.

Loud crouched down to her from the stage. "Glad you came."

"Let's go!" she said. "They're going to kick us out!"

"They're going to kick *me* out," Loud guffawed even as he jumped down into the waiting arms of two bouncers meaning business. As they ushered him down the aisle, they said they needed him to leave. That he wasn't part of the show and that he was being indecent. Loud started arguing with them, saying they were working for Ulmer Rhinehouse's ghost, just like Brawny Man. They weren't protecting anybody. They should be ashamed!

Aurora followed them: "It's okay. He doesn't mean it. I know him! I'll take him with me. You don't need to…"

She heard the crowd clapping. The guitar player finger-picked the opening to "Behind Blue Eyes." "This one is for our bare-backed stranger," the lead singer said into the mic.

In the atrium, Loud dropped his weight.

The bouncers grappled with him.

"Call the police!" one said.

"No," Aurora yelled. "Loud, stop!"

But Loud kept shouting at the bouncers. "You're going to let me say what I have to say to them. The way I want to say it.

Everybody needs to hear it!"

The band played.

The bouncer dudes dragged Loud along the red carpet, past the rounded glass of the ticket booth, and flung him onto the wet sidewalk. It was sprinkling. Loud tried to stand up, but the bouncers smacked him down again. He arched his back up, but the bouncers stood ready. So Loud hunched there, head bent down, the rain running from his loam-colored hair into his eyes.

The manager emerged with Loud's jean vest and backpack. He gave them to Aurora.

"He needs to stay off property. Or we'll call the police," he said.

"The police, Loud," she repeated.

"Okay, I'm going," Loud said, a hand stretched out defensively in front of his face, the other hand gripping the asphalt.

"It's raining," Aurora said to the manager.

The manager offered her an umbrella. "Get him some help," he said, nodding to Loud's half-naked form, muscles taut in the rain.

"He's just... trying to be a part of their pain," Aurora said.

The manager's brows furrowed. "Missy, they're just trying to enjoy themselves. They've had enough pain already."

*

Aurora and Loud walked under the umbrella, arm in arm. The rain hissed and stung on their faces like rice thrown spitefully into the faces of an absurd bride and groom.

"Look," Loud said.

Aurora saw a crowd gathering on the walkway over the Chehalis River Bridge. The drawbridge was raised, its tower of concrete looking like a slab floating in the sky. A timber barge with a red bow was surging slowly toward them. Its name, *Global Wisdom*, shown in white letters. Its deck was loaded with a forest of logs, the cut circles of their faces showing amber. As Aurora followed Loud up the stairs to the Chehalis River Bridge, she heard the ship's slow weight and endless groan. From above, the ship looked like a floating pallet of limbs bundled together off a Civil War battleground.

Those gathered were talking. It was Rhinehouse's last shipment of logs out of the Harbor. The barge's name rang out its true irony as the boat sounded its horn across Grays Harbor, putting shivers in their jaws and tailbones.

"See, Overalls," Loud pointed. "They use us and leave."

Loud started shouting at the boat, calling it names, challenging it to fight, accusing it of raping the town. But the barge—its cranes, its greenish stadium lights, its white control tower, its long, silent deck of timber—cruised by.

The others gathered shook their heads: at Loud, at the barge, at their fates.

"His dad worked for Rhinehouse," Aurora said, off-handedly. "He's…upset."

The crowd was silent and ambivalent. Soon they had all dispersed, and Loud was left emptying his lungs at the ship's stern, fading slowly toward the drying skies and the Pacific beyond.

*

"Loud," she said. "I'm cold."

"I want to go home," he said. "Not Lyle's turret house. I want my home."

Aurora texted Lyle. She told him she was going over to Jeremy's house to play some music, inspired by the concert. She would be home late.

Then they walked. Over the Wishkah's cantilevered bascule. Past Walmart. Through the marshes. Past the steaming towers of Sierra Pacific. Through the groves of alder and cedar and spruce. They arrived at the old McCrowley place, sagging, but still standing, its single dormer staring blindly down at them.

Though the Chehalis had receded in the weeks since the gale, the waters had left the house's main floor dank. The house, with its gray, splintery clapboards, didn't have much to offer in the way of warmth. It felt colder inside. And Loud, despite the long, draining trek, seemed to become even more manic once indoors. He broke the only remaining chair. He rambled about things Aurora only half understood: Pappy Rue's neck tattoo, Grandma Gin's five-finger discounts, his mother running away on a rabbit, his father as a pile of sawdust, his father as a bundle of sticks, his body devoured by Ulmer Rhinehouse. Cobain's ghost and Billy Gohl's ghost telling him to leave the Harbor forever.

"Loud," she said, putting her hands on the cold shelf of his shoulders. "I want to help you. I'm not going to leave you. And I don't want you to leave me."

Loud stopped but shook his head.

"But I *need* to sleep," she said. "How can I help you calm down? So, we can sleep?" she said, her face turned up, and her body leaning into him.

Loud went over to his backpack and took out a pinch of silver-tipped marijuana wrapped in purple plastic. "This helps sometimes."

After they'd shaken out the moth-eaten remains of his sleeping bags and sheets, they lay down and smoked. He stopped talking, stopped shivering, stopped running. He got up and built a fire with the broken chair. He lay back down and breathed regularly. The room filled with the hot, drowsy incense of marijuana and smoke from the fire. There was only the mild scent of urine. She found the high comforting. Mild. Like the feeling she got after a big dinner just before going to sleep.

As Loud lay there, he took something out of his pocket. A piece of paper.

"What's that?" she asked.

"It's a bus ticket," he said, showing her the blue, skinny-dog logo. "Pappy Rue gave it to me. I've kept it in case I ever needed to peace-out in a flash."

"Too bad he didn't give you two," Aurora said. "But I'll never leave the Harbor."

"Me neither," Loud said.

But Aurora couldn't be sure. She wondered about the woman on the rabbit—Loud's mother. Wondered if she was more like Aurora's dad, distant and uninterested. Or more like Aurora herself, wishing Loud would come back to her.

Her questions knotted together. She lay in the morbid silence. She was suddenly cold again. She didn't know what words she could say to fill the silence or the hurt.

Her fingers resting on her bare stomach suddenly gave her goosebumps. They felt like someone else's fingers. She wanted them to be Loud's fingers. She turned and put his hands there. She took his head in her hands and put his head there. Then she kissed his big cheekbones. His brow. His sturdy wedge of a nose.

His face turned toward her, and they came together like they had before, their bodies pressing in slow pulses. But as he started to work his way into that slow, rowing rhythm of his, that rhythm that always put him to sleep and ended their closeness early, she put a hand on his bare chest and pushed him off her.

"What?" he asked.

"No. Not like that." She couldn't help smirk at him as he watched with big, dumb hound-eyes as she slipped off her skirt.

He rose above her, and she placed her hands on the tight canvass of skin over his ribs. She looked through the lumberjack he'd painted across his pecs, nipples for eyes. She looked through that cartoonish ax cutting toward her to that skin of his. She locked her jaw so that she wouldn't cry out. She kept her cries in so that he would not stop, would not pause to consider the pain he was causing her. She knew that would make him run. She clutched him with her arms, her legs— boots still on. She worked through that stretching pain filling her and pushing again, again, again so that she could get as close as she could to him—let all of him in and hold him steady against her until he was rocking slower, slower, then silent. Asleep, an innocent boy.

*

She woke up around ten the next morning. Loud brought her a couple of breakfast burritos; he'd purchased them from a nearby gas station with the last of his monthly food stamps. She shoved the food down without tasting it. She was cold. She was sore. She looked blankly at the warped, gray floors. Through the edges of the plywood boards nailed over the windows, a thin, steely light was coming in.

"I'm not a virgin anymore," she said.

"I'm sorry?" He winced.

She looked up in surprise. He was tranquil.

"You don't have to be sorry," she shook her head. "*If* you go to treatment."

OEDIPUS WEIRD

Though early March, there were already hints of spring. At their tips, the bare branches of the trees were blighted by hard green buds that looked more like a disease than the promise of blooms to come. For his English class's unit on Greek tragedies, students could choose one of three: Medea, Antigone, or Oedipus Rex. For Jeremy, the choice was painfully obvious.

It seemed like around every corner, Jeremy ran into Aurora and the re-emerged Loud hanging on each other in compromising positions looking like they'd always just made out or were about to. Outside Psychology class. On the stairs by the tennis courts. Jeremy felt like he'd fallen in love with a sixteen-year-old version of his mother, just so she could go out with a seventeen-year-old version of his stepdad, who'd asked him to keep quiet about his accidentally revealed underworld. Jeremy's mind started scratching at ways he could break them up.

Given what he knew about what Loud had been doing at the Morck, how hard would it be? But he tried to take a gentler, more rational approach. Jeremy had been trying to diagnose Loud using their Psych textbook. So, he tried to show Aurora some of the connections he'd found between Loud's behavior and DSM disorders.

"Does this *not* sound like Loud?" Jeremy asked her after reading the description of schizophrenia. "They could have just put his picture in here."

Or schizoaffective disorder. Jeremy read the description out loud to her, convinced it was a fit. Aurora gave him a pitying look. His face hovered over the book, his eyes glowing at the promise the textbook offered: to make sense of the insensible world, to direct his steps through the untenable maze of existence.

Aurora took a deep breath and let Jeremy have it. She was

trying to get Loud to go to treatment, but she didn't see how the textbook's generalities could help them care for him. All this science just took all of life's mystery out of the picture. Diagnoses just put people in boxes, which were meant to control them. She thought it was disturbing and sad how excited he was to 'figure out' his best friend. She saw it as a sign that Jeremy just wanted to control Loud.

Jeremy looked away from her. They worked on a class assignment for a few minutes. Then Jeremy turned back to her. "But don't we kind of want to control him a little? I mean, wouldn't it be great if he like, did schoolwork, didn't talk to himself, or didn't randomly scream about stuff that didn't make sense? Wouldn't it be great if he could be stable enough to do things he'd be good at—like, be in a band? And not hurt people close to him? Like his mom, whoever she is? Like you?"

The band thing again? Aurora wondered. Did he ever let go of anything?

"Those things are good for *you*," Aurora said, shaking Jeremy's arm. "You'd like him to be in a band with him so you could be famous and finally get your dad's attention. You'd like Loud to not be with me so…I don't know. So I could be alone. Like you."

Faced with the flash pan of her anger, all Jeremy could do was stammer.

"Sorry. A little harsh. But it's what I think," Aurora said.

"You guys okay?" Ms. Pickett asked them. When they nodded, Ms. Pickett sent them to separate parts of the room to finish their assignment.

They met at lunch, Jeremy's face ashen as she sat down.

"You're mad at me," Aurora said.

"I just thought we wanted the same thing," Jeremy said. "Don't you want Loud to get better?"

"*I* don't want to control him," Aurora continued. "I'm just trying to give him a place he'll feel safe—something he's almost never had."

"That's what I want for him too!"

"I want him to be himself."

Jeremy shook his head. "He doesn't know who he is."

"Yes, he does," Aurora said, curling her hair around her ears. "We've talked about it."

"We talked about it too! You think because you're doing stuff with him, you know him better than me? He and I talked for hours about being in a band. He talked all about how he wanted to make a scene here. But none of it was real because Loud is crazy."

Around them, their peers squealed about sitcoms, Facebook wars, getting wasted, having oral sex. Jeremy pressed on. "Loud needs real help. Like from a mental hospital."

"You'd feel better if he was locked up, wouldn't you?"

"*He* would be better off."

She shook her head.

"You'd be better off, too," Jeremy said. "I have to tell you something."

"What?"

Jeremy's hands shook just like they had before blowing up the toilet. Fuck it. She was asking for it. "I know where Loud went."

Lunch was almost over. Kids were shoving stuff into their backpacks. Abandoning their ketchup-and-crumb-blighted tables. The hectic air made Aurora feel even more like she was being squeezed. Squeezed tightly by a tyrannical feeling that had no regard for her.

"Where?" she asked with her eyes closed.

"Loud was at the Morck," Jeremy said.

"The Morck?"

"Doing drugs. And…other stuff… With other people."

She saw the slightest of smirks creep across his face. Why was he enjoying this? Was it because he wanted her? Or wanted Loud? Or wanted everybody to stay alone like he was?

The bell rang. Kids started moving in big, bison-like herds out of the cafeteria.

"O...kay. How long have you known about this?" she asked.

"Since the day he left..."

"And you kept it from me?"

"He threatened to kill me if I told you. I was chickenshit, I admit it. But I can't keep it in anymore. He can off me for all I care."

She was shaking her head and looking up, trying to keep the tears in, and failing.

The warning bell for class rang. Jeremy stood up like he'd just completed an assignment, ready to sally on to the next one. An obedient little schoolboy.

He was squeezing her, Aurora thought. Trying to squeeze her free from the love she felt for Loud, trying to manhandle it out of her like a toy she'd swallowed, as if she were a little girl. And why? Not so he could be free to be with her. Which would have been bad enough. But so Aurora could be empty, just like he was.

She grabbed his hands. "I want you to stop," she said.

"Stop what?"

"Whatever it is you're doing. Loud... He's one of this life's great mysteries." She looked off into space. "You can laugh at me all you want. I agree he needs meds, but if you knew what I know, not just what's in your textbook, you'd know medication's only going to get Loud so far. You can't 'cure' away mystery. The only way to respond is with love. And I'm going to keep loving him in all the ways I can, in all the ways you can't. I'm sorry you can't.

But someone has to. And that's me. I know that's hard for you to accept. For whatever reason. Probably because you want me to go back to being your little tomboy friend or whatever. The whole town probably wants that. But I'm not what everybody thinks. I *love* him, Jeremy. And you need to deal with it."

*

That night, Jeremy strummed his guitar in his living room, looking at the *Starry Night* print. What the hell was that thing? The extra-terrestrial tree-shaped flame took up the whole damn painting. The black flame's tendrils floated witchy like an aquatic plant, dwarfing the pale steeple in the middle distance. Loud McCrowley superimposed over Aurora's body was all Jeremy could see or think about.

His phone buzzed. It was her. He picked up on the first ring. No point hiding how pathetic he was now.

"You were right about him being at the Morck" Aurora said. "He admitted as much."

Jeremy set his guitar on its stand, not expecting the conciliatory tone.

She said that Loud didn't remember threatening him and wasn't mad at him. "I know you're just trying to protect me," Aurora said. "Which is sweet. A little weird. But sweet."

Weird should be my last name, Jeremy thought, looking at the painting some more. Jeremy Weird.

Aurora explained that Loud's straying wasn't all-out betrayal because they hadn't been official yet. She hadn't fully opened herself up to him at that point, plus Loud felt she had betrayed him first by trying to dump him off at the hospital. He had reacted badly, no doubt. He had bad habits. But he was agreeing to give them up for her.

"And you believe him?" Jeremy asked.

"He's agreed to go to treatment."

Jeremy raised his eyebrows.

"And that's part of the reason I'm calling. I don't know

where to go. Or who to ask. I mean, other than trying the hospital again. Or DSHS. But I'm worried he'll freak out if we try to go there."

Jeremy gave her the name and contact for Dr. Leann Paul, the psychiatrist at Evergreen Mental Health Services his mom had tried to force Loud to go to. Aurora thanked him. He told her about how Loud reminded him of the dark flame in the middle of *Starry Night*.

"Is that what you'd wanted to tell me about the painting?" she asked.

"No," Jeremy said. "That…that was something different."

"The black flame is a tree, Jeremy," Aurora said. "It's just a tree."

"Yeah?" Jeremy cocked his head at the painting. "Then, I'm the little white steeple."

*

The weeks passed. Unsurprisingly, Charlotte bought Jeremy a car—the Tercel. Charlotte rode shotgun beside him while he got all his permit practice hours, which helped her work less. They took turns at the radio, talking about music.

Aurora was right about one thing. Loud didn't follow through on his threat to kill Jeremy. When Loud re-appeared in English class, he just went on not talking to him or anyone else.

In Psychology, Jeremy read the entry in the textbook for borderline personality disorder. He took a picture of the page with his phone to read later. They were starting a video about dementia that he'd have to take notes on. "I hope this one's more interesting than the one about the narcoleptic dachshund," Jeremy griped to Aurora.

"Yeah, especially since I've seen a lot of old people with the opposite of two minute sleeping spells. Like, they are sometimes spontaneously awake for two minutes."

At least Aurora was still his friend. She wouldn't listen to any more of his pet diagnoses of Loud, though. And she continued to wear distractingly revealing clothing, which made it harder for Jeremy to look at her platonically. She kept coming over to him in Psychology, always approaching him first, which wasn't hard because he was always early, and she was usually ten, fifteen, twenty minutes late.

Schoolgirl skirt with a white, backless crop top; black choker. Skintight, high waist jeans, plunge-neck, rose-print blouse. Each new outfit was like a blow to Jeremy's testicles. He passed whole class periods with almost nonstop erections. They were so fierce he stopped wearing skinny jeans. And after each class when the bell rang, there Loud would be, leaning against the opposite hallway wall, glance askew. Aurora would march right out to him as if wanting to make sure Loud left with her and not someone else. And Jeremy would be left in class, standing up slowly, his balls blue and aching like they were bungee-corded to an anvil.

Jeremy knew it wasn't all fun and games for Aurora. As the outfits grew tighter and more revealing as the days and weeks lengthened, and the temperature rose, Aurora seemed to get paler. Her face became more despondent. The lines under her eyes purpled. She got skinnier. The bumps on her spine and her ribs became more pronounced.

"Do you *want* to look like this?" Jeremy asked.

"What do you think?"

"Stupid question," he said.

"Do you…" she began, touching her black lipstick. "What do you think I look like?"

"I think you look pretty."

"Hmm," she said, sounding pleased. "I think I look dead."

"Pretty and dead," Jeremy confirmed.

"I'm trying to hold his attention," she said, touching his arm.

Jeremy hated it when she touched his arm. He loved it when she touched his arm. His diaphragm rose into his throat like he'd been in a car that had just soared over a bump in the road.

"It's not working," Aurora confessed. "He's drifting away. I feel like he could leave any minute. He has a Greyhound ticket. He could."

"Yeah," Jeremy said, biting his tongue. "That'd be…terrible."

"Yeah," she said. "I can't let him. I just can't. He can't become just some other…"

She trailed off.

Jeremy would get home from a shift volunteer marketing for *The Harbor Herald*—The Rejection Factory. He'd fling his stuff down, eat a Hot Pocket, and start plowing his way through the vicissitudes of Oedipus, collecting quotes for the upcoming five-paragraph essay. School offered what it always had—a lonely pursuit that, no matter how tedious, was orderly and accomplishable, unlike love and relationships and, apparently, work.

Then his phone would ring. He wouldn't need to look at the number. He wouldn't have to think about whether to answer or not, even though talking to her was like having a beautifully wrought knife dragged slowly across the wrists.

"What are you doing right now?" Aurora asked.

Jeremy switched ears. "Reading *Oedipus Rex*. Why?"

"I don't know. I just need to stay awake. So, I can watch him. He's out on the lawn doing his thing, and who knows how long he'll be out there. I don't want him to run off. So, can you just talk to me?"

"You sound like you're talking about a dog. Not your boyfriend."

"FML, right?"

The next thing Jeremy knew, an hour had passed, and they

were still talking. About bands, her love of old people, and books. "Okay," Jeremy yawned. "I have to get some shit done for real. This essay is not going to write itself."

"Okay, but you have to help me get him to come inside." She laughed.

"I don't fucking know. Shoot him with a tranquilizer dart," Jeremy said.

"You're so not helpful."

"So, don't call me."

"Please! Cal won't even answer me."

Cal? She'd tried calling *Cal*, that big, football-playing ox? Having her call and talk about Loud all night was bad. But her not calling at all?

"Jeremy!" Aurora said.

"Okay. Go tell Lyle to yell at him."

"Lyle's at some big meeting with the Chinooks. Otherwise, he would have a long time ago!"

"Tell him the neighbors called the cops."

"I'm not doing that. Could you…Could you come over? And help me get him inside? Please."

"He threatened to kill me, Aurora."

"He doesn't remember that. Please?"

Jeremy drove himself over to Aurora's. In back of Aurora's turret house, Loud was performing a deranged version of hopscotch across the prayer labyrinth. Jeremy tried to talk to Loud, but he could tell his friend was somewhere else. On another plane. The incarnate definition of 'far out'. So, Jeremy put one of his Conversed feet forward and began to walk the labyrinth. As he followed the curving stones, Loud would jump in front of him and make a face. At first Jeremy demurred until Loud jumped away. Then, he started pushing him playfully. Loud would laugh and hopscotch across the lines while Jeremy followed the stone path obediently in their reliable curving in and out. Midway through, Jeremy felt Aurora's hand in his and they walked together, Loud pouncing playfully in front of them. They'd push and pull at each other, laughing, until Loud would bound away.

The sun found the three in the center, collapsed in a heap, half asleep on the dewy ground.

*

Soon it was April. The crocuses petalled apart, and the trillium drooped, flowering red currant, Oregon grape, and salmonberry blooms taking their place. Still, the sky was often the color of concrete, feeling just as cold, heavy, and gray. In Psych class, though, the air crackled with a Friday's excitement over Spring Break.

While Ms. Pickett graded their finals and kids left for prolonged bathroom breaks, another PBS documentary droned on about the overprescribing of Ritalin for ADHD and, more recently, Adderall.

"Adderall," Jeremy repeated. "Adderall. Why does that sound familiar?"

The video broke the drug down into its chemical components, which include salts and stimulants. Jeremy turned to Aurora, "Do you remember that song he made up, 'Magic Lunch.'"

"Yes!" she gripped his arm.

"Add her all… Add her all… Adderall," Jeremy said.

"He was talking about his grandparents…."

"Feeding him bath salts," Jeremy completed her thought.

The flickering light from the video ran around the dark frames of their glasses. Jeremy realized that he and Aurora were two in a long line of neighbors that had tried to care for Malachi "Loud" McCrowley, who, in the meantime, made up myths about his past and present while rambling into his future.

They spent the rest of class in silence. Their peers passed notes, whispered about parties, and texted their friends, the class's content purely academic for them. The bell rang, and they fled.

Aurora didn't run out to Loud. He wasn't there.

Aurora turned to Jeremy. "The psychiatrist won't meet with him because he doesn't have insurance. So, he's been going to Ms. Ambaum, here at school. But…it's not working. He wouldn't sign the release, so she can't talk to me about him. He's still talking about more ghosts and about his dad and other stuff. And now I've got to get through a whole Spring Break with him and nothing to do."

Jeremy looked at the Psych textbook, then up at her. "He needs meds. The last thing he wants. But that's what he needs. And I mean, meds. Not pot… I can smell it on you, BTW."

Aurora blinked and ran a loose strand of hair behind her ear. "O…kay. Well, it calms him down. It calms me down too."

"Wow," Jeremy said.

"Don't judge me."

"Wouldn't *you* judge me?"

"No. I'm not a cop's kid."

Loud appeared in the doorway of the classroom. He was looking at the floor and smelling his hands. Aurora got up and walked off. "Call me if you think of anything helpful. I'm getting really, really tired of keeping this up."

She pushed past Loud as if ignoring him. Loud looked at her ass and loped after her with a grin on his face.

Jeremy felt that familiar twist in his stomach. Mingled with his jealousy, there was a new feeling of disgust. He despised the missionary element: the white girl trying to save the Native dude. Had that *ever* worked? He grimaced. Was that why it was called the missionary position? Because both would just end up getting fucked?

Aurora called that night around one a.m. "Sorry to call you," she said.

"Is he okay with you calling me so much?"

"He's out again," Aurora said. "I don't know where he is. Anyway, I don't think he knows I call you. He doesn't really seem to care about what I do too much. Or what anyone else does."

Jeremy shook his head. "Why don't you change the locks and call it quits with him? You did your best."

"I can't. He's been kicked out of everywhere else. And if I kick him out, he'll leave the Harbor."

"All the more reason to! You, me, everybody. We would be better off without him."

"You can't mean that," Aurora said.

"I do."

"He's your *best* friend," Aurora said.

"He's not acting like it. He hasn't actually talked to me in like two months. And he's hurting somebody I care about," Jeremy said. "I'm done with him. I wish you'd be done with him too!"

"I'm not going to do that. You don't understand. I've gone too far in to do that. Doing that would mean I wouldn't get back anything of what I've put into him. I wish you would just accept that."

"Well, I can't."

"Don't be angry," she cried. "I don't want him to leave. I don't want anyone to leave. Or die. I just want us all to be together."

Jeremy writhed, reminded of things Charlotte would say about Keith.

"Have you thought of anything else?" Her tone became flat. "Any way to help?"

Jeremy picked up his Psych textbook, heavily dog-eared and highlighted. He had started taking it home, though he wasn't supposed to. With Aurora still in his ear, he flipped through the pages, tearing one or two corners out of sheer rage. Why would she think he would want to spend the first night of Spring Break trying to cure her incurable boyfriend, his former best friend? Why didn't she get that he would rather cuddle up with her and watch a movie and talk to her about something else? Anything else! He flipped to the Abnormal Psychology section. Were it a witch's spell book, he would have read her a spell to make Loud disappear and leave them alone. He turned to the next best thing: the psychopharm section.

"Do you still see those old people?" Jeremy asked.

"Yeah," she said.

Antipsychotic medications, Jeremy had read, were also often prescribed for dementia. He started reading her the names of the drugs.

"How am I going to get ahold of them?" Aurora asked.

"With all those old heads-on-meds, are they really going to miss a stray bottle or two?"

BATH SALT HEART BREAK

Aurora had been volunteering with the elderly again, thanks mostly to Uncle Lyle's efforts to get her out of the house and away from Loud.

Uncle Lyle had done a good job hiding his distress when she'd brought Loud back in. He fixed them a big dinner and toasted Loud's return. But since, Lyle had become quite a nuisance. Since Lyle had quit his job at Rhinehouse and was home all the time, he used every opportunity to insert himself in their activities. Did they want to go with him down to the Museum of History? Did they want to go to a Duke Ellington tribute concert in Tacoma? The answers were obvious: no and no!

One morning, Lyle came to get Aurora up for breakfast, only to find Loud asleep with her in bed. Loud was fully clothed, but pillow marks were etched into his face.

It was as close to Lyle being through the roof as Aurora had ever seen him.

"It is absolutely unacceptable for you to lay with my niece in her bed under my roof, young man," Uncle Lyle chided at the breakfast table. "And it's a bit presumptuous of you to talk to *me* about minding *my* own business when all this is in *my* house which I am opening to you out of charity. That's what this is. Make no mistake. And my charity demands gratitude and respect, which means you do as I ask!"

In the face of Lyle's assertions, Loud could either walk away or accede. Aurora's eyes going big and pleading, told him to do the latter.

"Okay," Loud said.

"So it won't happen again?" Lyle asked.

"No," Aurora said and kicked Loud under the table.

"No," Loud echoed mechanically.

"Good. Because next time something like that occurs, I will start charging you rent," Lyle said, wiping his mouth and bustling away from the table.

But after that, of course, Loud started spending more time away—at his grandparents' abandoned house in the sloughs, at Whistle Punk Falls, and covert locales Aurora wasn't privy to.

A few days later, Lyle called her into his study for a sit-down. He felt she was becoming too attached to Loud. The relationship, though well-intended on her part, was having a negative effect on her. Look at her grades plummeting. Her extracurriculars dwindling. Take volunteering, for instance. The volunteer coordinator from Think-of-Me-Hill Retirement Community called and said she hadn't seen Aurora in over a week. True, Lyle hadn't thought it the most practical thing to do with her time, but *she* enjoyed it. Before Loud came along.

So, Aurora renewed her shifts, volunteering twice a week after school and on Saturdays. She started with her same old stations, doing crafts in the activity room, and leading Bingo games in the cafeteria. Soon she started asking to help with the more difficult residents: those less able-bodied, those who were more combative. Those that rarely came out of their rooms. She'd said she wanted this to have hands-on learning that paralleled her psychology class, that would prepare her for social work, a field she was considering studying.

Then Jeremy gave her that list of antipsychotics.

The first day of Spring Break, Aurora found herself on the first floor sitting next to a bed-ridden resident named Rufus. His room was like many of the patient suites. It was a mishmash of elderly living space and hospital room: a corner coffee table with a Bible, a musty-smelling chair, pictures of his family, bare linoleum floor, fluorescent lights, the omnipresent smell of sterilizer. The hospital bed the man was laying on seemed much more poised for movement than he was— its headboard straight, the foot of the bed cupped slightly upward. The bed seemed primed to swallow the old man's body the moment he gave up the ghost.

Rufus wore bifocals and a flannel shirt and sat on his hospital bed, watching television. Aurora sat next to him.

Aurora asked Rufus if she could look at his pictures on the wall.

He looked at her, and his mouth moved, but he did not speak.

Aurora got up and saw pictures of Rufus standing next to a woman with a white cottontail of hair, outside a familiar house with a single dormer window, surrounded by cedar trees. Then, a framed photo of a brown-skinned boy with a big chin and heavy brows—a space between his teeth as he smiled slyly.

"Ginny," Rufus said, voice struggling through what sounded like a swamp of mucus. "Where's our boy? What happened? What happened to him out there? At the mill…In the trees… In the city. Where is he?"

Aurora looked at him: his fine hair, his broad, age-swollen nose, and the tattoo of a Chinook salmon on his neck. He was reaching for her, arm trembling from the effort as if he were a shipwreck survivor reaching for the beach.

"What happened to our boy?" he asked again, this time with an edge of irritation.

"I'm Aurora," she said. "I'm just a volunteer here, Mr…Mr. McCrowley."

Rufus McCrowley waved her off and turned back to the TV.

Aurora had been told by the floor manager that Rufus had arrived two years prior but had declined precipitously since. At first, he'd lived with his wife on the third floor—a less-restricted wing. But the wife had been strange and had taken off one day on an outing to Olympia. She'd never returned. Alone, Rufus's dementia ramped up. He stopped leaving his room or speaking to others. So, management transferred him to the first floor. Occasionally, he'd blurt out something about his son who'd been killed in a logging or milling accident. He couldn't remember which. Other times, he'd call out for his estranged grandson.

Aurora returned to her seat by the old man and held his hand. Rufus held back reflexively. But when she looked over, he was crying.

A nurse walked in and asked how they were doing.

"Okay," Aurora said.

"It's sad sometimes, huh?" the nurse said. She turned to Rufus, "Now Rufus, time for your meds!"

The nurse took out a pill bottle from her apron and filled up a glass of water from a sink by the door. She wrote something on a whiteboard chart that hung above it. She was about to open the pill bottle when a scream erupted from down the hall.

"Get the fuck away from me! Get away from me," a voice bellowed. A fount of racial slurs followed, sounding the way a ruptured sewer line smells.

The nurse set the pill bottle on the counter and ran out to assist.

Aurora went over to the pill bottle. She looked at the label. *Depakote.*

Aurora heard Jeremy's voice say the word. It would do. She put the full pill bottle in her pocket and, by way of the exit stairwell, walked out of Think-of-Me-Hill Retirement Community for the last time.

*

Driving Lyle's old stake-body truck, Aurora got to Sierra Pacific's Mill and parked in its oversized lot, knowing nobody would tow it. Then she walked past the tickings and wheezings of the mill machines toward Rufus McCrowley's old house, where his grandson was currently squatting. Loud had texted her that since the weather wasn't bad, he wanted to spend Spring break with her there. They could scout around the sloughs. Visit Whistle Punk Falls. See what the ghosts thought. It was all starting to sound less fun to her and more like hell.

On the drive over, with the pill bottle rattling in her pocket, Aurora tried not to think about the consequences for what she'd done. Jeremy's mom flashed in her mind, blazer lapel pulled back to reveal her glaring badge. Aurora tried not to think about the nearness of Loud's grandfather or about what had happened to his beloved grandmother. Had she gone off looking for him? Aurora tried not to wonder. She had a more immediate concern. The big, pink pills.

As Aurora walked, the saliva in her throat thickened. She was walking with a backpack of groceries she'd picked up at Walmart on the way over. With each step, the straps of her backpack dug deeper into her shoulders.

She entered the cedar grove. There was a hint of wood burning slowly somewhere. The spring sky was a pale blue plate swirled with white, wispy clouds—a beautiful lid that covered them inside the observatory of sadness that the world seemed to be. The robins moved their auburn bellies swiftly and silently away from the gray, rotting house in the middle of the grove, from which a wild-eyed figure was fleeing.

"And you can keep your momma bike, you loon!"

A fat girl with dirty blond hair was blundering through the knee-high grass. She struggled to keep her sagging sweatpants from falling off her. Her massive, bra-less cleavage flopped in and out of her teeny white tank top.

"Well, well. If it isn't Ki's good girl? What's wrong? Hey,

you're *cute!*"

To Aurora's horror, the girl gave her a chuck on the chin.

Aurora jumped back. "Don't touch me...."

"What? Can't have a poor girl touch you, rich bitch-from-the-hill?"

"No...Just... Don't touch me. What did you do to him?"

"What did *I* do to him? Ha!" She threw her head back. "He's fucking crazy. You know that, right, rich bitch? Fucking crazy! Him and his 'ghosts.' I want me some real drugs after dealing with that one. You're his *only* bitch now cuz I'm done. I don't care how pretty he is. Jesus!" She walked out of the woods, waving her hands in the air as if trying to dry-shake them clean of something sticky.

Aurora's eyes centered on the discarded green trail bike on the porch, the derelict house's half-opened door, the darkness inside, and the ghosts that the darkness held. She walked ahead.

Loud was by the fireplace, looking into a fire's fading embers. He was completely naked and wore that wind-blown expression: brows together, mouth half-open. When he heard her footsteps, he looked at her with an unabashed smile. The smile faded quickly, his face mirroring the apprehension he saw on her face.

"I didn't do anything with her," he said, palms out as if Aurora was going to strike him.

"Then why was she here?" Aurora asked, arms akimbo.

"She followed me here. I told her I was done. That I only have one girl now..."

He stood up and placed his shaky hands on Aurora's arms. He kissed her cheeks. He kissed her on her lips—the slow and soft boyfriend kisses she'd gotten from him before they'd started having sex, the delicious and forbidden ones they'd first shared in her bed in Lyle's Victorian farmhouse. The kisses that led to nothing except dreams.

In the wet, warm darkness—her closed eyes, his open

mouth— she imagined for the first time, making Uncle Lyle's big turret house hers. Grandpa and Grandma McCrowley were sitting on the porch while Uncle Lyle served them tea and recorded their stories while jazz hummed from a radio. The garage was cleared and made into a studio with rugs and bright soundproofing and tapestries of alternative rock saints. She kept a steady beat for Loud to sing and dance to while Jeremy slid in his guitar licks. They would form a band after all and play shows at the D&R. Up the driveway, Cal was pulling in with Lyle's truck full of freshly cut beams from the lumber yard, and her father was in the backyard studying plans to build the McCrowleys a cottage. They were all together. And the grain silos and the warehouses and the empty lumberyards were not there. And the flat, smog-clogged river was not there.

Aurora felt the drag of Loud's cock up her pants. She pushed onto him, and they sank onto their tangle of sleeping bags and dirty sheets. He let her put him in, the only way she could do it without it feeling like a spear-thrust through her middle. Then she stroked her body along his like a swimmer, her eyes closed, trying to fight her way back to that vision of belonging. But her eyes opened in flashes, and through those small cracks of light, she would see Loud looking away from her, into the quiet fire, his mouth moving absently.

Afterward, Loud said he was hungry.

"I brought just the thing," Aurora said.

*

Before Aurora had showed up, Loud had been trying to catch a few winks in the dank, hollowed-out living room. Then Karla Potts barged in.

"Oh. My. God. You're naked. Put some clothes on!"

"How did you find me?" Loud asked.

"What a way to treat me. I was bringing you your momma's

bike back." But Karla demanded money. For the weed. For her court fees. Leaving her to get picked up by the cops! What kind of man was he? And the bike was a nice ride and all, but she wasn't stupid or made of cash. No, they weren't even. He never even got her off. She needed money or Larry was going to kick her out of her room at the 'Underbird. This time for real. The storm last November had shaken him up. He'd gotten off smack and was shaping up, which meant she had to get out. She started going through Loud's backpack and clothes.

"Sixteen dollars," Karla shouted at Loud. "That's it? Are you fucking serious?" She waved her arms, showing her sagging breasts and sand-dollar-sized nipples.

Karla left, Aurora walked in, and Loud did what he thought she wanted. He took her to that warm, hot place—a place he liked okay because he could let some of it out, but was otherwise uncomfortable in, mostly because Cobain always watched, shrugging at their panting, pushing, sighing. And now Gohl was there too! Though, to Loud's surprise, he turned his back on their display. Loud would see Aurora's face twist in what looked like pain, yet she dug her fingers into his back and wrapped her feet around his legs, and laid there until he couldn't take the hot, sticky pressing anymore and would squirm free. Like always, she was quiet and sad afterward.

Cobain's ghost stirred. *What does she want?*

It was a good question. Loud didn't want to hurt her. He said it to himself over and over and over again. Don't hurt her. Don't abuse the hookup.

Cobain pressed up against him. Loud had already hurt her, already drawn blood. Blood didn't wash out. And she was using that as a reason to suck him into her womb. Another womb! No breathing holes. Umbilical cord thick as a Bible wrapped around your throat. *Everyone dies alone, together, unhappily ever after, the end,* Cobain's ghost whispered. *Or she'll just leave you. Like your mom.*

Aurora had been mothering him a lot. *Have you showered? Have you gone to your counselor? Have you tried talking to Jeremy again? Have you, have you, have you???*

You wouldn't let Leah Ledbetter do this to you. Why are you letting this chick? Cobain asked. *Cuz she lets you have sex with her? Really? Why not just find a hole? A hole isn't going to mother you to death.*

"But she hasn't left me," Loud yelled. Aurora was in the next room, making him a bowl of Letter Betters. She was shaking up the box.

"What?" she called.

"Nothing. Just, just… You know. The ghosts get squirrely at this hour."

"O…kay," she said and kept shaking up the box for some reason. A lot. Guess she wanted to make sure the marshmallows were evenly mixed in and not all at the bottom. She was so great. Nicer than his mom had ever been. Nicer than his dad even.

"She hasn't left me," Loud said again. "She hasn't kicked me out. She hasn't tried to bath-salt-and-pepper me."

The ghost rolled his maggot eyes and shook the greasy hair that fell over his face. *She wanted to take you to a shrink! And you* know *what they would have done. It would have been back to bath salt breakfasts! And bye-bye to Loud's brain.*

"But I hate my brain," Loud said.

She does too, Cobain scoffed just as Aurora gave him a bowl of Letter Betters.

Loud looked down at it. The puffy-grained cereal and crispy marshmallows floating in the milk swirled and spelled out a message from Cobain that Loud more felt than read:

She probably just likes you for your skin. It's what she isn't. She wants to have it. All wrapped up inside her. But when her back gets sore, and she starts wanting money, she'll spit you out and leave you. When love leaves, it don't come back.

Loud slurped up big spoonfuls of cereal. Aurora was watching him. She said it was too sweet for her. She'd already eaten. He kept eating, avoiding her gaze by staring at the bowl's universe of bobbing red hearts, golden horseshoes, and rainbows, on the other side of which was the image of Loud's dad and him eating this same cereal after felling trees all day Orange shooting stars. Green clovers…. Hard, pink chunks???

Loud paused before dipping his spoon in again. He turned the spoon up. The pink chunks, like bits of an eggshell, ran down the spoon. His hand started shaking. He ran a fingertip over the stainless steel and scooped up a few of the pink bits. He put it on his tongue and in his teeth. Crunchy. Bitter. Bath salts.

Loud threw the bowl against the wall. "You're feeding me bath salts!"

"No!" she shouted.

Loud ran into the kitchen.

"I'm trying to take care of you!"

The ghosts roared.

Aurora tried to grab him, but he threw her down. He picked up the Letter Betters box and shook it out onto the floor. The sunlight creeping in through the half-open door caught on the crushed pills sprinkled amid the letters.

Loud buried his face in the crook of his elbow and sobbed as he started shoving clothes into his backpack. Aurora was pleading, she was crying, she was pulling on his arm, but he wasn't listening anymore. He shouted at her. He wasn't going to go into her womb. He wasn't going to be her good little Indian boy and go pee where she said he needed to go pee and go to Indian reeducation with the counselor twice a week. She'd been mothering him enough, and Loud did not have a mom, nor did he want one. She was racist and weird, and he wanted her to leave him the fuck alone.

Gohl's ghost was shaking his head and struggling to rip himself out of his bonds.

Round and round, little monkey-do, Cobain said. *That's all it is here. Better get clear.*

Loud put on his vest and went for the door, but Aurora caught him on the arm's loophole. She tugged with her whole body so that he almost fell over. But he wiggled his arms out of the vest loops, sending her and his vest to the ground. He walked out into the light, Greyhound bus ticket in hand. He pedaled off on his bike and didn't look back.

BLUE RAVE

Jeremy's search for Loud in Rat City dead-ends when he rounds a street corner and gets stuck up by some dude in a pair of Oakley's wielding a Bowie knife. The thief robs him of his wallet and whatever shred of urgency that he had left for finding Loud. At least the asshole let him keep his bus ticket. Shaking, pulse still racing, Jeremy boards a Metro back to Seattle's downtown.

Going back to the colonnade is a form of giving up. Somehow the fatigue he feels after a day of fruitless searching converts his anger at Loud into guilt. The pillars of the I-5 colonnade are Leviathan ribs trapping Jeremy in, the same way his guilt does over letting Aurora try to save Loud all on her own. Sure, her methods were self-debasing, but she tried. Jeremy isolated, wallowed in unrequited love's self-loathing, and, in his absence, she tangled herself up in the swamp of Loud's psyche. Then Jeremy gave her the idea about the meds—a spark that raged into a conflagration they were still getting burned by, each of them, alone. Aurora is probably flinging her unwashed body around in her bed in Lyle's turret house; Loud is tucked away in an inscrutable orifice somewhere in this city. Both lost to him.

He thinks on what Aurora said about Van Gogh's Starry Night. About how what he thought was a black flame was just a tree. She was right and wrong, Jeremy thinks. He's done some reading about it since. It was a Cypress tree. They were all around the region Van Gogh had been painting in. But she was wrong that it was just a tree. The thing that made it special was the artist who painted it. An artist lost to the world because nobody understood him. The same way Loud is lost. Only with Loud it's way worse because, unlike Van Gogh who we all get to know because of the great art he left us, Loud will never get to become an artist, because he's gotten lost too soon. Because his friends were too stupid to get him help sooner.

Jeremy kneels at the base of a blue light that clicked on between two ratty palm trees. Street kids, many of the same ones from earlier gather around. They set up speakers and stage lights. They ignore Jeremy for the most part, as do the pit bulls, rats, and ferrets they keep as pets. Then the brother with the tuxedo shirt and bone through his nose shows up.

"Name's Kenyon. Glad you came. How'd you hear about it? The travelers. Yup. They're good for that. They know what's on the down-low. Didn't find Link-nut? Yeah, I could tell. Well, hey, how about a little pick-me-up? Take this little wonder. Blue Mercedes, man! I know you've got those X's on your knuckles and that you 'don't do drugs.' Yeah, we all tell the normie staff that. It just keeps things simpler and lets them do their jobs and live their normie lives. There you go, down the hatch. In a half-hour, you'll be feeling pretty good and can forget about Link-nut. What's the story with you guys, anyway? You in love with him or somethin'? You from out in the boonies too? Out where they'd lynch a brother. Haha. Don't feel like talking? I respect that. If you asked 'bout me and my past, I'd tell you to go fuck yourself. Yeah. Well, I want to explain a few things before the bass gets cranking. It's dubstep. You're going to love it! Anyway, I can tell this is your first rave. Raves are about family. This is my family. Doily's my street daughter over there. Hopvine's my street son. Stacy's my street wife. Hey, baby! Feelin' good? Lookin' good. Yeah. Show me some sugar. Mmmwahh! And the rest are all my grandchillun. We like to chill, don't we chillun? Yes, you all my street chillun. Anyway, we're the Edgy family. Unlike you, we can't just go back home, see. So, yeah. Parents be trippin', wiggin', tweakin', or, even worse, Bible thumpin'! So, we can boo-hoo and be depressed and do heroin. Or… make a new family. So, that's what we did. I made them all my family one night by giving them what I gave you. Now, you my street son too. Which is why I want you to know all this. We live by PLUR: peace, love, unity, and respect. It's plur-fect. You see, my son, it's not just about drugs. Anybody who tells you it's all about the drugs is a normie idiot. We look out for each other. We'll look out for you too and make sure you have a boss night."

The music gets louder than a helicopter landing. It's a frenetic mix of bass, beats, and synth that sends the kids into a collective frisson. They wiggle, jostle, butt-pop, and grind against each other with the changing time signatures and the stomping uproar. The two tattered palm trees sway above. Meanwhile, Jeremy's vision churns. The music grows louder and the lights brighter, making him wince and bowl over. He gropes through the dancers and the blue light.

The music pitches, and through throbbing eyes, Jeremy sees Loud's face. The face is the same raisin of pain he'd seen that night on the beach. He reaches out to touch it. It becomes the annoyed face of the heavy-set girl with the far-off stare and furry-eared hat. Jeremy sees Loud's face again. It becomes the annoyed face of Stacy. Jeremy sees Loud's face another time. Just as he reaches for the face, it becomes the dude with the baby-blue beads covering up the cuts on his wrist. *Are you okay, bro?* Loud's face flashes over all their faces. The face arches and screams, *Stay away!!!*

Jeremy falls in a cloud of clay-colored dust. He sees a sky of hands and beyond them, the concrete beams of the freeway. His ears throb from the pulsing bass and manic shouts. His limbs go gelatinous; he feels stuck to the ground like a beached jellyfish. He is alone and wants to hold someone's hand.

The earth feels like it is moving beneath him and Jeremy's pulse yammers on with the music's hypnotic *hump hump hump.*

The dubstep drops into his head, and the faces of the ravers return as demons. Is this what it's like to be Loud? Jeremy closes his eyes, trying to be invisible, and only then does his skin stop crawling. When he opens his eyes, the demon-faced ravers swirl in a cabal, and his heart pounds in his chest like something buried alive. He closes his eyes. Calm. He opens his eyes. Hell.

"Sweet Nothings," he says in a daze. "Sweet nothing. Sweet, nothing. Jeremy Sweet is nothing."

PART THREE

Dear Malachi,

This will be my last letter for a while because I know what to do now.
Uncle Philip's been helping me. He finally retired. Heart attacks can
really reset a guy's priorities, I guess. He wants to be the uncle to you
he started out as, carving your headboard and everything.

You can be mad at me all you want. But I don't want you to be
mad at your Makah family. Especially not Uncle Philip. Trust me, I've
had my seasons being mad at him. But there's no point.

When things were okay and I was tending bar and sober, I
thought about asking Uncle Philip to come down to do some Native
things with us. Carve a canoe. Teach you some of our songs. Not that
you would have wanted to. Even as a toddler, you were stubborn. With
pretty particular ideas about what you wanted to do and didn't want
to do. Like your momma. Only with you, it was whatever Grandma Gin
wanted to do. Which makes sense, I guess, because she was the one
your dad took after most.

But anywho, I never did ask Philip to come down. I always felt
like Native ways and Aberdeen ways would be like oil and water. The
two just didn't belong together and I didn't want to rock the boat.
Your grandpa with all his military and union stuff...I assumed he'd
think it was all a bunch of nonsense. And your dad always got skittish
when I'd talk about my culture. Like I was talking about something
that wasn't for him. Like he had an allergy to it. Also, whenever I
could get Philip on the phone, he always sounded so tired. Of course,
there was his own family, which he's always put first. Then that job of
his. I could almost see him taking off and cleaning his bifocals, telling
me about the thieves stealing our salal for floral bouquets, about the

sneaky timber contractors cutting too much, about the kids getting carried away with drugs in the woods, the meth labs exploding and causing fires up in the hills. All of which it was his job to manage.

We Ledbetters have always been like our name: heavy. Land-lubbers. Watching from the hills as the whalers paddled off on their hunts. We cared for the trees, we built and cared for the longhouses, and carved the canoes. Or so the stories go. And so, your uncle was just being a good Ledbetter boy, the way he always was.

Growing up was not easy. Your grandfather was born early. Or had his family too late. However you want to say it. He was almost sixty when he had me, his youngest. Anywho, he got sent off to one of the boarding schools: Chemewa, all the way down in Oregon. And they messed him up real good. If that wasn't enough, he went off to WW2. Met and married my mom, your grandmother from the Quinault tribe, when she was working down there at the army base. But when he came back, he was a different man.

He could not hear us, his babies, cry. I heard my mother say it over and over again. It wasn't his fault. At the boarding school, he'd hear the children of our people crying and, especially after the war, he heard them crying all the time inside his head. Our cries—even whimpers—would trigger him. He tried to drown out the cries by boozing. What else? But it didn't work. It just made him stupid, clumsy, impatient. But his nature was so sweet. He never lifted a hand against us. When your other uncle, Roderick, and I would start hollering or carrying on, Dad would just run. Out of the house. Out of town. For days, weeks at a time. Until finally, he ran out of our lives. Mom always felt like an outsider so she made up for it by working up a storm trying to fit in, doing all the Makah things right so we wouldn't have any trouble. But this left Philip to help raise us and we were quite a handful. Especially me.

You should know it took incredible patience to do what your uncle did. Not just losing his childhood to sort of be my dad. But the patience he'd had to do his job. So much watching, waiting, tracking, and wading through bullshit. I could never have done it. Through his career, he has elevated our standing which just might help you get in with them, if you want it.

I hear you've run off from your haunts down there. But I want you to know I'm not waiting around for the cops to call me. I've got a bunch of vacation time stacked up. The fire under me's been lit again. Just like it had when you ran away from the McCrowley's and I looked for you day and night. Just like it had when I turned eighteen and set off to look for my dad.

The head of the house always hung out in a darker, quieter corner near the back of the longhouse, while the women and children played by the big fire near the front. That way, if raiders came, he could duck out and sneak up on them. But I imagined my dad lost in a dark corner somewhere, lost in his hurt, trying to wriggle out of the trap he'd got himself into, trying to get back to us in the best way he could. But he needed help. I never found my dad. But I am going to find you. Gotta go.

Love always, your mother,
Leah Ledbetter
Neah Bay, Washington

LA VERGUENZA

After fleeing from Aurora with the taste of Depakote still in his mouth, Loud biked eight miles along the highway to Saginaw where he finally cashed in Pappy Rue's Greyhound ticket. He made a trade with a drifter—his mom's trail bike Neil Young for a bag of dusty shake. Then he boarded a Seattle-bound bus. In Seatown, he spent a day bouncing around, taking a few photos of himself in favorite spots, and meeting street kids. At a library, he posted the photos on his Facebook to feel normal. Since he didn't remember telling Jeremy about the page, he figured no one would see the photos anyhow. Loud then followed the kids out to a tent camp on the outskirts of Rat City. The tents were precariously bungee-corded and tethered to trees on a sloping hillside, and Loud and the others slept like cave-dwelling bats, hanging in sheaths of frayed nylon. They partied in a dog park, and he got high with Kenyon. He hung out in and around the camp for another week, finding fewer and fewer real people around.

Did he smell that bad? *Yeah, dude*, Cobain's ghost said. *You fucking do.*

The ghosts had followed him.

"Why me? Why do you dead fuckers choose to bother me?" Loud demanded.

Choose you? Gohl snorted *I didn't! You're the only one who listens.*

*

The day after Rufus McCrowley's Depakote went missing, Think-of-Me-Hill Retirement Community's head nurse filed a theft-of-a-controlled substance report, the prime suspect being Aurora Lee Loftner.

Traffic impeded Detective Charlotte Sweet's progress to the oldfolks home. Bullfinch Boyd's Papermill and Lumberyard had announced that morning that they too were shutting down. People were angry and driving wild. Detective Sweet thought about Jeremy's friend Cal and all the pain in this little town. Somehow, it all seemed to be gathering around this kid, Loud.

Once at the retirement home, Detective Sweet interviewed the nurse, the floor manager, and an unresponsive Rufus McCrowley. She patted the old man's hand and told him she was sorry about his boys. As she was leaving the room, she stopped at the picture of their house. She took a picture of it. She asked the clerical staff for Rufus' intake form and copied the address listed as his prior residence. She was sure the picture of the house and the address would match up and that they'd be important.

Detective Sweet returned to her car. Given everything she'd heard from Jeremy, given her own blunders with Keith, she was sure that Aurora had stolen the medication to give to Loud. But as a detective, she tried not to suspect. Only to know. She tried not to tell herself stories as she looked at a crime scene, but to let the evidence tell the story to her. She worried about how all this was going to affect Lyle's health.

Lyle had called her a week prior and confessed his miscalculations taking Loud in and described his current predicament. Given an ultimatum to obey the house rules or pay rent, Loud was hanging out with Aurora at a nebulous location.

"She says they hang out at Loud's uncle's house. Because Loud is more comfortable there. But Pete McCrowley, may he rest in peace, was McCrowley Sr.'s only child."

"I've heard about this supposed uncle before. The one in Kansas."

"Nebraska."

"Uh-huh."

"I didn't believe it either," Lyle said. "But I am not sure how to proceed. I thought you might have some advice."

"You know, he has a place to stay," Detective Sweet said. "With his mother. He has a mom. He's not some kicked-to-the-curb orphan."

"Why isn't he with her then?"

"I don't know. She wouldn't talk to me."

Detective Sweet confided that she'd called Leah Ledbetter back in November when Loud had been staying with them. Upon learning that Loud was staying at Charlotte's by choice, Leah ended their conversation abruptly.

"He's never going to get treatment when he always has someone else to run to," Detective Sweet said. "And if that keeps happening, he could hurt someone. More so than he's already done…is doing…to our kids."

"With all due respect, Detective, that's why I'm calling you."

Detective Sweet told Lyle she'd think about it. Then the retirement community had called. Sweet didn't even ask the two other APD detectives if they could take the case. The men would either go gung-ho or ignore it. And she sensed there was something about the McCrowley kid at the bottom of this. Whatever it was, she needed to unearth it if she was going to interrupt his year-long caper through town and the collateral damage it was inflicting.

Back at the station's low brick building, she typed in McCrowley's old address into the department's database, Sierra Pacific came up as the property's owner. She put in a call to them, asking if she could investigate the property due to trespassing reports. Though it took Sierra staff until the end of the day to get back to her with the okay, it was still faster than processing a warrant.

The next morning, she and two officers, Moreno and Weets, set out and combed through the old McCrowley house. They found the floor littered with cereal, crusty marshmallows, and crushed-up psychotropic. They also found Loud's crumpled denim vest with the back-patch of the top-hatted skeleton. Inside the inner pocket, Charlotte's gloved hands found a wadded pink notice from Sierra Pacific Industries declaring No Trespassing.

The note proved Loud's occupancy of the residence under the "name of law" statute, which linked the stolen and crushed-up medication to him. It was now only a matter of sending the wadded-up sheets with their patterns of stains and stray hairs to the lab, and Charlotte would have a trail of genetic material to link Aurora to the scene, plus more than enough to establish her motivation.

"I hope she just confesses," Charlotte said.

They had the fluid on the bed sheets, the proof of Loud's presence on the premise, the spoon with Loud's saliva, the toothbrushes with their saliva, and the cereal sprinkled with the missing medication. Open and shut.

She'll confess, the cops said.

"People can surprise you," Detective Sweet warned as they packed up, all incidentals tucked in vials or rolled up in butcher paper for the lab.

Given her past with Keith, Detective Sweet didn't have to ask why the girl got so close to someone so unpredictable and corrosive. She understood the allure and why Aurora would have broken the law to help him. After making her son blow up the toilet, Charlotte had considered duck-taping Loud to a chair and forcing him at gunpoint to swallow some barbiturates.

*

Detective Sweet wrote her report, submitted evidence to the lab, and thought about how to approach Aurora.

At shift's end, she went with Moreno and a couple of others for burritos at La Verguenza, a Mexican restaurant owned by Moreno's brother Gustavo and his Venezuelan esposa. Theirs was one of the few family-owned businesses remaining in Aberdeen and a local favorite.

"Weets isn't coming?" Charlotte looked around.

Moreno shrugged. "He says the food here gives him the shits."

"Pussy," Charlotte said. The guys ate that one up.

Gustavo brought out tamales on the house. Buen porvecho!

Moreno talked to the cooks in Spanish, then began his meal by unplugging a bottle of hot sauce. ARROYO BUBBLE BATH, the label read. He shook some of the thin red droplets onto his burrito, while shaking his head. "Looks like I'll have to take a third one from that group to jail."

The men laughed. Detective Sweet was silent. "That group" included her son.

"You know, we could get McCrowley for trespassing too," Detective Dugan said. "They could be the Harbor's very own Bonnie and Clyde."

"Oh, yeah," another cop said. "That kid needs to get put away. You hear about him slinking around half-naked at the D&R?"

They all had. All agreed, he was a bad seed. First getting the detective's kid to blow up that toilet, then manipulating Lyle's cute little niece to steal some meds for him.

Moreno had finished his burrito. "What do you think, Char?" He looked at her with his small, dark, reflective eyes set in his handsome face.

Everybody got quiet. She was not eager to divulge her feelings about mental health and justice with this table of good ol' boys. She relied on them daily, but they could easily turn on her if they felt her going soft.

"I want the McCrowley boy found," she said. "So that he can be..."

Restored, she wanted to say. But these men didn't buy into her social justice gospel.

"I want him to be rehabilitated," Detective Sweet finished.

The cops nodded understandingly. Perhaps they admired her ideals, though none shared them, not even Moreno. They still believed in prisons—a job-creating, problem-containing, color-blind industry. They didn't believe in healing—something Charlotte herself wasn't sure she believed in. But at the table, thinking about the last year for her, for her son, for Aurora, for the town, she wanted to believe.

*

The next morning, Charlotte—re-transformed as Detective Sweet—knocked on Lyle's door and asked to speak with Aurora.

Lyle looked at her like she'd punched him in his gut. "Detective…What…is this about?"

"Hopefully, Aurora can clear this up for me. And then I'll tell you."

Lyle shook his head, wide-eyed, and shuffled upstairs. Lyle motioned absently for Detective Sweet to come in. She sat down on a couch to make herself appear less imposing.

Aurora walked in quickly and sat down across from her. She looked at the distressed arabesque pattern on the floor rug as if allowing the detective to inspect her.

Detective Sweet looked at her. Aurora had the look of a girl who needed someone. Her curly black hair, glasses put on over mascara-stained eyes, and lipstick a little too thick and red for that pale skin. Aurora had the mark of a girl without a mom.

In the wake of Aurora's silence, Detective Sweet began. "We have to have a conversation about what happened at the McCrowley house a few days ago. About why there are bits of medication sprinkled into cereal all over the floor. About why a certain senior-care facility has reported a missing pill bottle of…"

"I stole the medication," Aurora said, not looking up.

Detective Sweet gave a long, low nod. *Good girl,* she

thought. *You didn't even make me mention the cum-stained sheets.*

"And what would make you do a thing like that?" Detective Sweet asked.

Aurora closed her eyes, caught her lower lip with her teeth, and shifted uncomfortably. The walls seemed to get smaller. Aurora looked back at that day when she'd waved Jeremy off, mocked him, and accused him, while she tried to justify her savior complex. It made her bury her head in her lap. She felt like she was being squeezed again. But she knew now it wasn't Jeremy or Lyle or Loud trying to get something out of her. It was the feeling of some oppressive force bearing down on her, pushing her, boxing her in. It was the feeling of shame. And Detective Sweet's eyes radiating on her.

Aurora told Detective Sweet how she'd crushed up the pills, hid them in Loud's cereal, and fed it to him.

"I thought it was the only way to help him get better."

"You broke the law."

"I wasn't even thinking about that." She wiped her nose. "I just saw the pill bottle and ran."

"How'd it work out?"

Aurora told the detective how Loud had left.

"So, you didn't go after him," Detective Sweet clarified.

"No," Aurora said, voicelessly through her lips.

Detective Sweet asked where Loud was now.

"Who knows? I just know he's left the Harbor and probably never wants to see me again."

"Probably a good thing."

Aurora nodded and cried, looking at her black nails through her tears.

"We learn slowly, don't we?" Charlotte said. "Hopefully having told someone the whole thing, it will hurt a little less… Eventually."

When Loud left that day, it had hurt so bad, Aurora felt the pain from all their times together lance her through at once and she lay surrounded by all the letters on the floor in that filthy house for what must have been hours, the sun and the shadow lapsing over her skin. It was all made so much worse because she'd triggered the whole thing. Loud must have felt so violated—the girl he loved spiking his cereal with something he abhorred. Even someone without his issues would have reacted.

When she got home to Uncle Lyle's after it happened, Aurora collapsed in bed and continued replaying everything. She felt as wounded by Loud as she did by Fate, and all the town ghosts she couldn't see or hear. She felt like that old picture of a sparpole, the tree the old loggers used to set their rigging. The spar was the tallest, strongest tree in the grove picked clean of its foliage, left to stand naked, piked, and abused in front of all those men and their cables and donkey engines. After Loud, no one would want her again. Jeremy wouldn't. Cal wouldn't. The hurt and embarrassment of the whole thing felt like a hole bored inside of her, a searing column of pain that could never be filled or soothed by anyone. And there was still the pain of the consequences to come.

Charlotte leaned forward. "Thank you for being honest with me."

Aurora shivered. She watched Charlotte catch her lower lip in her teeth as if she wanted to say more but couldn't.

"I'm not going to take you to jail today," Charlotte said.

"Thank you?" Aurora suspected a catch.

"With your continued cooperation, I'm going to send a report to the prosecuting attorney's office, and we'll be in touch."

Aurora texted Jeremy and Cal the news. Jeremy brooded while Cal stormed off to look for Loud in the sloughs.

Back at her office, Charlotte did something she had even

less relish doing than interrogating Jeremy's love interest. She called Leah Ledbetter.

Loud's mom had a silence between sentences and an ominous timber in her voice that made her seem severe and spiteful. Charlotte kept the phone call short, simply confirming that Loud was not with her.

"What's he done now?" Leah asked.

"This time, it was something done *to* him."

"Is he okay?"

"I don't know. He's disappeared."

Leah thanked her and said she'd file a missing persons report. She said she was rallying her people to do something about this.

"I don't want my son to be a bother to you or anyone else in Aberdeen again," Leah said. Then she hung up.

To the tune of the phone's disconnect signal, Charlotte tapped the receiver on the back of her neck. Those silences from Leah. The curtness. Charlotte decided they weren't from spite but from hurt. And Charlotte understood a woman's need to protect her heart.

CRAZY HEARTS

The next evening, after ditching Jeremy in Seattle, Cal drove down the hill back into Aberdeen. COME AS YOU ARE, read the welcome sign.

"Kitschy bullshit," Cal sneered. He'd abandoned Jeremy—a kid one year younger and half his size— to look for their mentally ill friend in downtown Seattle's maze. He felt low. He remembered a time when he made fun of "emo" kids for being down in the mouth. Now, he found himself pulling into the empty parking lot of Bullfinch Boyd's just because he wanted to sit with his despair. To look at it in the face. To not be chicken-shit. At least the ruin looked beautiful. The sun was setting. The sky, as if in protest to the thinning light, brought out impromptu parades of color: pumpkin, fuchsia, lavender, smoke.

Cal had gotten into Western State. But after a day of hemming and hawing, he gave the university a definitive rejection. This decision resulted in a blowup with his dad, who told him he was short-sighted, ungrateful, and rash. Cal said he'd never leave the Harbor. He wanted to stay and work in the woods and didn't see what else he needed to learn to do that. But the recession sunk his plans. Most of his class would be peace-ing out in a few months, going to Olympia, Tacoma, Seattle, Portland, Vancouver B.C. Sure, he'd have Jeremy and Aurora to hang out with. But what else?

He texted Aurora to ask how she was doing. To his surprise, she texted back.

How are YOU doing? Your dad's mill! ☹Are you with Jeremy?
Cal told her via text what he'd done.

"Don't feel too bad," Aurora texted. "I would have left too. Jeremy will be okay. He won't last more than a day away from his guitar or his homework."

They agreed to go see a movie. They both needed an escape.

Cal would pick her up in a half-hour.

Aurora giggled. She'd unintentionally set herself up on a date with Calvin Gearhart, vulnerable and raw after the family mill's shutdown. A minute before he'd texted her, she'd been feeling like the ugliest person in the world. She felt like all the things she'd done with Loud had driven a hole through her middle that everyone could see. She worried no one would want to touch her again. Then Cal's text chimed her back to life. Now she was pumping Cat Power through her iPod's headphones as she pressed on her lipstick and swayed to Chan Marshall moaning. The blues-rock guitar always transformed Aurora's room into a smoke-filled lounge she was too young to be in. She stretched on her black tank with the plunging neckline and pulled up her tight jeans and gave herself an approving once-over in the room's little mirror.

Cal picked her up in the Forerunner. His usually grease-soaked hair was in a dry, frizzy mullet, indicating he'd showered recently. It was the only sign to suggest he gave a shit. He wore a jean jacket and Dickies. Instead of feeling miffed, she felt comfort.

He drove her to the movie theater, and they got out to look at the movie posters. A head taller than her and a year older, eighteen, Cal seemed out of place among all the other kiddies rushing in to see *Avatar*, *Jennifer's Body*, and *Where the Wild Things Are*.

"You pick," Aurora said.

He chose *Crazy Heart*.

After the movie, they sat in his truck. She had said she wanted to talk. She knew *he* probably needed to talk but wouldn't unless she cornered him. Being chivalrous, he couldn't refuse. They shared a joint he rolled with some dry Yakima shake and talked in the swirl of smoke and dull buzz.

"What I don't get," Cal said. "Is why that hot chick would get with that old guy."

"I do," Aurora said.

Cal laughed. "Why?"

Aurora shrugged. "He's sort of like your dad. But not."

"You're weird!" Cal said.

"I just mean, he's a musician. He's mysterious and, because of his age and all his drinking, kind of forbidden. And that's sexy."

"Damn, who would have thought Overalls, the Little Drummer Girl would know what sexy is. If Loud hadn't come along…" Cal tore his gaze away from her slowly.

Of course, he was right. Loud had invited her into the strange world of attraction. Cal intuited this. Yet he was still sitting next to her. He wasn't running away. He wasn't making it awkward.

"So, how are you really?" Aurora asked him.

"Fucked up," he said, flicking the rest of the roach out the window.

From where they were sitting, across the purple dark, they could see the silhouettes of the abandoned Rhinehouse hoppers in the foreground and beyond, the silent spire of Bullfinch Boyd's Papermill and Lumberyard.

"Working at the mill was my plan," Cal continued. "My livelihood. Now I don't have one. It's like one minute you're part of your family's legacy. You're making stuff. It's good stuff, made from things that grow in your part of the country. You're making it well, just like your grandfather did, and his grandfather did. You're a part of the past. You're a part of the future. And then, suddenly, you're not. You're nothing."

"Oh, Cal," she said.

For some reason, his words broke her. She trembled. She touched his arm.

"I've never lost anything before." He gave a sad smile, eyes red from weed and tears. "Loud's lost. Jeremy's lost. You've lost. The town has lost. Boy has this town lost. Now, I've lost. And it's dark. And it sucks. I don't know where I'm going to go. Or what I'm going to do."

He put the heels of his hands into his eye sockets to stop up his tears. After a moment, he lifted his hands away and looked at them, almost surprised to find them wet. He wiped his nose on his jacket sleeve and said he was sorry.

Aurora stewed in her seat, feeling like she was sitting on a hot kettle boiling over. She crept across the seat, widening her legs around him and putting her small, white hands on both sides of his face. She lowered her lips toward him when he asked her to wait.

"Look…I like you. I've kind of liked you for a while actually… But. I can't do this right now," Cal said, wincing.

She drew back. She felt the cold leather of the steering wheel press against her hips.

"Why?" she asked.

"It's just…Loud. Jeremy. The shutdown," Cal said, his eyes squeezed shut, and shook his head. "I'm just too fucked up right now."

Aurora slid off him and sat in the bucket seat. The silence felt like a fire peeling back her skin and tearing into her heart and lungs. She popped open the door and started walking home in the dark.

*

The next morning, Jeremy is walking the streets on the northside of Seattle's U-District. The morning sky is slate gray from the clouds glowering over the shrill waters of Puget Sound. In only his jean jacket, he is freezing.

The houses give way to churches and their rickety admin buildings. One of which he remembers as the yellow clapboard soup kitchen from his previous day wandering. Jeremy is going to cop some breakfast in the hopes of righting his still-spinning brain from the E that Kenyon gave him last night.

Jeremy's teeth chatter. A pile of ragged blankets steam outside a used bookstore. He grabs at one of the cleaner-looking pieces of cloth for warmth.

The pile growls. Out from the depths of the moldering sashes and caftans, an old woman's face rises. Her pale eyes are wide, and her white hair floats above her as if she's underwater. "What about me, Malachi?" she screams. "Why did you leave without me?"

Jeremy runs. Did she say 'Malachi'? There must be some Blue Mercedes left in his brain.

He runs to the yellow clapboard house and joins a line of kids waiting for breakfast sandwiches. Along the line is an older couple serving hot cocoa out of liquid dispensing backpacks. When kids accept the cups to warm their hands, the couple shows them a picture of a Native American young man with a gap between his front teeth and roguish good looks. The couple is asking each kid, *have you seen him?*

When it's Jeremy's turn and they ask, he holds up the same picture: Loud's school I.D. "I was about to ask you."

*

For most of their drive back to Aberdeen, Jeremy has rested his forehead on the passenger window. The sun shifts through the wayside hills of scotch broom and wild sweet pea.

Loud's mom, Leah, has a long mane of stiff-black hair. Her skin is the same leather as Loud's, though careworn with wrinkles and regrets. Loud's uncle, Philip, has the same face as Leah, but he's taller with closely cropped, salt-and-pepper hair with old-guy glasses.

The Ledbetters offered to give Jeremy a ride back to Aberdeen. They wanted to talk to all of Loud's friends. And their parents.

"To get everybody on the same page," Uncle Philip said.

Jeremy agreed.

"But call your mother first," Leah said. "Let her know you're okay. And that we'd like to talk to her. And to Aurora and her family."

Jeremy's eyes widened.

"Oh yeah," Philip said. "We know about her too."

They talked for much of the I-5 part of their drive to Aberdeen, the Ledbetters and Jeremy negotiating their way around rocky topics and navigating the currents of uncomfortable themes, none of which Loud would have wanted them to share. So they tacitly agreed to talk as if he were there, sharing just enough to understand each other.

The Ledbetters too had been looking for Loud the previously day and all that morning, canvassing with hot cocoa at every homeless youth service center they could. Jeremy's mom, apparently on the case, had called Leah as soon as she learned from Aurora about Loud's disappearance.

Jeremy shivers. He feels exactly as he would have had the adults discovered why they called their hideout Whistle Punk Falls. The jig is up. The adults have them surrounded. But Jeremy's feelings of shame quickly swap with feelings of relief. The teens had tried to handle it by themselves and look where it had got them.

"I filed the missing person report this time," Leah says. "Not much good that ever seems to do."

Why did they think to look for Loud in Seattle?

"He'd run away there before,"

Because of the protracted awkwardness of their conversation, when they approach the highway toward Aberdeen, Jeremy narrows his eyes enough so that they look closed and he pretends to sleep.

The sun paints the dingy dome of Olympia white. It fills the hourglasses of the abandoned Satsop nuclear towers, and turns the railroad tracks into bars of gold that descend with them down the hill toward Aberdeen. COME AS YOU ARE, reads the welcome sign. *Unless you're me,* Jeremy thinks. Maybe that's what Cobain had felt too. *Take your time, hurry up,* Cobain's lyrics continued, feeling alienated by the shifting expectations of others. But what expectations did any of them have on Loud other than he not annihilate himself?

From the highway, Jeremy sees Feller's Landing, the boat launch into the sloughs and their trailhead to Whistle Punk Falls. A backhoe eats into the old barn on the hill. With ease, the animate steel mashes the rotten planks.

Once downtown, he thanks the Ledbetters for the ride but asks them to let him off at the Smoke Hole. He needs some time to think. They exchange phone numbers; he gives them his mom's contact information so they can all talk. They seem nice enough, he thinks, confirming his belief that Loud is truly insane.

He retraces his Think-of-Me-Hill hike with Aurora through the hills along the outskirts of town. He thinks about what to say to Aurora and to Cal when he sees them next. He thinks about what to say to his mom. The wind tousles his hive of curly hair. Aurora could be the one tousling his hair just then if only he was man enough to make a move on her. Jeremy is suddenly angry at his mom. In divorcing his dad, she became his first rejection, rejecting the half of him that was his father, Malcolm. And marrying Keith was the equivalent to parading that rejection in front of his face, day in and day out for years, and asking him to respect it! This constant reminder of his dad's unworthiness hobbled Jeremy before the race began, making him unable to assert himself and risk in the ways a guy needed to get a girl.

Having replayed his entire weird walk with Aurora on his descent down hospital hill, Jeremy opens the door to the Canyon Court rambler, planning on asking his mom why she forever stunted his masculinity. Instead, he finds the house empty. A note on the fridge reads:

Had a good talk with the Ledbetters. Out now tying up some lose ends. Be back for dinner. Frozen meals in the freezer if you get hungry. Glad you're safe and home.

Love,

Mom

Out? If she isn't working, why would she be out? Who would she be out with?

A sickening feeling seizes Jeremy's stomach.

She has crawled back to Keith.

SEE THE CHILD

Around this time, a platoon of transit workers flanked by a squad of cops are razing the homeless encampment on the easternmost hill of Rat City. They'd given residents numerous warnings. And from all appearances it looks like most of the camp dwellers had gotten the message and cleared out. They only apprehend two junkies dozing in heroin comas and a gangly seventeen-year-old who calls himself Loud.

Officers zip-tie Loud's wrists and load him and the smack-heads into the back of the police van. They feed him into the juvenile justice system which strips him, wraps in a jumpsuit, and hides him behind one of the blue doors in the decaying juvenile hall until he can be arraigned. When he's brought before a judge, Loud declares, "I'm the Wild Man of the Wynochee. See these holes? These holes, man? These are all the holes they put in me. Cuz I just don't fit in anyone's boxes, and I'm too dirty to just give away. Guess you gotta shoot me."

The judge gives him a ninety-day, involuntary treatment assignment at Hartman House, a youth home nestled amidst the gothic manors on the northwest side of Queen Anne. There he's diagnosed with paranoid schizophrenia. Of course, his mother is contacted and, of course she consents to his treatment. Of course, Loud refuses to speak to her and tells the staff he won't see her even if she does visit. The staff balk. No kid has ever threatened to refuse a parent visit, no matter how bad the parent. When staff push the issue, Loud tells them that his mom is a heavy drinker who abandoned him when he was little. A perfunctory CPS file is opened. Hartman House staff scrambles to locate other family members they can tie into Loud's treatment plan, which makes Loud smile in silent glee.

He settles into the three-hots-and-a-cot routine of a defiant inmate, refusing school, activities, social interaction, and most food. In standard issue orange flipflops, he paces the floors of his room, whistling to himself and talking to the ghosts. Gohl bemoans the injustice foisted upon his life. Cobain kvetches about his stomachaches. The Wild Man of Wynochee, Loud's personal favorite, doesn't say much, just drools blood on himself in the corner and pokes at the bullet-holes polka-dotting his chest.

Sometimes the ghosts fade for just long enough for Loud to think a coherent thought or remember something. One memory is of the morning he realized his mind didn't work quite right. The first time he felt his thoughts turn in strange circles.

He had been about six, and the summer sky opened like hangar doors for the sun to burst through. Summers meant no school and tagging along with Dad and Keith as they drove through the narrow logging spurs in the early morning. Keith was always jumpy as if he'd just downed an energy drink. His dad, Pete, moved slowly and spoke in a voice flat and calm as one of the copper-colored pools deep in the sloughs.

Even in summer, the mornings in the Willapa Hills were cold. They all wore buffalo-plaid hickory shirts. And the sunlight was shy, slowly working its way through the trees, revealing more and more of their silvery trunks.

"What time is it?" Malachi asked from the back of the cab.

"Half past a monkey's ass, quarter to his balls," Keith said.

"It's five-thirty a.m., Ki," his dad answered. "Ready for some whistling?"

"Hell yeah!" Ki unrolled his window, put his lips together, and filled the woods with his shrill toot.

"Jeezuz," Keith said

They came to the grove that DNR had contracted their outfit to log. The trees, to little Ki, felt like a host of others receiving them in silence. They grew on a slope. The men carried their chainsaws on their shoulders as they walked. Loud carried a bag of two axes and red wooden doorstops called wedges. Along with salal and sword fern, salmonberry grew on the forest floor. They popped the orange berries in their mouths and laughed at the sour faces they made.

They hiked up the hill to the new tree line they'd made a few days prior, the two men's chainsaws flashing, spraying sawdust, and tearing into the trees. Keith and Pete worked forty to fifty feet apart. Loud stood where he could see them. He was to whistle twice if either of their trees fell toward the other. But they never did. They'd first walk up-slope and make little mouths into a tree with their saw. Then they'd come around, driving their saw into the sides of the tree. They'd hammer in the wooden wedges into these side slits. Then they'd make a final slice at the back of the tree, facing downslope. They'd hammer in a last wedge into this slice, and the tree would sway. They would run back to join Ki. The tree would pop and groan from the inside, and Dad would pinch his shoulders. Usually, Keith just lit a cigarette. Either way, Ki would perform his duty with solemnity, whistling once before the tree started to fall. While the tree would slice through the air, its branches rustling, Ki would brace himself, but no matter how much he tried, he always shuddered at the thunderous crash the tree made when it hit the ground.

Ki watched his dad walk up slope to a slanted, silvery tree. As his dad slowly dragged his chainsaw across the bottom of the tree, Ki saw a current ripple across his vision. His dad dragged his chainsaw up diagonally to meet the top cut he'd made. He used the butt of his ax to chip out the wedge of wood, and the little mouth appeared. And when it did, Ki felt things turning inside, and he heard something. The mouth in the tree spoke.

Ki stood transfixed as his dad finished fixing the tree. Ki didn't speak but kept trying to hear what the tree was saying. It was speaking to him in a low hum. He wanted to shout, but a sixth sense told him he couldn't let his dad or Keith know what was happening. Ki heard a clink as his dad knocked the last wedge into the back cut and saw his dad running toward him. The tree cried out. It cried out in pain.

The tree fell crooked, to the left toward where Keith had been cutting. It slammed into the ground a few feet from where Keith had been standing a few seconds before.

A mist of dust and debris washed over, and for a moment, Keith disappeared.

A moment later, Keith emerged, shouting. He had his hand over his face and was coughing. "Jeezus! Shit! You dumb shits almost fucking nailed me into the goddamn ground with that thing!" Keith pointed a finger at Ki, "And you, you little pot licker! You've got one fucking job, and you didn't do it! You done fucked up, whistle punk!"

"Keith, stop," Pete said calmly. "I know you're angry, but…. He's just…"

"Spacing out is what he's doing!" Keith said, his eyes red with splinters and dust. His voice quavered as a man who'd just seen his own ghost.

"And you, Pete!" Keith continued. "You're getting old. And stupid. Falling that thing crooked. What a sissy nube move!"

"It must have had some rot in it I didn't see. Or some branches crowding the left part of the crown," Pete said. "I'm sorry. I'm…glad you're okay."

"Yeah well, next time check your hazards a little better, damn it. Shit, Pete. I expected better from you is all!" Keith walked into the woods, cigarette in his mouth. "I just almost died by you fucking people!"

Pete looked at Ki. "It's all right," he said. "It…it wasn't you're fault. I cut it wrong. And we shouldn't both cut at the same time... I'm sorry. It's dangerous. We know better. We've been asking for it for a while."

Ki looked at the fallen tree. In that instance, Ki had the chance to tell Dad what had really happened in his mind. He shut his eyes tightly. He showed his teeth.

"Are you okay?" Dad lowered himself into a crouch and peered at Ki, his eyes searching, encased in a film that pleaded, *are you still you? Are you still my son?*

"Yes," Ki lied. "I'm okay." And he saw doubt ripple beneath Dad's face, and he raised himself on his haunches as if to spring away, even as he took Ki in his arms.

"Ki. I'm...I'm sorry," he said patting Ki's back, giving off his scent of canola oil and sawdust. "You just spaced out. All this must be boring for you. I'm sorry."

"Sorry..." Ki repeated, pulling away.

Dad's eyes shifted and his mouth gripped downward, against a current pushing up inside. "Would you...like to stay with your mom? For a little while? Instead?"

"No!" Loud's choked cry panged out and Dad drew back. "No," he said again with a coltish shake of his head to rid the thought from his mind. "I want to stay with you."

Dad thumbed his nose and said okay.

Had Ki the words, he would have said that what he really wanted was no more change. No more separation. No more cutting away of closeness by the wild serrations of the knife that seemed to wait in the violet of every dawn.

They quit for the day, taking Keith to a hospital to check his eyes and his hearing. He was okay. But they'd lost money. The day ended in the McCrowley basement with his dad telling him it'd be alright. They'd get the money back by working extra hard tomorrow. They slurped down Letter Betters in blue plastic bowls and fell asleep.

Loud was never allowed out with them again. Even on days where there was no school. He stayed at the house with Pappy Rue and Grandma Gin. Not that it mattered much anyway. In a few more months, Pete and Keith were to be laid off as they were every year, only this time the layoff was permanent. There just weren't enough board feet to cut anymore, Pete explained. Their days as fallers were over. Both men ended up with jobs in Rhinehouse's logging yards, and they counted themselves lucky.

As Loud stares out the narrow window of his little room in Hartman House on Queen Anne Hill, his toes wiggle in his orange sandals, and he wonders, "Why didn't I tell my dad that something was wrong with me?"

Because he would have thought you were crazy, Cobain answers for him. *And he would have left you first. Or had you locked up.*

All thoughts of his father, Keith, the trees, and his first inner turnings fly away in a great wind.

THICK AS CEDAR THIEVES

The Missing Persons alert on Loud has been lifted. Before Charlotte can even call, Leah Ledbetter calls her. Malachi has been involuntarily assigned to a treatment center in Seattle. Though he won't talk to her, he's safe. For now, at least.

For Loud McCrowley, Charlotte thinks, his father's death in the soggy cedar swamps of Grays Harbor has become a kind of iron core that the compass of his life has revolved around. Detective Sweet needs one more declination point to help her make sense of Malachi "Loud" McCrowley before she can help the Ledbetters get him back and away from Aberdeen. Away from her son. And, to her knowledge, there's only one person who can corroborate the details of Peter McCrowley's untimely end: Keith Chevelle.

Jeremy told her about his and Loud's encounter with Keith outside the Jack and the Box. Conversations she's had with others around town confirm it: the two were thick as cedar thieves back in the day.

The divorce has been finalized. They haven't spoken in months. But he answers her phone call.

"How are you?" she asks.

"Busy," he says. "Movin' on. To bigger and better things."

"That's good."

"What do you want?"

"I want to talk to you."

"About what?" he chortles sardonically.

"About how Peter McCrowley died."

The line goes quiet.

"What? Pete? Why?" Keith's voice sharpens into an icicle's tip. "Why the fuck would I want to talk about that? To you!"

"Because. It's part of what's driving our kids crazy. Jeremy's friend, Malachi, is…"

"Of course. This is all about little Lord Fauntleroy."

She bites her tongue, keeping her purpose fixed between her eyes. "There's still something you can do for him. For your friend. For his son. You can set the record straight for him. On how he died. He wants… He needs to know."

He asks her to meet him at the Olander's farm of all places. Stupid? Cocksure? She goes armed and plans to hold herself back from trying to snoop around inside.

Fenced and pitbull-guarded, the Olander farm sprawls along the Humptulips River between Newton and Copalis Crossing. Everybody knows its location, including most of the cops. American and POW-MIA flags flap in the wind off the river.

As she gets out of her blue Focus, she eyes the pavilion, imagining its contents: a campground of big grow tents, UV lights, water spritzers for the plants. Keith comes out of the ten-foot-tall gate, still in that camo-colored ballcap, blue jeans, and greasy plaid shirt. But he is now a sun-bleached skeleton of himself with new sores around his mouth, on his cheeks, and arms. He shifts his shoulders and bobs his neck like he's swaying to a dark song no one else can hear.

They sit on two stumps outside the Olander compound. The pitbulls bark in the background, and Keith tells her the story, which he lets her record:

"We were on strike against Rhinehouse, without pay. Our union was pissed because of shortened shifts and reduced benefits. All because of that damn spotted-owl bullshit. Those hippies turned bureaucrats shut down the woods! Well, me and Pete planned to open them up again. Both of us had bills to pay. I had my court fines and lawyer fees. And Pete? Well, Pete was a single dad now, for Christ sake. And he was getting older. A fifty-five-year-old man without health insurance…

"Then 9/11 happened. Because we were out of work, we

had all day to sit around and watch those hajis wreck shit. Then we lit out.

"So, we loaded up my truck with our tree-cutting gear. I'd pimped out the truck with some running lights so we could see better. We drove and turned down a logging road just outside of Raymond and followed it down into a cedar swamp.

"We drove deep enough so the lights wouldn't shine onto the highway. And our chainsaws wouldn't be heard neither. We came to this red cedar. A hundred years old. Shaggy as a fuckin' monster. Just sitting down there rotting away, getting used as nothing but a squirrel penthouse while Pete and I were damn near starved. It looked like red gold to us."

Keith takes off his hat and worries over the weak arch in its bill.

"The night was a little breezy. But not bad. We'd cut on worse days. We turned our headlamps on. Put 'em on our hard hats. We did a couple walks around the tree. Checkin' our hazards. I made sure of it. The tree looked clear. Clean, neat crown. Full foliage. Healthy. It shoulda been easy enough. We plugged our saw exhaust ports into buckets of water. To muffle the sound, see. Shouldn't really be tellin' you all this. Now you'll know our secrets! They'll make you detective of the year or something. But it doesn't matter much now. As the penalty for thieving is way up, don't nobody do it anymore. Plus, I'm on the ground floor of Olander's marijuana business now. And it's gonna make us *way* more money than cedar thieving did. And soon it's gonna be legal!

"So Pete is doing the slope cut. Arching it over, lining it up real nice, using his sights. I'm standing back, lighting it up, so he can see. I've got my wedges all ready and am sizing up where we gonna drive 'em. Then, shit hits the fan. Wind from the north cuts right down through the valley. And there's a lot of space between the trees in that swamp, so we got no protection. The wind hits right into the tree. Thwacks it. Like God flickin' a toothpick or something. Pete kills his saw. I hear the crack. I shout for him to run. But it's too late.

"A rotten branch from the mid-story level. In the night, we musta not seen it. Pete turns to run, but he don't get far. Thing musta weighed three hundred pounds. Cracks him right on his head. I'll never forget the sound. Even with a hard hat on, it downed him instantly. Yeah, I seen it. Seen him crumble under it. Lit it up with a fucking spotlight like a movie scene. Then the sky got quiet, and there was just me shining the light on my dead friend, his body half hanging out from the broken pile of branches. And me just crying. Crying and shouting like a crazy person."

"So," Charlotte prompts.

"Well. I didn't have manpower enough to cover up the job now. It was gonna take both of us to cover the truck's tracks. Besides, everybody in the county knows Pete'n me did every job together. And, as you know, I'm a shit liar. Which is too bad, cuz I do enough bad shit to need to lie about. Well. Whatever. I called the cops. Got booked. Phoned Leah. Phoned old man McCrowley. And, I guess that's the end."

Detective Sweet puts the recorder in her lapel pocket. She looks at Keith's moist eyes. His gaunt cheekbones make his thin goatee look bushy. He may be helping the Olanders grow reefer, but he's on tweak.

"I'm sorry that happened to you. And your friend," Detective Sweet stands and walks to her car.

"Say," he says. "You want to catch a movie sometime?"

And he was so busy. He'd moved on. She rolls her inner set of eyes.

"No. Sorry, Keith. That ship's sailed." But as she turns

around to face him once more, she sees he's asked it in irony, baiting her.

"Too bad. My ship is just taking off," Keith motions toward the Olander farm. "With this new cash crop, we're going to put this town back on the map."

She turns the engine over.

"And we've even got somebody in Olympia now. A name you'll recognize."

She looks squarely at him.

"He's helping us get the ears of all the senators," Keith says smirking. "Making up for all the hell his tree-hugging caused us."

She backs her car up. Malcolm. Jeremy's father. Her first husband. He's lobbying for legalization for the Olanders.

"I'll keep a candle lit for you, Char, is all I'm saying," he says, his face a sardonic mask. It's the face of a man owned by addictions, offenses, and numbered days extinguishing like cigarettes.

"Goodbye, Keith," she says, and with her foot on the accelerator, she turns him into a small, ranting man on a roadside.

CIRCLES

The next morning, Charlotte meets with the Ledbetters at Lyle's house. She gets along better with Philip than Leah as Leah's eyes glint with humor and mischief that would like to come out but is held back for reasons Charlotte can't decipher.

After their talk, Charlotte walks herself out of Lyle's house and stands on his wraparound porch. A lone bell tolls from the Catholic Church near the high school, expanding in a widening circle of sound until over the Harbor, over Think-of-Me Hill, it fades.

Charlotte sees the leaden circles of the law and the systems of their society swirl around her and the teenagers in her life. She thinks about how Malcolm has always been more interested in the circles of those systems than in the people inside them. Maybe these circles are closing around a center and that center is this kid, Malachi McCrowley. Maybe Charlotte can help the Ledbetters reforge these circles as flesh and blood, rather than law, lead, or iron.

*

Charlotte gives Jeremy an hour to talk alone with Aurora below the bridge above Canyon Court. A misting spring rain beads on the tips of the cedar branches, diamonding on stray strands of sun that sneak through the clouds. They sit for a while, moldering like twin silos filled with their separate secrets. Then it's like their grain hatches open and their secrets come spilling out. She tells him what happened with the pills. He tells her about the fruitless search in Seattle. He tells her about his ideas about the tree in *Starry Night*. About the drugs. She tells him about Cal.

"It doesn't change anything." Jeremy sighs. He might as well come out with it. "I love you."

"I'm sorry," she replies.

"Do you like Cal?" Jeremy asks.

She cleans her glasses. "I don't know. I like Cal. I like you. I don't know."

"Why not?"

"Because I'm fucked up!" she says. The statement echoes in the hollow of the bridge's arc. She'd shout it out of a goddamn digeridoo if she could. Broadcast it to the whole town via public radio. Of course, it'd probably just get *more* guys into her.

The raindrops whisper as they fall onto pine needles and pavement.

Jeremy stands up, feeling his soaked socks. Aurora shifts uncomfortably.

"Can't you just hold my hand while I figure all this out," she asks.

"It's been an hour," Jeremy says. "My mom wants to talk to you. And I've got a date with the Rejection Factory."

Charlotte drives Aurora back over to Lyle's turret house and they sit at the kitchen table.

Detective Sweet has submitted her report to the prosecuting attorney's office and lets Aurora know that they will be inquiring about Aurora's continued cooperation.

"So..." Aurora asks, trying to parse through the legalese.

"Do you really want to help McCrowley?"

Aurora flushes, curling a lock of hair over her ear. "Yeah... yeah, I do."

Detective Sweet tells Aurora how Loud is at a treatment center but is refusing help and refusing to see his mother. What Loud needs most is to get over his fixation with Aberdeen, forgive his mother for whatever passed between them, and give life a try with her up in Neah Bay, with her brothers, and their tribe.

Aurora looks away from Detective Sweet, who seems less

like a woman and more like a steel object—a jet, an aircraft carrier, an I-beam—slicing through bad air, problems, days, and people.

"O…kay," she says. "So…"

"So Loud's mom, Leah, and her brother, Philip, have given us a game plan. In case Loud ever comes back to Aberdeen."

"Why would he come back here?"

"She thinks he will. And I think she's right. He's magnetized to this place. He runs away and comes back. It's his pattern. Like a strange circle."

"Or a labyrinth."

*

Jeremy isn't going to *The Harbor Herald* to work a shift canvasing for the paper because there's no more point. And not just because he's completed his community service hours.

Jeremy sits with his back against *The Harbor Herald*'s vibrating brick walls inside which the press—that colossal block of drums, levers, and conveyer belts—is printing the paper's final issue.

All Jeremy's cold calling and cajoling the residents of Grays Harbor to subscribe and keep their local guardian of honest facts afloat, could not alter the paper's fate. The owners, a conglomerate based in Kansas (or is it Nebraska?), have sold the building, auctioned off the aging press for scrap, and laid off all the newspapermen in exchange for a team of equally talented, cut-rate journalists in the Philippines who can generate comparable content for the Harbor online.

The rollers pick up speed. There's the smell of warming ink and solvents. Claps resound from the warehouse as the sheets are stamped and whisked through the whizzing cylinders. The quickening speed changes tone, and, at Jeremy's back, the bricks quake.

As the machine whirs to a stop, its high-pitch carom decreases in decibels, and the bricks shake still. The press's drums spin their final circles, steam hisses off the dampers. And the paper is no more.

Jeremy keeps the newspaper's death rattle in his bones to fuel some invention down the line. Maybe an album. Maybe a novel.

HARD TRUTHS FROM LAURA LAW

As the days grow longer and the sun sends more fronds of warm light into Loud's dorm at Hartman House, the ghost of Laura Law returns. She emerges from the walls. Bent over herself sobbing, she looks like a wrinkled-gray pod.

She was only trying to love you! the ghost says.

The ghost lifts its head and stands. Aberdeen's most infamous unsolved murder victim wears a pinafore dress and a torso of open wounds. Her face would have been pretty if it weren't for the bludgeons in the top of her scalp and brittle pieces of exposed skull. When she speaks, she speaks in female version of Loud's voice. American. Native.

Loud shrinks from her and she fades for a time, but comes back again crying like before, this time with two fingers held to her lips, as if holding a smoldering cigarette. Between fits of weeping, she feigns a drag, propping an elbow up on a forearm and shaking her head.

The room sizzles with heat. Loud feels feverish. He asks her what she wants, but she just shakes her head and walks away.

Laura Law has a different texture than the other ghosts. She comes and goes even when Loud is calm and lucid. A strange warmth follows her.

She was only trying to love you, the ghost says again. *And you left her!*

"Go away!" Loud says. "I'm sorry, all right."

But the ghost continues: *The only one willing to love you no matter what.*

"Overalls tried to feed me bath salts, okay?"

She was trying!

"You're a vindictive bitch! Just like my mom."

The ghost folds on itself and returns to its kneeling position, weeping.

Loud spits at her. In the face of her wailing, Loud curls up on the green vinyl mattress, which smells faintly of urine, and he tries to sleep while keeping a wary eye on her.

The Wild Man of the Wynochee sits down next to Laura. He lets her cry on him, lets her rest her head on his bullet-hole ridden chest. She cleans the wounds with her tears. She kisses him and he kisses back. And Loud's hand takes over from there.

The heavy door opens. Loud tries to cover himself with a blanket. Too late.

"Doing okay in there?" a voice asks. "Oh, sorry…"

"Get the fuck out of here!" Loud shouts, drawing the blanket up over his naked waist.

"You can just draw the shade on the window if you want private time, and we'll know to knock," the staff person says.

"What the fuck ever. God!" Loud yells.

The staff person points to the door's window and models how to put on the little Velcro flap for privacy. "Of course, we still have to do checks every fifteen minutes at night." He points to their clipboard.

"Yeah, yeah!" Loud shouts. "Or I'll kill myself. Like that girl did a few months ago. I know all about it. So, take your stupid clipboard and shove it up your ass!"

The door shuts. And Loud finds himself unable to finish. He hears the staff talking into their radio on the other side of the door:

"It's really weird. It's really hot in there. Condensation on the window!"

"Stupid asses," Loud curses.

You're a judgmental little fuck, Cobain's ghost comments. He leans against the wall across from Loud's bed.

"So are you!" Loud says and sings a bar from "All Apologies," which Loud has always heard as less an apology, but more of an indictment on how awful everybody else is.

Well, Cobain shrugs sheepishly. *What can I say? People suck.* "Is that why you did it?"

Cobain just nods. *I saw black holes in everything and everyone. And the drugs stopped covering it up. So I figured I should put the black hole in me and spare everyone. You should think about it too, dude.*

Laura's ghost still sulks, searching herself for something, probably her Pall Malls. She steams like a mound of compost. "You fucking smell," Loud chides her.

At that, she leaves, Loud's mind clears. He understands that he has hurt Overalls in some horrible way. He isn't sure how. He heard her crying as he ran. His stomach hurts thinking about it. Sure, she tricked him into going on meds again. But she hadn't left him. *He* left her. All alone! And hurt. He wants to let her mother him a little. Maybe bring him some chocolate milk or make him some nettle tea. He's given up something special with her. Something they'll never have with anybody else again. Part of them will always be alone and it's all his fault.

Cobain lowers himself along the wall to sit on the floor. As he slides, the wound at the back of his head leaves a message on the wall: *Move on!*

But it's written in blood. The blood of a dude who 86'ed himself with a shotgun. He had a bombshell wife and a cute kid and people around the world who would pay to hear him play music. Why should Loud listen to this idiot? Fucking junkie!

"I should go back to Aberdeen," Loud says.

That night, an old vision rolls through his mind like a familiar fog: his father sitting alone in the McCrowley basement, humming a blues song, whittling his mother's face into a silent chunk of wood. Beside him is a bowl where letter-shaped cereal floats in leftover milk spelling something.

"Yeah, I know. 'When love leaves, it don't come back.'"

In the vision, his father sets down the carving and the knife and shakes his head.

"What?" Loud asked.

His father looks up, eyes blackened in death. *You haven't been reading my message right.*

"What's it say then?" Loud trembles.

When love leaves, it can't *come back. Because the darkness has taken its place.*

"So, I got to kick out the darkness!"

The next day, for the first time, Loud voluntarily takes an antipsychotic. Geodon. Loud switches up his behavior. He starts leaving his room. Starts showering. Stops shouting at staff. Starts going to groups. Volunteers to talk about his feelings. Eats regular meals. Says 'yes' a lot.

The Hartman House staff people are mostly nice, gay, and white. It sickens Loud how happy it makes the staff people when he comes out and minds his Ps & Qs. It makes him want to shout. *We are not all machines!* But he holds his tongue. He keeps his big mouth shut when the ghosts are around. He tries his hardest not to talk to them or look at them. He takes his drugs. He tells the shrink he doesn't see ghosts anymore and that he knows they're not real. He knows he has problems. He sits by staff and asks them what music they like and other anodyne questions. He watches movies with everybody and laughs when everybody else laughs.

After a few weeks of this, Loud is considered one of the good kids on the unit. He gets to go on outings to movies, to the pool, to a rock-climbing gym. Staff leave him alone in rooms by himself more often. Staff let him walk from the gym to the unit by himself. Staff stop checking on him every fifteen minutes at night, though they are still technically supposed to.

At night, Loud whispers to Laura Law, "Rest. It will be okay."

He's trying now. He's going back to find a way to make it all up to her. And if he can't, he'll kill himself.

He asks Laura Law who killed her. Everyone wants to know. *Men,* she tells him.

Staff even let him hang out in the cafeteria by himself sometimes! On a dusky evening in mid-June, Loud is chilling on one of the "spider" tables bolted into the linoleum. He's counting the salmon berries heavy on their prickly branches, mapping out his plan to go pick some for his journey back to Aberdeen. Nobody's Ghost walks in. Only no Pendleton this time. Just a fleece vest and a t-shirt with wolves on it.

"You found nowhere yet?" Nobody's Ghost asks.

Loud blinks. "Nowhere?"

"You said that's where your people are. Nowhere."

"Oh. Right. Sorry. The weed. Bad memory. Uh. I haven't been looking."

They catch up.

"So, what are you doing out here anyway," Loud asks.

"What do you mean?"

"I mean, don't all spirits who stick around have some kind of business left hanging. What do you want? And what's it got to do with me?"

Nobody's Ghost reaches into his fleece and takes out a Ziplock bag with some folded papers inside. "Someone... My sister. Started writing a book. A book in the form of letters. Letters to her lost son. But she never finished it. Not that anyone would have wanted to read it. Would you like to read it? Then at least one person would have gotten to read it."

Loud reaches for it. "Yeah. I guess. Okay. I could use something to read. I got some downtime coming up here real soon."

*

Back on the unit, one of the tweeners with the clipboards asks Loud how his visit with his uncle went.

"My uncle?"

*

A few days later, Loud and two of the other good kids get taken off the unit to go swimming at a neighborhood pool. But one of the boys starts arguing with the staff about who gets the front seat. The boy gets heated and calls the staff a fudge-packer. The staff radios for someone to assist. When the boy realizes he won't be able to go swimming, he kicks the staff in the shin. The staff tries to hook the kid's arm around his back. But then the other kid starts fighting. The staff struggles with the two. The clipboard gets in the way. He calls to Loud for help. But Loud is edging away. By the time backup staff arrives, Loud is five blocks north.

Wearing a t-shirt, a pair of tennis shoes he got from the unit store, and a baggy pair of jeans over his swimming trunks, Loud bounds a staircase that takes him to the bottom of Queen Anne Hill, which opens to an empty industrial strip. He's got nothing in his pockets other than the Ziplock bag with Nobody's Ghost's sister's letters, which he hasn't even read yet.

Loud prowls through the alleys and loading docks to a set of railroad tracks where he waits and waits and hops a BNSF freighter bound for Tacoma. The tracks are free of bulls. He lets the warm night wind through his hair as he rides the rails. He's free of Hartman House, its goody-goody staffers, its urine-glazed mattresses, and its drugs.

Cobain tells him it's a bad idea. *If this doesn't work out, you'll need to pull your plug.* Laura Law casts a look of clemency his way. She strokes his hair, furry and shapeless by this point. *She's waiting for you, whistle punk. She's been waiting for so, so long…*

How do you know which 'she' she's talking about? Cobain

asks. But Loud doesn't think it matters anymore.

As the rails curve along shorelines and hillsides, the moon's glint upon the winding steel reminds Loud of the rings of light that caught on Overalls' glasses. The curvature reminds Loud of his journey from Aberdeen to Seattle, Seattle to Forks, Forks to Aberdeen, Aberdeen to Seattle, and back again. Round and round. They are black circles swirling, swirling in a never-ending figure-eight.

He can't sleep, so he unfolds the letters and by the moonlight, he starts reading.

It's not much for a book. There are only three letters. A few sentences in, a green grimacing basilisk in the tank of his gut begins to squirm. The black tapes spin in his brain. He mashes the papers into a ball and squeezes them while he writhes on the boxcar's floor.

Nobody's Ghost. My uncle!

He makes to throw Leah's wad out of the window of the rushing train. But Laura Law stands in his way, jaw set, fists clench, shimmering in heat and old-world woe.

Loud curls his lip, but unfolds the papers, smooths them out, and, with the rising sun, begins to read, mumbling, "Guess Overalls wasn't the "she" you were talking about, was it?"

RETURN

Loud treads back into Gray's Harbor County on Saturday morning, July 4th.

Having train-hopped from Seattle to Tacoma, he used his charm to hitch rides to Olympia, but the Geodon wore off, and he started frightening away even the sturdiest Samaritans. So over a series of days, Loud walked the highway to the Harbor—the Wild Man of the Wynoochee reborn as a brown-skinned homeless boy with big brows and an overgrown mohawk.

The spring rains have lingered, along with their chill. His t-shirt and Greyhound blanket are rain-soaked. He spent a whole day drying off inside a Subway in McCleary, using his EBT card to get breakfast, lunch, and dinner. He spent another day beneath the belly of an iron cow—one of three sculptures adorning the wetlands below the vacuous Satsop cooling towers. Despite the estival time of year, there have been nights he thinks he might freeze. Part of him hopes he does. *I'll never be whole. I'll always be the boy with the broken brain.*

He's tried. He really tried to kick out the darkness. But he's failed. In his deranged slog, he's a fractured, rain-weakened fever-dream of himself. The ghosts form a cross—a splintered, bloody rood in his head. They chatter, berate, and whisper at him endlessly, and he shouts them down. Even when a car slows down in response to his extended thumb. He no longer has the strength to pretend he doesn't see or hear the ghosts. Confronted with his gesticulating and susurrating, any sympathetic drivers pull away. He's thought of hopping a train. There probably wouldn't be any Bulls on alert out here. But he hasn't seen a single train on his journey on foot through the Willapa Hills.

There have been occasional truces—moments when the ghosts let up their bombardment on his sensory cortex. In these moments, he has read and re-read his mother's letters and he thinks that maybe he's been wrong about everything this whole time. But he isn't sure. She did leave! Then, she lied. Lied in such a way that he still doesn't know how his fucking dad died. Was it the widow maker or the bandsaw? Neither? The same old tapes play and replay.

He looks west toward Aberdeen, the town where a beautiful girl loves him. He's sojourning back there for her. To make up for something. He can't remember what he's done but the thought makes him tremble. Did he push her? Abandon her? Cheat on her? Rape her? He can't distinguish dream from fantasy from reality from haunting from memory from imagining. All he knows is that when he gets to her house, he'll lay himself down at her feet and tell her he will do whatever she wants him to. She's the girl who knows! He hadn't listened to her, he remembers that much. But he will listen now. Even if she tells him to eat bath salts, go to the hospital, or go kill himself. If she won't talk to him, he will look for the standing cedar with the mouth cut into it, and he will lie down at its base until he freezes to death. Or he'll lay himself down on a train track. If she doesn't want him, he wants to go where his dad is. To pass through the curtain of darkness.

*

That morning, Teenage Graceland is slow. Molly Donahue is wrapping up an overnighter. The one kid checked in—a girl who'd been kicked out by her father for coming out—is still asleep. Molly is reading a book on family counseling for her MSW.

There's a knock at the door. Officer Moreno ushers in a soaking wet and salivating version of Loud McCrowley.

Moreno raises his eyebrows. "You know the plan."

Molly does.

"I've put in the call to Detective Sweet already, and she's making her moves," Moreno says. "But can you just watch him until she gets here? It's a busy morning out there."

Molly looks from the officer to McCrowley, whose stare is askance and vacant.

"He's not really with it. I tried a few times," Moreno says and takes off on a call.

Molly sits McCrowley down, and looks into his face. "Hey, kiddo."

He looks at her, and his light brown eyes dilate. "Hey. Hey! Cougar lady. Can…can…can you heat me up some breakfast? Like before?"

"Sure," Molly says. "But if you call me Cougar Lady again, I'm going to punch you."

Loud laughs and says sorry. "I don't remember your name. The weed. Weed is the cure for bad brains!"

"Yeah… I hear you," she says, acknowledging him. "While I make your breakfast, if it's okay with you, I'm going to get you a raincoat."

"K. Laura Law says you're okay," Loud says to her and then, to some invisible presence sitting next to him, he hisses. "She's not. She's not. She's not! You get outta here. Get! Git. Turd Cobain."

Molly tears up. She leaves Loud with the remote for the big screen. But Loud casts the remote from him like it's a used prophylactic. Molly returns with a coat from the clothing closet and a microwaved Hot Pocket, interrupting the following altercation he's having with himself:

"I wouldn't have been allowed in any of your unions!" Loud points to the skin on his arms.

Molly drapes the raincoat over him and offers him the plate, which he wolfs down.

Loud asks to see Overalls. Aurora. "Can you bring her here? I have to see her. I have to lay myself down for her. Tell her I'm hers."

"Loud. Loud, buddy," Molly says. "Don't be afraid. But here's what's going to happen…"

Loud swallows.

"You can't stay."

Loud's brows furrow, and his lip quivers.

"And you're not going to be able to see Aurora."

"Why? You're…You're going to kick me out?"

"No. Listen, listen, listen," Molly says.

Loud's face melts in a tribulation of wrinkles. "I have to see Overalls. She's the girl who knows. I've hurt her and have to make it up to her! And if she won't take me, then I'm going to kill myself."

"How…how are you going to do that?"

Loud shrugs. "Just lay down somewhere. Somewhere cold. Somewhere dead. Like on some railroad tracks."

"Okay," Molly says, patting his knee. "Thanks for telling me…"

Molly hears the girl call out. The voice is thin and panicked.

"Just… Stay here for a second," Molly asks. Molly checks on the girl. Just a nightmare. But when Molly races back, she finds the couch empty and the door ajar. She looks out the door down the empty streets, across the empty soccer fields and sky of chimneys and church spires.

At least he took the coat.

KILL THE WILD MAN

Loud runs across railroad tracks to a trail lined by stands of scotch broom and fireweed. The trail hugs the river and will take him to his grandparents' house. *I just want to see it one last time.*

Along the trail, tents crouch in the coarse, black-podded branches of the scotch broom. Rickety bicycles lean against rusted, mossy-roofed cars, some without wheels. One hunched over a snag. Motorhomes and car campers park behind butterfly bushes; unpaid tickets and unanswered letters clog the windows. There's the smell of campfire. Wild lilies droop and sway to the breezes of shaggy-haired people rustling, smoking, and fucking behind yellow-stained sheets and crack-slatted blinds. As Loud walks their hidden highway by the river, part of him wants to join them. Maybe they could cook up a can of beans together, share some stories, and go hobo out to Raymond, Kelso, or Spokane and forget all this. Maybe in another life. He stays on the trail. He has to see his grandparents' house one final time. Then Overalls. And then…

A riverside trek, a swim across Mox Chuck Slough, and a swamp sojourn later and he sees the opening in the trees.

As Loud creeps with high steps and ginger footfalls into the cedar grove of his grandparents' property, all his ghosts' whispery anger evaporates as if someone in his head opened a vent. But into this vacuum comes the cold beeps of dozers backing up and hydraulic whizzing and cranking from a backhoe's digger lifting, then crunching into wood and glass. A dump truck snarls into the grove. Loud calls the ghosts back because he can't handle this alone. But they don't come. He emerges from the Indian plumb and sword fern underbrush into the clearing to find his grandparents' house remixed as a jagged mountain of sticks.

All three machines are branded *Sierra Pacific Industries*. The white guys in their golfing polos are having their day.

Brock is at the wheel of one of the dozers. He's thicker now and has a full, black beard. In the cab of the backhoe is the Brawny Man. Two other similar-looking dudes wrestle with their steering wheels and twist their torsos inside their machines.

"My dad's in there," Loud screams and stomps toward them and their thick-wheeled bulls of steel—their tank-like tonnage and rumble be damned. "Oma's in there. Pappy Rue too. I'm in there! You can't…"

The lumbering, ochre-colored machines herkie-jerk quiet. A conspiracy of radios buzz.

Brock lifts himself up and casts his pale eyes at Loud in a way that makes him wipe his mouth to see if he is foaming rabid. Brock curls his lips around his snaggle teeth and waits at his dozer's door, arm resting on the roof. The big troll is afraid of him! Good.

"Put it all back, or I will," Loud orders. "Put it back, turn around, and leave us alone."

Loud sees movement to his left, and in seconds, the Brawny Man is before him. He is squattier than Loud imagined with a big, blonde walrus' mustache. His blue eyes have an iceberg hue and mercury to them that shows Loud he's craftier than he thought. Brock joins him.

"The hell you doing to my house, Brawny Man?" Loud asks. "I know you've been wanting to wipe us off the face of the earth for…"

"It'll be Mr. Olander to you," the man says, his mustache hairs fluttering from the assertion. "And this hasn't been your house for years. Blame your Grandpappy for that one, may he rest in peace."

"You kill him too?" Loud asks.

Brock, looking seasick, takes a step back and looks at Brawny Man for direction. Brawny Man is Brock's dad! *Why didn't I put that together sooner?*

"What are you guys doing this for? The ganja not bringing in enough bread?" Loud asks.

Both Brock and his dad's eyes shift. Finally, Brawny Man's, a.k.a. Olander Sr. gives his response:

"Everybody needs a day job."

Wearing Carhart coveralls, camo hats, sweatshirts, and work boots, the two others approach: that froggy-faced kid Johnny Mackleroy and the other thick, squatty white dude—Johnny's dad Loud guesses. Loud finds himself facing off against these linebacker-sized white guys who would much prefer he never existed. They move toward him. He tries to think of a way to break through them so he can dive into the pile of rubble that had been his family home and, beam by beam, raise it again. Or, more likely, slice himself into smithereens in the attempt.

The spaces between the dudes close as they tighten their line. They all take steps toward him. They have their hands out with curled fingers locked, Ken-doll style. It's like someone or something from an invisible control tower in the sky coordinates their movements—a coach, a foreman, a mayor, a god, some power that has always been against him trying to make a life for himself on the shores of the Chehalis. The closed visors of their heavy faces are swollen from labor and alcohol and beef grease and scramble.

Where are those guys? Loud thinks of the ghosts but realizes they're too scared. Pussies. It's just as well. These dudes want them gone just as much as Loud.

Loud turns tail and scrambles over to the nearest vehicle—the dumper. He crawls on the ground and shoves his head between the dirt and its massive tire treads.

"You'll have to kill me," Loud says. "This is my family's land."

Loud winces as he feels two sinewy mitts wrench him up and shove him offside.

He's faced with Olander's red, huffing jowls. He looks for a way to edge past him.

But the brawny men all lock together again and advance, inching him out and away from the demolition site.

Loud rushes them. If you're going to go, go out big, right? But it's like hitting a wall—only colder, whiffed with tobacco and coffee and body odor. He tries again and again, but each time they block him and buffet him back, leaving him unharmed, unwanted, and outside.

"Lynch me!" Loud shouts at their closed faces. "Fucking do it. You know you want to. You've wanted to for years. *Lynch me already!*"

Old man Olander grabs him and flings him to the ground. "The fuck you think I want to do that for? Lynch you? I got enough problems," he spits.

The others move toward Loud, but Olander holds out his arms to keep them at bay. He whispers something to them that Loud can't hear.

Loud gets up, "Well. Could you scalp me at least?"

Brock says how fucked up this all is.

"Wouldn't want to get your scalp between my fingernails," Olander replies. "I don't want even a drop of your blood left here. There's no place for you here. Not any part of you."

The man's bold, official words remind Loud of the broad lettering on a pink slip of paper that told him in as many words to get lost. And why doesn't he? Fuck this shithole.

"This is my home!" Loud argues. With himself as much as with them.

"No. It. Isn't," Olander says.

Loud looks at their clay-covered boots. He shifts on his

feet. The ghosts are still quiet.

"You *are* your daddy's son," Olander says. "Dumbest thing Pete ever did was *stay* here. We'd all leave if we could. 'Cept there's nowheres else for us to go."

Olander grabs for him, but Loud jukes backward. They surge toward him, but he's on his feet and running. He turns back the way he came, shoulder-deep into the sloughs before he looks back and sees their forms as dumpy lumps shuffling back to work, wiping all traces of him and his family off the land. Too bad they couldn't have hurt him a little, so he could have some outward way to show the world how much he hurts inside, his family home destroyed.

But what kind of family were they, anyway? They'd been the first to kick him out. His mom hadn't done that. They had! It's nothing to cry about. All he knows is that Overalls is his true family. And if she doesn't take him back, not only does he have nothing left in Aberdeen, he has nothing left in life.

*

Olander turns into his phone, "Hello. Yes, this is William Olander. We just seen him. He's headed toward Feller's Landing. I'd give him ten minutes. Yeah. Good luck with him. Sure got your hands full with that one, missy. Yeah. Yeah. You're welcome. I owe your Uncle Lyle. We all do."

THE WHISTLE PUNK DEPARTS

Cal doesn't answer his cell phone. It's Jeremy. Probably to ask for his help or something. He'll have to call him back later. He's gotten work on the big new project of the Chehalis. Eight aircraft-carrier-sized ingots are dug into the silty earth of Bulfinch Boyd's former sorting yard. Working people in hard hats, Cal among them, swarm the rebar ribs of these three-story deep casting basins. They've laid pipe and erected walls. Sure, the floating bridge they're building will be to benefit software engineers and latte-sippers in Seattle, but it's unionized work at a living wage.

The concrete pours.

The sluice gates open.

Tugboats pull the pontoons out.

The slabs of concrete float on air pockets preserved deep inside.

The leaden slabs drift out into a horizon soaked by the blinding sun that obliterates the divide between sea and sky.

*

"Cal's not answering," Jeremy says.

"We don't need him," Aurora says at the wheel of Uncle Lyle's Longhorn.

Though Jeremy likes the sound of that, he isn't sure. What if Loud tries to fight them? He looks past the black cottonwoods at the entrance to Feller's Landing, the new beams of the barn being built in place of the old, and the glossy leaves of the Oregon grape growing along the wide field that rolls gently down to the river's dashing blue. His eyes follow the river and the train-track rails that withdraw to a vanishing point in the east to where a young man is standing near the tracks. They hear a distant train whistle blow.

"There he is!"

Aurora rolls the truck onto the launch and steps on the

e-brake. She calls to him. Loud keeps staring at the train tracks. She calls to him again, and he turns.

Around his blinking eyes are red rings of hurt. Aurora calls him into the cab, and he lopes toward her with a cautious smile.

"Hey!" Loud calls. Then, upon seeing Jeremy, he skids to a halt. "Hey."

"I can go."

"No. It's okay," Loud says. "It's good! We're…all together. We're all good! The band is back!" He guffaws and pogo-jumps and holds their hands.

He pushes them left, he pushes them right, and begins spinning their circle. They spin a ring-around-the-rosy spiked with glee, carbonated with pain, until they collapse.

In Washington state history, Jeremy's teacher led a lesson on plants. Jeremy's favorite is still trillium, sprouting its three white petalled flower in April, the cruelest month, as Elliot said. Ms. Rigby'd finished the year with *The Wasteland*. April, that month when their trifecta imploded. They are a crumpled, dizzied sprig of trillium, white petals curling and dying purple in its twilight. He looks at them. It's lasted longer than he thought it would. Longer than it should have. *It's alright*, Jeremy thinks, removing his hand from Loud's to wipe his face. *It's a lot more than most get to have.* He's the first to rise and shakes off the dust.

"Whoa. No 'x'"s!" Loud notices Jeremy's hand.

"Yeah. I'm kind of done with all that."

"Sweet! Like your name. Ha! Now we can all go get high! And play dope music. And have a sleepover at Whistle Punk Falls."

Jeremy looks at Aurora. She returns his gaze. Her face mirrors his, he realizes—twisted and sick.

"What is it?" Loud asks.

"We… We should talk," Aurora says, then looks at Jeremy

again, pleadingly this time.

"K. I'll...leave you two alone. I'm going to go watch for... You know. Her car."

Aurora and Loud look at each other.

"Just....Remember to... Be careful," Jeremy says.

"Jer. You can go," Aurora says.

"Yeah. Okay..." Jeremy stomps up the hill toward the highway.

When Jeremy has disappeared over the crest of the hill, Aurora grabs Loud. As if in one embrace she could absorb his essential oil—his loamy hair, his unsteady song, his inconvenient fire, his stinging tea— and then she leans him back. He moves easily in her arms now as if the days and months have eaten out his marrow, and he walks on bones hollow as a windblown bird's.

"Loud, we've hurt you," she says.

He shakes his head. His mouth moves, but nothing comes out.

"I've..." he struggles. "I've hurt *you*."

Aurora nods. A breeze carries the smell of the new wood from the golden beams of the barn. "That's what happens."

"But I'm here now," Loud says. His eyes are shining mall fountain pennies.

A train approaches. It sends out a heavy circle of sound that thickens toward them.

"Loud." She closes her eyes. "You have to *go*."

Smelling his hands, he says he knew she would say that. He nods and turns away from her.

"You have to go to your mom," Aurora says.

He nods. Then shakes his head, "But. She...My dad...She lied!"

"Malachi," Aurora says. "Your dad died stealing a cedar tree. A wind came and caused a branch to fall on him. I'm sorry."

"You sure?"

"Yes. That guy Keith told Jeremy's mom all about it."

"Keith…"

Aurora plays Loud the recording of Keith telling the story of his father's death. Loud listens, smelling his hands, pacing, and nodding. The story ends and Loud's brows freeze into a furrow that makes him look middle-aged.

"Loud," Aurora says, struggling through what feels like thick bands of time strangling her. "Your mom… She's trying. She's been trying. More than any of us have."

Loud turns toward the train that has become as big as a school bus and is rocking the ground beneath them.

"Will you go back to your mom?"

He nods, not looking at Aurora, saying to himself, "She *was* trying. She is trying. She…has been trying. This whole time."

Aurora shouts above the din of the train for Loud to go home to his mom.

Then Loud starts running.

The train's face is an orange battering ram lined with black war paint. Its empty center-beam flatcars form a queue of picture frames that undulate around the curves of the track. They divide the land from the river. Its lading shakes the earth, and its frantic whistle bores hollows of sound into their ears, stomachs, and bones.

Jeremy tears down the hill, yelling at Aurora, "What are you doing?"

"It's okay," Aurora says, trying to grab him. "He's going to ride the train home!"

But Jeremy pushes past her. "He's not going to ride it, you idiot! He's going to throw himself in front of it!"

A shrill column of fear goes through her. How could she be so stupid?

"Loud! Don't!" She joins Jeremy in a mad dash after Loud.

Sirens wail. Moreno's squad car bursts from the hill, Charlotte riding shotgun. The vehicle bounds through the rotten fence squaring the launch from the field and growls through the gravel in pursuit of the figure who is inches from the train, his body small and erratic next to the beam of steel hurtling through the air. The boy's big limbs scramble, kicking up dust, and his running path arcs so that for an instant, he is parallel to the train before he jumps up to grab the rung of a ladder. He tucks his legs as he lifts himself up the rungs until he's clear of the gnashing wheels beneath, and he begins to climb.

The squad car fishtails to a stop. Aurora and Jeremy skid to a weak-kneed halt.

Jeremy sees it suddenly. The fire inside Loud has never been at risk of going out. It will always smolder, warm, and burn.

They all watch Malachi "Loud" McCrowley, seat himself cross-legged on the freight car roof diminishing as the train thunders away. Even beneath the train's whistle, the boy's gaze remains fixed on them. The huddled group of them watch as the train carries him to the Harbor's wide arms, ever stretching toward the sea.

*

At the end of the line, Loud rids himself of the train. He roams north. He isn't sure why. Something about cereal, bad tapes, and the Aurora Borealis. But north, north, north. It's in his mind. Between his eyes. The voices of the ghosts titter and wheel in his head like gulls, constant but far from him now and he is glad. He hums punk rock as he follows the Hoquiam River and climbs the hill up the 101. He doesn't look back. He's done with that town. It's not his scene! Prophets and rock stars alike are hated in their hometown. What could you do?

The trees convene, forming their citadels of green. He's tired. He's hungry. He's cold. This July's gotten off to a rough start. But it can only get better. He holds out his thumb, hoping something will happen.

A bubble-gum blue Rav-4 pulls over onto his side of the highway.

A woman steps out. Her skin is brown like his, her brow worried like his.

"Malachi?" the woman asks in her deep voice.

He stands there. He locks eyes with hers and sees his eyes reflected back at him—two clay-bottomed pools the sun hits in such a way that makes him want to wade into them. There's something for him in her eyes. A gift of some kind. Maybe many gifts.

"New car?" he asks.

"Figured it was time for a change," she says. She walks around the SUV and opens the passenger door.

"Start over with me?" she asks.

Loud looks at the open door.

"You can," she says. "*If* you want to."

He gets in. "Can I choose the music?"

"I can live with that," she says.

ACKNOWLEDGEMENTS

The gray chubby faces of the boys fogged up the second story window of their clapboard split-level. They were looking down at me in my traipse through their cul-de-sac. The place was simultaneously phantasmal and familiar: Aberdeen Washington.

This was on my second or third trip out to Aberdeen in that many years, though the town had haunted my imagination for far longer. In the mid '90s, my Cali-born parents and I were doing what millions of other tourists do every year: highway-cruising through the town's moldering core on their way to coastal getaways. Yet an uncanny foreboding filled me. Aberdeen's awful beauty and mystery snagged in my consciousness and fused with my earliest impressions of Washington.

So in my early twenties, with my heart set on having my first novel be a teenage disaster romance, I knew I wanted to set it in Aberdeen. The Seattle suburbs I'd lived in— Covington, Maple Valley, Issaquah—offered me little intrigue.

But the boys in the window didn't know any of this. I could almost hear them asking each other who I was. I asked this question many times over the course of writing this book, along with the question of who am I to write about this town?

Of course, the Aberdeen in this book isn't THE Aberdeen, but MY Aberdeen, a fictional version limned for the work's poetic and formal concerns. In his Aberdeen novel, *The Land of Plenty*, Robert Cantwell doesn't mention the town's name. Murray Morgan renames his Aberdeen "Cove" in *Viewless Winds*. But these options weren't available (or desirable) to me, given my featuring of town legends Billy Gohl, Laura Law, and Kurt Cobain—all by now inexorably linked with the place's real name.

As Jonathan Franzen observed, with contemporary fiction, voluminous research isn't necessary. To contemporize this, no amount of research will prevent the ire of the internet and the perfectly understandable annoyance of Aberdeeners, indigenous peoples, female police officers, and others that a person like me (Scotch-Irish-English-German American white male) has written fictional characters like them. As Thomas Mann said, he learned the most from his critics. As Phillip Roth writes in *American Pastoral*, "the fact remains that getting people right is not what this is all about anyway. It's about getting them wrong…That's how we know we're alive. When we're wrong… Writing turns you into somebody who's always wrong. The illusion that you may get it right someday is the perversity that draws you on." In that spirit, I welcome any and all critiques. This notwithstanding, voluminous research, I did.

And here's as good a place as any to note that I did this research and subsequent writing primarily on Duwamish land stewarded by a people whose effort to be seen and understood is ongoing (find out more at www.realrentduwamish.org).

In his critique of Jeanine Cummins' *American Dirt*, David Bowles exhorts white-bodied authors writing about brown-bodied people to "hold their babies". I've held the next best thing: their stories. My reviews on the following works by indigenous peoples can be found online: M. Scott Momaday's *House Made of Dawn*; Denis Staples's *This Town Sleeps*; Sasha taqʷšəblu Lapointe's *Red Paint* and *Rose Quartz*; and Oscar Hokeah's *Calling for a Blanket Dance*. Joshua L. Reid's *The Sea is My Country; The Maritime World of the Makahs* provided vital cultural knowledge and background, as did my tour and interview with June Williams at the Makah Cultural & Research Center Museum.

I'm indebted to the following Northwest books. For novels, Ken Kesey's *Sometimes a Great Notion*; and David Guterson's *The Other*. For nonfiction, Andrew Mason Prouty's *More Deadly Than War: Pacific Coast Logging, 1827-1981*; William Dietrich's *The Final Forrest*.

In addition to my 2 years working and volunteering at mental health treatment centers, my 3.5 years working at a youth center for youth who were houseless, my nine years in public schools, and my 30-ish years living with subclinical depression and anxiety, the following works informed my depictions of mental illness and people who are unhoused: Pete Earley's *Crazy*; Elyn Saks's *The Center Cannot Hold: My Journey Through Madness*; Kay Redfield Jamison's *An Unquiet Mind*; Margaret Moorman's *My Sister's Keeper: Learning to Cope with a Sibling's Mental Illness*; and Craig Rennebohm's *Souls in the Hands of a Tender God: Stories of the Search for Home and Healing on the Streets*.

For background context of the '09 housing crisis, I read Andrew Ross Sorkin's *Too Big to Fail*. For information on Gray's Harbor and its many misunderstood ghosts, I read Charles R. Cross's *Heavier Than Heaven: A Biography of Kurt Cobain*; Aaron Goings' *The Port of Missing Men: Billy Gohl, Labor, and Brutal Times in the Pacific Northwest*; Anne Cotton's *The History of Aberdeen*; and of course, John C. Hughes and Ryan Teague Beckwith's *On the Harbor: From Black Friday to Nirvana*.

And now comes the procession of 'thank you"s.

Thank you to Sandra Tudor for everything. But specifically, your decades of knowledge of being a police officer, patrol lieutenant, detective, mental health counselor, and my mother.

Thanks to a Gray's Harbor police department which shall go unnamed, as requested. Thanks for granting me a lengthy phone interview and issuing me a ride along. Thanks to Erin Pankey for the phone and email interviews and tag-along while you were at Gray's Harbor Youth Center. Thanks to Forks Lumber Mill Tour.

Thanks to my first readers and encouragers: Eli Hastings and Kaitlin McMichael. Thank you especially to Kaitlin for staying married to me despite all my breast beating and sackcloth and ash-heap moods during the various stages of writing, revising, and querying for this novel. Thank you to the Rough Writers Dan Magill, Grace Kingara, Irene Jung, Abbi Engel, and Angelo Grosso (my best friend since 5th grade!). Thanks to readers Kyle Larson and Chris Bridges.

Thanks to Anna Katz, who provided developmental feedback early in the querying process. Thanks to my first editor Jim Thomsen who helped me hone the swampy early version. Thanks to Theresa Burton for suggestions, edits, and praise in your kind read-through.

Thank you to Novelist Dennis E. Staples for your friendship and for delighting in this novel. Thanks to Harry Kirchner, who believed in this book and worked with me on the manuscript off and on for about two years. Whose guidance helped me trim about 25% off a baggy monster of a draft. Who believed in this book so much you went to bat for me. Thanks to Novelist Thomas Kohnstamm for introducing me to Jim, Dennis, and Harry.

Thank you to my therapist Cameron Lewis who cheerleaded for my bruised ego during the painful final months when rejection deluges were daily.

Thank you to Tracy Haught for updating your LinkedIn profile; if you hadn't, my manuscript would probably still be in digital slush piles on servers throughout the country. I'm incredibly lucky.

A final thank you to my best buddy, my son Adam. As a baby, you napped, swaddled on my chest in the front back while I edited this book. Forgive me frequently becoming distant as I've gotten lost in the slough of my own thoughts thinking about this and other ambitions.

Through my readers and editors, I've felt seen, heard, and validated. I'm painfully aware that many in our world—perhaps most—do not and have not felt seen in this way. Thinking about this, I want to go back to the boys in the window. I want to call them down. I want to sit with them. I want to ask them to tell me some stories. And then I want to help the world listen to them.

--Seattle, Washington
May 25th, 2025

PHOTOGRAPH BY ROBERT FOREHAND

Shaun Anthony McMichael is the author of THE WILD FAMILIAR short stories (CJ Press, 2024) and the poetry collection JACK OF ALL…(New Meridian Arts, 2024). Since 2007, he has taught writing to students from around the world, in classrooms, juvenile detention halls, mental health treatment centers, and homeless youth drop-ins throughout the Puget Sound region. Over 115 of his poems, short stories, and reviews have appeared in literary magazines, online, and in print. WHISTLE PUNK FALLS is his first novel. He lives with his wife and son in Seattle where he attends church most Sundays. In addition to teaching English to immigrants and refugees at a public high school, he hosts an annual literary arts reading series, Shadow Work Writers. Visit him at his website shaunanthonymcmichael.com.

www.ingramcontent.com/pod-product-compliance
Lightning Source LLC
Chambersburg PA
CBHW020657110726
47901CB00001B/227